LIQUID GOLD

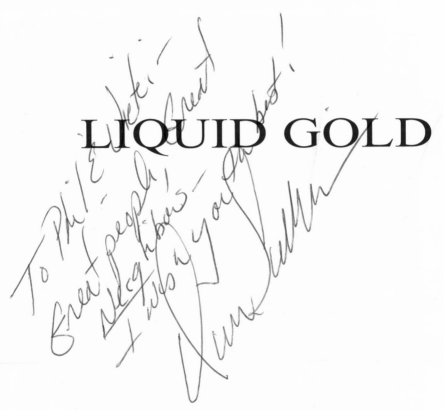

OWEN SULLIVAN

TRIWEST
PUBLISHING

This is a work of fiction. Names, characters, places, and incidents either are the product of the author's imagination or are used fictitiously. Any resemblance to actual persons, living or dead, events, or locales is entirely coincidental.

Liquid Gold
By Owen Sullivan

1. FIC 000000 - Fiction / General 2. FIC 002000 - Fiction / Action & Adventure
3. FIC 020000 Fiction / Men's Adventure

ISBN: 978-0615823522

Cover design by
David Flanagan
Misfit Agency
1013 7th Street, Sacramento, CA 95814
916-290-9660
www.agencymisfit.com

Printed in the United States of America

To Preston, Nicole, Jessica and Jolene,
and their spouses, Pete, Aaron and Ben.

ACKNOWLEDGEMENTS

This book would not have been completed without the expertise and tremendous help from Andrea Hurst of Andrea Hurst and Associates, and also Jessica Schmitz and David Flanagan at Misfit Agency. I'd also like to thank Jolene Childers for her untiring social media and technical assistance; Ed McGowan and Nicole McKane for their helpful feedback; and Genevieve Sullivan, my loving wife, for her invaluable work on this project and for always believing in me.

ONE

Thoroughbred race horses aren't dumb. They're graceful, athletic and are bred, raised, pampered, and groomed to do two things: run fast and win races. They know what they're supposed to do, and most do their jobs with enthusiasm and joy. But thoroughbreds, like all animals, including humans, have good days and bad ones. When they have a bad day, they don't do what they were raised to do. That creates havoc for those who bet on them.

For the fifth time this Saturday afternoon, Matt leaned forward against the Turf Club railing above the grandstand of the racing track at Cal Expo in Sacramento and watched the horse he bet on, Riding High, have a bad day, crossing the finish line three horses off the lead.

Matt methodically tore up his betting slips, letting them flutter to the ground. There goes another twenty bucks well spent, he thought to himself. Well at least I'm improving; the last four horses were fifth or lower.

He had a soft spot for all animals, but his exposure was limited primarily to dogs and cats. When he was down in the paddocks before the last race, he couldn't help but admire the majesty and beauty of the horses. He'd rubbed their noses and petted them while they stood passively in their stalls, sizing him up. It was a good thing he didn't own a ranch, he'd go broke taking in every race horse that came along. He could see the sign now above the entrance: Matt Whiteside Ranch.

He turned from the racetrack to see his close friend, Drew, standing in triumph, hands held straight up, high-fiving everyone within reach of his palms. Even though Drew was dressed casually in a white polo shirt and khakis, he carried himself as if he'd just stepped out of a photo shoot for *GQ Magazine*. His black wavy hair, mischievous hazel eyes, and surfer tan caused many a woman to do a double take.

Drew aimed one of his hands at Matt, who slapped it back and smiled wide. "How about that, Mattie-boy? Another winner! If I keep this up, I might be able to retire soon. I told you, you should have gone with that number five horse. You need to listen to me next time."

Matt smiled at him. "Drew, you know as much about horses as I do, which is just about nothing. I'd keep my day job if I were you. I don't think you're going to retire on two hundred dollars in winnings."

Drew had turned his attention to three attractive women, two blondes and one brunette, who were sitting in the booth directly above where they sat. All three were well-dressed and jewelry sparkled from their hands, ears and necks. Their natty attire of flowery sundresses and the three bottles of champagne at their table suggested they were there for more than the horse races. They were rather conspicuous for the venue, as the more typical attire was blue jeans and a tank top.

Matt sat down in his seat and rested his chin on the railing. The noise had subsided from the previous three minutes, when everyone had been on their feet and screaming at their horse to win. There was still plenty of shouting and laughter, but because there were only a few thousand people in a place that held fifteen thousand, the sound was not deafening. Matt sipped a beer from a frosted glass and watched the throngs of people milling around the track. To his left on the floor level, about a hundred yards in front of the finish line, a circle of tough-looking guys spoke loudly to each other. Most of them had lit cigarettes, and the smoke blew everywhere while they made sweeping movements with their hands, as if every gesture were an important part of a story.

Matt's gaze took him to the infield, which was a neatly manicured lawn area with a large lake in the center, accentuated by a fountain that shot a geyser of water twenty feet into the air. Four swans paddled lazily around the fountain. About forty yards away from the fountain, a flock of geese chased each other around the lake as if they were arguing about some unknown grievance.

Matt's eyes swept past the finish line toward the paddock area, where another set of horses was being prepped for the next race. What a nice day for racing, he thought. July usually is hot around here, but it's only in the nineties. I can live with that. Besides, it's Friday, the company is paying for this outing, and it beats sitting at a desk.

He turned in his chair and watched Drew holding court with the three women in the other booth and shook his head. That boy can't help himself, he thought. They just flock to him, like bees to honey. One thing is for certain, he'll never be lonely for lack of company. Drew caught his look and moved back to their table.

"Hey, Matt," he said as he waved a couple of tickets around in the air, "do you want to come with me and see where the winning window is? I mean, if you listen to me, you might be able to use it today."

Matt laughed. "No, go ahead." He nodded in the direction of the paddocks. "I'll look over this next batch and see if I can come up with a winner. I think this is the race where my luck will change."

"I doubt it. By the way," he said as he turned his head toward the three women, "that blonde in the middle with the bright lipstick thinks you look a lot like Matt Damon. She thought you were taller, cuter, and had pretty blue eyes. She called you doe-eyes; like in a deer. Those were her words, not mine."

He looked over Drew's shoulder at the woman who was staring at him and seductively running her tongue over her champagne glass. He smiled back at her and said dryly, "Well, she obviously has impeccable taste."

Drew laughed. "Or she needs to visit an eye doctor. That would be my guess. I'll be back in a second with my winnings."

A waitress came up to the table where they were sitting. "Would you like another round?"

Matt drank the last swallow of his beer. "Yes, thanks, that would be great."

He noticed some pieces of betting slip had stuck on his blue Brooks Brothers shirt and his shorts, so he mindlessly brushed them off. The phone in his pocket vibrated, and he fumbled with it before answering.

"Hello?"

He heard the familiar sound of his fiancée, Stephanie's, soft voice. "Hi, sweetie, are you winning big bucks for us? I could find all sorts of ways to spend that money."

Matt smiled. "Not yet, but I feel a roll of wins coming." He thought about how she looked when he left her this morning. Stephanie was on her way to a meeting in downtown Sacramento with a group of bankers, and even though she didn't try to look sexy, she couldn't help it. The light-colored dress would work for most women in a business setting, but Stephanie managed to make the outfit stunning. Her wavy brown hair was pulled back in a ponytail, accentuating sparkling blue eyes, and she rounded out the outfit with a pair of taupe heels. He wished she were here with him today.

"How is work going? I almost feel bad sitting here betting on horses and drinking beer while you're at work. Let me make that clearer; I said almost."

"Don't worry, Matt, I'll get even. I'll make you take me to dinner tonight, so win some money so it can be expensive. Everything at work is cool. They were happy with the results of my last assignment, so they want to put me on some bigger things. They weren't real specific with the job I'm taking on, but it has something to do with land development deals."

Drew sat down and threw a wad of twenties on the table. He pointed at them excitedly like a toddler discovering his first chocolate rabbit at Easter.

Matt nodded and waved him away as if to say, 'Go away, you're boring me.' He spoke into the phone. "Wow, that's great, Steph. Your new assignment sounds interesting. There's nothing like land deals to get my blood pumping."

"I hope so. Well, I've gotta go, Matt. I just wanted to say hi. I'll see you later tonight."

"Okay, I'll see you then."

The waitress had returned and set their beers on the table.

"That was the lovely Stephanie, I presume?" Drew asked matter-of-factly. "Are you two going out tonight?"

The brunette wandered over from her table, a champagne glass in her hand, and was cozying up to Drew.

Matt watched his friend and then answered. "It was. We're celebrating our birthdays tonight. Mine's not for a couple weeks, but hers is Wednesday and she's going to be in San Francisco that day."

Drew raised his glass. "Cheers to you both. I knew your birthday was coming up. How old will you be anyway? Forty?"

"Nice try. I'm still four years younger than you, which will make me thirty-two."

The brunette cooed softly to Drew. "Aren't you going to introduce me to your good-looking friend?" She had her elbow propped up on Drew's shoulder. Her lipstick had made a red impression of her lips on her champagne glass.

Drew grinned. "Of course I will. Matt, this is Annette. She

5

works at First Republic Title as a title rep." Drew turned to Annette. "This is Matt Whiteside, my poor friend who keeps picking the wrong horse."

Matt tipped his head as if he were wearing a hat. "It's nice to meet you, Annette. Are you and your friends having fun today?"

She smiled, showing off a perfect set of white teeth. "Oh, absolutely, we're all having a blast, and I think it's just about to get more fun." She took a sip of her champagne, her eyes locked onto Drew's face.

Drew turned to Matt. "This was a great idea. I appreciate you inviting me on one of your corporate outings. You must thank your boss, Diane."

"Lucky for us, the company reserved four boxes for this and I snagged a couple of the box seats. It was a great idea of hers."

A groom in white pants, black riding boots, and a red coat stepped up to a microphone on the track, right at the finish line. He pulled the long brass horn out from under his arm and played the call to race. After a polite applause, he started to play a jazzy song that got the audience to clap along. Matt shifted in his chair to watch as the first horses for the next race started to parade in front of the grandstand.

Drew scanned the racing forum in his hand, looking for the horse lineup for the next race. "How often do the thoroughbreds run? Is it year round?" he asked.

Annette looked intently over his shoulder.

"The State Fair runs from July tenth to the eighth of August," Matt answered. "The thoroughbred horses only run for fourteen days during the fair. I haven't been to the races in ages, but it's always fun. I wish the fair would extend the time they run."

Annette whispered something to Drew, and then returned to her friends.

Matt thumbed through his forum. "So, how is everything at Hartford Financial, Drew? It's got to be a different place since the housing market collapsed?"

Drew took a sip of his beer. "You better believe it's different. I don't think I've seen a transaction involving mortgage-backed securities in three years. I've been instructed to start looking at institutional real estate properties and will be checking out some Class A office buildings, high-end apartment complexes, and even a few exclusive land deals. This market has shaken loose some impressive properties." Drew pointed at the third horse from the head of the line. "I like that black horse right there, Midnight Train. He's my boy."

Matt followed his gaze. "Yeah, he looks impressive, but they all do. If you're betting on him, I think I'll go with Never Surrender." He pointed with a rolled up forum to the sixth horse. "That's my first winner."

"Matt, Matt. You never learn. Listen to the horse whisperer," Drew said, fingers pointing inward at himself.

"We'll see who ends up at the winner's circle. Seriously, Drew, I would like to talk to you more about where you are looking to invest. At General Tech I don't get to see what's behind the investments I'm overseeing in the pension fund, and I'd like to get educated. I miss the learning I did at Franklin Smith before the market tanked. It was really exciting."

Drew had his wallet out and was counting out twenty dollar bills on the table. "Anytime, Matt, I'd be happy to fill you in. Even though things have changed in the last few years with investors steering away from the housing market, there is still a lot of activity in real estate. When one door gets shut, you have to find another one to open. Let's go. The horses are at the posts, and it's time to make our bets."

Annette returned with her drink in hand. Drew extended his arm. "Why not have a seat. We'll be back in a second."

Matt was almost out of the box when he felt Drew's elbow in his side. He looked toward Drew, who was staring straight down the aisle. Matt followed his gaze. Walking toward them was a middle-aged, portly gentleman dressed in dark slacks and a white silk shirt buttoned halfway down his chest. A large amount of chest hair was the resting place for three gold chains with a big gold medallion dangling from one of them. His full head of salt and pepper curly hair looked as if it had been permed, and a bushy, but nicely trimmed, mustache matched the color of his hair.

On each arm hung a young, attractive, well-endowed, and equally well-inebriated blonde. The one on the right wore a red, skintight miniskirt, and the one on the left wore tight jeans, a flimsy blouse, and black stilettoes. Both stumbled as they walked and held onto the man for balance.

The man caught Matt's eye, and he gave a slight expression of recognition. They passed and made their way to a booth three down from where Matt and Drew were sitting.

Drew spoke first. "Did that guy take a bath in Polo cologne? I thought for a minute I just walked through the perfume aisle at Macys."

Matt chuckled. "I don't know. I was trying to focus on the guy and not his company. I'm guessing those are not his daughters."

Drew turned and started down the aisle to the bettors windows. Matt followed in stride. "Uh, I would say that would be a negative. That's probably how I would walk in high heels if I were forced to. Did you catch his hair? It looks like a salt and pepper Chia Pet. Do you know that guy?"

Matt turned back for another look. "I know of him, but we've never been introduced. He's a real estate developer, mortgage broker, contractor, and who knows what else. I've seen his picture in the paper. He was charged a few years ago with being part of a mortgage scam. They dropped the charges against him recently."

Drew got in line at the betting window and looked back at the man. "He looks like quite a character."

Matt nodded. "I've heard rumors about him and his business

practices. He is said to be pretty ruthless. He was friends with Taylor Whitney."

They came up to the betting window and got in line behind an elderly, bald man who was chomping on a cigar butt. He held a racing forum closely to his thick glasses, making notes as he shuffled to the window. His rumpled shirt was stained with various condiments from the food vendor.

"Taylor Whitney?" Drew asked. "Wasn't he the big developer who was murdered along with his girlfriend at his mansion in Granite Bay?"

"That's the one. They still haven't figured out who offed them and I don't think they ever will."

"If they were friends, do you think he knows anything about Taylor's accusations against you?" Drew asked.

Matt shook his head. "I don't know, but it's possible. I hope not." Matt glanced back over his shoulder. He spoke in serious tone. "I recognize that watch he was wearing."

Drew looked back. "You do? From where?"

"Taylor Whitney wore that exact watch, a diamond-encrusted gold Rolex. You can spot one from miles. I guess birds of a feather flock together."

Drew gave the woman behind the window his bets for the next race. Scanning his tickets, he stepped aside for Matt to bet. "Maybe that watch is bad news," he said.

Matt slid ten dollars to the clerk. "Give me number six to win." He turned to Drew. "It's not the watch that's bad news; it's the person who wears it. And my instincts tell me that guy is bad news."

Two

Yuri Kletcko reached the booth at the racetrack where his friend, Ivan Brosky, sat sipping a vodka Martini out of a frosty tall glass. Ivan was about the same age as Yuri, around fifty, but had less hair and dressed like he found his clothes on the floor of his closet. Crumbs from his half-eaten hamburger stuck to his sweat-stained shirt, standing out like sprinkles on a cupcake. He eyed the two young women hanging on Yuri lecherously, as he poured them into their seats. Subconsciously, Ivan rubbed his hands up and down his thighs.

Yuri smiled at Ivan mischievously then turned his attention to his guests. "Ladies, what would you like to drink? How about a couple shots of Jager and tequila, eh?"

Both girls wiggled and squealed with delight. "Oh, Yuri," the blonde in the red slurred, "that would be awesome. You are the best." She slumped back in her chair, almost knocking her friend out of her seat. They both giggled.

Yuri motioned at a waitress to come over. He sat down, pulled a handkerchief out of his pocket, and wiped his forehead. "It's a warm one today, no? Not as bad as last week, but still warm."

Ivan nodded. "It is, but it is a good day to be alive." Nodding at the girls, he continued. "We have come a long way, my friend. Who would have believed we would be sitting here with these two gorgeous young things, with wealth to our name, and many more good things to experience? It has been a wild journey since we left Russia."

Yuri paused for a moment. He hadn't thought about his homeland in a while. Growing up under Communist rule wasn't that horrible when your father was a player in the Politburo. His family didn't live a life of luxury like some of the higher ups did, but they had a nice apartment and enough food to eat.

His father was a loyal party member, but could never rise very far because a man named Nicolas Trolsky never allowed it. For whatever reason, Nicolas kept Yuri's father down and insulted him at every opportunity. Yuri didn't understand why his father put up with the insults; and as time went by, he grew to hate Nicolas, swearing to one day get even.

When the Communist rule crumbled in 1989, Ivan made plans. He wanted out of Russia and worked to get to the United States. It took him a year and many thousands of dollars, but he finally secured a visa. But before he left, he had one task to finish.

Yuri remembered this as if it were yesterday. He lured Trolsky, with a promise of a big business deal in the Ukraine, to a seedy area of Moscow where he had rented a room and had hired an attractive hooker. When Trolsky entered the room, his eyes lit up in delight as he saw the half-dressed woman. He nodded approvingly at Yuri and moved toward the woman, who didn't seem to mind his fondling. While he was fumbling with her nightie, Yuri spun him around and stuck a six-inch knife in his belly. He pulled the knife straight up, slicing open his front torso. Trolsky stumbled forward, grabbing his bleeding belly, and fell face down, bouncing off the bed onto the floor. The hooker stood stunned in the corner of the room after Yuri wiped both sides of the knife on her gown and flung it onto the bed.

He rushed out the door and yelled at the first person he saw to call the police there had been a fight next door. He sprinted out into the night as the sounds of sirens filled the air. He slowed down to a walk, trying to look as casual and inconspicuous as possible.

Yuri grinned at the memory of the expression on Trolsky's face when he had seen the knife. He would never forget the bulging eyes and the look of hideous fear on his face.

Yuri was on his way out of Russia on a freighter before anyone figured out the dead man's identity. It caused quite a commotion in Russia, and the hooker was sent off to jail to stand trial for the killing. He smiled to himself. Everyone has a weakness; you just need to find it and exploit it.

Yuri's attention was brought back to the present as the waitress came up and set the drinks on their table. He saluted his friend. "Yes, Ivan, it has been a long trip. Do you remember when we first arrived? How we bummed around New York for a few months before my cousin sent for us in California? We lived in that two-story house in Rancho Cordova and ran the chop shop. What a mess that place was." He sipped his drink, smiling. "We had to be the world's dumbest criminals, yet we never got caught."

Ivan laughed. "Do I remember? How could I forget? How many cars do you think we stole during those years? Two hundred? Two fifty? I'm glad those days are over. That's a young man's game. What about the loan business we had a few years ago? We made some good money off those banks, but I'm glad we got out when we did. It was getting pretty hot there for a while."

"It was getting hot, but it gave me a good bankroll to do legitimate deals," Yuri said. "But where else can you go with no money in your pocket and end up with a million dollar empire? As that crazy boxing promoter Don King used to say, 'Only in America.'"

Ivan shook his head approvingly. "Only in America."

"Did you get the papers signed on the Johnson Ranch deal?" Yuri asked. "That one will put us over the top."

"They're signed and on your desk. Congratulations, you're one step closer to owning one of the most undervalued seventeen thousand-acre ranches in all of California, and it's only ten miles from downtown Sacramento. You're going to get filthy rich on this one, Yuri."

The blonde in the jeans came over and sat on Yuri's lap and nuzzled up to his neck. Yuri adjusted his watch, rolling it up from his wrist, and smiled. "Filthy rich is good. I still am amazed at how easy it is to make money in this market. My company, Wealth Management, Inc., is almost printing money with those mortgage deals we're doing. We can't foreclose on those houses fast enough." He reached into his pocket, pulled out a large wad of bills, then peeled off ten crisp hundred-dollar bills and gave five to each girl. "Why don't you girls bet on a couple of horses and win some money." He winked at Ivan, who was watching the scene. Ivan smiled back.

The girls screamed with delight and stumbled out of the booth toward the betting windows, unaware or uncaring of the amount of flesh they were exposing.

Ivan watched them leave then nodded toward the betting window where two young men were standing a few feet from the window talking. "Do you know those guys?" he asked.

Yuri looked up. "I recognize the taller one, with the brown hair. His name is Matt Whiteside. He threatened my friend, Taylor Whitney. It had to do with some issues about a house Taylor built. Before Taylor was knocked off, his house was shot up. Matt was arrested for it, but quickly released when the cops found the real shooter. Taylor swore something fishy had happened at his house that night, and he was sure Matt had a hand in it."

He pulled a cigar out of his breast pocket and bit off its end. "I know Whiteside's type, and I don't like them. Always sticking their face where it doesn't belong and asking too many questions. One of these days it will catch up to him."

Yuri felt a vibration in his pocket and pulled out his phone. He stared at the number for a second then sent the caller to voice mail. "It was the wife." Then he smiled and laughed. "I haven't got time for her right now, I'm busy."

Ivan laughed.

Yuri raised his glass. "Yes, filthy rich is good, and here's to getting even more filthy rich."

THREE

Caroline Bennett rested her chin on her hands as the speaker standing in front of the committee droned on about the merits of the real estate development project he was representing. She stole a glance at the clock on the right wall of the Board of Supervisors' chambers, noting it was almost ten o'clock. She stifled a yawn and pretended to pay attention, but her mind was wandering, as it normally did with these proceedings. Mellissa Burns, a close friend, was sitting in the second row, furiously scribbling notes. Caroline thought about how far back the two of them went, back to their freshman year at the University of California at Berkeley, where they were roommates for four years.

They were disappointed that they were too young to be involved in the Vietnam era protests that had brought turmoil to the campus along with notoriety to heroes of the free speech movement, Mario Savio and Angela Davis. They were happy though to be involved in whatever protest came along at the University.

There were striking differences. Caroline came from a wealthy rice-farming family that traced its roots to the gold rush and was one of the pillars of Yolo County society. She never had any worries about money, unlike most college students, as her father made sure she did not go without anything. Being an only child and her father's pet made her life growing up rather pleasant.

Mellissa, on the other hand, came from more modest means; her mother had raised her and her sister on a school secretary's wage, living month to month and hand to mouth. Early on in her life, she acquired a love for animals and the environment, which grew obsessive as she aged. Even though she had a good job and made good money, she spent it on every animal or environmental movement that came her way.

Caroline thought about the long talks they had in their dorm room late into the night and how they would make a difference in society. After they graduated, they stayed close, cementing their friendship by getting deeply and religiously entrenched into the environmental movement, much to her father's chagrin.

Caroline had to keep her political views quiet lest it irritate her father, who was a committed Republican and an advocate of capitalism, so she allowed Mellissa to do most of her bidding on controversial issues. When her father passed away in 1989, he left her a great fortune, such that she would never need to work again. His death devastated her, and she spent months depressed. Finally, she started to get over her grief by immersing herself into local political and environmental causes. Now the fortune left to her by her father allowed her to not only pursue her passion, but also fund it.

She glanced up at the sixty-inch television monitor hanging at the back of the auditorium showing the proceedings, which went out to a small, but dedicated TV audience. She tilted her head slightly to the left to check herself out from that angle, and then she tilted her head to the right. She fluffed up her blouse and adjusted herself discreetly. Smiling to herself, she thought, I'm looking pretty good for a gal closing in on forty.

Caroline snapped out of her daydream and focused on the speaker at the microphone. She knew the speaker, David Parker, well. As an attorney from Wilshire-Pitt, a prestigious law firm in Sacramento, he had appeared before the board many times, representing numerous landowners in Yolo County.

She stared at him vacantly as she listened to him speak. How long will this high-paid windbag go on about this parcel? It's a request for a Smacky Burger restaurant for god's sake. Nothing good comes out of a Smackys. She sat in the center of the Board of Supervisors' panel as the head supervisor. She glanced to her right at two other board members who were nodding their heads in agreement with the speaker. Caroline turned to her left to watch the other three board members seemingly hanging onto David's every word. She caught a glimpse of the California state flag hanging in the corner. Ah, the great flag of California. What a great state we live in, she thought sarcastically.

As she scanned the crowd, she took notice that the amphitheater chamber was sparsely populated, due in part to the mundane items on the agenda and the fact that it was the middle of summer.

Focusing back on Mr. Parker, she chuckled to herself, too bad you didn't know that I funded most of these board members' campaigns and they vote as I say. I don't dislike you, but I don't like your client. Therefore, there's no way this project will be approved.

After he finished speaking, Dave gathered up his notes then added one final thought. "That is all I have to say about the merits of this project, and I hope you will vote to approve it."

Caroline leaned into her microphone "Do any of the supervisors have any questions for Mr. Parker?" She looked one way at the panel then the next. None of the Supervisors spoke. "No, then I move to open up the discussion to the public. Please come up and state your name and address for the record."

Mellissa stood up and waddled up to the microphone. She plopped her papers on the podium. "I'm Mellissa Burns, and I live at 4021 D Street, Davis. I want to point out to the eloquent Mr. Parker that Yolo County doesn't need another Smackys, as we already have four of them within a twenty-mile radius. But besides that fact, the County Staff did a horrible job on its California Environmental Quality Act, or CEQA, study. This business's traffic will triple the 5,000 cars per day and generate twenty-five tons of carbon emissions per day more than the report. There is no community benefit for a business like this, and I think the application should be denied. Thank you." She piled her papers together and shuffled back to her seat.

Caroline smiled at Mellissa. How ironic it is she's speaking out against Smackys, she thought. A hamburger and french fries are two of her basic food groups. "Thank you, Miss Burns. Any other comments before we close the meeting to the public?"

Five more people, one after the other, came up to the podium, echoing Mellissa's comments about CEQA, traffic, and crime. After the last one spoke, Caroline asked again, "Any more comments before we close the meeting to the public?" By now, fewer than fifteen people were in attendance, and five of them were seated with the applicant and Dave Parker, his attorney. She glanced up at the clock, and it read 11:15. "Then I will close the meeting to the public." She slammed her gavel on the mark and set it aside.

"Supervisors, do any of you have any comments?" Caroline listened politely as each Supervisor had their say, and it finally came around to her. Caroline set her jaw and spoke deliberately. "I have to agree with Miss Burns and the other concerned citizens who came up here to speak. This CEQA study is embarrassing. This project is an environmental disaster, and I see no reason to allow it. We already have another Smackys within two miles. I think we have enough fast food restaurants. Do I hear a motion to vote?"

The vote was 5-3 against the project and the meeting was adjourned. Caroline got up to leave when she caught David Parker glaring at her. She forced a fake smile and gave him a dismissive wave. Sorry, Dave, your client just blew eighty grand to find out this project isn't going anywhere, she thought to herself. Don't bring crummy projects before my board again.

Leaning back into the microphone, she spoke sternly. "I believe that will conclude our agenda for tonight's meeting. Do I hear a motion to adjourn?"

Supervisor Roth chirped in. "I move we adjourn the meeting."

"Is there a second?"

Supervisor Garfield spoke up. "I second."

Caroline slammed her gavel down. "A motion has been moved and seconded to adjourn this meeting. I call this meeting to an end."

Before Caroline had set her gavel down, Mellissa had moved out of her seat and made it to the front of Caroline's position at the dais.

Breathlessly, she patted Caroline's hand. "That was beautiful. That hotshot, five-hundred-dollar-suit attorney is steaming." She turned and looked back at Dave Parker, who was conversing excitedly with his client. "That ought to set them back a few bucks."

Caroline smiled, obviously gratified. "I think you're right. He doesn't look too happy right now. He might want to think twice before he brings in any other stupid development projects before me."

Mellissa gave Caroline a stern look, which Caroline knew meant something was brewing. "Caroline, you know that big ranch between Woodland and Sacramento? The one that runs right under I-5, just west of the airport?"

Caroline nodded slowly, acting like she was trying to envision it, even though she knew it like the back of her hand. "I think so. It's the one that's been in the Johnson family for some 200 years or something like that? It was one of those old Spanish land grants, I believe."

She knew exactly which ranch Mellissa was referring to, as her ranch almost abutted it on the south. She had been trying quietly for years, as had her father before her, to purchase it. The Johnson Ranch was not the greatest farmland around, but it had one thing in abundance and that was something Caroline's ranch could use more of: water. Caroline could hear her father's deep, thunderous voice in her head. "Always remember, Caroline, water is everything. Nothing on Earth survives without water. You can't drink precious metals, and you can't raise crops and livestock with bonds or securities. You can never have enough water; it's liquid gold." Caroline's ranch had a lot of water, but she wanted more. More water meant more crops, and more crops meant more money, money she needed to reach her ambition of being elected a U.S. Senator, where she could pursue her passion for saving the environment through the power of the U.S. government.

Unfortunately for Caroline, the Johnsons and the Bennetts were not on good terms and hadn't been so for generations. But recently she had almost gotten title to the ranch when the Johnsons overextended themselves and found their ranch in foreclosure.

I had the money to buy that land in my account and was ready to purchase their ranch right off the courthouse steps, she thought to herself. Then, at the last minute, someone stepped in and bailed them out with a new loan. Damn them, whoever they were. How did the Johnsons manage to get a multimillion-dollar loan on ranch land in this horrible real estate market? That had to be a magic trick Harry Houdini would have been proud of. She clenched and unclenched her fist.

"Yeah, that's the one," Mellissa answered. "Anyway, I hear there is something afoot about that ranch, and if it's one of the usual suspect developers, it can only mean bad news for that environmentally sensitive area. I don't know much about what's going on there, but you can bet I'm going to find out. I just wanted to give you a heads up."

Caroline smiled at her and patted Mellissa's head as if she were a small child who had just cleaned up her room. "I know you will. You are the greatest. Let me know if you find out anything." She looked toward the back of the chamber, where a young, handsome man about half her age was sitting quietly. She mouthed to him to get the car and then motioned toward the back door of the chambers. He nodded, rose, and brushed through the substantial wooden doors out into the hallway.

Caroline gathered her papers and wished everyone around her a good night. As she was getting ready to leave, she spotted a skinny man with balding hair come down the stairs of the amphitheater heading towards her. He wore a nice white shirt with pressed slacks and a pair of thick black-rimmed glasses. She sighed and thought, oh god, here comes Bill Miller. I hope he plucked those nose hairs and cleaned himself up. Last week he looked like he had an overused toothbrush coming out of his nose, and I was about ready to puke. If he asks me out again, I'm going to slug him.

Bill made it down to the dais and stood in front of Caroline. "Hi, Bill," she said in a dull monotone, as if she had just signed up for a root canal. "I'd like to talk to you, but I'm in a hurry. Is it something that can wait?"

He stuttered a bit as he spoke. "Of course, Miss Bennett, I understand. I'll catch up with you when you have more time."

Caroline faked a smile and hurriedly left the chamber room. Whew, she thought. I dodged that bullet. Opening the back door, she found her brand new black Mercedes Benz CL600 Coupe waiting at the curb, its engine running. She loved the car's sleek outline and didn't care that it had a 5.5 liter biturbo V-12 engine, which left most other cars in its dust. All she knew was it drove like it was riding on air. The young man leaning against the driver's door came around the car and opened the back passenger door for her. She slid in, throwing her papers and files next to her.

"Where to, Caroline?" He looked into her eyes from the rear-view mirror and awaited her response.

She stifled a yawn and spoke without looking up. "I think we should go back to the Davis house, Brett. I'm not hungry. I think I'll take it easy tonight." She reached down to pick up an open bottle of

Dom Pérignon champagne and poured herself a full glass. She drained the glass and poured herself another. Oh, that tastes so good, she thought. These long meetings are killing me. I would have paid a thousand dollars for some of this halfway through that meeting.

He put the car in gear and pulled away from the curb. "Did you want me to stay tonight?"

She looked up at the back of his head then closed her eyes. She envisioned his naked body, perfectly tanned, rippling with well-defined muscles, sculpted by hours at the gym. It made her tingle. Hmmm. That body is too gorgeous to not use, but I'm too tired tonight. She opened her eyes, poured herself some more champagne and focused. "No, go on home tonight. Call me tomorrow in the morning. You can help me wake up and face the day with some spring in my step."

Brett shifted his position. "Uh, you haven't mentioned anything about the cashier's check you said you would get me last Wednesday. I'm supposed to close on my house in two days. I don't want to be a pain, but I was counting on the money from you."

"I told you I'd get it to you!" she snapped. "Tell your broker to give you an extension. Nobody's going to buy that house from under you, what's the hurry?"

He started to plead. "I've gotten an extension twice, Caroline. I'm not sure they will give me another one. I know it's thirty thousand dollars, but you told me you'd take care of this for me. I really want to buy this house."

Caroline leaned forward and spoke into his ear. "Listen, Brett, I know what I said I would do, and I know what I will do. There is nothing keeping you here to do this job. If you think I'm treating you poorly, drop me off, pick up your car, and then keep on driving once you leave my property. There are dozens of guys like you at the gym that would love to have your job. I'll get you the money when I'm ready, so get your little broker friend to work a little harder and get you an extension."

They drove in silence for the next fifteen minutes, passing through various subdivisions in the more affluent part of Davis. He turned into a cul-de-sac and drove straight onto a long circular driveway that was lit up on both sides by soft Malibu lighting. Even in the dark, the landscaping looked enchanting. The sprawling two-story home sat back sixty feet from the driveway. A dozen carriage lights lit its exterior displaying even more wealth than the rest of the tony neighborhood.

After driving into the garage, Brett opened her door and she breezed by him as if he weren't even standing there, carrying her full champagne glass in her left hand. She entered the house without a word and slammed the door shut behind her.

Caroline tossed her purse on the kitchen counter and smiled to herself. *If he wasn't so hot, I'd fire him tonight. I think I'll make him sweat out the money thing for a couple of days. Thirty grand is nothing to me. Oh, I love it when a man needs me, and boy he needs me. Of course, I need him for other things, many more things.* She raised her eyebrows and smiled seductively.

FOUR

General Technologies' office was located in the brand new Breckenridge Building, at the beginning of the Capital Mall in downtown Sacramento. They occupied the twenty-first floor of the twenty-five story, elegant glass structure. The offices had a commanding view of downtown, the Sacramento River, and the Capitol.

Matt, sitting in his corner office looking directly down on the State Capitol was parked at his computer studying financial reports sent from various asset managers. The credenza behind him held photos of him and Stephanie: the trip to Tahoe in June, and a camping trip to Union Valley Reservoir over the July fourth weekend. A couple of golf trophies stood next to the photographs, along with a pair of well-read financial books.

Two oil paintings of bright flowers in a meadow hung on the wall across from his desk, a reminder of his previous position as a mortgage-backed security trader at the prestigious firm of Franklin Smith. Unfortunately, the real estate crash made that stint far too short.

He had a stack of reports on his desk, and every time he studied one particular report, he kept going back to one section that didn't read right to him. Why are these assets going down in value? he thought. This shouldn't be happening. Since the real estate crash and subsequent recession, General Technologies' employee 401(k) plans had taken a financial hit. Many U.S. company employee plans had suffered also, although General Technologies had fared better than most. Matt knew he wasn't the cause of the losses, but he wanted to make sure he did everything possible to keep the portfolio from falling further. He sent an email to his boss, Diane Amory, requesting an appointment to review his concerns. She asked him to come immediately to her office in downtown San Francisco, almost two hours away.

Matt printed the reports, took the elevator to the garage, and started driving. Two hours later, he sat in front of Diane's expansive desk and laid out the reports. Diane was an attractive woman, in her mid-forties, in great shape and always dressed to impress. Today she didn't disappoint in a tailored beige suit, with a colorful scarf around her neck. Her dark hair was long and wavy and gave her a soft look. Matt knew she was anything but soft. She had a degree from Stanford and a work ethic that was second to none. She knew her job and worked hard at it.

"Diane, this is what I'm confused about. We've invested approximately $100 million with Wealth Management Inc., WMI. Almost all of these investments are apartment complexes in California. They were all brokered to us by the same company, WMI."

"How much in commissions did WMI earn on these deals?" Diane asked.

Matt punched some numbers into his calculator. "It looks like they made around $8 million on the deals. Not bad. But what I'm concerned about is all the assets are underperforming. The executive summaries that were shown to the board before they were purchased show an effective rate of return on equity of 8.5%." Matt flipped through a couple of reports. "We've owned these assets now for over two years and we are bouncing around a 3.5% return on equity."

Diane put on a pair of reading glasses and studied the reports. "Hmm, that doesn't look right." She handed the reports back. "What do you think is causing them to be underachieving? Is it the real estate market in general?"

Matt made a grimacing face. "It might be that, but I don't think this market would have that great of an effect. These projects are apartments, and they usually hold their own during tough times unless they are overleveraged, which these aren't. These projects were scheduled to bring in $8.5 million annually. They're only bringing in $3.5 million right now. I would say if they were down by eight hundred thousand-dollars or maybe even a million dollars, the market could be the culprit. There's got to be more to this than the real estate market."

Diane nodded in agreement. "WMI was introduced to us by one of the Board of Directors of General Technologies, Morton Bain. He swears by them and he's a powerful board member so he usually gets what he wants." She folded her hands on the desk. "Matt, can you find out what the problem is here? Why these numbers are so far off? Go through the reports and get through the numbers. See what you can find out about Wealth Management, Inc., or WMI or whatever they're called. Keep what you find to yourself, and bring your report back to me. Whatever you find, good or bad, will have to be reported to the board. Every employee in this company has an eye on their 401(k). Whatever is causing this devaluation needs to be stopped, or we will hear about it."

Matt gathered up the reports. "I can look into these projects, Diane, but I'll have to visit each project individually and talk to the onsite personnel. That'll take some time, because these projects are scattered all over the state."

"I don't care how long it takes, Matt. Find out what you can and hopefully there haven't been some shady dealings with WMI in this portfolio. As you are probably aware, whenever you get projects that cost big money, there is always the possibility that someone's going to have their hands out."

Matt got up to leave. "Okay, Diane, I'll get started on it Monday. I'll need to wrap up a few loose ends at my office, and then I'll be on it right away."

Matt was dialing his phone before he hit the elevator. A familiar voice answered. "Hello?"

"Hey, Drew, it's Matt. I'm in the City at General Technologies. It's after five; want to meet for a drink?"

"Absolutely, old buddy," Drew answered. "How about the Thirteen Views at the Hyatt, our favorite haunt?"

"That would be perfect; I was thinking about the same spot. I can be there in about 30 minutes."

"I'll see you then, Mattie boy."

Matt arrived first and picked a spot at the bar where he could look out the huge floor-to-ceiling window and see the San Francisco Bay. About fifty sail boats of different sizes tacked back and forth across the expansive water. The sun shone brightly in the afternoon sky and the water reflected its brilliance. An older pianist in a black tuxedo softly played a Billy Joel tune on an ivory-colored piano. He appeared to be in a trance as he methodically struck the piano keys. Businessmen in suits and secretaries in skirts half-filled the normally placid bar. Matt took off his coat and laid it over a bar stool.

Before he could place an order for a drink, or loosen his tie, he felt a firm grip on his shoulder and turned to find a grinning Drew standing behind him. "How's it going there, buddy boy? What brings you here to my fair city?"

Drew pulled out a bar seat and motioned for the bartender to come over. The place was slowly adding more bodies and the noise level was rising. "I'll have a Corona, and he'll have a Coors Light."

"Thanks Drew. I had to meet with Diane regarding some underperforming assets in our 401(k) portfolio. I'm scheduled to be hitting the road here soon to visit about ten projects all over the state.

That ought to be fun. How's everything at Hartford Financial? Have you worked your way out of the subprime mortgage mess yet?"

Their beers arrived, and Drew took a swig of his. "Man, Matt, you don't know how lucky you are to be out of the industry. Every day is a new adventure in unraveling bad real estate loans. I've seen some real doozies lately. You can't imagine how hard it is to separate pieces of bad loans from a whole security. Whoever thought up that type of financial instrument should be locked up in a room full of them for six months and told to figure them out."

Matt reached for a bowl of pretzels that had been set in front of them. The music, laughter, and clinking of glassware made speaking in a normal voice a challenge. "I guess it was a blessing in disguise that I got out of it."

Drew's eyes wandered as he checked out the women in the room. "The new thing is we get a hundred calls a day from investors trying to buy our securities at a huge discount. Fortunately, we don't have very many bad ones, as we were the first to spot the change in the housing market."

Matt loosened his Perry Ellis tie. "Why are investors trying to buy mortgage-backed securities? I thought they were so toxic nobody wanted them; they were worthless."

Drew smiled. "They are toxic assets to a huge bank or hedge fund because it's too expensive to sort them out. Besides, they are a public relations nightmare if the big guys foreclose on these homeowners who are part of the securities."

Matt stared at him intently as he paused to sip his beer. "Keep going, I'm listening."

"Well," Drew continued, "some banks are selling these securities at a discount just to wash their hands of them. The buyers of these securities try to foreclose on the bundled mortgages as fast as they can. Most of the time homeowners are trying to modify their loans with their original banks and are doing so in good faith, and suddenly their house is foreclosed out from under them."

I wonder if that's what happened to Mom and Dad, Matt thought. When the market changed and dad got sick, they tried everything to save their house, but ended up losing it anyway. "But if these investors foreclose on these houses, don't they end up with homes that are worth less than the investor paid for the note?"

"Here's the kicker," Drew said, poking his finger on the bar for emphasis. "These investors turn around and sell the homes, then file a claim with TARP—which is the acronym for the Federal Bailout, the Troubled Asset Relief Program—for the difference between what they sold the house for and the full amount of the loan they foreclosed on." He set his beer on the bar. "Let me give you an example. Let's say I sell an investor a mortgage-backed security, which has a face value of one hundred million, for twenty million. That investor forecloses on those securities and eventually sells the homes they took over for the twenty million they had in the security. The investor then files a claim with TARP for the one hundred million the securities were originally worth, less the twenty million they received for selling the homes."

He paused to let the numbers sink in. "Once TARP pays the claim, the investor pockets eighty million on a twenty million dollar investment. Pretty slick, isn't it?"

Matt whistled softly. "Wow, no wonder you hear so many people crying foul over their foreclosed homes."

Drew nodded in agreement. "Let me tell you one more thing. I guarantee you the foreclosure process is being done fraudulently. There is no way the people signing off on these foreclosures could unravel these securities without cutting corners and forging some signatures. You watch, sooner or later the press will pick this up, and these people are going to scatter like cockroaches."

Matt shook his head in amazement. "I wasn't even aware that anything like that was going on. I just figured people were losing their houses because they were over their heads and couldn't modify their loans."

"Well, some are losing their houses because of that, but there are a lot of others who are getting screwed. Actually, there are more than a lot of people getting screwed. "

"Not to change the subject, Drew, but you know something about multifamily investments, right? In the portfolio that I manage, there are several projects where the income they are generating is way off of our initial projections. I've been asked to figure out why there are discrepancies."

Drew had been staring at an attractive blonde sitting with her friend at the end of the bar. She had obviously noticed Drew and was communicating with her eyes, which usually meant Drew was only half paying attention. He looked back at Matt. "What? Oh, yeah, apartments. I'm familiar with how they're valued. We have a whole division that buys and sells those babies. There can be lots of reasons your income isn't as high as projected."

Drew shot a quick glance back at the blonde. "I mean there could be major repairs that are needed, or the real estate taxes could be higher now because the value has been pegged to the sales price. It could be a lot of things. Are you going to look at the income and expense reports and the operating budgets?"

Matt nodded as he watched a large pleasure boat leisurely cruise by the piers jutting out into the bay from the shoreline. "I'll be looking at all those things by visiting each site and walking the grounds. Hopefully I can figure out why there are differences in the projections versus reality."

"Make sure you talk to the onsite people and not just to the property manager," Drew said. "The property manager only visits the site periodically and will try to tell you what he or she thinks you'll want to hear. The onsite people know what's really going on at those projects."

He paused for a second, looking back at the woman across the bar. "I've got to send that gal over there a drink. She's just too cute."

Matt shook his head, smiling. "Drew, you never fail to amaze me. You don't miss a beat."

He smiled and shrugged with an indifferent look on his face. "Hey, it's what I do. I can't help it if she can't take her eyes off me."

FIVE

The large conference room wall was paneled with a rich walnut wood and ornate crown molding ran along the ceiling. The dark, oblong central table was ringed by fourteen black leather chairs. A pitcher of ice water sat in the center of the table on a polished silver tray with eight sparkling crystal goblets. Six men in suits of various colors of grey sat around the table. Stephanie, dressed smartly in a dark-blue business suit, sat to the left of her boss, Dennis Willis. Directly across from her sat Alan Hubbard along with two of his colleagues. She didn't recognize the other two, but she knew Alan. He had a reputation as a ladies' man, mostly in his mind, but there seemed no female that he hadn't hit on, including Stephanie.

Dennis stood up. "I think most of you know me, but I want to introduce Stephanie Bernard, one of my top investigators." He held out his right hand in Stephanie's direction. "You've all probably heard of the Rocklin Wealth Management mortgage scam we cracked a couple of months ago. It was one of the most sophisticated mortgage Ponzi schemes ever discovered in the United States. These people were generating millions of dollars in loans with straw buyers and phony appraisals. If they hadn't been so greedy, they might have gotten away with it." He turned to Stephanie. "But Stephanie and her team managed to figure out who the players were and what they were up to." He smiled at her. "She's investigated a couple of these now, and she's quite good."

As he addressed the group, a couple of the men took notes, while the others sat back in their seats. He turned to his left and waved his hand. Dennis poured a glass of water and sat down. The room was eerily quiet.

He nodded to Alan. "So give us a little background on this case and bring us up to speed."

Alan adjusted his red tie, which matched smartly with his light grey suit and navy-colored shirt. He had a square jaw, tan face, and a youthful look with his full head of wavy brown hair. He came across as a confident man who knew he had good looks and a brain to match them.

He stood as he addressed the group. "Mr. Parker, as you know, is a prominent land use attorney here. He's been practicing law for over twenty years and is concerned about some practices coming out of the Board of Supervisors of Yolo County."

Alan handed out file folders to Stephanie and the others. "I've made you a copy of five development applications that the Yolo County staff processed. None of these applications called for a zone change, a variance or anything controversial." He set his folder on the table in front of him. "The land use was consistent with the zoning and all of these proposed projects were within the conditions of the general map. They should have been a slam dunk for approval, but instead they were all turned down."

Stephanie spoke for the first time, locking eyes with Alan. "They were turned down by the Board of Supervisors, right?"

Alan kept eye contact with her for a moment. "Exactly. There was no good reason to turn these down except that the current board seems to be against all development. They have a NIMBY attitude when it comes to any real estate project, especially commercial projects."

Stephanie asked, "What's NIMBY? I've heard that expression, but never knew what it meant."

Alan leaned forward, putting his pen down. "It's an acronym for Not In My Back Yard. Developers face neighbors all the time who don't want certain things built in their neighborhood, including the same type of house they live in. It's okay for the neighbors who currently live there but not for anyone else who follows behind them."

Alan continued but kept his eyes on Stephanie. "We see that a lot when we're trying to rezone a project or put a more intense project like an apartment near a single family subdivision. But it's rare that we see it used on a project that fits the zoning and is not controversial to the public." He finally shifted his gaze.

"The board is controlled by its chairwoman, Caroline Bennett. She's one of the largest landowners in Yolo County and by far the wealthiest person there. Mr. Parker can't figure out why she is so against development. There doesn't appear to be a financial incentive for her to turn everything down."

Dennis jumped in. "I've heard about Caroline. She's a confirmed liberal who sees herself as a protector of the environment. But she is beyond normal activists. You might say she is a zealot. She also has lofty goals she has set for herself, and the Yolo Board of Supervisors is just the starting place for those goals." He leaned back in his chair, twirling his pencil with his fingers.

Alan sat down. Stephanie tried not looking at him but could feel his eyes boring through her like the sun through a magnifying glass. She thought, Please, take a picture, it'll last longer. This guy is a dog. She glanced around the conference room, noticing the watercolor prints that John Parker's wife had painted hanging on the wall. I wish I could be that talented. She thought about Matt and their upcoming wedding. It was six months out, but there was still so much to do.

Thinking about him made her smile, and she was getting antsy to get out of this meeting and see him. Alan interrupted her thoughts.

"Caroline has a close friend named Mellissa Burns. They were roommates at Berkeley and see each other every day. If you can believe it, Mellissa is a bigger environmental nutcase than Caroline."

Dennis asked, "This is all interesting stuff, the background of the Board of Supervisors and all, but what can we do for Mr. Parker? What does he want us to do?"

Alan cleared his throat. "Excuse me. I was just getting to that. We think there is a reason behind Caroline and Mellissa beating-up every project that comes to the board. Mr. Parker can't afford to be turned down every time he presents a project to the board as he will lose clients, which means losing money."

He let the words hang over the room for a second. "He thinks there is something else going on with these two. Why is the board so antidevelopment and what is behind their agenda? What type of project will they accept? Caroline Bennett must have a method to her madness. That's what we want you to find out."

He handed Stephanie a stack of business cards that read: Horizon Films, Stephanie Bernard, Assistant Producer. She read the card and looked up, giving him a confused look. Alan continued. "We need to get close to Miss Bennett and Miss Burns. Here's how we think you can do it. Stephanie, you and I are now in the documentary business. I've gotten you an interview with Caroline at her ranch house next Wednesday, ostensibly to talk about Yolo County ranchers. She was thrilled at the idea of being in a documentary."

Alan tapped his pen softly on the table. "I'm interviewing Mellissa Tuesday. She thinks she's part of the film, also. She should be able to give us some information that will be useful, but we have to handle her delicately." He looked directly at Stephanie. "I need you get close to Caroline and figure out what makes her tick."

Stephanie nodded her head. "I'll be happy to meet with her Alan. It may take a little time, but I'll get to the bottom of her agenda. I have some questions for you though." She couldn't help but notice that he was good-looking, but she wasn't interested in anything other than working together. He didn't seem like the type of guy who would take no for an answer.

She looked down at the yellow notepad in front of her and underlined a sentence. "From the little research I've done, Caroline seems to have higher ambitions than the Yolo Board of Supervisors. What if she is just passionate about the environment and hates all development." She looked up from her notes. "What if all she wants to do is be the largest landowner in Yolo County and keep all development out?"

Alan shrugged. "If that's the case, then I'm sure John will want to go with plan B, which will be to help put up another candidate to run against her in the next election and vote her out of office. The next election is not for two years, so if she has other reasons for her tough stance, we'd like to find out in sooner than two years."

"What is your timing? How soon do you need to get a report on this, and what will you do with the information once you get it?" she asked, tapping her pen on the notepad. "I know Mr. Parker and he's used to getting results quickly, but I think this is going to take some time. I hope he understands."

"He understands, Stephanie," Alan said. "But he does want results. So if you can produce those, he will be patient." He kept eye contact with her. "Can I get your cell number, please? I'll need to keep in touch with you frequently."

I bet you will, she thought, just don't abuse it. She brought her black patent leather purse from around her chair and handed him a card. "Here are my numbers. Call me if you need me." She glanced at her watch. "Is there anything else? If not, I'm going to have to leave. I've got another appointment I need to make."

Dennis looked around the room. "Is there anything else, Alan?" Alan shook his head. "I guess we have what we need for now. Shall we meet in another ten days and compare notes?"

They all nodded. "Okay that's it, we'll be in touch."

Stephanie hadn't reached the door when Alan called out, "Hey, Stephanie, can I walk you out? I want to speak with you about a couple things." He reached out and held the door for her.

Stephanie hesitated for a second. "Sure, my car is in the parking garage downstairs, third floor. Where are you parked?"

Following behind her as she exited, he answered, "I'm on the same floor. You might be wondering why this is such a big deal and why Mr. Parker would be willing to pay your firm to dig up information on this woman; but believe me, there's more here than meets the eye."

Stephanie felt him checking her out as they walked. This guy is unbelievable, she thought. I wonder how long I'll have to be around him.

As they descended down in the elevator, he continued. "Parker has had ten projects turned down in the last three years. No matter how many times he's met with Caroline privately, either at her office or other places she'll agree to meet, he ends up getting stonewalled, and she and her cohorts end up trashing his projects." He held the door when they hit their floor.

Alan lifted his arm out and checked his watch. "You know, it's only 5:00. Why don't we go down to the 4th Street Bar & Grill, and I'll buy you a drink. There's a lot that I need to fill you in on, and it's hard to do in a short period of time."

Stephanie stopped in her tracks. "Alan, I appreciate the offer, but I never mix business with pleasure." She held up her watch and pointed to it. "Besides, I'm meeting my fiancé for dinner in a half an hour. Maybe another time we could go over this, although it's probably not a good idea over drinks."

Alan smiled and leaned against a pillar. "I saw your ring. It's pretty impressive. Look, Stephanie, we're going to be working on this case for a while, so you might as well get used to me. Heck, you might even end up liking me."

She had started walking, so he sped up to catch her. He reached out and pulled her arm. Stephanie turned a surprised look on her face. He released his grip. "Look, I promise, I don't bite. I just want to get to know you a little better. I like it when I know who I'm working with, versus being around a robot."

Irritated that he'd made her feel defensive, her face flushed. She stopped at a white Honda Accord. "This is my car." Without taking her eyes off him, she fumbled through her purse for her keys. "How did you end up working for Mr. Parker? Are you an attorney?"

He leaned on one elbow on the top of her car. "I am. I went to law school at Vanderbilt and passed the bar in '96. I went to work right away for the FBI chasing money launderers and drug smugglers." He paused. "I liked the excitement but got tired of moving and traveling all the time. I've known Dave Parker for years and he asked me to come to work for him. I get to practice a little law and still do investigative work. It's great. I'm on interesting cases all the time."

Stephanie nodded toward the bulge in his jacket. "Do you always pack a gun?"

He shrugged and spoke nonchalantly. "It's a force of habit. I've got a concealed weapons permit, but I haven't had to pull it out since I left the Bureau." He looked up and smiled. "You never know who you'll run into in this business."

"Hopefully you won't need it when I'm around," she said.

He opened the door for her. "I'm sure I won't." He nodded at some pictures lying on her passenger seat. "Is that you and your fiancé? May I look at them?"

Stephanie picked them up, thumbed through them briefly, and then handed them to Alan.

He studied them one at a time then handed them back. "You make a nice couple."

Stephanie smiled thinly. "Thanks."

Alan turned serious. "Send me as much information as you can on Caroline and I'll see what information I can find."

"I will," she answered. "You said in the conference room that you would be handling Mellissa. What did you mean by that?"

Alan shrugged. "We feel she is a needy person and will probably be more than willing to talk to us. You and I will be trying to get to know her, get close to her and see if we can get her to help us. I'll start with her first."

"So you're saying she's vulnerable and you're going to use her to get to Caroline?" Stephanie asked a mild note of irritation in her voice.

Alan grinned, showing off an almost perfect smile. "I wouldn't use such a harsh term as 'use' her. I like to think we'll all find some common ground that could benefit everyone, including Mellissa. Just wait, you'll see. My methods are very good for all concerned."

Stephanie sat and swung her well-toned and tanned legs into the car. Alan didn't miss any of it. "I can't wait to see this," she said. "This ought to be a real education in human relations. I'll speak to you later."

Driving down the parking ramp toward the exit sign, she started to wonder. Why would Caroline act this way? What is to be gained by having your board turn down projects that follow existing zoning and land use laws? How will Alan get Mellissa to trust him? This is definitely going to be an interesting case.

Highway 50 toward Folsom was fairly busy for a Thursday afternoon. Traffic in both directions was moving at a slow pace, as was typical for the weekday commute. Beyoncé sang out a soft ballad with her rich voice as Stephanie drove, and she tapped her well-manicured nails on the steering wheel to the beat of the music. She had arranged to meet with Matt at Folsom Beer Gardens for happy hour, and then they were to meet with a local florist regarding the floral arrangements for the wedding.

She couldn't believe it would be happening in six months. She thought of the night at Il Fornaio when he got on his knees in front of a packed restaurant. The waiter had slipped her diamond engagement ring into a champagne glass and had totally surprised her.

Matt, what a wonderful guy. I'm so lucky. The phone interrupted her daydreaming.

"Hello?"

"Hi, Stephanie, it's Dennis. I just wanted to get your thoughts on the Caroline Bennett case. Have you had a chance to digest anything that was discussed this afternoon?"

Stephanie steered the car to the right lane as her exit approached. "Not really, Dennis, but it seems this lady must wield some major power for Mr. Parker to hire us. This is not a small project. We're expected to dig up a bunch of information on a very public figure without creating a lot of fuss. That won't be easy, nor cheap. Does being a member of a board wield that much power?" she asked.

"Oh you bet it does, Stephanie," he answered excitedly. "The board of supervisors has the final say on land use. If you own land in any county, what that board allows you to do with that land will determine what it is worth."

As she listened to Dennis, Stephanie fiddled with her blue tooth headset, adjusting it to hear him better. He continued. "In Yolo County, Caroline carries a big stick. The projects she and her board are turning down already have the proper zoning designation. They are often very sizeable projects and come before her board for a final blessing before they can be developed."

"I see," Stephanie said as she turned into a shopping center parking lot. "I guess that does explain why Mr. Parker wants to understand her rationale for being antidevelopment. Well, listen; I'm where I'm supposed to be, so I've got to go. I'll see you in the morning." Stephanie adjusted herself in her mirror and made it inside the restaurant where she spotted Matt sitting in a corner booth. There were seven other patrons in the place, and five were sitting at the mahogany bar that sat against the wall with a large ornate mirror behind it. Bottles of alcohol were stacked on wooden shelves on both sides of the mirror.

Stephanie waved at the blonde bartender, who was busy mixing up a tropical drink in a blender. The jukebox in the opposite corner of the bar played a Carrie Underwood tune. Matt spotted Stephanie and rose to greet her.

He gave her a hug and kissed her on the lips. "Hey, gorgeous, how are you doing?"

"I'm great, Matt. Did you order something to drink?"

"I ordered a beer, but I wasn't sure when you'd get here so I didn't order you anything. Here comes Jenny now. I'll get you a glass of wine." They settled back into the booth.

"So, how was your day, anything exciting going on?"

Stephanie set her purse next to her. "I got a new case today that might be interesting. Have you ever heard of a ranching family from Woodland named Bennett? Supposedly they own quite a bit of land in Yolo County."

Matt sipped his beer and nodded. "Yeah, I've heard of them. Mark Bennett, the father, was a bigwig with the California Republican Party. He was kind of a king maker for them. I remember that the family owned the largest amount of land in the county and were very powerful people."

Stephanie reached for his hand and squeezed it as he spoke. Matt smiled at her and continued. "I think the father died a few years ago."

Stephanie perused the appetizer menu. "Well, now his daughter, Caroline Bennett, has inherited everything and is the power player in Yolo. I bet her dad would be rolling in his grave if he knew what her politics are now."

Matt raised his eyebrows. "Really, why do you say that?"

"Apparently she's a diehard liberal and is very committed to the environment. She sits on the Yolo Board of Supervisors and controls it. The board is raising havoc with developers. They won't approve anything that is development related."

"What are you supposed to be looking into?"

Stephanie straightened up in her seat. "This law firm that specializes in land use hired my firm to check out Caroline. They want to know why she's turning down every deal that comes before her board. She doesn't need money, so that can't be it. Can you think of why she would be doing this?"

Matt rested his hand underneath his chin. "Usually real estate deals revolve around money. When you take that element out of the equation, it starts to get a bit murkier. You say she's a committed environmentalist. Is it possible she's so radical there is no development project on Earth that she would approve of?"

Stephanie sighed. "I guess she could feel that way. Maybe her political ambitions need the support of the environmentalists." She turned the menu around and studied the back. "Are you hungry? I'd like to get a salad or something before we go to the florist."

Matt handed her a menu that was sandwiched between a bottle of ketchup and a jar of mustard. "This is the full menu. I think I'll get the French dip sandwich." He snuggled closer to her. "All I know is one thing. Mr. Parker hired the right person for the job."

Stephanie smiled at him and sipped her wine.

SIX

Matt turned the immaculate blue BMW into the circular driveway of the large apartment complex in South Sacramento. He had spent three hours over the weekend washing and detailing his car, and even though he had driven to San Francisco and back, it looked as if had been driven off a showroom floor. As he got out, he subconsciously wiped a spot off the hood. He parked in a spot with a Reserved for Future Tenants sign, and then he walked past the circular driveway leading up to the clubhouse. A spectacular fountain shot water fifteen feet in to the air, which then tumbled down an artificial waterfall into a waiting pond. Large colorful Koi swam lazily in the water, periodically diving under an available lily pad at some unseen danger. The glass door to the clubhouse had the words Welcome to Pheasant Crossing painted in white letters in a semicircle.

Wow, he thought to himself, this is an impressive project. If I were in the market for an apartment, I wouldn't mind living here. He looked toward the first building to the left of the clubhouse. It was a two-story, walk-up building surrounded by a well-manicured lawn and mature trees. Brightly colored snapdragons, pansies, and daisies filled the flower beds. He could see beyond a sprawling string of similar buildings, each positioned a bit differently than the one next to it. The only sounds he heard as he walked toward the entrance were the water from the fountain and an occasional bird singing in the nearby oak trees.

He introduced himself to the young woman sitting behind the first office outside the main community room. "I'm Matt Whiteside. I'm with General Technologies, and we have this project in our portfolio. I'm here to look over the project and to ask you a few questions, if you don't mind."

The woman, with a nametag Brenda on her lapel, initially seemed friendly, but once he told her the purpose of his visit, she seemed to become more edgy, shifting in her chair often. Matt guessed she was probably in her late twenties. She was a little heavyset but not overly so. She nervously ran her hands down her dark slacks then tugged at the sleeves of her blue blouse. She sure wears a lot of makeup for a young woman, Matt thought. She cleared her throat and spoke. "Of course, Mr. Whiteside, whatever I can do to help you, ask away."

Matt took a yellow pad out of his briefcase and scanned his notes. "The property management firm that oversees this project is Wealth Management Inc.?"

She nodded. "We go by WMI, but that is correct."

Matt continued. "What is the name of the property manager you report to?"

"My PM is Mika Menski. He oversees this and, I believe, five other projects." She tapped the top of her desk nervously.

Matt nodded. "Do you know the names of the other projects, by chance?"

"Yes, I believe he oversees Stanford Gardens, Mayfair Grove, Carmichael Gardens, Folsom Downs, and The Oaks at Arcade Creek."

As she ticked the projects off, Matt noticed all five were in General Technologies' portfolio. He spent the next three hours with her going over the rental rates, the monthly expenses, and the construction work, and finally they took a walk around the complex.

Upon returning to the clubhouse, Matt commented, "You have an impressive complex here, Brenda. You've done a nice job maintaining it, and I can see why you keep it full."

She shifted her stance, holding her hands at her waist. "Thank you, Matt, but I'm only one of six persons on this staff here. Everybody who works here contributes." She looked up and out toward the buildings. "It can be quite a challenge sometimes. Mika is a demanding person to work for."

Matt clicked his car keys to open the door. "One last question before I go. You were telling me about ongoing construction projects here." He looked around the complex, his Oakley sunglasses deflecting the bright sunlight from his eyes. "This project looks fairly new. Why is there so much work going on here? We spent over one million dollars last year on capital repairs." He looked at her. "Aren't these repairs part of the original builder's warranty work? And who is the contractor that's doing all this work?"

Brenda's eyes widened and she started to stammer as she spoke. "I really don't know why the work was requested or required. I'm only told that certain buildings are to be worked on and to notify the tenants. WMI is also the general contractor on this project and on all projects they manage. Mika doesn't tell me more than that."

Matt edged his sunglasses to the bridge of his nose. "So you're saying the company that does the property management also approves itself to do repair work on the same project?"

"I don't know how all that works, Mr. Whiteside," Brenda replied. "They don't tell me much about that side of the company."

"I see," Matt said. "Well thank you, Brenda, you've been very helpful. You can call me Matt. Here's my card with my cell number. If you ever have any problems, give me a call. Keep up the good work."

Matt pulled out of the driveway and began thinking about the conversation with Brenda. Something doesn't add up here. The management company is ordering repairs and giving work to itself without competitive bidding. Almost ten percent of the units are vacant because they're waiting for renovation that doesn't seem necessary on such a new project. Brenda has a waiting list for those units but can't rent them because the construction isn't finished. As he was mulling over all this, his cell phone went off.

Not recognizing the number, he answered, "Matt Whiteside."

A male voice in a heavy middle-European accent answered back. "Yes, Mr. Whiteside, this is Mika Menski. I understand you were just visiting Pheasant Crossing, and you might have questions. I can answer them for you."

That was fast. "Yes, Mika, I am just leaving Pheasant Crossing. Your manager, Brenda, was very helpful. She seems very knowledgeable about the project. Right now I'm on my way to look at Stanford Gardens in Rocklin and all the other projects you manage. After I've seen them all, I'm sure I will have plenty of questions for you."

"Mr. Whiteside, I don't like having people snoop around my projects," he said curtly. "In the future I would like you to make an appointment and I will show you around. I know everything there is to know about these projects, so if you want any information on them, you need to go through me."

Matt steered the car into the fast lane as he spoke. "Pardon me for correcting you, Mika, but you've got the tail wagging the dog. General Technologies owns these projects, and they are a critical part of the assets in our 401(K) portfolio. I don't need your permission, or your presence, to look these assets over. However, if I feel I need your expertise, I will let you know."

Matt felt irritated with Mika's attitude. He added, "Like I said, I'll let you know what questions I have when I'm finished reviewing all of these projects. I can tell already I'm going to have a lot."

Mika responded condescendingly. "We shall see where your

inquiry goes. You'll be hearing from me again." Matt heard the phone go dead.

Twenty-five minutes later he found himself turning into another Sacramento project, past a monument sign that read Stanford Gardens. It, too, was a large apartment complex, with similar architecture, except that the first project had a beige body color with crème trim and this project was light grey with charcoal trim. Matt was impressed with the well-maintained grounds and the overall appearance of the project. But he also noticed it too seemed new and shouldn't be requiring major construction.

He spent the next two hours with the property manager; an older gentleman named Bill, and walked the grounds with him. After thirty minutes they ended up back at the clubhouse. "Bill, I appreciate your time and the information you've provided. I left my briefcase in your office, so I'll snatch that and be out of your hair."

Bill held the door for him and followed him into the clubhouse. Matt noticed a tall, slender woman with wavy blonde hair standing in front of a desk of one of the rental agents. She wore a pair of jeans that fit her snuggly and a red halter top, showing off an area of bare skin on her back.

Next to her stood a small child, no more than two years old, quietly sucking on a lollipop.

Hearing footsteps behind her, the woman turned to look back to see who was coming up behind her. Matt's heart almost leaped out of his chest. She looked at him with astonishment. "Matt, Matt Whiteside, is that you?" She turned all the way around to face him.

Standing in front of Matt was a gorgeous woman, one with soft skin, pouty lips, and bright blue eyes. The little girl turned to see who her mother was talking to.

"Kathy Ann," Matt croaked. He cleared his throat to talk in a normal voice, but he was sure she noticed it was quavering. She moved over and hugged him. Immediately he smelled her Tommy Girl perfume, and it brought back memories of an earlier time when they were both attending Santa Clara University. He was the star quarterback for the football team and she was the head cheerleader. They were the king and queen of the campus. They had spent many intimate times together and the scent of her perfume brought it all flooding back. Matt backed away. "What are you doing here, Kathy Ann? The last I had heard you were living in San Jose with your husband."

"I was," she replied as if she had answered that question a million times and it bored her to death. "I just moved to Sacramento last month." Her daughter looked up at her quizzically. "I don't know if you've heard, but Keith and I are divorced."

"Keith?" Matt asked. He was going to add more but she kept on.

"You remember Keith, don't you? He was the tight end at Santa Clara. You guys used to play together. We started dating after you and I broke up."

Oh, I remember Keith alright, he thought. I also remember you dumping me like a bad habit and breaking my heart after I blew out my knee. It took me years to get over it. "Yeah, I remember Keith. What happened to him? I lost track."

"He transferred to Fresno State after Santa Clara cancelled its football program to finish up his eligibility. I followed him there, and we got married right after graduation. The Packers drafted him, and we both hoped he'd have an NFL career, but he got cut in training camp."

Matt just listened, but thought, Keith, the guy with the worst hands in school and probably in all of college football, couldn't catch a cold, let alone a fastball thrown by Brett Favre. He was so dumb he couldn't remember his own phone number, let alone a 200-page NFL playbook. He got cut? What a shocker!

"Wow," he said, feigning surprise. "I didn't realize you got married so fast." He kneeled down on one knee in front of the little girl, who smiled shyly. "Who's this pretty little girl?" Matt couldn't help but notice she had olive skin and a flat nose like her dad. Too bad she didn't inherit her mother's looks.

"This is Brittany. Britt, can you say hi to Matt?" Kathy Ann spoke to the girl sternly. "Matt and I used to be really close friends."

Looking up and smiling, she responded in a high pitched voice. "Hi, Matt."

Matt smiled at her, "Hi there, cutie, how old are you?"

Brittany held up two fingers. "Two."

Matt straightened up. He nervously straightened his tie and addressed Kathy Ann. "So, you live here at this complex?"

She nodded. "Yeah, I live here and I work at Macys at Sunrise Mall in Citrus Heights. Remember, you took me there once a long time ago during Christmas vacation?" She gushed as she spoke. "I can't believe I ran into to you. I think about you all the time, Matt. I wish I hadn't been so rash in my decisions a few years ago, but we all make mistakes." She grabbed his hand and pulled him closer, almost inches from his face. She batted her eyes. "I've really missed you."

Brittany was watching everything with a quizzical look on her face that said she wasn't sure why her mother was standing so close to this stranger.

Matt was breathing quickly, trying to gather his thoughts. You missed me, he thought. Then did you break my heart like you did?

"I missed you too, Kathy Ann," he stammered. "You look great, just as I remember you."

"Why don't we go do lunch or grab a drink soon?" she asked. "I'd love to catch up and find out what you've been doing all these years. Do you have a number where I can reach you?"

Matt fumbled through his wallet and handed her his card. He looked down at it and spoke. "Here you go. Listen, it's been great seeing you, but I've got to run. I've got another project to look at before the day is up." He smiled down at Brittany, who continued to watch everything with wide eyes. "It's nice to meet you, Brittany."

Kathy Ann came up and kissed him on the cheek. "I'll call you soon, Matt."

By the time Matt had reached the freeway, his mind was in a jumbled mess. Why, of all places, did she have to end up in Sacramento, and why did she rent an apartment he was overseeing? Why did she have to look so good, and why did he give her his phone number? He remembered how pushy she could be, and if Kathy Ann wanted something, she usually got it. *I should have told her I was engaged.* He mumbled to himself, "Why didn't you level with her about things?"

SEVEN

The hood of the green John Deere tractor pointed in a parallel line to the greyish-brown, tilled earth that it had swept past five minutes earlier, going in the opposite direction. The flat expanse of earth in front of it seemed to go on for miles into the horizon. Ken Johnson sat in the dusty enclosed cab, listening to a Tim McGraw CD, almost in a trance, as he gently steered the tractor down the row at a steady pace. He'd been disking this field since dawn, and even though it was 2:00 in the afternoon, he still hadn't finished half of it.

His cell phone vibrated in his pocket, and he looked to see a text message from his wife. "Yuri's here. Come back to the ranch house."

Ken had been expecting Yuri, but not until after three. He hopped out of the cab and after a few minutes of working a large wrench, had disconnected the disk behind the tractor, which stretched out eight feet across the field. Within minutes he was headed across a dry alfalfa field that stood four feet tall and was a week away from harvesting.

A group of ring-necked pheasants, three colorful roosters, and two drab hens burst straight up about ten feet in front of the tractor, cackling and squawking as they pulled away in a flurry of wings and feathers.

Even though this happened almost every day, Ken jumped, temporarily losing control, before righting the tractor. As he watched them fly straight ahead for six or seven seconds before dropping into the field ahead, he thought to himself, I never get tired of that sight.

He pulled up onto a levee road leading toward the house. A couple miles straight up the road, he could see the bridge that carried traffic along I-5 from Woodland to Sacramento.

Two minutes later he pulled up to the older two-story ranch house that sat fifty yards off the levee road. As he parked the tractor, he couldn't help but think how long this house had been in his family and how his great grandfather and great granduncle had built it in the twenties after the original home, built in 1875, had burnt down.

It hadn't change much in ninety years. The porch was the same as he remembered growing up. A worn wooden swing hung from a thick chain in the center, and two old rocking chairs sat unused on the other side of the brown front door. The white painted exterior, with matching trim, although dusty, had been kept up over the years. Except for the added rooms in the back, an updated kitchen, and an indoor bathroom, it was the same as when it was built in 1920.

Back in early 2003, with real estate loans being so available and so easy to get, they had refinanced their ranch, using the extra funds to upgrade some equipment and bring some excess land under crop. The loan had a five year balloon payment, and by the time they tried to refinance again, the market had changed. Credit had dried up and their lender had no intention of modifying the loan, as the ranch was worth much more than the loan. The lender would have been happy to foreclose on it and own it.

Ken and his wife of forty-five years, Betty Lou, had looked everywhere for a loan and they were weeks away from losing their house when they were introduced to Yuri Kletcko. He came up with a unique loan that saved their ranch, and they were forever grateful.

Ken entered the house to see Yuri sitting at the kitchen table sipping tea from a blue diamond tea cup with matching saucer. The scent of fabric softener filled the house, and he could hear the sounds of the dryer in the laundry room adjacent to the kitchen as it rumbled through its cycle. Yuri was talking to Betty Lou who sat across from him. She looked alternately from Ken to Yuri with a worried look on her face. Ken placed his stain-ringed, straw cowboy hat on a wooden hat rack in the corner of the kitchen and pulled up a chair. He ran a hand through thinning white hair that barely covered his pale forehead. He looked older than his seventy plus years, as his ruddy complexion was lined with wrinkles from years of overexposure to the sun.

"You're early, Yuri. I thought our meeting was at three." He noticed Yuri was wearing a pair of Wrangler jeans that looked way too tight to be comfortable and a long-sleeved, George Strait dress shirt. A pair of gaudy cowboy boots made of exotic reptile skin rounded out the department store cowboy look. "I didn't realize you had gone country."

Yuri smiled. "I'm starting to like the look. I'm sorry I came early, but I had business in Woodland and finished early. I thought I might come by and see if I could catch you."

"Could you fetch me some lemonade, please?" Ken said to Betty Lou.

Without hesitating, she leapt up and moved to the refrigerator. She was quite agile for a woman her size, in spite of her snug jeans.

"You know you can find me here, Yuri." Ken waved around the room in an arc. "This is where I am all the time. It just takes me some time to get from where I am on the ranch to here. You mentioned we had some things to discuss. I thought everything was done now that we closed the loan."

Yuri nodded. "Everything is complete, but I wanted to go over a few things with you. As I was explaining to Betty Lou, you have the absolute right to run the ranch as you have in the past. You can continue to raise rice and whatever other crops you wish."

"Don't forget the duck club," Ken chimed in. "This ranch has the best duck hunting in California."

"Of course you have the rights to use the duck club," responded Yuri. "I might request a couple of blinds from you at some time in the future, but that's a discussion for another time. I will need your cooperation on certain filings regarding the ranch with the State Water Resources Board. I believe you indicated you wanted to put this ranch into some type of wildlife conservation when you both pass on."

Betty Lou brought a couple of glasses of lemonade to the table and spoke up for the first time. "Ken and I feel very strongly about donating this land to UC Davis upon our deaths, as we discussed with you. We have no children and there is no one we want to leave it to. We don't want the state to take it for taxes, so we want to make sure it ends up where we want it to go."

Ken bobbed his head in agreement. "I know it was a condition of the loan to insure our lives in the amount of the loan, but those insurance proceeds go to pay off the loan and the land goes to the University, right? That's how John Roth, our attorney, explained it to us."

"Your attorney is correct," Yuri said somberly. "That's what we agreed to. I am on title with you as a joint tenant. Once you pay off the loan in a couple of years when the market improves, everything will revert back to the two of you alone. I'll move on to another project." He smiled a thin smile.

Betty Lou patted Yuri's hand. "You don't know what a godsend you have been to us. If you hadn't come along and made that loan, we would have lost this ranch. We were only a few weeks from foreclosure and I could almost feel Caroline Bennett pacing the courthouse steps waiting to snatch this place up. She'd put us out on the highway as fast as her high-powered attorneys could move."

Ken rose and opened the well-used refrigerator. He held up a pitcher of lemonade. "Anybody else want some?"

Yuri shook his head. "I'm okay."

Ken set the lemonade on the white tile counter next to a porcelain rooster. He leaned back in front of the sink. "Yeah, Yuri, Betty Lou's right. We tried every bank in the county and every credit union we could find. None of them would help us out. I thought we were out of options."

Yuri leaned back in his chair, resting his folded hands on his bulging stomach. "Well, that is what I do for a living. My lending methods are a little unconventional, but I'm glad I could help. I only ask that you assist my endeavor as long as it doesn't interfere with your farming"—he nodded at Ken, smiling—"your duck club or your eventual donation as a conservatory ranch to last in perpetuity."

Yuri reached for some papers in a briefcase sitting next to him. "I'm going to leave these documents for you to review. I know you get an annual allocation of water that is sufficient for the current operation of the ranch, but there have been some changes at the State Water Resource Board." He picked up the teacup with chubby fingers and took a small sip. "I want to apply for as much water as this ranch can be approved for."

His face turned serious and he leaned forward, speaking in almost a whisper. "You and I can't afford any reductions in the amount of water that is allocated to this ranch. If you don't get your water, you can't flood your fields and harvest rice. If you can't harvest rice, you don't make money. If you don't make money, you can't pay me." He leaned back, satisfied he had made his point. "I want you to be able to pay me, so I'll make sure you don't get shortchanged by some bureaucrat."

Betty Lou rubbed her hands nervously. "Do you really think the Board would cut back our allocation, even after our family has been farming this land for over a hundred years?"

"I don't want to find out, so I intend to be proactive," Yuri answered. "If you trust me, I promise you, I will help you accomplish what you want to do with your land." He smiled at one then the other. "These documents also help me because if they approve the additional water we're requesting, it gives me more collateral for the loan." He spread the papers across the table. "If you have any questions, please contact me. I will be back in two days and would like to pick them up. If you are satisfied with them, please execute them for me."

He stood and half bowed. "Thank you for the tea, Betty Lou, and thank you for coming in from the field, Ken. I'll see you both in a few days."

They stood at the front door and watched as he made his way to a dusty, silver Lexus parked past the white picket fence surrounding the front yard. A flock of brown chickens milled around the car, clucking and pecking at the dirt. Ken and Betty Lou both waved as Yuri drove off down the dirt road toward the frontage street, a great cloud of dust trailing behind him.

"What do you think, Ken? Do you think it's possible for the Water Board to cut our allocation of water? Yuri is probably right, we should get as much as we can."

Ken turned and stepped back into the house. "I don't know, Betty Lou. I never pay attention to those blowhard politicians in Sacramento, so who knows what they're up to." He plopped down on an antique rocking chair in the corner of the room. He set his dusty boots on a well-worn, leather footrest and slowly rocked back and forth. The living room looked like an antiques dealer showroom with centuries-old chairs and an oak and glass cabinet in the corner filled with knickknacks. Betty Lou slumped tiredly onto a couch covered with a handmade quilt of various colors.

"Should we show the papers to our attorney?" she asked. "He was sure Yuri was legitimate when we signed the loan documents."

"I don't know. Do we need to spend money on an attorney?" He scratched at his forehead thoughtfully. "I think I'll go over the documents, and if I have any questions, I'll give John a call.

EIGHT

Caroline sat quietly in the back of the car, flipping through the latest edition of *Town and Country Magazine* while Brett steered the Mercedes up the asphalt driveway that stretched a mile from the street to the main house. Tall, majestic eucalyptus trees lined both sides of the driveway. Just outside the trees, a white three-board fence ran for miles in either direction. She hadn't seen Brett for a few days since the board meeting. She decided he'd been punished enough and asked him to come to her house in Davis the previous day. He pulled the car up to the front of the low-slung, single-story ranch house that was surrounded by an expansive, immaculate lawn. White and yellow daisies, snapdragons, and mums flooded out of the crowded landscape beds.

Brett leapt out and hustled over to open the passenger door. Caroline, still reading her magazine, breezed by him, paused, lifted up her Gucci sunglasses, and whispered to him, "You were wonderful last night. Be a dear and wait with the car for me. I won't be long." She wandered up the curvy walkway toward the entry of the house.

Throwing open the hand-carved oak door, she stepped into the high-ceilinged entry. Stepping through the expansive foyer, she stopped to observe the gaily decorated living room with its collection of vibrant oil paintings. She had personally picked out the pastel green color of paint for the walls and trim. The couch and two matching sitting chairs covered in an expensive, light red and green floral fabric were accented by pale blue pillows. All the furniture was sitting on a bright gold, red, and blue Persian rug with intricate patterns of peacocks and roosters.

She turned and made a beeline to a large office to the left of the living room. Shelves crammed with books lined the walls from top to bottom. It was apparent this was a man's office at one time, with three mounted elks' heads gracing one wall and a large, overstuffed chocolate-colored, leather couch sitting off to the left. Caroline went straight to the oak desk in the center of the room and sat down. She rifled through the stack of documents sitting neatly if front of her, pausing every few seconds to scan something that caught her eye.

A soft tapping on the door made her look up. Her ranch foreman, Morris, stood there looking sheepish, his dirty cowboy hat held in both hands. "Are you ready for me, Miss Bennett?"

Without speaking, she gestured to the chair in front of the desk. She left him sitting in awkward silence while she continued to go through the papers. After about fifteen minutes, she addressed him without looking up. "How many acres do we have planted at this time?"

He answered, his voice higher pitched than normal, "We have thirteen thousand acres of rice, twenty-five hundred acres of corn, three thousand acres of alfalfa, eight thousand acres of wheat, and five thousand acres of soybeans."

She looked up at him, a scowl on her face. "How much land are we not farming?"

He cleared his throat. "We have about ten thousand seven hundred acres that are fallow."

She looked up from her papers. "I assume that is because we don't have the water to sustain crops on that, especially rice."

"That's right, Miss Bennett..."

She cut him off and snapped, "It's Caroline. Do you get that? How many times do I need to tell you to call me Caroline?"

"I'm sorry, uh, Caroline," he stammered. "But you are correct; that land is not planted because of the lack of water. We would need twice the amount of water we've been allocated if you want to plant rice on that acreage. Rice takes a lot of water."

"I know that, Morris." She bristled. "I was raised here, remember? I'm well aware how much water is needed for rice growing. Go find Elliot and tell him I want to see him. He should be in the outside offices."

"Yes, ma'am, I mean, Caroline." Morris bowed and backed out of the door.

She shot him an irritated look.

A short stocky Mexican woman in a long dress with a white apron tied around her waist came into the room carrying a silver tray with a silver pot and a single cup and saucer.

She tentatively approached Caroline and stopped a few feet in front of her. She spoke meekly, her face staring at the floor. "I brought you your tea, ma'am."

Without looking up, Caroline said in an even tone, "Set it on the table by the window, Rosa. You did remember to put two cubes of sugar?"

"Yes, ma'am," Rosa replied. The woman did as she was instructed and left the room.

A few minutes later, a middle-aged, balding man with a barrel chest appeared at the door. Elliot Spencer, dressed in khaki slacks and a short-sleeved shirt, was the ranch manager.

"Hi, Caroline," He stepped into the office. "Morris said you asked for me?"

"I did." She pointed at a chair with a pencil. "Take a seat. How much money per acre are we losing by not planting rice in that ten thousand acres we have fallow over by the causeway?"

Elliot looked down, a serious look on his face. After a few seconds, he looked back up. "You're leaving millions of dollars on the table by not utilizing that land for growing."

Caroline threw her pencil on the table and walked over to one of two eight-paned windows on either side of the desk. Heavy beige curtains were pulled back and tied, leaving a commanding view of the front of the ranch. She stood for a moment, arms folded. "Millions a year," she said the number out loud. "That number never gets smaller. It's all because those ignorant hillbillies, the Johnsons, wouldn't sell me their land. They will take it to their grave and then do something stupid like donate it to charity."

She turned back to Elliot. "How much more rice could we grow if we cut back on the other crops?"

He fumbled with some numbers on a note pad. "As you know, Caroline, rice takes massive amounts of water. The crops we are growing are a good balance for this ranch. Besides, some of the fields where we are growing other crops are not conducive to rice." He winced as he spoke. "I don't think we can squeeze out any more rice without more water."

Caroline paced the floor. "Given our current allocation, of course we can't grow more. Well, here's the deal, Elliot." She stopped and leaned forward on the desk. "I've got plans, and my plans require a lot of money. I don't know how I'm going to do it, but I'm going to get more water for this ranch. Start figuring out how to get those fallow ten thousand acres ready for next spring's planting." She paused and then smiled. "I want it all planted."

Elliot's eyes widened. "Of course, Caroline, I can get it ready. What will we plant?"

She sent him a chilling look. "Rice."

A moment of silence hung over the room and then she waved him off.

He started to leave but then stopped. "Ah, before I go, can we go over the issues I brought up last month, the ones you asked me to ask you about this month?"

Caroline rounded her desk and sat down. With a bored look she sighed and asked, "Remind me about the issues again, Elliot. I've forgotten."

"May I sit down again?"

She gave him a disinterested nod.

"Our workers are barely making above minimum wage. I want to give them a small raise to give them more money to live on."

"Don't I supply their housing and utilities?" Caroline asked, clearly irritated. "How much more do you want me to give them? I'm running a ranch, not a charity."

"I understand that, Caroline," he pleaded, "but these people have been with you and your family for years; they are tremendously loyal."

She rested her chin on her folded hands. "And a lot of them are here illegally. If I don't give them more money, what are they going to do, turn me in? Of course they won't." She scolded him with a pen. "I've been very good to my workers, way better than some of my neighbors, I might add."

Elliot seemed to ignore her comments and charged on. "You mentioned their housing. There are a considerable number of repairs needed, as there has been deferred maintenance on quite a few of the units over the years. I'm afraid if the health department came out, they'd fine you heavily, and..." He let the sentence hang in the air for effect. "You wouldn't want the newspapers to pick that up. It would be bad publicity."

The last phrase caught her attention. "What needs to be done?"

"Here." He handed her a piece of paper with figures on it. "I've made up a list of things that need attention." Caroline glanced at the paper, focused on the last number, and threw it on the desk. "I'm not spending seventy-five thousand dollars on those shacks. Figure out a way to do it for half."

Elliot made some notes. "What about the wages?"

She paused a second. Every year this bleeding heart hits me up for a raise for his workers, she thought. I'd rather give that money to the Save the Earth Foundation. I may need to start looking for a tougher ranch manager. She signed the paper. "Alright, I'll roll over this time. Give them a quarter an hour raise. Now get out of here, I'm busy."

Elliott gathered his papers, gave Caroline a quick bow, and exited the room. Her phone rang and she answered it.

"Hello?"

"Hi, Caroline, it's Mellissa. I need to see you. It's about the Johnsons' ranch. I've got some scoop you'll want to hear."

She cupped the phone. "Hold on, Mellissa." Caroline shut the door to the office. She spoke in a whispered tone. "Listen, dearie, can you meet me for lunch at Del Paso Country Club in about an hour? I want to hear what you found out."

"Oh, Caroline, I forgot you were a member there. I just love that place, it's so glamorous. What time should I be there?"

"Be there at eleven thirty. Don't forget there's a dress code. You can't go in there in jeans and sandals," Caroline reminded her.

"Don't worry, Caroline, I remember," she answered then hung up.

I hope you remember, dear Mellissa. I almost died when you showed up a few years ago at the country club looking like a ragamuffin who had just spent the morning dumpster diving. Thank god I had a skirt I could throw around you and a loose blouse that fit, but barely. I don't mind when you come to the Board of Supervisors meetings dressed like that, but not at the country club. How she can stand living with those five mangy cats in that dinky house is beyond me. The smell alone would force me to take them to the pound. Ugh!

The expansive formal dining room, with its twelve-foot high, boxed-beam ceilings at Del Paso Country Club, overlooked the first tee and the eighteenth green of the pristine golf course. The room held seating for three hundred people, but less than twenty-five occupied the white-clothed tables with gold chargers. They all spoke in hushed tones, as if worrying their voices might ruin a delicate soufflé.

Caroline sat at a table in the far right corner of the room, staring vacantly through the floor-to-ceiling windows at the golf course outside. A group of four men in knee-high, neatly pressed shorts and short-sleeved golf shirts milled around the tee box, waiting for the group ahead of them standing in the fairway to clear out of their way. Tall, leafy oak and redwood trees lined both sides of the narrow first fairway as it hooked to the left about two hundred and fifty yards down from the tee box. A white flag stick could barely be seen four hundred yards away, hanging listlessly in the hot air.

Mellissa arrived at the large entry, paused under a dazzling chandelier, and hurried past a startled maître d' to Caroline's table. She wore a drab, olive green dress without a belt, and it hung down to the midpoint of her shins. Her hair was pulled back tightly in a bun and two plastic knitting needles jutted out like a pair of rabbit ears from an old black-and-white TV. On her sockless feet were well-worn, brown flats. She plopped herself in the seat across from Caroline and set her large, overstuffed purse on the floor beside her.

Out of nowhere, a slender waiter in black slacks, white shirt, and white tuxedo jacket with a black bowtie appeared and helped push her chair in for her. He took the white, folded napkin from its place in front of her, snapped it open, and gently laid it across her lap.

"Oh, Caroline," she gushed. "This club is so exquisite. I just love it. I hope they're serving the cream of mushroom soup today. I've been dreaming about the tomato avocado sandwich with sprouts all morning."

Caroline answered her in a dull voice. "Today's your lucky day.

That's the soup de jour." She perked up a bit. "Now tell me. What's the big news you wanted to share with me?"

Mellissa looked over both shoulders and leaned closer to Caroline. "You knew the Johnsons' ranch was in foreclosure a while ago. Well, a wealthy Russian developer named Yuri Kletcko stepped in and gave them a loan." She stopped to catch her breath. "Well, ever since that developer lent the money, there have been some strange things going on over at that ranch."

Caroline raised her eyebrows. "Like what, for instance?"

"Like someone has been making inquiries about developing the ranch into a big planned community with commercial offices, homes, and apartments," Mellissa replied. She pulled the napkin off the basket of bread that a waiter had brought, and she helped herself to a fresh baked roll. She lathered some butter on the roll and stuffed half of it into her mouth. Still chewing, she continued, "I ran into one of my friends from the Sierra Club who knows a couple of land use attorneys. The Russian developer's representatives had contacted them. They've only made inquiries about developing the ranch, as far as I know. They haven't filed any formal applications with Yolo County yet."

Caroline turned to the window and watched a heavyset man drive his ball off the first tee dead left into a large oak tree thirty yards away. The ball bounced back at him as fast as it had left his driver, and he had to jump quickly to the side to dodge being hit by the ball. She was amazed a man his size could move so nimbly.

Caroline, along with everyone else watching, chuckled at the sight. She took a roll out of the basket and set it on her plate. "Melissa, there is no way anything like that would ever be approved. That ranch has so many wetlands and vernal pools, it would be impossible to get an Environmental Impact Report that wouldn't kill any project proposed. It's habitat to so many species of ducks and wildlife, the public would come out with pitchforks if anyone tried to develop it. What are the Johnsons thinking?"

A waiter in a crisp white shirt with a black bowtie appeared, and she paused so he could take their order. After he left, Caroline whispered, "I never told you this, but I offered to buy them out at a great price about a year ago. I can't understand why they won't just sell out and retire."

"Well, that's not all, Caroline," Mellissa continued. "I heard they are making a request to the Water Resources Board to increase their allocation of water to reach that ranch's maximum. You know what that means, don't you?"

"Of course I know," Caroline replied irritably. "That means if the Johnsons are successful, the resources board could cut back on my water and I'll have to plant less."

"Exactly, Caroline. I know you want to grow more rice so you can build up your war chest for your political run."

The waiter came up and served their soup. He slipped away as quietly as he had arrived. "Oh my god," Mellissa spoke after her first sip, closing her eyes and leaning back in her chair. "I'm in heaven." She heartily attacked the soup, finishing it in a matter of minutes. She looked around the room before continuing. "Well, you realize the reason the Johnsons didn't take up your offer is they hate you. Your family and theirs have been at war with each other since your grandfather was alive. You could've offered them their own sheikdom with a thousand oil wells pumping out a million barrels a day, and they would have turned you down."

Caroline sighed. "I know, but why couldn't those two old goats have taken my money, stuck it in a bank, and gone to the beach. Imbeciles, I tell you." Now it was Caroline's turn to glance around the room like they were surrounded by CIA agents and she was passing on classified information. She spoke softly. "There is more than one way to skin a cat, Mellissa." She caught herself and raised a hand to her mouth. "Oh, that's probably not a good analogy for you, sorry."

Mellissa made a hurt face. "You're right, it is a bad analogy, but go ahead."

The waiter slipped in to deliver their order, and then he disappeared.

Caroline continued. "I've got an idea that is going to get me as much water as I need to get my ranch running at peak production. It will take a little time and some ingenuity, but I know I can get it done." She clasped her hands together and smiled. "And, for the most part, it will be legal."

"I love it when you come up with new ideas," Mellissa spoke excitedly. "So, what is it? Tell me, tell me!"

"I can't tell you yet," Caroline said smugly, "because it is imperative I keep this under wraps until all my ducks are in a row. I don't want to tip my hand to the Johnsons or that slime ball, what's his name, Yuri?"

Mellissa sat there with her eyes wide and alfalfa sprouts hanging out of the corner of her mouth. Oblivious, she spoke sternly, spitting out sprouts as she spoke. "You can't leave me hanging, Caroline, that's not fair. Give me a hint or something. I won't be able to stand this. You always tell me everything. You know I can keep a secret."

Caroline allowed a look of satisfaction on her face, knowing she knew something no one else did. I can't tell you anything, Mellissa, she thought to herself. I love you to death, but you couldn't keep a secret if your life depended on it. You don't have an unspoken thought and my idea would be all over the county by tomorrow if I told it to you today. If Yolo County needed a town crier, you'd be perfect. But I'm going to be nice today and give you a morsel to chew on. "Okay, Mellissa, here's your hint." Caroline paused to get maximum effect. She spoke two words with authority. "New London."

"New London?" Mellissa asked, surprised. "That's it, that's my hint?"

"Yep, that's it." Caroline smiled knowingly. "Mull it around for a while. The answer will come to you soon. Let's eat up. I've got to fly over to the Pebble Beach house this afternoon. I'm meeting with Jerry Spanos this afternoon."

"You mean the political consultant?" Mellissa asked between bites of her sandwich.

"That's the one. He wants to discuss timeframes and a strategy for my campaign."

"Isn't that election a few years off, like in ten years?" asked Mellissa.

Caroline shrugged as she patted her lips with her napkin. "It is, but Jerry thinks you can't start on these things soon enough. Either that or he's milking me for a paycheck."

Mellissa laughed. "It's probably a combination of both."

"Well, do some research while I'm gone, and maybe you'll figure out my plan. I'll get in touch with you when I get back next week, and I can give you a bit more information if you haven't guessed what I'm up to."

"I can't wait to find out, Caroline," Mellissa exclaimed, clapping her hands together. "Oh, did I tell you I'm meeting with Alan Hubbard, that producer who's doing the documentary on you?"

Caroline smiled and waved her hand as if to say, I don't believe you, even if she did. "Oh stop it, Mellissa; it's not all about me. It's about a lot of ranchers in Yolo County, and I just happen to be the largest one. I'm meeting with the assistant producer, Stephanie Bernard, next week. I checked out their production company, Horizon Films, and they do nice work. A lot of their films are puff pieces, but you can't get enough publicity is what I always say."

Mellissa nodded in agreement. "So, New London is the word of the day. I've got my homework cut out."

The shiny white twin-engine King Air 200 with a red and gold stripe sat in front of the open hangar as Brett pulled the Mercedes to a stop a few feet from its stairway. The four-blade pops glimmered in the bright sunshine. Although Caroline only flew on the plane on short trips such as this, a two hundred mile flight to Monterey, the plane was capable of flying two thousand nautical miles at a cruising speed of five hundred miles per hour.

Caroline preferred this plane more for its comfortable and roomy leather interior rather than its speed and range. Waiting by the stairs, two pilots in pressed uniforms tipped their caps to her as she climbed out of the car. One of the pilots, a young, dark-haired man, looked more like a model for Abercrombie and Fitch than he did a pilot. Before she headed up the stairway to board, Caroline turned to Brett. "I'll see you in a couple of days, sweetie." She leaned forward and kissed him on the lips, then bounded up the stairs and ducked into the plane.

Two and a half hours later, she was seated at her granite breakfast bar, staring out over the eighteenth green at the Pebble Beach Country Club. Waves crashed against the sea wall across the fairway, sending white water spaying high in the sky. The sun was beginning to set, and the water looked like it had thousands of diamonds bouncing light off it. The golf course was empty and looked like a picture out of a magazine.

Caroline's kitchen would make a gourmet chef salivate, with two five-burner Viking Stoves and two full-sized Bosch double ovens. A pair of copper vents hung over the stoves, each having an assortment of stainless steel cooking utensils ranging from spatulas to ladles hanging from them. Caroline never cooked herself—she had hired help for that—but she enjoyed showing off her homes' kitchens, all of them, as she knew others would be envious. That pleased her.

She picked up her wine glass and the bottle of Scribner Bend's Syrah and meandered through her family room to the outside patio. She'd been with Jerry Spanos for the last two hours going over campaign strategies, and he had just left. A gentle breeze blew in from the ocean, bringing the temperature down to a comfortable level.

The doorbell rang. "It's open, Randy, come on in," Caroline called out through the screen door to the patio. The front door opened and the young pilot entered the foyer with two brown bags with the name Monterey Cannery written across them. The smell of garlic and lemon quickly permeated the room and the house.

"Come on out here and let's watch the sunset. Put the food on this table and we'll eat in a few. Help yourself to a glass of wine. It's delicious."

Randy set the bags on the table and poured some wine. "Did you get through your meeting okay?" he asked.

"It went fabulously and was very productive." She leaned across the table and playfully pulled his tie. "Why don't we loosen this up so you could be more comfortable? I don't want you to feel like you're on duty."

He smiled. "I don't. Thank you for letting me stay here with you. I really didn't want to return to Sacramento." His eyes drifted to the golf course and the sunset. "This place is so peaceful and serene. I don't know why you ever leave it."

"I've got things to do and places to be," she answered. "Besides, I can't stay in one place all the time. I like being on the go." She got up from her chair, hiked her flowery skirt up past her slender thighs, and straddled his lap, putting her face an inch from his nose. She slowly unbuttoned his shirt never taking her eyes off his. She massaged his muscular chest with her fingers.

Her hair fell across his face, and he softly brushed it aside. He held her head with both hands as he kissed her on the lips. "Maybe we should take this inside, what do you think?" he asked.

Running her hands up and down his chest, she stopped and pulled her blouse up over her head. She reached around her back and unclasped her bra and let it fall. "I think right here is just fine."

NINE

A series of ceiling fans spun lazily, pushing the air across the expansive restaurant. The midday heat was warm, but not as hot as it usually was in Fresno in August. Even though it was one o'clock in the afternoon, Pismo's Coastal Grill was bustling with customers, including Matt. Young waiters, dressed in shorts and bright shirts, shuffled back and forth from the busy kitchen to the array of tables and booths spread across the sealed concrete floor. A large, rectangular bar sat in the center of the room with the bartenders in the center, and a few patrons ate their lunch there rather than at a table. The voice of Frank Sinatra singing "It Was a Very Good Year" flowed through the sound system, which reverberated around the restaurant. The smell of fresh cilantro, lemon, and basil drifted delicately through the air.

Pismo's was noted for its fresh seafood dishes, and although he didn't get down to Fresno frequently, Matt always made it a point to eat there whenever he was in town. He sat with Adam Roberts, the onsite property manager of Lake Ridge Apartments, the sixth project on Matt's tour of General Technologies' properties.

"How's that steamed crab?" Matt asked Adam as he checked out the dish. "If I didn't love the signature dish, I would have ordered that. It looks good."

Adam shook his head enthusiastically, giving him a thumbs up, not wanting to speak with a mouthful of food.

A man in his late fifties with short grey hair came up to their table. He was fit and tanned and carried himself as if he owned the place, which he did. He was greeting customers, checking on the kitchen and making sure everyone's dining experience went well. Matt stuck his hand out to shake. "How are you doing, Dave?"

"I'm doing well, thanks, Matt. How's that Sea Bass? It just came in this morning from Monterey."

"Awesome as usual, Dave."

"Excuse me. I see my chef is waving at me." As he turned to leave, he said, "I want you to try this new dish I came up with. It's calamari with an aioli sauce and jalapenos. I'll send it over in a minute. I'd better go check what he needs." He headed back toward the kitchen before Matt could answer.

"Dave's a piece of work. He never stops trying new dishes. I love being one of his guinea pigs," Matt said as he wiped his hands on his napkin and set it on the table. "How old did you say your project is, Adam, ten years?"

Adam nodded. "Yeah it was built around 1998. The builder did a great job in the construction of the project. The rumor is that it was supposed to be sold as condominiums, but the project was sold before that was accomplished due to a change in the market. It was turned into a rental project and was owned by a big real estate investment trust out of New York before General Technologies bought it up."

Matt picked the last bite of Sea Bass off the plate with his fork. "Well, you and your crew have done a nice job maintaining it. It looks brand new. Let me ask you something. There has been a lot of repair work done on it in the last year and a half." He looked down at a sheet in front of him. "Something in the neighborhood of two million dollars." He looked at Adam with a quizzical look. "Was all that work warranted?"

Adam looked surprised. "Well, it seems to me to be a lot of construction. I realize this is a 320-unit project, but I think that number is excessive." He scratched his head. "I mean, I don't get into the construction side of things, but that seems like a lot of construction, and I don't remember seeing that much work going on."

Matt leaned on his elbows. "Would you be aware if there was major construction going on at your project? I mean is it possible something was going on inside the buildings that you didn't know about?"

Adam paused for a moment as if collecting his thoughts. "There's no way, Matt. If there were any major construction going on like what you're describing, we would have to notify the residents so they wouldn't be in the way. There would be parking issues and all sorts of things that would require you to give a heads up to the tenants."

He took a sip of water. Even though the restaurant was busy, the noise level was low due to the large open windows on three sides of the restaurant.

"Also, I wander around the grounds on a daily basis, and I would see major activity," he said. "I don't remember any such stuff going on."

Matt shrugged as if to say it was no big deal. He didn't want to alert Adam that anything was amiss. He was seeing the same pattern at all the projects he'd visited so far. They are all newer projects, all well maintained, but each had huge construction expenses that seemed out of whack.

Matt felt his phone vibrate in his pocket. He answered, "Hello?"

"Hi, Matt, it's Diane. Where are you?"

Matt looked at Adam. "I'm in Fresno having lunch with the onsite person at Lake Ridge, Adam Roberts." His eyebrows furrowed. "Is everything okay? You sound stressed."

She paused on the other end. "No, everything is okay, but I need you to cut your trip short. Can you get back to San Francisco?"

Matt glanced at his watch, noting it was 1:30. "Do you mean today? If I left right now, I could probably make it to the city by five o'clock, but it will probably be later because of traffic."

"Why don't you come up tonight and meet me first thing tomorrow morning?" Diane asked. "I want you to fill me in on what you've found with our properties. I just saw a report out of accounting and the value of our apartment portfolio has dropped again. We have a report due to the Board of Directors and they are not going to be happy when they see this. We need to figure out what's wrong and correct it fast. I don't want to be inundated by unhappy employees after they look at their new 401(k) reports, like what happened in 2006 after the subprime meltdown. They will be out for blood."

He had hoped to be back in Sacramento by six. Since he had been on the road for a few days, he was looking forward to being with Stephanie and taking her to eat at her favorite restaurant, Paragary's Bar & Oven. She would understand, of course, but he missed her and was tired of being on the road.

"That works for me, Diane. I'll be in your office at eight o'clock tomorrow."

"Great, Matt, I'll see you then."

After he hung up, Adam asked, "Is everything alright? Is there anything I can do?"

Matt smiled at him and patted him on the shoulder. "No, Adam, don't worry. I just have to take off from here and drive to San Francisco this afternoon."

"Is it anything to do with my project or what we're doing?"

Matt looked at him. It doesn't have anything to do with you, but something is going on with your project, which I doubt you know anything about, and I need to figure out what it is— quickly, Matt thought. "No, it's more about a lot of things in general with the

73

office," he answered calmly, not wanting to give Adam any reason for concern. "I oversee a lot of investments for General Technologies and yours is one of them. But you are doing fine with the project, so keep up the good work. Keep those vacancies and expenses down like you've been doing."

Matt waved at the waitress to bring him the bill.

"I appreciate the time you've spent with me, Adam. You've been a wealth of information. If I have any more questions, I'll give you a call."

He slid out of the booth and as he shook hands Adam said, "Thanks for lunch, Matt. Have a safe drive."

"Thanks, I'll do that."

As he hit the on-ramp to Highway 41, Matt fumbled with his stereo, trying to find a country station. Being unfamiliar with the call numbers, he set the stereo on seek and hoped it would trip over something. He headed north on Highway 41 to Avenue 12, where he cut across for eight miles before he ended up on Highway 99.

The projects he'd seen really bothered him. Who was authorizing these major construction projects, and who was overseeing the payment? Something was amiss. Normally a project would have a budgeted number for repairs, and if that number were large, like more than a hundred thousand dollars, it would be bid out to several contractors to get a competitive bid. From what he could determine, this wasn't being done. Also, large invoices would be administered and paid by a third party. This wasn't being done either. No one was paying much attention to the income and expense statements other than Matt, and he had almost caught the discrepancies by accident.

He put on his headset and dialed Stephanie. She answered on the second ring. "Hi, sweetie, how's it going?" she asked.

Matt glanced into his rearview mirror before changing into the fast lane. He set the car on cruise control and adjusted his seat further back. "It's all good, Steph, it's all good. I got bad news for tonight though. I have to head to San Francisco for a morning meeting with Diane tomorrow. After we talk, I'm going to call Drew and see if he'll put me up for the night."

"Oh, I'm sure he'll let you stay," she said. "Oh, baby, that's too bad. I was looking forward to seeing you. I guess I'll have to reheat a pizza and watch a bad movie with Smokey."

Matt laughed. "Hey, you treat that cat better than me sometimes. Did you have that interview with Caroline Bennett today? How did it go?"

"We did meet today at her ranch home. She was running late, as she had just come back from Monterey," Stephanie answered. "She's an interesting woman, and very striking. I was told she was in her early forties, but she looks ten years younger. It might be the cosmetic surgery she's had. She is also certainly very ambitious. One thing that came out loud and clear is her stint on the Board of Supervisors for Yolo County is just a stepping stone."

"How do you know she's had cosmetic surgery? Did she say something about that or was it that obvious?"

"Matt," Stephanie answered in a scolding tone, "there are some things we women notice, and that is one of them. Trust me, she's had surgery."

"Uh, okay, I believe you. Do you think she has an agenda? Do you think you can find out what drives her to turn down all these development projects?"

Stephanie answered, "Oh, I think I can figure out what she wants. It will just take a little time. I can tell you she likes to talk about herself—a lot. Caroline loves the idea that there is going to be a documentary and that she will be a major part of it. Or so she thinks."

"Are you going to meet her again soon?" Matt asked.

"I'm meeting her next Friday and she wants to show me her ranch. Then we are scheduled to meet twice more in the next week. By the time I'm done with her, I will know her like I would know a sister, if I had one. I'm looking forward to getting the tour of her ranch. From what I saw this morning, it's cool and there are a lot more scenic spots on the property."

"That sounds like fun," Matt said

Stephanie paused a second. "There were a couple things she did that I found odd."

"What was that?" Matt asked.

"When I was sitting in Caroline's office talking to her, a young man came into the office. He was probably around twenty-five and was really good looking. I thought at first it might be her son or something. He stood silently for a second until Caroline finally acknowledged his presence."

Matt tried to picture the scene and asked. "Was he her son?"

"No, she introduced him as an employee. I'm not sure what he does for her. But he asked her a question regarding a pending escrow, and she just lit into him. It was like I wasn't even there. I felt sorry for the man, because she made him look so small. Finally, she dismissed him, telling him to wait outside until she was done with me."

"Wow, that's strange," Matt said.

"That wasn't all. A small Mexican woman came in quietly right after that with a tray of tea and proceeded to set it on a table in the corner of the room. Apparently, Caroline has a particular way she wants her tea prepared, and this woman didn't follow her instructions. If you didn't know better, you would have thought the woman was trying to poison Caroline."

"What did the woman do?" Matt asked.

"I thought she was going to cry, but she just stared at the floor, apologized quietly, and left. Then Caroline turns back to me as sweet as pie, as if none of it happened. It was really awkward, to say the least."

"That's some interview, Steph. It sounds more interesting than what I've been doing."

"How has your trip been, Matt? I've missed you."

"It has been enlightening. Diane called me out of the blue a few minutes ago, and she didn't say what it is she wants to go over with me, but she sounded anxious."

"Well, I hope it's nothing major, but if it is, I'm sure you can handle it," Stephanie said. "I better let you drive without distracting you any further. I guess I'll see you tomorrow."

"That's right. I should be home in the afternoon, and I'll take you out then. I love you."

Stephanie made an exaggerated kiss on the phone. "I love you too, bye."

Matt took the headset off and set it in the console. He turned up the radio and hummed along to a Toby Keith song. His phone set off a dinging sound and he looked down to see a text message: "can u meet 4 a drink 2nite? Kathy A."

Matt stared at the message. I meet Diane at 8:00. Our meeting will probably take about an hour and a half. I can be on the road to Sacramento by 10:00 easy. He texted back quickly, and tried not to get into an accident as he drove. "In SF 2nite." He paused for a second before completing the text. "Meet tomorrow at 4th St Grill at 12:00 4 lunch." He hit the send button and heard the swish as it whisked out into cyber space. He immediately regretted sending it, thinking a lunch meeting with Kathy Ann was a bad idea. "Oh well," he said to himself out loud, "nothing to do about it now."

Matt sat in Diane's office early the next morning, nursing a Starbucks Latte Grande in one hand and clutching a manila folder in the other. While he waited for her to make a couple of copies of documents he'd given her, he couldn't help but notice how similarly she had decorated this office to the one she had at Sun Systems where he used to work. The two famed pictures of her children, along with various photos of her and her husband on different trips, covered the credenza behind her desk. Her diploma from Stanford University hung on an adjacent wall, along with numerous awards from business affiliations. Her office had a view of Highway 88, which was constantly flowing with commuter traffic.

She stormed back in, closed the door, and sat behind her desk. She looked sharp in a dark, blue pantsuit with a white blouse and light floral scarf. Her dark hair was wavy and bouncy and her fiery blue eyes had a lot of sparkle in them.

She handed Matt a stack of papers, and he put them in the folder. "I received the strangest call yesterday, Matt, and that's why I asked you here. Morton Bain called and asked if there was someone from this office checking on the apartment projects in our portfolio."

"Who's Morton Bain?" Matt asked.

"He's on the board of directors of General Technologies, basically both of our bosses. He's supposed to be the second in line to the Chairman of the Board."

Matt nodded knowingly and rubbed his chin with his hand. "Now I remember who he is."

She continued. "He wanted to know who was checking on the projects and what the purpose of the investigation was. I told him you were the person who had noticed the discrepancies between what was presented to the Board at the time of purchase and what is the reality."

She paused and sipped some coffee.

"I told him you hadn't mentioned to me anything you had found and you were scheduled to look at five more projects between Fresno and San Diego. Once you had finished visiting all the sites and speaking with all the onsite personnel, you were going to report your findings to me.

"Before I could go on about the purpose of the investigation, he cut me off. He told me to call you back, as he would personally take over checking out the projects. He made it clear he didn't want anyone to interfere with the projects or for anyone other than himself to speak further to anyone onsite."

Matt looked confused. "Doesn't that seem strange to you? Why would a director in his position step in and take over this investigation? It doesn't make sense. I'm in charge of looking out for the company's 401(K) and he's in charge of making sure his stockholders are protected, many of whom are employees. Why would he prevent me from doing my job?"

Diane shook her head. "I don't know, Matt, but it seems strange to me, too. There's no reason for him to get involved." She leaned across her desk. "Here's what I want you to do. I want you to continue to check out this issue. I didn't tell him you gave me a little information, specifically that the property management firm that manages the projects and the construction firm that is doing all the work are one and the same. This doesn't pass the smell test, especially when someone as high up as Bain steps in. Besides, Bain's not the only Director on the Board and you can bet we will be hearing from some of them if this value slide continues. They all own a lot of General Technologies' stock and will be very vocal if they start losing money."

Matt shifted in his seat. "I agree, Diane. I'm not an apartment expert by any means, but something is off here. I'll keep this low key from now on, and I'll make a report on what I've found so far and send it to you. Maybe you will see something I miss. If there's any mismanagement going on here, we're the ones who will get the blame if we don't find it. "

Diane took a deep breath, "We've done a good job at keeping the losses on the employee 401(k)s low so far despite this horrible market. If anything happens on our watch to drop those values any further, you and I will get the blame, and you know what happens after that."

Matt nodded. "We'll be out of a job."

"Exactly. But you need to keep this under the radar." Diane

leaned forward on her elbows, narrowing her eyes. "We'll keep this investigation between you and me. If you find out anything, let me know immediately. Start with the property management company, the contractor, and Bain. There might be a hidden connection between them. And please be discreet."

Matt rose and headed out the door. "You got it, Diane. I'll let you know what I find."

Matt pulled into the underground parking garage below the Macy's department store, which was located across the street from the 4th Street Bar & Grill in downtown Sacramento. He glanced around the half-empty lot. When he didn't see any car he recognized, he turned off the ignition and contemplated his next move. Last night, when he stayed with Drew, he'd confided in him that he'd run into Kathy Ann and was meeting her for lunch. Drew's reaction was predictable—that Matt was making a horrible mistake and he should cancel it and rid her once again from his life.

Matt knew Drew was right and he should forget the whole thing, but he felt like the proverbial moth drawn to the flame and he couldn't help himself. He missed the spontaneity of Kathy Ann. The memory of the trip to Napa came to his mind. After the wine tasting while driving home that night, he'd almost died when she took off all her clothes and insisted he get off at the nearest side road. He'd been so nervous climbing into the back seat and was sure a police cruiser would pull up at any second. He chuckled as he reminisced. If that episode took more than two minutes, he would be shocked. *Do I miss that part of my life?*

He stepped into the restaurant. *I might as well get this over with. I'm here, and there's no harm in having lunch with an old friend.*

Kathy Ann was sitting in the corner of the restaurant, a glass of white wine in front of her. As he approached the table, Matt could see she had gone all out for the occasion. Her hair was pulled back in a ponytail with a white scarf tied in it, similar to the way she used to wear it. Her flowery blouse was low cut, accentuating her perky breasts, and she wore the pearl necklace he had given her for Christmas many years ago. Her red lipstick matched her manicured nails and he could smell the scent of her perfume. She looked fabulous, but he couldn't figure out why she looked different than how he remembered her. Her figure seemed more filled out than before. Then Matt remembered his conversation with Stephanie the day before about cosmetic surgery. Now I know why, he thought.

She smiled when she saw him and patted the seat in the booth next to her. He slid in, trying not to look conspicuous, but at the same time trying to see if there was anyone at the restaurant he knew. He kept trying to convince himself it was an innocent lunch, but his conscience wasn't buying it.

She put her arm through his and scooted up next to him. "I'm so glad you came," she said. "I've been thinking about you nonstop since we ran into each other last week."

Matt smiled at her and shifted his weight away from her nervously. "It's nice to see you again too. You look great as always. Have you had a chance to look at the menu? I'm a bit pressed for time today."

She gave a fake pouty look. "Oh, Matt. Where do you have to be that's so all-important? You can relax and spend some time with me." She reached up and played with his hair. "Why don't you loosen your tie and enjoy yourself?"

She reached up and started pulling on his tie when he waved off her hand. "Listen, Kathy Ann, I would love some time to kick back with you, but today's not the day. How is your daughter, Brittany? Why didn't you bring her along?"

Kathy Ann waved her hand dismissively and checked out the menu. "She's doing fine; I left her with my neighbor's daughter."

"How old is your neighbor's daughter?" Matt asked.

Kathy Ann kept studying the menu. "Uh, I think she's around twelve, but she's mature for her age." She looked up and batted her eyes. "Trust me, Brittany's fine. I think I'm going to have the Chinese chicken salad. What are you having?"

Matt quickly perused the menu before answering. "Uh, I think I'll go with a pastrami sandwich." He put the menu down, and cleared his throat. "You know, Kathy Ann, I'm engaged and am getting married soon."

She raised her eyes, but didn't act surprised. "I thought I'd heard that, but I don't care. Your marriage is a lifetime away. We've got plenty of time to reconnect."

Over lunch they talked about the old times and about her failed marriage. Mostly Kathy Ann did the talking. Matt sat and listened, still feeling awkward. He looked over her shoulder and saw a man who seemed to be staring at him from the hostess desk. He had a firm jaw, neatly trimmed hair, and brown eyes. He was well dressed in a dark suit and tie, as if he had just come out of a high-powered business meeting, and appeared to be in his early forties. The man turned and looked through the mirror behind the bar, and it appeared to Matt he was sizing up Kathy Ann.

Who is that guy? Matt thought. He sure seems interested in us. I don't think I've ever seen him before.

The man turned his gaze back to Matt, shook his head, and walked out of the restaurant. Kathy Ann had continued talking, unaware of the stranger. Matt turned his attention back to her, hoping the man wasn't someone who knew Stephanie.

Finally Matt interrupted her. "I'm sorry, Kathy Ann, but I've got to return to work." He felt guilty but at the same time enjoyed being around her.

After paying the bill, Matt started to slide out of the booth when Kathy Ann pulled his arm. She slid up to him and whispered. "Brittany is going to be with the neighbor all afternoon. We could go to my place, and I'll do the things you used to love me to do to you," she cooed softly. "You still remember don't you?" She lightly ran her fingers up his arm, smiling into his eyes.

Matt cleared his throat and moved away. "Come on, Kathy Ann, I'll walk you to your car."

"I enjoyed lunch, Matt. I want to see you again. Please call me."

"I enjoyed it too. I'll be in touch," he said, feeling as if he were playing with fire.

As Matt drove to his office, his mind was spinning in. Why am I putting myself into this position? I know she is bad for me and I should put her out of my mind. Do I really want to revive this relationship? Taking a walk down memory lane is exciting, but is it reality?

TEN

Yianni's Restaurant was located on busy Fair Oaks Boulevard in the heart of Carmichael, an affluent area of Sacramento. It was a small venue, and if a person wasn't aware of its location, it would be easy to drive by it twenty times without ever seeing it. It was situated between a Salvation Army drop-off building to the north and an auto repair shop to the south. Three years ago, it was a pizza parlor. The new owner, a transplanted Chicagoan of Greek descent, spent a ton of money to fix up the place.

Alan sat at a corner table with Mellissa, nursing a glass of champagne and listening to her talk about the loves of her life, her cats. She wore a nondescript grey dress with a white frilly collar and brown sandals. Her thick, unkempt grey hair hung straight over her shoulders. Alan pretended to be interested as she went on and on about her felines' antics, but he wasn't a cat person. If someone left a stray on his doorstep, he would more than likely take it to the pound than anything else.

The restaurant held twenty-five persons at a sitting, along with another twenty at the u-shaped bar, which surrounded the island of liquor, where the lone bartender hung out. There was one other couple in the eating area and another three people at the bar rolling dice. Background music from a local rock station played a Glenn Frey song. The door to the kitchen was open and from where they sat, they could see and hear the chef busily cooking up the lunch fare. The special of the day was mussels in garlic and wine sauce, and the pungent smell of shellfish and garlic hung over the small venue.

Mellissa paused in her monologue to finish off the last remnants of a Caesar salad. She paused for a second, rolling her eyes in an exaggerated manner. "Oh, Alan! This is the best Caesar salad I've ever had. I've got to get the recipe." She took a gulp from a bubbling glass of champagne. She held up the glass. "And this is divine!"

Alan pulled a bottle from a silver bucket next to their table and refilled her glass. This was the opening he was waiting for. "When John, the owner, comes back, I'll ask him if he'll give the recipe to you. He's a good guy and I'm sure he'll let you have it." He took a sip of his champagne. "Mellissa, we've talked about a lot of things this afternoon, and you are very insightful as to the goings on around Yolo County." He paused and looked over his reading glasses at her. "You and Caroline go way back, and you probably know her better than any other person." Alan flipped over a page in the notebook in his hand. "What would you say is the thing that drives her most? She's successfully taken over her father's business and made herself a player in this county. What's next? What does she want to accomplish that she already hasn't?"

Mellissa shifted in her seat and smiled. She acted thrilled to be thought of so highly as the closest confidant of Caroline Bennett. She took a deep breath and spoke. "I think Caroline sees herself in a more powerful position than the Board of Supervisors and feels she can do more for people and the environment from a higher platform."

Alan was scribbling notes and asked, "Does she have theological aspirations or political aspirations?"

"Oh, no, Caroline? Definitely not theological." Mellissa laughed at the suggestion of Caroline as a religious person. "But definitely political. She wants to run for a higher office sometime in the future. She loves being on the Board of Supervisors, but there is a limited amount of good you can do on a small board."

Alan set his pen down to sip some champagne. "There has been some talk around the development community that Caroline and the Board are antigrowth, and that it is almost to the point of a radical agenda. How do you think she would respond to that?"

Mellissa's eyes squinted, and she almost spit her words out. "Developers only want to tear up the land, asphalt over everything they can, and rape the environment, all in the search for the almighty dollar. They don't care what they destroy in the process. Caroline and I don't feel those are the values we want to promote in our community." She drained her glass of champagne. "Many of Caroline's backers fully support her position against developers and applaud her for taking them on." She glanced about the room. "If she wants a powerful political appointment or to run for higher office, she's going to need those backers' support." She paused. "And their money."

"You mean like the Friends of the Planet and other environmental groups you're involved with?" Alan asked.

"Yes, exactly. She'll need their support down the road and then some. She can't be involved with these groups, as it might create a conflict of interest with her being on the Board of Supervisors, but I can."

The owner, a tall slender man with a mane of white hair, came by their table and started picking up their plates. "How was everything?" he asked in his booming voice and East Coast accent.

"It was great, as usual," Alan answered. "Hey, John, this is Mellissa. She's been praising the Caesar salad and wanted me to ask if you could possibly give her the recipe."

He slapped Alan on the back. "Well, seeing as it is Preston Carson's recipe, and I stole it fair and square from him, I don't see why not."

"Who's Preston Carson?" Alan asked.

"He's a local builder who comes in here a couple times a week with his lovely wife, Karen. He's a great guy and a wonderful cook, and I know firsthand, as I've been to his house many times for dinner. I love his salad so much; I pestered him into giving the recipe to me. It's one of my biggest sellers."

"Oh, thank you so much, John," Mellissa gushed. "It is incredible, the best I've ever had. The romaine lettuce was so crisp, with the blend of Dijon, garlic, parmesan, and I think a hint of anchovies; it was heavenly. "

"You've got an excellent palate. I'm glad you enjoyed it," John said. "Give me a minute. I'll get it and be right back." He slapped Alan again as he headed toward the kitchen.

Alan refilled her glass and referred back to his notes. "If you are running for, say, a seat in the United States Senate, that takes a lot of money. I know Caroline is rich, but is she that rich?"

Mellissa smiled a knowing smile, her cheeks flushed. "She is rich, and she's going to be richer, and I'm going to help her."

That phrase caught Alan's antenna. "Really? That's interesting. How so?" This might be the break we're looking for he thought. Keep flirting and keep her talking. And drinking.

"Well, Caroline's ranch is operating based on sixty-five percent of the land being farmed. She's got a plan to put the balance of the land into rice production." She tapped her fingers on the table absent mindedly. "That will almost double the income to the ranch and she will save that extra money and use it somewhere down the road as she needs it." She gave Alan an I-know-something-you-don't-know look.

His eyes lit up, and he pretended to be impressed with this insider knowledge.

He tilted his head inquisitively. "How is she going to accomplish that? I'm not a farmer or a rancher, but I know rice takes a lot of water, and every rancher already has a certain amount of water allocated to their land. How will she manage to get that much more water?"

She sat up straight, her chin in the air, as if she were being defiant. She flung a lock of hair out of her eyes. "I can't tell you that; it's confidential."

Alan set his pen on the table and folded his hands. "Okay, how about if we talk off the record? This is fascinating."

"Off the record, for sure?" she asked.

"Off the record, I promise." He held his hand up as if he were a boy scout, which he thought was ironic because it would be the first time anyone accused him of being that. Besides, he justified to himself, I'm never going to print any of this conversation.

She squirmed in her seat and moved closer to the table, holding her glass out. "Please pour me some champagne. It is so good." She cleared her throat. "I'm not completely certain myself what she's planning, but I will give you the same hint Caroline gave me: New London."

Alan filled her glass and stared at her blankly for a second. "New London?"

She nodded her head as she sipped. "Now you know what I know. But I promise you the next time we meet I'll know a lot more." She caught herself hiccup. She looked at him with wide eyes and started to laugh. "I think I'm getting tipsy."

Alan smiled at her and thought to himself, I need to keep the dialogue going and gain her confidence. She may not know everything, but she knows enough. Maybe I can get her to slip up. "So, what do you do when you're not helping Caroline with her politics, Mellissa? What is your daytime job?"

She scanned the room. "I work for a developer at a company called Wealth Management, Inc., or WMI for short. I loathe the owner, by the way. He's scary and gives me the creeps. Anyway, I'm in charge of doing documentation to facilitated foreclosures on defaulting homeowners."

Alan cocked his head to the side. "Really? What does that entail?"

She played with the last bit of the sandwich on her plate. "I'm what is referred to as a 'robo-signer.' I sign thousands of documents a day saying this procedure was followed correctly or that signature is correct so my company can complete foreclosures and take possession of homes. Sometimes I think the documents are fraudulent, but I don't have the capacity to do anything about it. I'm scared that if I say anything I'll get fired."

"Why do you think they're fraudulent?" Alan asked.

She leaned in to speak closer. "Because the mortgages we're foreclosing on were all bundled into securities and sold all over the United States in pieces. Nobody knows who owns what part of what mortgage. I'm forced to sign that my company owns the deeds and because my signature is notarized, it looks official and we can take it to court for confirmation."

She waved her glass at Alan, spilling some champagne. "I don't like this; it makes me sick to think we're putting all these people out of their homes. But I've got news for you, Alan." She leaned back and looked at him smugly. "I'll let you in on another secret. Off the record, of course."

Alan winked at her.

Mellissa rambled on. "WMI won't be able to get away with this for long. They're foreclosing on homes illegally. I've been keeping detailed files and a diary of all that's been going on the past year, and when the time is right, I'm going to spill the beans. I'll start with *The Sacramento Bee*."

Alan made a mental note to follow up on WMI. "That's interesting. You're a brave woman. So you're only afraid of your boss firing you, or is there something else?"

She looked at him with a sad expression. "Can I confide in you, Alan?"

He leaned forward and held her hand. "Of course, Mellissa. Anything you tell me will be confidential."

She squeezed his hand "I've only told my friend, Amber Behrendt, who works with me at WMI about this, and I've given her copies of my files for safekeeping just in case something happens to me."

Alan squeezed her hand. "Are you that worried?" he asked.

She nodded her head. "I think my boss is a ruthless gangster who will do anything for money. I've heard him speak to people on the phone, and it makes me feel he would not think twice about doing harm to people."

Alan listened intently. "Have you thought about going to the police?"

She sighed and leaned back into her chair. "I've thought about the police, but I don't have enough information yet. But I will soon enough."

Alan let her hand go. "Be careful, Mellissa."

John came up to the table and handed Mellissa a sheet of paper with the recipe typed neatly on it. "Here you go, Preston Carson's Caesar salad recipe. Enjoy it."

She beamed. "Thank you so much. I can't wait to try it at home." She glanced at her watch, an old Timex with a frayed band. "Oh my, I didn't realize it was way past 3:30. It's been great talking to you, Alan, but I need to get home and feed my cats. They get upset with me if I'm late."

After she left, Alan sat collecting his thoughts. He wrote down the name Amber Behrendt on his notepad and underlined it. John stood next to him until Mellissa had left the restaurant and nodded in the direction of the front door. "Who's the babe, Alan? Either the law business is worse off than I thought, or you've really lowered your standards."

Alan looked up at him and gave him a dirty look. "You're a jackass, John. That wasn't a date. I am trying to get some

90

information out of her for a client. Thanks for not coming up and blowing my cover with one of your lame jokes."

John held his hands up in mock protest. "Me, come up and antagonize one of my best clients on a date, err, I mean, on an undercover operation? Never."

"Please, you're killing me." He pointed at the bar and said, "Make yourself useful and pour me a Stella, will you?"

Alan sat for a minute then dialed his phone. A female voice answered. "Hello?"

"Stephanie, it's Alan, how are you?"

"I'm fine, Alan. What's up?"

"Can you meet me at Yianni's in Carmichael? I'd like to go over what you've gotten from Caroline and run what I've found with Mellissa by you. I don't know what to make of what she told me, but I think it might be important."

"What's Yianni's, is that a bar? Why can't we meet in my office or your office like most business people do?" she asked.

"Yianni's is a restaurant where I just had lunch." He glanced up at the bar that was five feet from him then back at his beer. "Normally I'd agree with you and meet at the office, but it's almost four and I don't want to drive all the way downtown and fight the traffic. You live in Carmichael so it's on your way home."

She paused for a moment. "Oh, all right. Give me forty-five minutes, and I'll meet you there. I can't stay long. I'm meeting Matt for dinner."

"Great, it shouldn't take us long to compare notes."

Stephanie stepped inside Yianni's and surveyed the place for a second. Alan watched the five men seated at the bar turn when they heard the door open and do a double take as she stood in the doorway. She looked striking in a tailored beige suit with a white silk blouse and light-colored high heels. Her hair tumbled across her upturned collar, and a stylish necklace of white beads adorned her neck. She spotted Alan sitting at the same table as he had before, studying a notepad. Alan looked up and watched her wander over to him as the men at the bar followed her every move.

She stood over him, her arms crossed. "Alan, I thought you said this wasn't a bar."

Alan gave her a quick once over with his eyes and gestured to the seat across from him. "Well, it's not exactly a bar." He waved around the room, pointing to the tables behind him.

She sat down. "It's not exactly a restaurant either." John had seen her and approached. He looked at Alan and said loudly, "This is much better. Your taste is improving by the minute."

Stephanie looked at Alan, confused.

"Stephanie, let me introduce you to John, the owner of this fine establishment. I try to ignore him most of the time."

John bowed slightly, "Nice to meet you. Would you like a drink?"

"Yes, I'll have an iced tea, thanks." She turned to Alan. "You met with Mellissa today, right? Did you glean anything out of her?"

"I think I got some useful information, but I need to do more digging with her." He paused and flipped a page on his notepad. "Caroline does have a monetary reason for being antidevelopment. If she continues along this path, she will have the support of some of her well-heeled environmental friends to build up cash when she decides to run for higher office."

Stephanie contemplated that for a second, and then asked, "What political position is she aiming for?"

"That question came to my mind too," he answered. "I don't know for sure, but it's possible she may want to take an appointed position somewhere, maybe an ambassadorship somewhere. I don't think she can make a leap from Board of Supervisors to, like, a United States Senator. There's got to be something in between, and my guess is it will take money."

Stephanie sipped her ice tea and asked. "You mean like some type of political payoff?"

Alan shook his head. "No, nothing illegitimate. I'm talking about raising money for other politicians and once they are elected, getting them to appoint her to the position. The question is what position would she want to be appointed to? I didn't ask that question, as I didn't want to be too obvious. Next time I meet with Mellissa, I'll try to get her to talk about that."

"Do you think you can get her to do that?" Stephanie asked.

Alan smiled. "I've got her right where I want her. She's so happy to be interviewed for this piece, she can't stand it. She'll talk, all right, but I don't want her to think I'm prying. I'll let her do the talking and she'll tell me. I actually think she likes me." He paused for a second, and then continued, "Mellissa told me some interesting things about her boss. She thinks he's doing some illegal things with mortgages. She's is planning on ratting him out, even though she's worried he might take revenge on her. I can't figure out what to make of all of it."

"Who's her boss? Did she say what kind of revenge he might take on her?" Stephanie asked.

"She didn't say his name or what he might do. Maybe she has an active imagination." He shrugged. "How about you, Stephanie?" he asked. "What have you found out from Caroline? Has she spilled out anything earth shattering?"

A loud bang shattered their conversation. Stephanie turned toward the bar to the source of the noise. Three men were noisily playing dice, alternately taking turns at banging the dice cup against the wooden bar top.

"Is this place like this all the time?" she asked.

Alan chuckled. "Only in the afternoon, when these contractors get off work. They come in here before they go home. They'll do this for a couple of hours and then John will kick them out before the dinner crowd rolls in."

Stephanie played with the straw in her tea. "Caroline has confirmed what Mellissa said, in that she wants to run for a higher office. She didn't elaborate but hinted her final goal wasn't at the state level. She's kind of elusive as to what she's aiming for, but I hope to find out."

Alan signaled to John to bring another round. "My guess is she will try to get appointed to some high-level board first. Stephanie, are you sure you won't have a glass of wine or something? You're making me feel guilty drinking alone."

She shook her head. "No thanks, Alan. But don't feel guilty. I don't care if you indulge."

He looked into her eyes and reached across the table to touch her hands. "I know this is not an appropriate thing to say to you, as we are colleagues, but I can't help myself. You are one beautiful and intelligent woman. Matt seems like a nice guy, but I wish you weren't spoken for." He cleared his throat.

Stephanie pulled her hands back from his reach and her face flushed. "Alan, I am totally flattered, but I am not interested in anything other than a professional relationship with you. I would appreciate it if we keep it that way. If you can't, either I will resign from this case or you will."

Alan smiled slyly, pulling his hands to his lap. "I knew you would probably react like this, and it only makes me admire you more. I can keep things professional as you wish, but don't think I won't be thinking of you in a different way." He thought for a second. Should I tell her that I saw her fiancé at the 4th Street Bar & Grill today or let it go? I don't know who Matt was having lunch with or why, but I doubt it was about business.

Stephanie interrupted his thoughts. "I've seen how you are, Alan. You were flirting with that receptionist at the law firm the other day, and I see you with a different woman all the time. I know your type."

He shrugged his shoulders in indifference. "I'm single, so I'm free to date." He looked into her eyes.

She sipped her iced tea through the straw and raised her eyebrows.

He looked down at his beer. "I don't want to cause trouble between you and Matt, Stephanie, but I think I need to tell you about something I saw."

She sat in rapt attention as she waited for him to speak. After an awkward pause, she said to him, "Well, go ahead, let's hear it."

Should I do this? he thought. It's probably my only chance to get close to her. He spoke softly. "I had to meet someone at the 4th Street Bar & Grill before I met Mellissa this afternoon." He looked up into her eyes. "Your fiancé, Matt, or a man that looked just like him, was having lunch with a pretty woman I didn't recognize. It looked pretty cozy. I just thought you would want to know."

Stephanie sat frozen in her chair. Her expression didn't change. Finally she said, "I'm sure there is an innocent explanation for whatever he was doing. I'm very comfortable with my relationship with Matt."

Alan stared at her and thought, Well, I just opened a can of worms in that relationship. She's trying not to show concern, but I can read women, and this woman is going to want some answers. This should be interesting. He patted her hand soothingly. "You're probably right, but I felt you should know."

"Thanks, Alan," she said giving him a steely look. "I should be going. Thanks for the drink and the info."

ELEVEN

Yuri sat with Ivan at a circular glass table while a wide umbrella shielded them from the hot afternoon sun. The table sat on an expansive wood deck that overlooked the seventh hole at the Serrano Country Club in El Dorado County. Serrano was one of the most exclusive country clubs in the greater Sacramento Area, and the immaculately manicured grounds were surrounded by mansions that rose above the golf course. Yuri's mansion sat farther back off the course than most of the houses around it, and since it sat at the top of a knoll, it had a commanding view of the lights of Sacramento to the west. He had purchased the home from a struggling custom builder who ran out of money before he could complete the house. Yuri stepped in and paid two million in cash and finished it to his tastes.

A pair of golfers drove their cart by Yuri, and he and Ivan lifted a glass to them. They in turn waved back. About a hundred yards from Yuri's deck was a pond where a dozen ducks swam casually around an island. A large waterfall stood in the center, and gurgling water cascaded down the manmade stream. A majestic weeping willow sat in the center of the island, creating shelter from the bright sun.

A clear pitcher of ice sat on a white cloth next to a fifth of

Stolichnaya Vodka. Yuri reached over and filled Ivan's glass, then his own, with the vodka. He clinked Ivan's glass. "Cheers my, friend. Here's to another million dollar deal closing. That retail center was a steal. Literally."

Ivan lifted his glass high. "I have to hand it to you, Yuri. You make it look so easy. I never thought you'd get Markham to agree to your price. He was so indignant when you guys first talked. I guess he ended up seeing it your way, eh?"

Yuri smiled. "Of course he saw it my way. He just needed some persuading."

"How'd you do it, Yuri?" Ivan smirked as he sipped his drink. "He seemed so set on his price."

Yuri shrugged his shoulders. "Ivan, everyone has a weakness. You just need to figure it out and expose it." He sat back in his chair. "It seems Mr. Markham has a young girlfriend he's been supporting in Folsom. I had my nephew, Mika, pick her up from work a few weeks ago and take her to Markham's personal residence a few minutes before his wife was due home from a church service."

Ivan interrupted. "Did the girlfriend go willingly?"

"Not exactly, but Mika has a way of convincing people they should do what he is asking. Anyway, he shows up with the girl and has a short conversation with Markham and Markham quickly figures out it would be cheaper to take the discounted price I offered than to risk a messy and expensive divorce." He smiled and lifted his drink. "I think Mika also told him it might not be in his best health interests if he didn't take my offer seriously."

Ivan smiled back. "That was good, Yuri, but you must be careful. This is not like the old days. You can't go around making threats to people or make them disappear. We're past the days of Russia after the wall fell when it was like the Wild West, or even our chop shop days of the '90s. There are too many ways to get caught."

Yuri reached across the table and picked up a Habanera cigar that was resting in a redwood-lined, silver box sitting at the center of the table. He flicked his lighter and took his time lighting the thick cigar. He took a deep drag, then fell back and blew grey smoke slowly into the air.

"I'm not making anyone disappear, Ivan, not yet anyway. Let's just say that the thought that I might do such a thing is just as effective as doing it." He waved his hand with the cigar in the air, dissipating the smoke. "But if I did have to, as you say, make someone disappear, trust me, they won't be found and I won't be caught."

Ivan reached for a cigar. "All I can say is be discreet, Yuri. You are becoming more visible due to your wealth, and you do draw attention to yourself. You can't work in the shadows anymore."

Yuri waved his hand dismissively. "Okay enough about Markham. It's done; we won and we're richer. Let's talk about the Johnson Ranch. We are in process to get the extra water rights I applied for from the water resources board. I want to figure out what those rights are worth without alerting the Johnsons."

"How are you going to accomplish that?" Ivan asked. "They've got to know the extra water has value and they're entitled to it."

Yuri saw out of the corner of his eye an older woman with grey and white streaked hair come through the French doors from the house and approach them. She wore a full-length, beige smock with a collar up to her neck. She wore old sandals on her feet and no makeup. She shuffled up to the table and stood there silently.

Ivan nodded to Yuri, who finally acknowledged her presence. He snapped at her, "Woman, why do you interrupt us? Can't you see I am busy?"

The woman bowed subserviently. "I'm sorry to interrupt you husband, but I need supplies from the store and don't have any money. I wanted to wait until you were done with your business, but it has been two hours. I want to get to the store before it closes."

Yuri exploded, "Did I not give you four hundred dollars three days ago? What is wrong that you can't run this household without coming to me for money every other day?" His voice kept rising and he stood up, towering over her. "Why don't you take lessons from the Khabensky lady down the street? She feeds her family on eight hundred dollars a month and she doesn't run around looking like an old hag all the time."

He was screaming at her now, and he raised his hand to strike her. She cowered and turned away from him in a reflexive mode, as if this weren't the first time he had struck her.

"It is time for you to learn the proper way to take care of your husband and his family." His fist glanced off her head as she shrieked and fell to the ground. Yuri balled up his fist and wound up to strike her again, when Ivan caught his arm.

Yuri gave him an angry look. "Let go of me, Ivan. I know how to take care of my own matters."

"Calm down, Yuri. I know you can take care of your household, but you don't need to alert the whole neighborhood." He directed Yuri's eyes to a pair of golfers who were standing outside their cart watching the whole scene.

Yuri relaxed his arm and put it at his side. He turned to his wife and snarled, "Woman, get into the house. I will deal with you later." She scurried through the French doors and disappeared.

Yuri turned to the golfers, adjusted his collar of his shirt, and smiled. He indicated with his arm for Ivan to sit. He then sat down and relit his cigar. The golfers got back into their golf cart and slowly drove away, watching Yuri until they rounded a corner on the fairway and were out of sight.

Yuri waited until they were gone. "Okay Ivan, where were we before we were interrupted by my stupid wife? Oh yes, you were asking how I'm going to keep the Johnsons from getting wind of the value of the extra water. That's easy. I will tell them there is more value for the water and will give them some additional cash once I sell the allocation." He blew smoke at Ivan and smiled. "I just won't let them know how much I received for it. They'll be happy with what I give them."

"Are you sure they won't find out?" Ivan asked. "I wouldn't think it would be too hard to find out how much extra you could make."

"It wouldn't be if the Johnsons were suspicious, but they love me. I am their savior. As long as I share with them some of the money, they will be happy."

Ivan rolled his cigar in his fingers. "You never told me, Yuri, how you managed to come up with that money to loan to the Johnsons."

Yuri took a deep drag on his cigar. "Remember the group we had been doing business with when we were scamming the banks, putting phony loans with phantom buyers? The guys who Taylor Whitney used to gamble with?"

"You mean the Mexicans, Carlos Diego's Cartel?" Ivan asked, raising his eyebrows. "That's a rough crowd."

Yuri yawned. "That's the one and they are tough. But remember, they were the ones who warned us about the mortgage meltdown and helped us get out in time before the feds got wind of us. When I showed Carlos this deal on the Johnson ranch, they were all over it. They also lent me the money to start WMI."

"They did? Are the Cartel interested in the ranch itself?"

Yuri spit out a loose piece of tobacco. "Carlos doesn't want his name on anything here in the U.S. He wants what I want: the water rights. That's where the big money is and that's how he'll get his money back. The only thing I worry about is that neighbor of theirs to the north, you know, the one that's on the Board of Supervisors."

"Caroline Bennett?"

"Yeah, everyone knows she wants to expand her operation to grow more rice, but she doesn't have the water allocation. I don't understand why she wants to grow more rice." He shook his head. "She already grows more than anybody in the county."

Ivan tapped his cigar in a porcelain ashtray. "She's the

wealthiest woman in the greater Sacramento Area already. Why would she want to take on the headache of farming more land?"

"That's a good question. I know she's tried to buy the Johnson ranch, but they wouldn't consider it." He rested his chin on his closed fist. "She's got a friend who's her lap dog at all the board meetings and seems to do all her dirty work. Her name is Mellissa Burns, and she works for me at WMI. She has been sniffing around the Water Resources Board, asking a lot of questions. I've got to believe that those two are up to something, and I want you to find out what they're up to. The other thing is Mellissa has been compiling information on all our foreclosure activities at WMI. She thinks she's going be some Don Quixote whistle blower. No one will believe her, but I'm going to have to deal with her very soon. I don't want her screwing around with my operation at WMI."

Ivan picked up a cube of ice with silver tongs that were resting in the ice bucket. He poured himself more vodka and topped off Yuri's glass. "Have you any idea what Caroline and Mellissa might be trying to do? You've already got the extra allocation of water in process. Is there any way they can interfere?"

"No, not to my knowledge. But I'm not a politician and that's where I'm at a disadvantage. Caroline and Mellissa might be able to do things behind the scenes that I'm not aware of. I also don't want any type of bad press." He stared hard at Ivan. "Here's what I think needs to be done. I want you to put someone on Mellissa and watch where she goes for the next couple weeks and who she talks to."

Ivan nodded. "I can put Marc on it. He's good and reliable."

"Yes, that's a good choice. I may just be paranoid, but this Johnson project is too important to take any chances. We are close to meeting our goals and I want to make sure nothing goes wrong. I'm going to have some of my people at WMI keep an eye on Mellissa there also. She's in a critical position and I don't want her causing problems. Tell Marc to look for any files that she's been rumored to be keeping on WMI." He pulled back, rubbing his hand on his face reflectively. "My instincts tell me there is more going on than we are seeing, and it could come back and bite us hard. I need you to turn over every rock on this."

Ivan raised his glass. "You know you can count on me. If anything is going on with Caroline or Mellissa, I will find out. I'll start with Caroline's ranch employees. Employees always know a lot and they love to talk."

"Good idea, Ivan. But make sure you are doing it on the sly. I don't want to tip our hand to anyone. It is imperative we beat everyone, including Miss Bennett, to the prize."

Yuri saw his two young grandchildren, a boy and a girl, poke their heads out the sliding door and bolt toward him. They yelled as they ran towards him, arms outstretched. "Papa, Papa!"

Yuri put his drink down and bent down on one knee with his arms extended. He embraced the children when they reached him. "Nicholas, Annicia, you're early! How was school today? Are you two the smartest kids in the third grade? I only want to have smart grandchildren, you know."

The children giggled and snuggled against him. In chorus they both answered, "Of course, Papa, of course."

They pulled away and Nicholas asked, "Papa, can we hit balls on the golf course today?"

Annicia chimed in, "Yes, Papa, can we, please?"

Yuri surveyed the course, seeing a few foursomes backed up on the course and others in the distance. "Yes, children, we can hit balls today, but we have to wait until a little later. Once the golfers get off the course in a couple of hours, we will swing some clubs." He turned back and tousled Nicholas's hair. "Where are your mommy and daddy? Are they inside?"

Annicia pointed at the house. "Mommy is talking to Grammy. Daddy was sick today, so he stayed home. Why was Grammy crying, Papa?"

He bent down and hugged the little girl. "Oh, Grammy was just happy to see you. She's fine. Why don't you two run inside for a while and I'll come fetch you to go hit balls in a little while?"

They both turned and sprinted into the house. Yuri watched them, a proud smile on his face. Turning to Ivan he spoke in an agitated voice. "That lazy son-in-law of mine. I know he got drunk again and is too hung over to come for dinner." He punched his fist. "I swear, Ivan, I'm going to have to deal with that bum soon. I gave him a job at WMI, but he never shows up for work."

"How is WMI doing, Yuri? You haven't asked me to help you on any of the construction projects you're managing lately."

"WMI is going well. The money is flowing in and Carlos is happy." Yuri held out his wrist and pointed proudly at a massive gold Rolex. "He's so happy he sent me a present."

Ivan stared down at Yuri's wrist. "I saw that on you at the horse races the other day and wondered where you got it. It's impressive."

Yuri rolled his wrist to let the diamonds sparkle in the sunlight. "My friend, Taylor Whitney, had a watch almost identical to this one, and I always admired it." He smiled broadly. "Now I've got one for myself!" Yuri's expression turned serious. "I got a call from Morton Bain, my inside guy at General Technologies, yesterday. He oversees all the acquisitions for the 401(k) program there, and he's approved the purchase of five apartment projects in Fresno and Bakersfield that consist of 1200 units. There will be at least five million dollars in reconstruction work on those projects and we'll net half of that."

Ivan yawned and stretched his arms out. "Why is Bain involved in this? Didn't he already make a fortune when he sold his start-up to Yahoo a few years ago?"

Yuri nodded. "He did make a fortune, but he's also pissed most of it away. His wife is a big time socialite and spender. Morton likes to take trips to Vegas to gamble and always loses." Yuri looked around and leaned closer to Ivan. "He also has a major secret. He spends bundles of money on a boy toy. Gives him lavish gifts, bought him a house in Hawaii, and meets him at the Bellagio anytime he can get away from the wife."

"Bain is gay?"

"He's a closet gay, which is just perfect. Between his wife and his lover, they've blown almost everything, so he needs money, and I help get it to him. If I ever encounter any problems with General Technologies, Bain will help me out."

Ivan turned his head and asked, "What problems are you having?"

Yuri flicked his cigar, the ashes making it partway into the ashtray and onto the wooden table. "One of the asset managers at General has started questioning the construction and management fees we've been charging the projects we're managing. He's becoming a pain in the ass."

"Who is he?"

"Matt Whiteside, that guy I told you about at the racetrack." Yuri stood up and paced the deck. "I have called Morton previously and told him to get this Matt off our projects, but somehow I don't believe he will back off. We've got a few more projects to complete before we can get out of that business."

Eight days later, Yuri sat behind the desk in his office, going over information from the State of California. The door to the office opened and Ivan stepped in wearing his usual dark slacks and a white shirt, this time less wrinkled than normal. He sat down in one of the chairs in front of Yuri's desk and waited for Yuri to speak.

Yuri put his hands behind his head and asked, "Well, have you found anything out yet?" I hadn't heard from you in a few days, and I thought maybe you'd forgotten about me."

Ivan grinned. "Forgot about you? Come on, Yuri, you know me better. I just wanted to get something useful before I bothered you."

He leaned forward and spoke softly. "As we talked about, I had Marc follow Mellissa around. He checked out her house while she was at a board meeting, and I guess she is quite the hoarder. He wants to talk to you about paying him more for going into that smelly pigpen. Apparently he went into the place after dark and lost his footing in all the clutter. He stepped on an unseen cat's tail, and it screeched like it was being skinned alive. He was suddenly attacked by two other cats that appeared out of nowhere. One leapt on his back and the other wrapped itself around his calf, scratching and biting him. He sprinted out of the house and was about a block down the street before he realized that the cat on his calf was still attached to his leg. It took him five minutes to peel it off," he said laughing.

Yuri motioned for him to speed it up, trying not to laugh. "I can talk with him about that later. Get to the point. Did he find the files?"

"No, he didn't get to stay long enough to look around. He'll have to go back. But she's been really busy the last few days," Ivan continued. "She checks the calendar of the Yolo Board of Supervisors every day. She never misses a meeting and is constantly meeting with the county staff. She went to the State Water Resources Board six times in the last eight days. One of those was a meeting, and Caroline also attended." He paused. "Do you mind if I get some coffee?"

Yuri pointed to a Keurig Elite coffee machine in the corner of his office. "Help yourself, but please continue."

Ivan sat back down with his coffee. "Last week, she had a meeting with a man who looked like a business professional. You know, white shirt, tie, and pressed slacks. They met at a place called Yianni's. The only reason Marc mentions this is it didn't look like the typical person Mellissa would be meeting."

Ivan sipped his coffee. A phone rang a couple of times in the other room before it stopped.

He continued. "Anyway, Marc found a seat at the bar and overheard most of their conversation. She talked about a lot of things and the conversation included Caroline and her need for more water. Marc couldn't get everything that was said, but he did hear her say that the key for Caroline getting more water had to do with something called New London."

"New London? What does that have to do with anything?" Yuri asked.

"I don't know, Yuri, but Marc felt the way she was talking about it was important. The next night she was at a Yolo County Board meeting." Ivan leaned forward and set his cup on Yuri's desk. "She was at the podium railing against a new development project cited the same old issues: CEQA, more traffic, more crime, and devaluation of property. She had a group of like-minded people with her at the meeting and each followed behind her and spoke against each proposed property."

Yuri yawned. "So, what else is new? We know she and Caroline are against any development in Yolo. It would be more surprising if she didn't protest a proposed development."

Ivan had moved to the window looking out over the parking lot and leaned against it. He half turned back toward Yuri. "This is true, but at the end of the public comment section of the meeting, Caroline asked the audience in attendance if there were any further comments on items not on the agenda."

He paused for a few seconds. "Mellissa came up to the podium and wanted to point out an alarming trend. According to her research, there were numerous landowners who had gotten water allocations from the State Water Resources Board but had no intention of using the water in Yolo County. Instead, she said, all they were going to do was sell the water rights to a third party outside the county and pocket the money. She said it was almost a crime that any water would be leaving the county."

Yuri had sat up straight and was paying close attention.

Ivan continued. "Mellissa rambled on that, to her, this was inhumane, as the water could be used to actually grow things that could help feed a lot of people here in Yolo County and that a lot of wildlife depended on that water for food and habitat. Therefore she asked the Board if there was a way for Yolo County to block the sale of the water and make sure it was used in Yolo County."

A man with a cell phone walked past the window and started talking rapidly. Ivan looked over at him for a moment.

"Caroline applauded her, as did a couple of other members of the Board. She suggested to the staff that they look into what legal means might be used to force landowners to keep their water here in the county. She asked Mellissa if she would be willing to help staff with this study, which Mellissa readily agreed to."

Yuri looked stunned. "They can't do that. The county can't do that. If they got ahold of that water, it would cause a drop in the value of the Johnson ranch along with every other ranch in the area. There would be lawsuits flying all over the county if they tried that. Caroline and the Board know this, they're not that stupid." He stood up and paced behind his desk. "There has to be something else they're up to." He pointed a finger at Ivan. "I don't like this, Ivan. These two are dangerous to our plan. If they continue down this road, we'll take some dramatic action."

"Like what, Yuri?" he asked.

"Leave that to me, Ivan," Yuri replied, his eyes narrowing. "I'm not going to do anything yet, but if these two continue to make trouble, well, let's just say they will need to be educated. Tell Marc to keep up the surveillance and promise him I'll make it up to him for his adventure with the cats."

Ivan left the office and Yuri stood staring out the window. He pounded his fists on the desk. "I'm too close now. I won't let anybody get in my way!"

TWELVE

Ken leaned over the front of his 1999 Ford F-150 truck and wrestled with a stubborn bolt inside the engine block. The hood was held up by a rod protruding from the motor casing and hung over his upper body as he leaned halfway into the open area. His belly rested on the chassis and was shielded by a dirty towel upon where he had spread out an array of tools. His overalls had grease stains covering every inch. It was difficult to tell where the brown color of the truck started or the color of the dust covering it ended.

Betty Lou walked out to the mailbox perched above two flower boxes filled with pink, blue and red petunias that stood at the end of the dirt driveway. The mailbox had two flower boxes below it filled with pink, blue, and red petunias. They blended with the surrounding flower beds below it that were filled with an assortment of pansies, snapdragons, and daisies.

As she walked back to the house, she thumbed through a stack of letters and stopped as she came to one in particular. She opened the letter and read it. Still reading, she came up to the truck. "Hey, Ken, get a hold of this. Remember Yuri told us he was going to sell our excess water rights from our new allocation and give us forty thousand dollars?"

Ken kept working on the truck without looking up, banging on the engine to loosen a stuck nut. "Yeah, I remember. What about it? Did he send us a check or something?"

"No, he didn't. But I'm looking at a letter from a Southern California firm that wants to purchase our new water allocation when we get it. They don't say how much they'll pay, but they give testimonials from different landowners who have sold their water rights and the figures they are throwing out are in the millions of dollars."

Ken pulled himself out of the truck, rubbing his hands with a dirty rag. "Did you say millions? Are you kidding?" He held out his hand. "Can I see that letter?"

She kept reading, ignoring his request.

He kept wiping his hands with the dirty rag and tried to read the letter over her shoulder. "Wow," he said. "Are any of the testimonials from anyone we know?"

Betty Lou read the letter a second time then turned it over to see if she missed anything. She shook her head slowly. "No, I don't recognize anyone. It doesn't say where the landowners are from in this letter. I'm not familiar with the company the letter is from, Westwood Land Company." She looked up at him and held the letter out. "Are you?"

"Nah, I've never heard of them, but that doesn't mean much," Ken said matter-of-factly. "I don't pay attention to much outside this ranch. What I'm wondering though is do you think Yuri knows about this? Is it possible he's not telling us everything about our water?"

Betty Lou folded her arms. "I don't know, Ken. I don't think he's the type to take advantage of people. Besides, why would he have gone out of his way to help us out? He's already got millions and millions. He doesn't need to try to cheat us out of money. The loan he gave us is secured, and like he said, the extra water allocation makes the security better." She scratched the back of her head as she reread the letter. "It doesn't make sense that he would try to short change us, because the more money we make, the faster we can pay off his loan."

Ken contemplated that thought. "Yeah, it doesn't make sense that he wouldn't tell us if the water rights were worth much more money than he originally thought. Should we give these people who are on the letterhead a call and see what this is about?" Before Betty Lou answered, Ken glanced down at his watch and asked, "It's almost four o'clock. Where is Westwood located?"

Betty Lou looked at the letter again. "Pasadena. That means they're in the same time zone as we are. You keep working on the truck. I'll call and see what I can find out. It's probably nothing to get excited about. I'll be back after I talk to them."

Betty Lou placed the handset to her ear to hear a dial tone. With her other hand, she placed her index finger in the hole and carefully began to dial each number on the rotary dial. She held the handset to her ear as the curled, white cord stretched from the wall to the square kitchen table where she was sitting. While she waited on hold for John Anderson, the author of the letter from Westwood Land Company, she sat doodling designs on a yellow notepad. She daydreamed about going to dinner at one of her favorite places, Café Italia, in downtown Davis.

She had just pulled out two loaves of bread from the oven and had set them on the kitchen counter to cool prior to making the call. The warm, yeasty fragrance of fresh baked bread wafted through the kitchen. A television set in the family room outside the kitchen droned on with a talk show host recapping the news of the day.

After twenty minutes of waiting, a male voice came through the receiver. "John Anderson, how can I help you?"

Betty Lou sat up straight. "Hi, Mr. Anderson, my name is Betty Lou Johnson. My husband and I own the Johnson ranch just outside of Woodland. I'm calling you about a letter you sent us regarding purchasing the excess water allocation we've applied for from the State Water Resources Board."

There was a pause on the other line. "Hold on a second, Mrs. Johnson."

"Please call me Betty Lou."

"Okay, give me a second to find that letter." She could hear him rattling paper on the other end of the phone. "Ah yes, thank you for waiting, I've found it. So you are the owners of about seventeen thousand acres up there in Yolo County, Betty Lou?"

"Yes. That's our ranch."

"Our records show you've been allocated about half the acre feet of water annually that your ranch is eligible for. Recently you've applied for the full allocation of water. I don't know if you intend to use that extra water allocation on your ranch, but if you aren't, Westwood Land Company would be interested in purchasing your excess water when you receive it. Is that something you might be interested in doing?"

Betty Lou cleared her throat. "My husband and I had thought about selling. We just don't know what it's worth. You're the first people that have contacted us, so I thought I'd call you back and see what you're offering."

"Well, Betty Lou," John said, "I'm sure we won't be the last to contact you. Water is a valuable commodity these days. Even more so with all the environmental restrictions put on the Delta, which affects how much water gets to farmers in the central valley. Since the Delta water flow has been cut back, some of the farmers can't get the same allocation as they have in the past. If they want to farm their land, they must buy other ranchers' water."

Betty Lou made some notes. She thought, I wonder why Yuri hasn't said anything about this. He made it sound like we were only requesting water as a precaution, not as a money grab. "Okay, I get that part. But you haven't told me what the extra water is worth."

"Hold on, let me do some calculations." Betty Lou could hear him hitting buttons and the sound of a printer kicking out paper calculations. "If you decided to keep the same amount of water as you've used the last five years and sell the rest..." The calculator went into overdrive. "I think we would be willing to pay you in the range of two million two hundred twenty-nine thousand dollars annually. Of course, this would all be subject to a field audit, but it should be fairly close. Is this in the range you had in mind, Betty Lou?"

Betty Lou had dropped her pencil after he had mentioned the word million. She hadn't heard the rest of the conversation. Catching her breath and feeling her heartbeat increase in speed, she asked, "You did say two million annually?"

"Yes, ma'am, that's the number I gave you." He replied like he had just told her the price of a head of lettuce. "Do you have any questions?"

Betty Lou's head was spinning. "Ah, Mr. Anderson, I do have a lot of questions, but I need to speak to my husband first. Is there any way you can send me that quote in writing? I'd like to show it to my attorney and get his opinion on it."

"No problem, Betty Lou, I can get it in the mail to you today. If your attorney has any questions, I can put him in touch with our legal department."

Betty Lou's breathing had finally slowed down to a normal level. "Thank you, Mr. Anderson, I appreciate your time. We'll be in touch after we receive your offer."

She hung up the phone in stunned silence. Her hands were shaking as she headed out the door to tell Ken the news. She repeated what John Anderson had told her and waited for Ken's reaction.

The expression on his face never changed, but he whistled and said softly, "I think we should make an appointment with John Roth as soon as we get that quote from Westwood. Did Mr. Anderson say how long it would take to get to us?"

"He said he would put the offer in the mail today. We should have it in a couple of days. How about if I make an appointment for next Tuesday? Tuesdays are pretty slow around here."

Ken nodded in agreement. "Yeah, make the appointment for Tuesday. I hope John can tell us this is legitimate."

The following Tuesday, Ken and Betty Lou sat in John Roth's office in two older leather chairs. Their attorney sat reading the offer from Westwood Land Company. His office was a classic located on 2nd Street in Old Sacramento. It sat just across from where the turn-of-the-century river boat, the Delta King, permanently docked. The front door to his office spelled out in gold leaf with a black border "John Roth, Esquire" in a style reminiscent of the 1800s gold rush days.

For the meeting, Ken wore a clean pair of Wranglers with a western shirt and a cowboy hat, which he had removed upon entering the office. Betty Lou had her hair pulled back and wore a light blue sundress with white flats.

John's office was cluttered with law books and periodicals that he had accumulated over the forty-five years he had practiced law. The paneled office was small but comfortable as Ken and Betty Lou waited in silence for John to finish reading.

He finally stopped, took his wire-rimmed glasses off one ear at a time, and addressed them. "Well, this is quite interesting. Before you got here, I checked into Westwood Land Company. They are new in the sense that there are companies like this that have been around for a hundred years, but these guys have been in business since 1992. They have listed some references on their website, but I haven't had a chance to call them."

Ken shifted his hat on his lap. "Betty Lou and I did the same thing and we came to the same conclusion. But if they are legitimate, how much of this money are we entitled to? Yuri indicated we would be getting around forty thousand dollars for our extra allocation. Do you think he didn't know it could be worth this much?"

"I can't answer that question, Ken, as I don't know how Yuri thinks. But I do know that water rights have always had value. Recently they have begun to become more valuable since water taken from the Delta has been cut back to save endangered Chinook salmon and some Smelt. For the past few years, central valley farmers have been complaining that their water allocations were going to be cut and they wouldn't be allowed to farm with unlimited water as in the past."

He leaned back in his chair. "Now their fears are coming to fruition, and firms like Westwood are coming in to broker water from people like you who don't use all your water to farmers who need it because their allocations have been cut. I think what we're seeing is just the beginning of a gold rush for water rights."

He stood and walked to the front window that looked out over the wood sidewalk outside his office. "But in answer to your question, I find it hard to imagine that Yuri would not be aware of such a substantial increase in value." He turned back to Betty Lou and Ken. "Didn't you tell me it was his idea to apply for the higher allocation?"

Betty Lou and Ken looked at each other. Betty Lou spoke first. "It was Yuri's idea. But the way he presented it was we should apply for more water so we would be protected from being cut back, which would affect our ability to farm and consequently affect our ability to pay his loan."

Ken chimed in. "Yeah, it was all about keeping us financially healthy so we could pay him back. I mean, if we could collect this amount for a few years, we could pay him off altogether and have financial independence."

Betty Lou reached over and put her hand over Ken's. "John, how do we find out if Yuri's been honest with us, and how, if we are given the extra water, can we get our hands on the money so we can get out from under Yuri's loan? We're grateful for all he's done, but if there is any way we can get away from being obligated to him, we would like to go that way."

John pulled out the drawer to his left and thumbed through the files. He found the file he was looking for and opened it on his desk. "This is the loan file for you and Yuri. It's been a few months since it closed, so I need to refresh my memory about the details." He looked up at them. "Give me a few days to research this file and we'll get together to map out a strategy. In the meantime, I think a little heart-to-heart with Yuri and you would be in order. Maybe he didn't know and will do the right thing. Who knows?" He pulled out a pocket calendar and thumbed through it. "How about we meet again a week from today?"

Betty Lou nodded. "Okay. We'll speak with Yuri about Westwood Land, and meanwhile maybe we'll get a higher offer."

The next morning, Betty Lou sat at the kitchen table, a buttered English muffin on a saucer in front of her. The morning paper sat folded on the table unopened. Ken sat across from her his hands cupping a steaming cup of coffee. Nervously, she dialed Yuri's number and listened as it rang. About the third ring, Yuri's familiar deep voice answered. "Hello?"

"Yuri, it's Betty Lou Johnson. Did I catch you at a bad time?"

"No, I always have time for you. What can I do for you?"

Betty Lou paused to gain her composure. "Well, I'm calling about the extra water allocation we applied for." She put an emphasis on the word *we*. "We got a letter from a company called

Westwood Land expressing interest in buying the excess water from us. The numbers they are willing to pay are much more than the numbers you mentioned."

Yuri responded quickly. "I'm familiar with Westwood Land and they can't be trusted. They throw out offers all the time, but they never come through with any money. I am careful who I deal with because I don't want someone like a Westwood to tie up the property and then string it out while they try to find someone to sell the water to. Their reputation is terrible in the industry."

Ken listened intently as did Betty Lou. He mouthed a question for her to ask.

"So you're saying Westwood never performs?" she said. "If that was the case, wouldn't they be getting sued on a regular basis? We looked up their status with the Secretary of State's office, and as of yesterday they were a corporation in good standing. Wouldn't there be red flags with the state if there were lawsuit issues?"

Yuri became agitated. "Look, Betty Lou, I know the market for this water. It is higher than we discussed a few weeks ago, but in no way is it in the millions like this Westwood is throwing around. However, to ease your concerns, I will put the word out that we are interested in bids on the excess water and we can see what turns up. How does that sound?"

Betty Lou looked at Ken, with a "now-what?" look. He raised his shoulders and shrugged. Betty Lou spoke. "I guess that sounds okay to us, Yuri. How long do you think it will take you to find anything out about the value? Should we be looking into this also?"

Yuri snapped into the phone, "No, that won't be necessary. Let me handle things, Betty Lou. If too many people start putting out their own version of what's available, it'll create confusion in the market place."

"When will you get back to us?"

"You tell Ken I will have some figures to go over with both of you by the end of next week."

"Alright, Yuri, we'll wait to hear from you." She hung up and looked at Ken. "That wasn't the same kind and gentle Yuri of a week ago, was it?"

"It sure wasn't. I think we should do some more homework on Westwood and other companies like them to find out for ourselves. Let's see if John could expedite his research in figuring out what we can do about the loan with Yuri."

"Don't forget, Ken, that Yuri has an insurance policy on the both of us. I want to believe that it is only the insurance for the loan and not for some nefarious scheme."

Ken sipped his coffee. "I had almost forgotten about that policy. I wouldn't worry though. I've heard of that type of policy covering a loan before, so it's not that uncommon."

"I don't know, Ken. I'm getting a bad feeling about all of this."

THIRTEEN

The large banks of florescent lighting lit up the playing field at 3-Com Stadium, home of the San Francisco Giants, as the players on the field got into their positions, awaiting the next pitch. Matt and Drew were on their feet along with the other 55,000 fans stomping, clapping, and screaming at the top of their lungs. The dreaded Los Angeles Dodgers were in town. Thirty minutes earlier, in the top of the ninth inning, the Giant fans were screaming encouragement for their ace closer, Keiichi Yabu, as he trotted in from the bullpen to face pinch hitter, Juan Pierre, with a runner on second, two outs and a one-run lead. On the third pitch, Pierre smashed a 0-2 curveball over the right field side of the ball park and into McCovey Cove. One third of the fans in the stadium cheered deliriously, waving their blue and white Dodger colors as Pierre rounded the bases and touched home plate, giving the Dodgers a 2-1 lead.

It was now the Giant's turn to make a comeback. They had runners at second and third with two outs and their all-star third baseman, Rich Aurilla, at the plate. On the third pitch he ripped a line drive toward the gap in right and center fields. The stadium exploded as the Giants fans anticipated the ball going to the fence and scoring both runners. But right fielder Randy Winn got a great jump on the ball. Just as the runner from second base was rounding third with the winning run, Randy leaped and extended his body, snagging the ball inches from the ground. He slid forward on his belly in the damp grass, rolled on his side, and held up the ball. The second base umpire, sprinting toward him, signaled an out and the end of the game.

A collective groan from two thirds of the stadium came out as the other third danced in their seats and in the aisles. Matt stood silently with his hands on his head in disbelief and watched the Dodger players sprint onto the field to congratulate their right fielder, whose wide-eyed, joyous smile could be seen as far away as the press box on the second level of the stadium.

"I can't believe that catch," Matt said to no one in particular. "Those damned Dodgers are so lucky. Every time we play them, it's like it's the World Series."

Drew, standing next to him, nodded. "They always seem to bring their best when they play us." He shrugged as if resigned to the loss. "Oh well, we're still in first place and they aren't going anywhere but home for the post season." He sat down and slumped in his seat. "You have to admit that was an incredible catch. I thought that ball was in the gap for sure."

Matt sat down. They were fifteen rows directly above the first base dugout in General Technologies' season seats that Matt had reserved five weeks earlier. There were two other guests sitting in the other two company seats, neither of them known to Matt, and worse, both were Dodger fans. "It wasn't that great a catch. I could have made that play," Matt said dully.

Drew looked at him and rolled his eyes. "Yeah right, in your dreams."

"Hey, Drew, I'm not that old and I'm still pretty fast. Some of my coaches at Santa Clara said I had moves like Barry Sanders."

Drew grunted loudly. "Yeah, that was then. Today you'd look more like Colonel Sanders."

Matt laughed. "You're just jealous." He looked around the crowded stadium as fans in the black and orange colors of the Giants made their way up the stairs to the exits as Dodger fans razzed them the whole time. More than a few of the Giants fans responded to the good-natured ribbing by showing a finger, sometimes used as a signal for "we're number one," except that it was the wrong finger.

"We might as well hang out here for a few minutes and let the crowd disperse," Drew said as he watched fans starting to leave the stadium. "Besides, I've still got half a beer left."

"Yeah, I'm in no hurry. It's a good thing the stadium stops selling beer at the end of the seventh inning." He turned his body to catch a better view of the fans leaving. "Could you imagine 50,000 drunken knuckleheads heading out of the stadium together after a game like this? It would be nothing but ugliness."

Drew watched the exodus and responded sarcastically. "Really, I would have never thought that any problems could occur between these fans. Mutual hatred and alcohol—it's probably not a great mix."

Matt cracked open a peanut shell. "Hey, Drew, you were talking earlier about your hedge fund's positioning on investments, now that the mortgage-backed securities markets are dead. I didn't catch some of what you explained due to the crowd noise, so explain it again, if you don't mind."

Drew reached down between his legs and retrieved a half-full cup of beer. "Not a problem." He took a swig of the beer. "First of all, the mortgage-backed securities market is not dead. It is still active, but all packages are more closely scrutinized nowadays. The biggest problem I see in the real estate industry is that banks don't have a handle on the loans in their portfolios."

"What do you mean by that?" Matt asked.

"I see a lot of investments that banks are trying to unload to my fund. Some of these loans are in some state of delinquency or foreclosure. The banks are willing to give us a guarantee, either on the full amount of the loan or give us title to the houses if they are foreclosed upon."

The two Dodger fans sitting next to them bade them farewell and offered their condolences as they headed to the aisle on their way to the exits.

Drew continued. "But we know what the banks are doing, and they're going to get caught sooner or later. We don't want to be part of it."

"What are they doing that your people are worried about?" Matt asked.

"They have so many loans that are convoluted because they are tied together with a bundle of other loans. They have no way of identifying which of these loans are good and which ones are bad. Some of the banks are foreclosing on everything," Drew responded. "We know some of the banks are not following the proper legal procedures to foreclose on properties."

"Why would they do that? They've got to know this will come back to get them."

"I agree with you that they have to know this is not good. But they have so many bad loans; they're not going to be bothered with laws to get these houses off their books. Bankers for the most part are idiots. They feel they're above the law and nobody will mess with them because they wield so much influence. But I think they are going to be in for a rude awakening when this foreclosure stuff comes to light, especially the illegal stuff. Mark my words."

Matt sat silently digesting the information. "That's interesting. I always wondered how all those bundled loans would get straightened out. I guess we'll find out soon enough."

Drew stood and stretched his arms. "Have you made any progress in your investigation regarding the investments in your company's 401(k) program? The last time you were in the Bay Area you told me you had been told to pull back."

Matt looked up at the scoreboard as if some way magically it might have changed. It hadn't.

"Like I told you earlier, my boss, Diane, asked me to come here to review what I had since I met with her a week ago. Since I was asked to pull back, I haven't found much other than the property management company and the contractor is basically one and the same, and one of the Board of Directors of General Technologies wants me to quit my investigation."

"Did you check and see if the corporations were in good standing with the State of California?" Drew asked. "Sometimes that can give you a reason to check their books."

Matt nodded, yes. "I did and they're okay. I figure whoever owns one of the companies either owns the others or has some kind of control over them. I'm waiting for some information from one of the onsite property managers I've gotten close to." He picked out a couple of peanuts from their package and started to shell them. "Apparently, one of the owners of the property management company uses the Pheasant Crossing project as his satellite office. My gal there, Brenda, thinks he might have left some documentation around."

"If your gal knows the owner, why doesn't she just tell you who he is?" Drew asked.

"It's not quite that simple," Matt answered. "She's never been introduced to him, doesn't know his name, and she's not positive who the man is. It's strictly speculation at this point. The only thing she did know was the guy looks foreign. He also has a taste for young women. Whenever he shows up onsite, some hot babe is not far behind."

Drew's eyes lit up. "Hmmm. I might like to meet his guy. Maybe he could use a little help with some of his companions. You know, I'm always up to help a guy out if he has too many women on his hands."

Matt laughed. "Of course you'd like to meet him. And, of course, because of your magnanimous nature, you'd be happy help the man out with excess hot women. I would only think less of you if you didn't feel that way."

Drew bowed. "I'd be at his service."

"I'll bet you would," Matt said, shaking his head. He kicked at the pile of peanut shells mounded at his feet, scattering them down the next row of seats. Dozens of hot dog wrappers swirled around the park in the evening breeze. A flock of seagulls had been waiting patiently on the edge of the stadium's roof for people to leave, and they began swooping down on the empty field to scrounge for morsels. "Anyway, I might find out who this mystery man is tomorrow. The other thing that's bothering me is why a General Technologies board member would take on interest in stopping an investigation of the company's 401(k) program, especially when there seems to be some funny things going on. It would seem to me he would want to find out what exactly is going on for the good of the company."

Drew threw the last of his beer down. "Yeah, that is a real head scratcher. But he's on the board for a reason. They don't normally elect stupid people to these boards. I'm sure he has reasons to stop you that you're not aware of."

"Yeah, you're probably right," Matt agreed reluctantly.

Drew slapped Matt on the back. "So, big boy, how many more months before you tie the knot? Your time as a single man is slowly running out. How is everything with that beautiful fiancée of yours? I still can't believe you talked her into saying yes to marrying you."

Matt flinched, which didn't go unnoticed by Drew. "I think it's less than six months, Drew." He hung his head and stared at the shells strewn about the floor under his seat. "This wedding stuff is all happening so fast. Sometimes I think I'm not ready."

Drew turned his head sideways, as if to hear Matt better. "Uh, have you lost your senses? This woman you are about to marry is one of the smartest, nicest and most gorgeous I have ever met and I *know* you have ever met. What seems to be the problem? You should be counting the days on the sidewalk, not looking like you've been sentenced to Pelican Bay Prison."

Matt took a deep breath. "I know you're right, Drew, but sometimes I find myself wondering if I'm doing the right thing. Stephanie is a wonderful person and I love her very much, but I keep having doubts about this whole marriage thing. I don't want to make a mistake."

Drew sat back down in his seat. "You know what I smell? I smell a skunk and I can only think of one person who would put out that smell: Kathy Ann." He stared at Matt and spoke as if he were scolding him. "Does she have anything to do with all this sudden marriage remorse?"

Matt stood silently. Finally, he spoke, though not very convincingly. "No, it's not her, exactly."

Drew shook his head in disgust. "I should have known. Look, Matt, I know you two were close at one time and you have a history together, but that was years ago. To be honest, I was happy to hear about your breakup. She's always been chasing after something she couldn't have. Even when you were dating, she had her feelers out for a second option in case things didn't work out with you."

He stopped for a second, and then added, "Don't you remember how fast she ditched you after she thought your football playing days were over at Santa Clara? If I recall, she hooked up with one of your teammates when his NFL prospects looked better than yours. How did that work out for her? Not very well I'm assuming."

Matt thought, Everything Drew is saying is right. Why can't I get her out of my mind? Is it her looks, or the sex? It can't be that; Stephanie is the most amorous and sexy woman I've ever known. Is it some forbidden fruit thing?

"Look, Drew, I'm not thinking of getting back with Kathy Ann. It's just seeing her made me question whether or not marriage is for me right now. It's true her marriage didn't work out and she's now free, but she's not the reason for my angst." He ran his fingers through his hair. "I don't know what I think anymore."

"Matt, you and I go back a long ways, and I don't get into your business very often," Drew said sternly. "You've got to get this woman out of your mind and out of your life forever. She is only going to bring you heartache and could ruin one of the best things that you have going, your relationship with Stephanie." He poked Matt firmly in the chest. "Don't let her screw this up for you."

Matt leaned back, surprised at his friend's forcefulness. "I hear you, Drew. I just don't know. Maybe I'm just a glutton for punishment."

Drew nodded toward the exits. "Come on. Let's go over to Lefty O'Doul's and I'll buy you a beer. Maybe it'll help you clear out your mind and get you headed in the right direction. Even if you don't need a beer, I sure as hell do."

Matt smiled weakly. "Okay, old friend, that sounds good, but I can't promise you anything."

The next morning, Matt sat at his desk in his Sacramento office reviewing the weekly investment reports from the accounting division. He had gotten an early start by leaving Drew's house at 6:30 to beat the traffic coming out of the Bay Area. During the two-hour drive down I-80, his mind wandered over a variety of subjects. He thought of his parents, Barbara and Stan, and how they had coped with all the drama they had gone through during the last two years. He remembered how excited they were and their euphoria at buying a new house, only to lose it to foreclosure less than two years later. I wonder how they managed to keep it together through all of that. He thought about what Drew had told him about the banks doing illegal foreclosures. Was that what happened to his parents? I remember them going through all those hoops the banks put them through, doing everything they could to hang on, only to lose their house and their savings in the end.

Kathy Ann crept into his head. Why do I keep thinking about her and questioning whether I'm ready for marriage to Stephanie. Do I really want to get involved with Kathy Ann and start an instant family? Is she really who I think she is, the sweet, caring woman I knew in college who felt like my soul mate, or someone different?

He cleared his mind and started focusing on the reports when his cell phone rang. He glanced at his watch to see it was just after 9:00 a.m. He answered after the third ring.

"Hello, this is Matt."

"Hi, Matt, it's Brenda, the onsite manager from Pheasant Crossing. I've got some information on the person who I believe owns the property management company that oversees this place."

Matt's ears perked up and he grabbed a pen that was lying across a yellow legal pad. "Go ahead, Brenda, I'm ready."

"His name is Yuri Kletcko. He is a local developer here and dabbles in numerous investments. As you know, the property management business is called WMI. But his contracting and development business is called Centennial, Inc."

"I know of Yuri Kletcko. Did you find out anything about him?" he asked.

"I don't know anything more than he immigrated to the U.S. in the 90s and found his way to Rancho Cordova," she replied. "I will keep checking if you'd like and see what I can find."

Matt wrote the names Kletcko and WMI on his notepad. Next to that he added Centennial and underlined it. "I would appreciate that, Brenda. But please continue to do this discreetly. I don't want anyone to know you are looking into this guy's background."

"Okay, Matt, no problem," she said. "I'll keep it quiet."

"Thanks." Matt leaned back in his chair and put his hands behind his head. "Yuri Kletcko, how did he get involved in this?" He went to Google on his computer and punched the name in. He waited a second and watched the screen. There was a Boris Kletcko that owned a car repair shop and a Victor Kletcko running a mortgage business, but no Yuri.

His cell phone rang again and he answered, "Hello, this is Matt."

"Matt, this is Mika from WMI. I understand you are talking to my onsite personnel again. You have to go through me if you need information, understand?"

Matt frowned. How did he know I had spoken to anyone onsite? Brenda was the only person he spoke to and that was just a few minutes ago. "I don't need you to run interference for me, Mika," he answered firmly. "I appreciate you offering your assistance, but I really don't need it."

"Matt, you don't understand. I'm not offering any assistance. I'm telling you if you want information on any projects, you go through me, got it? We know who you are, Matt, and we don't need you snooping around our projects."

Matt took a deep breath then answered, "Sure, Mika, I got it. We'll be in touch." Click.

Setting his phone down gently, he mumbled to himself, "What did he mean we know who you are? Who're *we*? Why would the personnel of a property management company continue to confront us, the owners of that property? That's not a smart way of doing business."

His phone rang again. He recognized he number. "Hey, Stephanie, how are you?"

"I'm great, sweetie," she answered cheerily. "How was your trip? How's Drew?"

Matt leaned back and put his feet on the desk. He thought he detected a different tone in her voice, but he shook it off. "Drew's doing great. We went to the Dodger-Giants game last night, and those stinkin' Dodgers pulled another one out of their hats. I couldn't believe it."

"I know, I saw the game on TV," she said. "I miss you. What

time are you getting off work? Would you like to go out to Club Pheasant for dinner? That band we both like, Neckbone, is playing there. I have a craving for some authentic Italian food."

Matt hesitated a second before answering. "Uh, that's right, I forgot today's Friday. Yeah, that sounds good."

There was silence on the other end of the phone, and then Stephanie asked, "Matt, is everything all right? You sound like something is bothering you."

Matt sat up and took a deep breath. Maybe I was right. She does sound different, a bit anxious. "No, Steph, everything is fine. It's just been a long couple of days. I'll swing by your place around six and we'll head over there. We haven't heard Neckbone in a while, and Italian sounds good to me too. I'll see you a little later."

He hung up and stared at his computer knowing that he'd have to make a decision soon.

FOURTEEN

Stephanie hung up and focused on the road ahead. She was looking for the Woodland off ramp just past the Sacramento International Airport. An orange and blue Southwest Airlines jet screamed over her head as it climbed upward to gain altitude on its way to some unknown destination. She was on her way to meet with Caroline again, this time to do a tour of the ranch Caroline owned and ran.

Something is going on with Matt. He hasn't been himself for the past two weeks and I don't know what's bothering him. My woman's intuition tells me it's more than just a mood change. I haven't gotten the nerve to ask him about the woman Alan saw him with last week, but I think we need to have a talk. I don't want to be the last one to know.

She found herself in the circular driveway of the Bennett ranch house. Caroline came bounding out of the house in a pair of Wrangler Jeans and a red-and-white checkered blouse, her diamond earrings and matching bracelet sparkling in the morning sun. The Tony Lama boots and black felt cowboy hat she wore added inches to her height.

She clasped her hands together playfully and greeted Stephanie with a hug. "Howdy, partner. Are you ready for your tour?" she asked gaily.

Stephanie stepped back, admiring Caroline's garb. "Wow," she exclaimed. "I didn't know cowboy outfits could look so glamorous. Look at me." She pointed at her jeans and well-worn black boots. "I look like a bum."

Caroline threw her head back and laughed, her wavy hair bouncing about. "It's just my cowboy chic. You, look like a bum? If so, you are the best-looking and best-dressed bum I've ever seen. Shall we get moving?" She pointed to a shiny olive-green Range Rover idling about fifty feet from them. "You've met Brett. He's going to drive us while I do the narration." They hopped into the vehicle and Caroline said sharply to Brett, "Take us to the northern rice fields, and we'll start there."

Brett nodded silently and started driving.

Caroline reached down to the silver ice bucket that set between them on the floor. She pulled up an open, chilled bottle of Dom Pérignon champagne. "How about a mimosa to wake us up? There's some orange juice in that other container." Before Stephanie could answer, she quickly picked up two champagne flutes. She poured champagne into the glasses and added some orange juice. Caroline held a glass out, and Stephanie took it from her.

I don't think Caroline will take no for an answer, she thought. I'm sure Mr. Parker wouldn't be too irritated. She clinked glasses with Caroline. "Thank you." Stephanie took a sip and pulled out a notepad and pen and set them on her lap, holding her champagne in her left hand. "Caroline, you've told me a lot about the ranch business and your ambitions. What about your childhood growing up?"

Caroline looked out the window of the Rover as they crossed a small wooden bridge going over a bubbling stream. A pair of Mallard ducks stood on the banks of the stream, eyeing them warily as they drove by.

"My childhood was rather dull," she stated still looking out the window. "I was raised here at the ranch by my father. When I was eight, my mother decided that San Francisco was more suited to her needs and left us both. They never divorced, but I rarely saw her after that. She was killed in a car accident a few years later." She turned back to Stephanie. "Initially I cried a lot," she stated, not showing any type of emotion. "After a while I forgot she ever existed."

She paused and fiddled with the volume button on the radio, turning it down. "I was involved in 4-H and all kinds of animal raising here on the ranch during high school. My dad let me get into many projects, and I fell in love with ranching. As you know I went to Berkeley. I loved it. After graduation, I came back here."

"You were married for a while, correct?" Stephanie asked.

Caroline's eyes narrowed. "Oh yes, for about eight years." She pointed to a white structure that jutted out over a picturesque pond behind the house. "We were married right there in that gazebo." She paused, as if reflecting on the moment. "I have been told it was one of the most extravagant weddings in the county. I had quite a guest list, thanks to my father." She smiled wickedly. "United States Senators, the Governor, anyone who was anyone in Yolo County was there."

She sighed and sipped her mimosa. "Unfortunately, it didn't work out. Richard was a great personal injury attorney and made a fortune chasing ambulances." She smiled at the thought. "That part I liked about him. But after two kids, and being stuck in suburbia, as B.B. King sang, the thrill was gone." She looked over at Stephanie with no expression. "So we split up and he took the kids. I didn't fight him for them. He was the better parent and could offer them more. They're way better off with him."

Stephanie was furiously taking notes. She stopped and asked in a sincere tone. "Do you see your kids much, Caroline?"

Caroline shrugged. "Oh, once in a while. They're engrained in the big city culture and have no interest in what I do, so they don't come here and I don't get up to San Francisco often. It's probably just as well." She tapped Brett on the shoulder. "Pull over there by the water tank. I want to show Stephanie the rice fields."

Brett did as instructed.

Caroline stepped out and put her hands on her hips. As far as the eye could see were wispy, thin, green plants shooting up through flooded fields. A mound of dirt dams, about one foot high, set in a huge swirling pattern separated one field from another. Every half mile or so, on a square grid, an elevated road crisscrossed through the fields. There was barely anything but the green shoots to be seen in three directions. Flocks of mallards, widgeon, and teal flew overhead, noisily moving across the sky.

Caroline swept her hand across the fields and proclaimed proudly, "Here it is, the heart of the ranch. It's these thousands of acres of rice that make me the most money. That field we passed about two miles ago is all wheat but gets nothing like the yield we get from the rice."

Stephanie took in the view, shielding her eyes from the sun. Dozens of white egrets gracefully stalked the four-inch-deep water about a hundred yards from where they stood. They would walk slowly, stopping every ten feet to strike a statuesque pose, waiting to hear the sounds of an unsuspecting frog or crawfish, and then spear the hapless victim. "That looks like a lot of rice," Stephanie commented. "It looks like it goes for miles. You were saying you wanted to increase your production next year. Is that the area you're going to plant?" She pointed to some vacant ground about a half mile to the east.

Caroline looked to where she was pointing. She nodded her head excitedly. "Exactly. I hope to have that area planted sometime next year." Caroline's eyes sparkled as she spoke of the barren land.

Stephanie rotated her gaze to the south, where in the distance sat a barn and a few other tall structures. A wide ditch stood between where they stood and the structures. A dead oak tree stood next to the ditch, and a lone red-tailed hawk circled silently above. "Is that part of your ranch also?" she asked innocently.

Caroline gave a look of disgust, and for a moment Stephanie thought she might spit on the ground. "No, that's part of my hillbilly neighbors' ranch, the Johnsons. I've tried for years to buy them out, but they won't sell." She kicked at the ground in front of her. "They got into money problems a while ago. I almost had the opportunity to buy their land in foreclosure, but someone came out of nowhere and saved their bacon by lending them money."

Stephanie looked at her then back at the farmhouse. "Who was the lender?"

Caroline dusted her pants off. "I think his name is Yuri Kletcko." She looked at Stephanie. "Ever heard of him?"

Stephanie shook her head. "No, I haven't." But I'm going to find out, she thought to herself. I wonder what the problem between Caroline and the Johnsons was? Most neighbors get along and look after one another, especially out here in the middle of nowhere.

"Me neither," Caroline said, looking out over at the neighbors' land. "But I've got some big ideas and I'm not done with the Johnsons yet, or with Mr. Kletcko. I don't know how he did it, but he managed to get his name onto the title of their ranch." She looked at Stephanie. "That's pretty strange if you ask me." She looked back at the buildings. "Well, this is enough of this side of the ranch." She yelled to Brett, who had been standing by the Range Rover with one foot in the vehicle and the other on the dirt road. "Take us to the stock yard and I'll show Stephanie that part of the operation. I'm sure she'd love to see some of our livestock."

He tipped his hat in acknowledgement and slid into the vehicle, but not before making eye contact with Stephanie and winking.

They drove around the ranch with Caroline doing most of the talking, giving Stephanie an ongoing narrative of the ranch's history and the various functions of it. Brett kept glancing in the rearview mirror, but Stephanie avoided his gaze. They arrived back at the house at a few minutes past noon.

Caroline got out first and came up to the driver's side. "Brett, park the Rover in the garage and go see Elliot. I texted him while we were driving and he's got your last check. You're done here."

Brett's eyes grew large. "But, Caroline, what have I done? I've been working for you faithfully for two years, I'm sorry if I said anything offensive." He got out of the car and pleaded. "Please, tell me what I've done."

Stephanie stood there awkwardly before speaking. "Uh, maybe I should be on my way, Caroline."

"Nonsense, Stephanie, don't go anywhere. Stay and have some more champagne with me." She turned back to Brett, who nervously fidgeted with a ring on his left hand. "I'm done with you, Brett. Next time don't insult my company. Now beat it."

Stephanie started to say something, but Caroline put her hand up and cut her off. "I know you had nothing to do with this. You probably weren't paying attention, but I was." She pointed at the office to the left of the house. "Get out of my sight, Brett, before I call the police."

Brett hung his head and wandered off toward the direction she had pointed.

Caroline smiled, slid her arm through Stephanie's, and led her back to the house. "Now that that nastiness is over, let's go get us another drink, I'm parched. Don't worry, sweetie. There are fifty more where he came from."

A few hours later, Stephanie was in Yianni's, sitting at a white-clothed table, sipping from a tall glass of iced tea. Across from her, Alan was drinking a frosted glass of beer. His pressed white shirt was rolled halfway up his arms and tucked into his dark slacks. John, the owner, was flitting in and out of the kitchen, alternately coming up to their table and that of an older couple having a late lunch in the corner of the restaurant.

Stephanie had filled Alan in on her morning with Caroline and was awaiting his reaction.

Alan let it all digest before speaking. "Caroline is a tough gal, isn't she? She just up and fires her boy toy in front of you?"

Stephanie raised her eyebrows and nodded. "She did it like she was dismissing a naughty puppy, and once it was done, she never gave it another thought."

He leaned across the table. "So explain again about the neighbor. Some wealthy Russian lends these people a large sum of money to save their farm, but as part of the deal he manages to put his own name on title?"

"That's what Caroline said," Stephanie answered, fidgeting with her spoon. "The name of her neighbors is the Johnsons, and there has been bad blood between the two families for years. But Caroline says she has a plan for them and for Yuri Kletcko. Do you think this plan she has is the reason she's been turning down every development deal that comes in front of the board?"

Alan rubbed his chin. "I don't see how the two things could be related. I talked to Mellissa again." He leaned back and got serious. "I've got to tell you this story. When I was talking to her, I was sitting across a table from her and I held her hands for a second. After she left, my eyes got real itchy and I had to stifle sneezing like I had an allergic reaction or something. It had to be a reaction to her cats. That woman's a walking hairball."

Stephanie put her hand to her mouth to hold back laughing out loud.

He continued. "Anyway, she reiterated to me that she and Caroline are up to something. It has something to do with New London, whatever that is. I have done some research and asked around, but nobody knows what New London could mean."

Stephanie leaned in and was less than a foot from Alan's face. She spoke softly. "We know she wants to attain a higher political office than the Board of Supervisors. We know she wants to have the environmental community on her side as she runs, and that's part of her reasoning." She sat back and sipped her iced tea. "She told me she wants to farm more of her land to bring in more money. Is there a reason she hasn't done that already? I mean, why hasn't she been farming the balance of her land for the last fifteen years? She's already hugely rich, why does she need more money?"

Alan cocked his head and asked her, "You sure you don't want a drink? I hate to drink alone, and it's already after three. Why don't we order a bottle of wine, get a little drunk, and maybe the answer will come to us? By the way, did I tell you, you look hot in jeans?"

Stephanie could feel herself blush as she sipped her iced tea. This guy doesn't miss a chance. If things were different in my life, he might actually be fun to hang out with. "Thank you for the compliment, but no thanks. Not this time." She looked at him sternly, but smiled playfully. "I thought we were going to keep this professional, Alan."

He shrugged. "I'm sorry, I can't help it. You bring out the worst in me."

Matt gripped the steering wheel as he steered west on Highway 50 and Stephanie stared silently out the passenger window. She tapped her fingers on the console to an Adele song playing on the radio. They arrived at the Club Pheasant and were greeted by Patty, a striking brunette and one of the owners.

"Matt, Stephanie, what a pleasure it is to see you," she said. She grabbed a couple of menus. "Follow me and I'll take you to your seat." She seated them in a dark red tuck-and-roll leather booth toward the back of the restaurant. The oak-stained, paneled walls accented by brass sconces threw off a dim yellow light. Stuffed pheasants of different breeds were scattered throughout the restaurant. The smell of garlic and pasta sauce permeated the main dining room. The place was packed as usual, and the noise level made speaking in a normal tone impossible. The friendly staff seemed to be sprinting back and forth to the kitchen.

Stephanie looked into Matt's eyes. "You've been so quiet lately, Matt. Is everything going okay at work?" She watched him carefully, trying to detect anything out of the ordinary.

Matt sighed and rested his chin in his hands. "Oh, everything's okay, except I keep getting pulled this way and that trying to figure out everything that's going on with some of my projects." He unfolded the napkin in front of him and placed it on his lap. "I mentioned to you that there were some irregularities with some of our assets, but I've been called off by of the higher ups."

He sprinkled some parmesan cheese over a bowl of minestrone soup that had been placed in front of him. Steam rose from it and emitted a fragrant aroma. A waitress appeared over his shoulder and refilled his water glass. He continued. "But then Diane wants me to keep pushing forward discreetly to see if there's something going on. It's kind of nerve-racking, as I don't know who to trust and who to confide in, and if I don't figure out what's going on I could lose my job."

Stephanie delicately played around with her Caesar salad. "Do you think there is something going on with those projects that aren't above board?"

Matt nodded excitedly. "Oh, absolutely I think something's going on that isn't right. Every time I try to get information from the onsite people, I get a call from a guy named Mika telling me I need to go through him for information."

"Who's Mika?" Stephanie asked.

Matt finished the soup and pushed it aside. "He's a property manager for WMI, the property management firm that manages all the projects. It's owned by a guy named Yuri Kletcko, but he's also the owner of...."

Stephanie straightened up and put her hand up. "Whoa, wait a minute. Who did you say owned the company, what was it you said, WMI?"

Matt looked up, surprised. "What, you mean Yuri Kletcko? I was saying it seems a clear conflict of interest for him to own the property management firm and to steer construction work to his other company, Centennial, Inc. Why, what do you know about Mr. Kletcko?"

"He's the guy who bailed out Caroline's neighboring rancher, the Johnsons, with a unique loan and prevented Caroline from acquiring it. She's bitter about that," Stephanie explained, her eyes widening. "The woman who's Caroline's' best friend, Mellissa Burns, works for WMI. I wonder if Yuri is her boss."

A steaming plate of chicken cacciatore was placed in front of her, followed by veal piccata for Matt. She closed her eyes and savored the flavor. "Mmmmm, this is the definition of euphoria."

"What was so unique about the loan Mr. Kletcko made?" Matt asked as he cut his food.

"He got on title with the Johnsons as joint tenants," she answered, cutting a piece of chicken. "I've never heard of a loan like that, have you?"

Matt shrugged. "That seems to be an extreme way to collateralize a loan."

A group of waitresses and waiters surrounded a table across from theirs and burst into a happy birthday song to one of the occupants. After the horrible rendition, people at nearby tables, including Matt and Stephanie, applauded the celebrant.

Matt returned his focus to his meal. He took a small bite and relished the flavors. "I've never heard of a loan like that, but in this market, who knows? Yuri has his hands in a lot of things, and maybe this is the new normal. By the way, Yuri was a friend of Taylor

Whitney's."

Stephanie pondered that for a moment. "Taylor Whitney? The dead Taylor Whitney?"

Matt nodded. "The one and the same."

"Wow. That's a strange coincidence." She paused for a second. "This Yuri is a busy guy. I think I should talk to the Johnsons. I don't know why I hadn't thought of them before, but maybe they could shed some light on Caroline's motivations." She buttered a piece of steaming bread that was just brought out and placed in front of them. "There might be more involved with Yuri than just a bailout loan."

They heard the distinctive opening notes to Van Morrison's "Brown Eyed Girl" being played in the room around the corner from where they were sitting, and the mellow voice of Neckbone's lead singer, Mitch. Matt turned toward the music. "Sounds like Neckbone is tuned up and ready to go. I hope his friend who writes original songs shows up and plays Hall of Fame with them. I love that song."

Matt pulled into Stephanie's driveway and cut the engine. The manicured lawn of her house fit with the well-maintained neighborhood. "That was a wonderful dinner, Matt, thank you. Are you planning to spend the night?" she asked as she reached out to hold his hand.

Matt paused before answering. He looked down at his lap. "No, I'm going back my folks' tonight, Steph. I haven't seen them for a while and I thought it would be good to spend some time with them."

Stephanie squeezed his hand softly. "Matt, I need to ask you something, something that's been on my mind for a while." She reached up and gently turned his face toward hers.

Matt looked at her. "Go ahead."

Stephanie took a deep breath. "A friend of mine saw you with a strange woman the other day at the 4th Street Grill." She paused, watching his reaction. "I didn't want to think it was a big deal, but I wanted to hear from you. Who were you meeting and was it just an innocent lunch? I need to know."

Stephanie felt a knot grow in her stomach as she watched Matt squirm. Oh no, she thought. Alan was right. I've been a fool.

"Uh, well, it was innocent, Stephanie," he stammered. "I, uh, well I was having lunch with an old friend who moved into town recently." He looked into her eyes, almost pleading. "It was Kathy Ann, my old girlfriend."

Tears welled up in Stephanie's eyes and she did everything in her power to hold them back. She dropped his hands. I should have known, she thought. Matt has never gotten that woman out of his system. "Why didn't you tell me, Matt?" she asked, her voice quavering. "Why did I have to hear it from someone else?"

Matt fidgeted uncomfortably in his seat, staring out the windshield. "I didn't think having lunch with Kathy Ann would be a big deal." He reached for her hand but she pulled away and got out of the car. She leaned down and spoke forcefully through the open window. "Matt, perhaps you need to take some time and think about things. I don't think you know what you want right now."

She walked quickly away, leaving Matt sitting in his car. She unlocked the front door, and turned to him. "I think we should put our wedding plans on hold. Let me know when you figure it out. Good night."

Stephanie stepped inside and locked the door. She turned her back and leaned on the door, slowly sliding down it until she was sitting on the floor. She buried her head in her hands and began sobbing. Her black cat, Smokey, came around the corner and paused. He sensed, as animals often do, that something was amiss with his mistress and rubbed up against her left leg. He arched his back and moved to her right leg, meowing mournfully. She put her hand down and lovingly stroked his back. "I'll be okay, Smokey," she softly spoke between sobs. "I'll be okay."

FIFTEEN

The well-polished, sleek Azimut 64 Flybridge yacht cruised leisurely up the Sacramento River. At a comfortable sixty-six feet in length from bow to stern and powered by twin 1,015-metric-horsepower Caterpillar C18 straight shaft diesel engines, it cut a formidable form on the river. Its baby-blue, painted hull with white trim around the top made for a stunning sight as it gently cut through the water. Although the yacht could cruise up to twenty-eight knots and had a range of 325 nautical miles, more than enough to get to San Francisco and back several times, it was moving along at twelve knots. The banks of the levees that kept the Sacramento River from flooding all the agricultural land around it were heavily wooded with sycamore and cottonwood trees, along with a sprinkling of smaller, bushier trees. Periodically, a flock of ducks flying inches off the water flew past the boat on their way to someplace down the river.

Except for the sound of the purring engine and the sound of the Bose sound system softly playing a Harry Connick, Jr. song, the river was quiet. Occasionally another ski boat, or cabin cruiser, would drift past, and Yuri, standing at the upper helm located on the starboard side forward of amidships would take his left hand briefly off the wheel to give the occupants a friendly wave, his right holding a frosty Cuba Libre. He wore a colorful Tommy Bahama speedo, which his belly hung over and made the speedo look tinier than it already was. His head was covered by an old San Diego Padres cap, which shielded his head from the sun, and he had flip-flops on his feet.

Ivan sat in a cream-colored leather seat adjacent to Yuri, also dressed in a speedo, just as ill fitting. He leaned forward, looking through the large windshield, and ogled at the two young women in skimpy bikinis sunbathing on the padded deck below. Their tan, toned bodies glistened with suntan oil. Both women were topless, half sleeping with big Gucci sunglasses covering their eyes, and a couple of tropical drinks by their sides.

Yuri steered the yacht with one hand, alternatingly looking over his shoulder for traffic coming up behind him and looking out for traffic ahead. He held up his glass to Ivan. "Could you fix me up, old friend?"

Ivan smiled and nodded. He hustled to the fully equipped bar that made making any type of drink an easy and enjoyable task. He was back in seconds with a fresh drink. Yuri took a sip and tipped his hat to Ivan. "I'm thinking we need to move up the timetable for our plan. I've figured out what New London means and what Caroline and her little troll are up to."

Ivan looked surprised. "Really, when did you figure it out?"

"Just recently, like in last night," he answered looking straight down the river. "It is a pretty ingenious plan, but I'm not going to let her pull it off. I want you to listen carefully because it'll require some coordination. It will also require bringing in Marc and Mika."

Ivan looked over at the women, who had rolled over onto their stomachs, their bikini bottoms leaving a lot of skin bared. "I will make some calls this afternoon." He looked back at Yuri. "How soon do we move? Will you fill me in on what New London is, or do I have to guess the whole time?"

Yuri smiled and laughed. "Of course I'll tell you, Ivan, but just not yet. You know I trust you, but I'm not taking any chances with this information. There's too much at stake." He nodded knowingly. "But once you know, you will know why we'll need to move fast."

He looked up and down the river and steered the boat to the right, towards an unpopulated cove. As it inched toward the shore, he reversed the engines about twenty feet from the shore, and hit the anchor release button. "Ivan, watch the anchor as I back this beast up to make it catch."

Ivan did as instructed and Yuri maneuvered the boat away from the anchor. Satisfied it was secure on the bottom, he shut the engines off.

Yuri lifted himself on his tiptoes and looked down on the women, licking his lips lecherously. Smiling, he turned to Ivan. "Shall we flip a coin to see who goes first?"

Ivan laughed and stood up and plucked a coin in the cup holder next to his seat. He flipped it into the air, and slapped it down on the back of his wrist. He smiled widely. "Go ahead, you call it. Heads you go first with Katrina, tails I go first with Anna."

"I call heads," Yuri said as he studied Ivan's wrist.

Ivan slowly lifted his hand and checked the coin. He then smiled wryly. "It's heads, you lucky bum. You're first."

Yuri slapped him on the back affectionately. "I'll see you in an hour or so." He cupped his hand and called out to the women. "Hey, Katrina, come on up here. I've got some plans for you."

The blonde woman rolled over and sat up, shielding her eyes. She looked at the other woman and gave her a naughty smile. She picked up her bikini top and her drink and sashayed up to the deck where Ivan and Yuri were standing. Yuri grabbed her hand, winked at Ivan, and led her down through the cabin to the master suite.

A week later, Mika sat on the corner of Yuri's desk, his back toward him. His bald head displayed a couple of scars from past fisticuffs where he had gotten more than he'd given, and on his left cheek sat a large brown mole. His Fu Manchu moustache was neatly trimmed, showing tiny flecks of grey mixed with black, and he chewed on a toothpick. His white silk shirt looked sharp and was tucked neatly into his dark Armani slacks. His black Mezlan Crocodile loafers dangled inches from the floor.

Ivan sat across from him in one leather chair and Marc sat on the other chair in a pair of faded jeans and a light blue La Costa shirt with a red alligator logo. His dirty white tennis shoes were unlaced, and he wasn't wearing any socks.

Yuri thumbed through a report and then set it on his desk. "Okay, Mika, you've been tracking these people for some time. Do you think you've got their routines down?"

Mika's beady brown eyes shifted from one person in the room to the other, almost as if he were at a tennis match. Without turning, he spoke. "I do, Uncle Yuri. They are as regular as clockwork. If I had to, I could tell you where they are and what they are doing right now. This job will be a cinch."

Yuri grunted. "There is no such thing as a cinch in this business, and don't forget that." He turned his attention to his other nephew, who sat quietly taking everything in. "Marc, what about you? Is everything covered on your end?"

Marc gave him a knowing nod. "I'll be fine, Uncle. I'm assuming Ivan has explained our plan to you. All I need from you is to tell me when you want us to make our move."

Yuri picked up a cigar out of a silver container, stood up, and lit it. Taking in a deep draw, and then exhaling, he spoke to Ivan. "Here's what I want to happen. There's a Board of Supervisors meeting in six weeks. I want everything ready to go prior to that. That means everything needs to go in a sequence with Mika going first. Once we start, I want no communication from any of you except you, Ivan." The room started to fill up with smoke. Ivan nodded at Yuri. "I want all of you to keep cell phone use and email to a minimum. Communicate with Ivan only as necessary. Does anybody have any questions?"

Mika spoke. "Yuri, what about those two directors doing the documentary on the ranchers in Yolo County? One of them is supposed to meet with the Johnsons this week, and she's been spending a lot of time with Caroline. Should we be concerned with them?"

Yuri paced behind his chair. "Yes, I am concerned about them, but I don't think they will cause us any problems just yet. As long as there is nothing leaked to the press about WMI, we can deal with them in due time." He stopped and waved his cigar at the two younger men. "But don't let them interfere with what you've been assigned to do. Use discretion, but do whatever it takes. When you report back to Ivan, the only thing I want to hear is that you have succeeded."

He looked at every face in the room. They all stared back at him in silence. He clapped his hands loudly. "All right, I'll let you know when I want you to execute the plan. It'll be soon, so be ready. Ivan will let you know when it's safe to meet again."

SIXTEEN

The white Honda drove slowly up the dirt road, trailing a cloud of dust behind it due to the dry, hot conditions. Betty Lou sat in a wicker chair on the wooden porch with Ken, rocking slowly back and forth. She cooled herself with a faded Chinese fan she had bought in San Francisco fifteen years earlier. They'd been observing the car coming towards them since it had left the paved road, about a mile ago. It finally came to a stop just outside the white picket fence that surrounded the front yard. A frisky, short-haired retriever came up to the driver's side to welcome the driver, spinning circles in excitement, its bobbed tail working in overdrive. An attractive, young woman in colored light jeans and a flowered blouse stepped out of the car. Her curvy brown hair fell about her shoulders, and she carried a brown satchel under her arm. Bending over, she gave the dog a loving rub above his ears, then opened the small gate and strode up the walkway.

Stepping up on the porch, she smiled a wide smile and extended her hand to Ken. "Hi, I'm Stephanie Bernard. Thanks for seeing me."

Ken shook her hand. "I'm Ken, and this is my wife, Betty Lou." He got up and pulled a chair from his left and set it near a small table sitting in the corner of the porch. "Come have a seat." He and Betty Lou scooted their chairs up to the table.

The porch was covered from the sun and had two sets of hanging pots filled with bright yellow and white daisies. A single ceiling fan, which had seen much better days, spun lazily above the center of the table, off balance, as it was missing a blade.

Betty Lou set a tall glass in front of her. "Would you like some iced sun tea? I made it fresh today." Before Stephanie could answer, she had already started pouring.

"Uh, yes, thank you, Betty Lou. That would be great." Stephanie took a sip and smiled at her. "This is just what I needed."

Betty Lou sat back and folded her arms across her lap. "So, tell us about this documentary you're making. We've heard bits and pieces about it, but this is the first time we've heard it from the horse's mouth."

Stephanie spent the next hour and a half explaining the documentary: who was in it, what it was about, and what Stephanie and her group hoped to achieve by making it. The Johnsons were very interested in what she had discovered and were more than happy to add the history of their ranch to the story.

Betty Lou was telling her some stories when she asked, "I know you spoke to Caroline Bennett. Did she get into the dealings we've had together?"

"No, she didn't get into that," Stephanie answered.

Betty Lou poured another round of tea for everyone. "That surprises me. She's been trying to buy us out or run us off for years. Her father was a mean cuss, but we managed to get along. Ever since he died and she took over, it's almost been like war between us."

Stephanie looked across the porch to the rice fields spread out beyond where she had parked her car. She could barely see, but could hear, the traffic going north and south across Interstate 5 in the distance. "Why do you think Caroline wants your land so badly?" she asked innocently. "She's got a huge spread already."

Ken spoke up for the first time. "She really could care less about the ranch itself. She just wants the water we are allocated." He could tell by Stephanie's confused look that she didn't understand. He pointed in the direction of I-5. "See how high that freeway is?"

Stephanie followed his hand, looking where he was pointing, and nodded.

"Every year," he spoke slowly, "after the rice is harvested, all this land floods from the winter rains and spring runoff. It fills about halfway up that bridge over there. That's a tremendous amount of water that accumulates because we have so much low-lying land, and that water will eventually flow down into the Delta. Caroline wants access to that water, or, more importantly, the water rights."

Betty Lou joined in. "She almost got it, as we were in deep trouble financially, and Ken and I were sure we were going to lose it. But a man named Yuri stepped in and saved us. We were at the end of our rope and didn't think we we'd be able to keep the ranch."

Stephanie put her pad down on the table. "These are tough times to get a real estate loan, especially one for land. That must have taken a lot of work."

Ken shook his head. "Not really. With Yuri it went pretty fast." He added nonchalantly, "We did have to put him on title to the ranch, and to protect the loan, he made us take out a life insurance policy on ourselves to pay it off if something happened to us. He is the beneficiary of the policy."

Stephanie almost spit out her tea. "Really? You took out an insurance policy on yourselves to secure a loan? I've never heard of that. Did you have legal counsel for this loan?"

Ken nodded assuredly. "We sure did. We also made sure we changed our will so that if anything happened to us, our ranch would be donated to UC Davis since we don't have any heirs. We both attended school there years ago and love the place. Our attorney, John Roth, looked the documents over and signed off on it. He wasn't crazy about the deal, but he knew we were in a bind and didn't have many options." Ken tapped his index finger on the table. "As a matter of fact, he's got all the original documents at his office, including the will and the insurance policy."

Stephanie gathered her things. "That would make sense. Is there a chance I could speak to Mr. Roth? I'd love to speak with him about the history of this area."

Ken glanced at Betty Lou. "I don't see why not. I'm sure John is full of great information about this area and the old families here."

Stephanie arose from her chair. "I can't thank you enough for letting me interview you, Ken and Betty Lou. I'd like to get my crew out here in a week or two to shoot some film of your place."

Ken stood and shook her hand. "That would be fine. You can call us anytime. It was nice meeting you."

Ken and Betty Lou stood on their porch and watched as Stephanie returned the same way she'd come, creating another dust cloud going in the opposite direction. Ken put his arm around Betty Lou's waist and said, "What a nice young lady. She's so polite and respectful. I get a good feeling talking to her. She'll make someone a wonderful wife."

Downtown Woodland could easily be mistaken for a Norman Rockwell painting of 1950 small town America. Main Street still had parking spaces that ran at an angle to the sidewalk. Old-time parking meters stood at the front of each spot. The Capital Hotel sat on the corner of Main and First Street, one of the oldest buildings in the town, built in 1923. The Value Rite Drug store, directly across the street, still had the neon sign spelling out DRUGS affixed to its facade, a throwback to a bygone era. The traffic on the street was slow and quiet, and pedestrians were polite and friendly, even to strangers.

Ludy's Main Street BBQ sat on the north side of Main Street, about ten businesses down from the hotel. Two red canopies covered the three tables that were outside the restaurant, which were enclosed by a three-foot tall rod iron fence.

Ken and Betty Lou sat inside in their usual booth at the front of the restaurant, near the front window. If it was Friday night, this is where they could be found. The interior paneling, aged planking made grey by years of exposure to the sun, had come off a nearby barn, and the walls were covered with antique metal signs promoting everything from Coca-Cola to Pennzoil Motor Oil. Old black and white pictures of Woodland dating back to the beginning of the 1900s hung on the walls. All the square tables were covered with red and white checkered tablecloths, and every table was filled.

Ken was finishing off the last of the beef ribs he'd ordered with the baked beans, and Betty Lou had finished her barbequed chicken. In his faded jeans, newly pressed George Strait dress shirt, with a Bolo tie and a turquoise slide, Ken looked the part of a rancher. He looked across the table at Betty Lou in her yellow sundress with white flats and her hair pinned up in a bun on her head. He watched her wipe her mouth delicately with her napkin and nod to a familiar face two tables away. The smell of smoke and barbeque filled the restaurant, along with laughter and loud conversation.

"It's been a couple days since we heard from that documentary maker, Stephanie," Betty Lou said. "She hasn't called back about filming the ranch. I wonder if she's had a chance to speak with John Roth."

Ken looked up from his ribs, wiping his hands with a big paper napkin. "Yeah, she said she would call us this week. John hasn't called back since I let him know she might be calling, so I don't know. Like I told you, I placed a call to Yuri a few days ago. I want to see if he had any further information on the offer we received from Westwood Land. If I don't hear from him in a day or two, I want John to look into what our options are."

Betty Lou sighed. "Good idea. I know we didn't have many

choices but to take the loan as Yuri dictated, but everything seems different with him lately." She neatly folded her napkin and placed it on the table. "Are you ready to go?" she asked. "I'm tired and have a couple of things to do at home."

Ken stood up, picked up his light brown Stetson cowboy hat from the chair next to him, and placed it on his head. He nodded. "I'm ready, let's go."

They drove through downtown Woodland, the radio softly playing a Buck Owens tune on a local AM station. The black antique streetlights lit up the area, throwing off a soft yellow glow on the buildings on either side of the street. As he drove, Ken rolled his window down and a gentle breeze from the Delta drifted through the car. Leaving downtown, they left the lighted area and drove down the road in darkness, the only light being that from the headlights of their car. They passed under I-5 and turned left onto Road 102. They hadn't gone more than a quarter mile when a dark Mercedes passed them and cut right in front of their car, forcing Ken to hit the brakes. Ken leaned on the horn and yelled at the driver, "Hey, jackass, where did you learn to drive? Baghdad?"

The other car slammed on its brakes and stopped. In their headlights they could see the driver, a bald man in a dark sweat suit, jump out of the car and come toward them, his fists in a ball and an enraged look on his face.

Betty Lou reached over and grabbed Ken's arm. "Go around him, Ken. We don't want any trouble."

Ken grumbled to himself but hit the gas and sped around the man, who stood in the middle of the street. As they passed, he pulled a gun from his sweatpants waist and waved it menacingly at Ken and Betty Lou's car. Once they were past the man, he leapt back into the car and accelerated after them.

Betty Lou leaned over the front seat to view what he was doing behind them. "Ken, speed up, he's chasing us." Her voice rose in excitement. "He's coming really fast!"

Ken looked up nervously in the rearview mirror. "Call 911, Betty. This guy is crazy. Tell them to hurry." He pushed harder on the accelerator.

Betty Lou fumbled through her purse for her phone and then dialed furiously. A male operator came on the line. "911, what is your emergency?"

Betty Lou blurted into the phone, "We're driving near Woodland, down Road 102 just south of I-5, and we have another motorist who's waving a gun and chasing us. We need some help right away." She turned to look out the back window as she spoke. Her eyes grew wide as she saw that the Mercedes was two feet off their rear bumper. Suddenly the Mercedes lurched and smashed into the back of their car, causing their car to lurch forward and Ken to temporarily lose control.

The operator could be heard talking to the police dispatcher as Ken tried desperately to shake his attacker. The operator came back on the line. "Ma'am, there is a Highway Patrol about six miles behind you and he's in the process of responding," he spoke calmly to her. "Do not try to engage the other motorist. Try to find a lighted area to drive to and wait for the police."

Betty Lou screamed into the phone, "We can't stop! He's slamming his car into us! He's trying to run us off the road."

They came upon a street that veered to the left. Ken turned the wheel hard, with dust and gravel flying, and then he headed the car down the dark, narrow road. He checked the rearview mirror, the lights from the Mercedes lighting his face. Sweat was pouring from his head, forming a wet ring around his cowboy hat as he struggled to control the car. "Damn, he's still following us," he said. "I think I can shake him off at the end of this road. It's going to take a hard right up here, and he won't be able to see it. He can't keep this pace up forever." He held the steering wheel tightly as the car bounced and flew over the pock-stricken country road.

The operator came back on the phone. "What is your position

now, ma'am?"

"We've turned east on Road 26A," Betty Lou answered, her voice filled with fear. "He's still following us. Please tell them to hurry. He's trying to kill us!"

The Mercedes sped up and pulled up next to them on the driver's side. The driver's face was fixed with rage and he pointed the gun at Ken. Betty Lou screamed as Ken held a death grip on the steering wheel, his face twisted in terror. Their car was approaching eighty miles an hour and he was having trouble with it on the narrow, bumpy road.

Betty Lou screamed into the phone, "Help us, please! He's got a gun, he's got a gun! He's about to shoot us!"

The Mercedes turned and scraped against the driver's side, knocking the car to the right shoulder of the road. Ken turned to look out his window when he suddenly clutched his chest and let out a guttural groan. He rolled his eyes and slumped forward, hitting his head on the steering wheel. The car veered farther to the right as Betty Lou reached out to try to straighten the car.

She shrieked, "Ken, Ken!" as she grabbed the wheel she turned to see where she was steering through the front windshield. A huge oak tree appeared in the headlights, dead in front of the car and three feet off the bumper. It happened so fast, she never heard the crash, felt the dashboard crush her body, or the subsequent explosion.

SEVENTEEN

The streets of Old Town Sacramento were quiet for a Monday morning. Workmen with trash bags roamed the area, picking up the remnants of the blues festival that had been held there the previous weekend, where 20,000 revelers had spent the better part of the weekend. Bonnie Jacobs sat at the reception desk outside John Roth's office, reading the regional section of *The Sacramento Bee*. She had been John's legal assistant for twenty-eight years and looked over John like a daughter to an aging father. She shook her head as she read the article about the Johnsons and their fatal car crash along Road 26A on Friday night. "No suspects as of Sunday night," she read out loud. "A possible case of road rage that turned violent." She set the paper down. "What's this world coming to?"

She had come to know the Johnsons over the years, as they met with John regularly. Her eyes welled up with tears at the thought of their deaths. "They were such wonderful people," she muttered to no one. "I can't believe they're gone. They had just called last week to authorize John to speak to a reporter who was working on a documentary. I better call that lady and reschedule that appointment for next week." She searched in the article for the date of the funeral and saw it was scheduled for the Friday coming up at 11:00 a.m., so she made a notation on John's calendar.

She looked up at the closed door to John's office. The very low muffled sound of voices came through the door, but nothing that was discernible. He was meeting with a new client this morning, a young man who wanted some advice on a real estate deal he was pursuing. Bonnie had a strange feeling about the man, but shrugged it off as her being paranoid. She never liked the bald look that so many young men sported these days, and the look of this young man was no exception. "I wonder why he is spending so much time on an initial meeting," she spoke out loud. She glanced up at the antique clock hanging on the opposite wall. "It's been over an hour and John normally moves new clients along in half that time."

Suddenly the door burst open and the young man charged out. "Call 911, I think John's had a heart attack," he yelled. "Quickly, I think it's serious."

Bonnie speed-dialed the number, trying to look through John's door and explain the situation to the operator. Assured that help was on the way, she hurried past the man and into John's office. Out of her peripheral vision she noticed the man was carrying an armful of files, but she pushed that to the back of her mind as she rushed to John's side. He lay sprawled on the floor behind his desk. Blood was coming out of a small gash on his forehead from when he hit the floor.

She turned and called out to the young man, "Can you throw me the towel from the bathroom to your left?" There was no answer. She called out again, but there was still no answer. She got on her knees, lifted up John's arm, and felt for a pulse. She then laid her head on his chest to listen for a heartbeat. Although she wasn't a trained nurse, she knew it was over. She remained kneeling on the floor, buried her head in her hands, and started to cry.

EIGHTEEN

The afternoon sun beat down on the apartment building set in the back of the Pheasant Crossing apartment complex, the farthest away from the rental office and recreational building. The landscapers had been through the complex earlier in the morning, leaving the lawns neatly mowed and the balance of the foliage trimmed. A couple of grey squirrels played tag, alternating chasing each other from one redwood tree to another one twenty yards away.

Brenda, the onsite manager, nervously fumbled with a large ring of keys as Matt stood a few feet behind her and watched. Her dark hair was pulled over to one side and held with a barrette, but a few wisps of hair hung about indiscriminately. She had fit into her black slacks better when she was ten pounds lighter, but she still looked much younger than her actual age. Matt could tell by her concerned look that she didn't feel comfortable doing what she was doing.

Matt moved away from the door and looked up a stairway that rose to service two units above them. He pointed up and asked, "Have these tenants said anything unusual about Mr. Kletcko? Have you had any complaints about his guests?"

Brenda turned around, stopping her attempt to find the correct key to the apartment. She looked at the two units above them and the unit directly across from the one she was attempting to open. "Nobody lives in any of those units," she answered. "They're all vacant."

Matt gave her a look of confusion. "They're vacant? Why is that? You've got a waiting list for any available units. What's wrong with these?"

Brenda shrugged. "Those were my orders from Mika. These units are to be left vacant until we are told different. I don't ask questions when a request comes from my boss."

"Don't these units each rent for eleven hundred a month?" Matt asked.

She corrected him. "Eleven hundred and fifty a month."

Matt did some quick calculations. "That's forty four hundred a month, over fifty thousand dollars a year, we're not receiving. That's crazy."

After the sixth key, Brenda found the correct one and opened the door. She walked into the unit, followed by Matt. "I don't like this, Matt. If Mika finds out I did this, he'll fire me, or worse."

Matt walked around the unit, taking in the layout. "What do you mean by worse?" he asked as he surveyed the apartment.

"It's nothing that's been said, Matt, but Mika scares me. He has a reputation as a hothead, and I've heard he's not above using his fists when he gets mad."

"Don't worry, Brenda," Matt said reassuringly, not completely convincing himself what he just said. "Nobody's going to fire you, and nobody will physically harm you. I've got a right to inspect properties General Technologies owns." He stepped inside and glanced around. "So, this is Mr. Kletcko's secret hideaway," he said.

They were standing in the main living area. A gas fireplace stood on the wall across from the entry. A brown leather couch and a loveseat sat up against the wall opposite the fireplace. A 42-inch flat screen TV hung above the fireplace. Numerous prints of landscape scenes decorated the walls and a dark coffee table in the center of the room had numerous copies of *The Wall Street Journal* laid out on it. Well, at least Yuri's a good housekeeper, Matt thought. This place is immaculate.

Matt moved into the master bedroom. A double bed sat in the center of the room, covered in a colorful comforter with multiple pillows accenting it. A mirror the size of the bed was glued to the ceiling. Matt looked up at the mirror, then over to Brenda. "That looks kinda kinky, don't you think?"

She giggled. "I thought the same thing. But you know the saying, different strokes for different folks."

Matt moved into the second bedroom, which had a simple desk with two chairs and a computer with a sixteen-inch monitor. On one wall hung a framed aerial photograph of a large land parcel near the airport. Matt moved up closer and studied the picture. He recognized Interstate 5 running east to west over the area known as the Yolo Causeway situated between Woodland and Sacramento. That looks like the ranch Stephanie was talking about the other day, he thought to himself. I wonder why Yuri would have it hanging on a wall in his office.

"Brenda, this place is so clean it looks like it has maid service. Does it?" he asked.

"Yes. We have about ten units we rent to corporations for when their people come into town for an extended stay and don't want to stay at a hotel. Those units come with daily maid service and we include that service with this unit also."

Matt surveyed the place again. "Well, that's convenient. He brings his playthings here, has a party, and doesn't have to clean up. It must be nice. Is this apartment complex the only place where Mr. Kletcko has a unit for his own use?"

Brenda shook her head. "I don't know firsthand, but I think this is the only one he has in Sacramento. He might have other ones in other cities."

Matt pulled a drawer open from the desk. "Brenda, do me a

favor. I'll be looking around here for an hour or two. Go back to the office and call me if anyone from WMI shows up. I don't want to be surprised by any visitors. I'll come get you when I'm done."

"Okay, Matt. Try to hurry." She left and closed the front door.

The apartment was eerily quiet. Matt sat at the desk and went through the drawers, thumbing through the files he found in the desk. Finding nothing of interest, he turned on the computer.

He clicked on the My Document icon. A list of files popped up and many of them appeared to be photographs. Matt clicked on one. A young, scantily-clad woman appeared on the screen. He looked at the image closer. Hey, that woman looks a lot like the one Yuri was with at the horse races, he thought. He clicked on a few more pictures and saw more of the same woman, only in different poses.

He moved past the pictures and stopped at a file in the center. It read Morton Bain. Matt stared at the name for a second, before it registered. He said to himself, "What's a file of a board member of General Technologies doing on a WMI computer?" He clicked on the file and waited for it to open.

Outside the apartment, a nearby car door slammed shut and made Matt jump. He froze in the chair, listening for any other sound. He looked around to see where he might try to escape if anyone came through the front door. The window across from the bed looked like the best option, and he readied himself to make a move. After a minute of silence, he relaxed.

He looked around the desk for a printer and found one on the floor to the left of his seat. He checked to see if it had paper, which it did, and he proceeded to print the contents of the file. While he waited for the printer to finish, he scrolled around through other files. At the bottom he noticed one final file: Johnson Ranch. Matt remembered the photograph on the wall. That's the ranch Stephanie was talking about, he thought. He printed the contents of the file.

Matt gathered all the papers, put them in a manila envelope, and strode out of the apartment. He had just walked past the corner of the building when he heard Brenda's voice speaking in an exited tone. "Wait for me, Mika, you're moving too fast. Hold on, what's your hurry?"

Matt turned and sprinted in the opposite direction. He turned the corner in time to hear Mika angrily answer her as he rounded the corner of the building where he had been standing. "I know that Matt guy is here somewhere, Brenda, and you better tell me where he is. I know his car, and that's his car out there."

Matt moved quickly down the building about thirty yards, hugging the walls. He stopped to catch his breath and checked behind him. Seeing nothing, he crept to an old fir tree and paused, looking around the tree to the front door of the apartment. He figured Mika had entered the unit, so he made a beeline to his car, which was sitting under a carport across the parking lot. He hoped Mika would spend a few minutes inside so he could get out of the complex.

He jumped in the car and gingerly pulled out. As he headed toward the entrance and out of the complex, he saw Mika exit the apartment and start sprinting toward him. He accelerated and sped away, wiping perspiration off his forehead as he adjusted his mirror.

His cell phone rang. He recognized the number and answered, "Sorry, Mika, I have another appointment and I'm late. Next time, I'll set aside some time to talk."

Mika was breathing hard and shouted, "Listen up, Matt. I meant what I said. If you know what's good for you, you won't come around here again. I'm getting tired of your games."

Matt eased up on the accelerator and slowed down. His breathing had slowed also, so he answered in a measured tone. "That sounds like a threat, Mika. What are you hiding? Your boss is taking some liberties with apartment units that my company owns. I'm going to find out what you guys are up to." He looked into his rearview mirror, half expecting Mika to be on his bumper, but relaxed to see a white-haired lady with horned rim glasses driving a

1990's Cadillac behind him.

"I warn you, Matt," Mika snarled into the phone. "Go back to pushing numbers around at your desk."

An hour later, Matt was at his desk, absorbed in the documents he'd printed. His cell phone rang and he recognized Stephanie's number. His heart skipped a beat. He had not spoken with her since their dinner a week earlier, and he missed her. "Hi, Stephanie, how are you?"

"I'm fine," she answered, not sounding entirely believable. "Can we meet, like soon? I don't know if you've been paying attention to the news, but there have been some terrible things happening in Woodland."

Matt put the files back on his desk and sat up straight. "I haven't been paying attention. What's been going on?"

Her voice was strained. "Meet me at the Fat City Bar & Cafe in Old Town in an hour and I'll fill you in. I'm meeting Alan Hubbard there, the guy I'm working with on the Caroline Bennett case. I think we all need to compare notes."

Matt set the files he'd been studying back on his desk. He knew by the sound of her voice that something major was going on. "I'll be there."

He hung up and stared out his window. The past week had been agonizing for him. He had tried to immerse himself in his work, but his thoughts always wandered. Kathy Ann had been pestering him to meet with her, but something told him that was a bad idea. The more he thought about Kathy Ann, the more he realized she was not the person he had known in college. The person he knew in college was carefree but focused. The person she was now seemed desperate. Her persistent texts and phone calls were a new side he'd never seen. In the past, she was more aloof and played hard to get. She was self-assured and had a plan for the future. That person he'd known no longer existed, and the one that had taken her place he didn't recognize.

The more time he spent without Stephanie, the more he realized how badly he missed her and how much he loved her. But she had cast him off because he had violated her trust, and he would have to start over to prove to her his love was genuine.

The Fat City Bar & Cafe was empty except for an elderly couple enjoying a late lunch and a pair of men in suits discussing a deal at the bar over a cocktail. Matt stepped into the foyer and looked past the bar area into the restaurant. As his eyes adjusted to the dim light, he saw Stephanie sitting with a man at a window table looking out onto Front Street. The man was a few years older than Matt and wore a dark suit with a white shirt and a blue tie that he had loosened. Matt couldn't help but notice he was good-looking, and he felt a twinge of jealousy when he thought about how much time Stephanie had been spending with him.

He came up to the table and waited until they had finished their conversation. Stephanie, as always, looked like she had just come off a photo shoot. She saw him and smiled. "Hi, Matt."

He stood there awkwardly, hoping she would stand up so he could give her a hug, but she remained seated. "This is the guy I've told you about, Alan Hubbard. Alan, Matt Whiteside, my… " She paused, "friend."

Alan stood up and shook Matt's hand. "Matt, it's a pleasure. Stephanie has told me a lot about you."

Matt sat next to Stephanie with Alan across the table. Suddenly Matt remembered Alan. That's the man I noticed was staring at me while I had lunch with Kathy Ann, he thought. Is he the one who told Stephanie? He stared at Alan for a second as he adjusted his tie, then he spoke. "I checked the internet before I came. Is this regarding the ranch couple who were killed in the car crash Friday?" he asked. "I don't know how I missed it."

Stephanie reached into a file folder and pushed a newspaper article to Matt. "Here's the article from Sunday's *Sacramento Bee*," she said. "As you can see, it was all over the front page. I was telling Alan before you arrived, I'm not convinced this was an accident due to a spontaneous road rage incident."

Matt scanned the article as she spoke. Without looking up he asked, "Why do you think that? Do the police think something happened?"

"They're not saying, but we know there was a 911 call made while the couple was being chased. They drove into a tree at a high rate of speed." She spoke softly but intensely. "These people were a wonderful couple. They were in their seventies. There is no way they would have gotten into a confrontation where they would have to drive for their lives."

A waiter brought a round of water, and then moved on to another table. Another couple had come into the restaurant and parked themselves at the bar. Canned music played softly from the speaker just behind their table.

Alan sipped from one of the waters then spoke. "The word from the initial coroner's inquiry is that Mr. Johnson died from a massive heart attack. The crash probably would have killed him, but he was frightened to death. There's one other thing, Matt." He nodded to Stephanie. "Tell him, Steph."

She turned to Matt. "The Johnson's have an attorney named John Roth, whom they have used for years for all their legal work. He was an older man in his eighties, but still actively practicing law. He had a heart attack at his desk last Monday while consulting with a new client."

Matt played with a spoon while he listened. "Maybe all of this is a coincidence."

Stephanie glanced at Alan and then back at Matt. "Maybe, but a lady named Bonnie Jacobs, his longtime administrative assistant, called me to cancel an appointment I had to meet with Mr. Roth later this week. She was distraught and spoke with me for over an hour." She paused as the maître d' walked a patron past their table to their seats. "The person Mr. Roth was meeting with when he collapsed was a new client referred by a colleague. Bonnie called that colleague after Mr. Roth's death, but he had never heard of the new client and obviously had never referred him."

Matt shifted in his chair.

Stephanie checked over her shoulder and continued. "When the paramedics were working on Mr. Jacobs, he had a small bruise by his neck that Bonnie hadn't noticed that morning when he first came into work. She thinks he might have been given something to induce the heart attack."

Matt folded the article and handed it back to Stephanie. "That sounds like a pretty big reach. A strange person comes into the attorney's office, stabs him with a drug to induce a heart attack, and disappears? Sounds like a scene out of a John Clancy novel."

"It gets better," Stephanie said. "Bonnie isn't positive, but she thinks the client walked out with an armload of files. Guess whose files are missing from the filing cabinet Mr. Roth kept in his office?"

Alan answered evenly. "The Johnsons'."

"Exactly, the Johnsons'," Stephanie said.

Alan nodded in the direction behind Matt and to his left out the window. "Hey, Matt, is that your blue BMW over there? What are those two guys checking it out for?"

Matt turned and glanced out the window. Two men—one bald, wearing dark slacks and a black shirt with dark sunglasses and another man with tattoos along his arms and continuing out from under a short-sleeved white shirt, up to his neck—were circling Matt's car. They alternately looked up and down the cobbled street and toward the restaurant. They both crossed the street and walked to the front door.

One man remained outside leaning against a lamppost menacingly. The man in black noisily entered the restaurant, slamming the door behind him. The noise along with his hostile demeanor caught the attention of several people in the restaurant. The bald man looked around the restaurant and stopped when he spotted Matt and the others. He moved toward the bar, leaned against it, and ordered something gruffly, not taking his eyes off the group.

Alan had his back to the man and cautiously reached inside his coat. "You know that guy, Matt?"

Matt kept his eyes on the man. "We haven't been formally introduced, but his name is Mika Menski. He works for Yuri Kletcko as a property manager and is also his nephew, but I think he has an expanded job description: hired goon."

Alan slowly turned in his seat. He pulled his coat back, barely revealing the holstered gun he was carrying.

The bartender poured a shot of Petron Tequila and set it in front of Mika. Without taking his eyes off Matt, Mika downed the shot and slammed his glass down on the bar. He pulled some money out of his pants pocket, threw it on the bar, and stormed out.

Alan, Matt, and Stephanie watched wordlessly as he and his tattooed partner crossed the street and jumped into a black Mercedes with tinted windows. The car hung a U-turn on Front Street and peeled out as it made its way out of Old Town Sacramento.

They all breathed easier when the car pulled out of sight. Alan was the first to break the silence. "What was that all about, Matt? Was that some sort of shot across the bow?"

"I'm not sure," he answered. "I've been trying to quietly find some information out about his boss, Yuri, but either he or Yuri isn't happy about it."

Matt became aware of a person standing just behind their booth. He turned and looked up at a stocky, bald-headed black man in a perfectly tailored suit, wired-rimmed glasses, and striped blue tie. He was also watching Mika drive away. Matt smiled. "Johnnie Gibson! What are you up to?"

Johnnie looked down and grabbed Matt's shoulder playfully. "I'm just watching out for you, my man. I was making sure you didn't need my services." He winked at Matt.

"I appreciate that, Johnnie," Matt responded. He turned to his companions. "You remember Stephanie, Johnnie, and this is Alan Hubbard." He nodded to Alan. "This is Johnnie Gibson, my defense attorney; the best defense attorney in Sacramento, I might add."

Alan raised an eyebrow. "It's nice to meet you, Johnnie." He turned to Matt. "Your defense attorney?"

Matt shrugged. "It's a long story. I'll bore you with it another time."

Johnnie laughed. "Yeah, fill him in some time. I've got to get to court, Matt. Try to stay out of trouble."

"I'll try, Johnnie," Matt yelled as Johnnie hurried out the restaurant.

Stephanie covered her mouth. "Oh my god, I forgot."

Alan and Matt spoke in unison. "Forgot what?"

Her eyes were wide and she spoke excitedly. "Yuri Kletcko, he's got an insurance policy on the Johnsons and he's on title with them on their ranch. If they're dead, he collects the insurance money and he becomes the new owner of the ranch unless their will can be found."

Matt looked confused. "What are you talking about?"

She filled him and Alan in on the loan for the ranch, the insurance policy, and the Johnsons' desire to donate the ranch to the university.

She took a drink of water and continued. "Don't you see? It's the Johnsons' files. If their will was in those files and is missing, that means there is nothing keeping Yuri from collecting the insurance money to pay off his loan and keep the ranch. It's a double bonus."

Alan scratched his head. "That is a pretty weird way this thing is falling into Yuri's lap. But here's a problem." He spoke to Stephanie. "You and I were hired to find out why Caroline Bennett was turning down development projects in Yolo County. Mr. Parker was sure there was something behind her actions. I'm about to report our findings to him, and as far as you and I can determine, she's turning everything down because it appeals to her political base and she feels it will help her get into a higher office." He folded his hands on the table. "If I convince him that's her whole agenda, he will pull us off the case and work on getting her defeated in the next election."

Stephanie pleaded with him. "Alan, you've got to hold off that report. There's more to this than Caroline's political ambitions and you know it." She nodded at Matt. "Matt's onto something and so are we. If we could get a couple more weeks to investigate, I know we will turn up more. Now that the Johnsons are gone, Caroline has to deal with Yuri. We know she's got her grand plan, but she doesn't know what she's dealing with."

"I know Yuri is dirty," Matt said, "but how dirty, I don't know. Would he harm someone? I wouldn't put it past him. But I'm getting the feeling that he's getting antsy and nervous about something. I agree with Stephanie, Alan. We've got to keep on this case a little longer."

Alan folded his hands under his chin and thought for a few seconds. He took a deep breath and sighed. "Okay, I'll hold back. Much as I don't want to, I'll meet with Mellissa one more time and see what I can glean out of her. Also, I know John Cranston, the Sheriff of Yolo County. I'll call him and feel him out about this. Maybe he can shed some light on this recent string of accidents. Stephanie, you meet with Caroline and see what you can get."

He stood up and pushed his chair in. "I think I'll be on my way. Both of you be alert." He reached into his pocket, pulled out a small black device, and handed it to Stephanie. "I don't know if you'll need this or not, but keep it on you. It's a GPS that will tie into my cell phone." He shrugged sheepishly. "I'm sorry. It's my old FBI training. If you get into trouble, hit the red button and it will activate the system. I won't know what your emergency is, but I'll be able to find you. We may be overreacting, but it's better to be on the safe side." He gave a half salute to them and headed for the door.

A minute of silence hung between them before Matt spoke. "I miss you, Stephanie. Can you stay around for a few minutes to talk?"

She smiled at him. "Sure, I've got a few minutes. How are your mom and dad? Is everybody doing well?"

He looked at her smiling. "They're all doing well, thank you. They always ask about you." He signaled to the waiter for an order. "I'm sorry how things were left, Steph. I've been doing some real soul searching, and the longer I'm away from you, the more I miss you. I would like to try and start again."

Stephanie sipped her water without expression. She let his words hang in the air. "That's it? All of a sudden it's clear to you I'm the one?" She ran a finger over the rim of her glass. "I'm sorry, Matt, but I'm not the type of person whose emotions you can stop and start at the drop of a hat. I've also had time to think, and although I do miss you also, I'm not investing all my emotions into this relationship right now. I want to see that this is for real with you and not a game." She studied his eyes for a few seconds. "I don't know what caused you to question our relationship, but until I'm convinced you are all in, I'm leaving things status quo."

Matt wanted to kick himself but kept up the façade of everything being okay. He resisted the urge to get on his knees and beg for her forgiveness. "I understand, Stephanie. Would it be all right if we start seeing each other again? I'm not trying to rush anything, but I really do miss you and I enjoy your company." He reached over and put his hand over hers.

She sighed and squeezed his hand. "Yes, we can see each other." She bent her head and looked at him with a furrowed brow. "Just don't get any ideas about picking up where we left off. I'm not ready for that."

Matt smiled faintly. "I promise to be on my best behavior."

Matt's phone, which he had set on the table between them, vibrated. Matt looked down on it to see a text massage. It read: "can u meet 4 a drink tonite? KA xox."

Stephanie saw the message, reached for her purse, and stood up to leave. Matt pulled at her hand. "Wait, Stephanie, this is not what you think." She yanked her hand away, rolled her eyes, and left the restaurant. Matt sat at the table and watched her as she headed to her car. "Kathy Ann has incredible timing," he muttered. "No matter what I say, Stephanie will never believe me that nothing has gone on. I've screwed this up royally."

NINETEEN

The drab, grey concrete building stood forty feet from the curb of Mechanical Road in Rancho Cordova. High up on its twenty-five foot walls, eight high-density floodlights aimed down upon the area in the front and side of the building. Although not in use on this hot afternoon, the photosensitive lights would activate when the sun went down. Any movement within twenty yards of the building triggered the 500-watt lights that were strong enough to illuminate a high school football field. Just before the entrance to the building, a rod-iron gate ran from one corner of the building to the redwood fence that enclosed the property. Razor wire looped across the top of the tall rod-iron fence. Three high-powered ski boats, dusty from years of neglect, sat behind the fence. Various parts of boats and car engines were spewed across the driveway. Toward the back of the property, a black and tan German Shepherd paced back and forth behind a wire enclosure, barking and growling excitedly and ferociously.

The inside of the building was just as cluttered as the outside. The warehouse was stacked, floor to ceiling, with engine parts. Two modified boat engines hung from heavy chains in the center of the building, attached to bulky beams that spanned from wall to wall and carried the weight of the roof.

Mika paced back and forth in the small, dingy office just past the front door. The well-worn carpet had grease stains every two feet, and the walls, once white, where discolored by years of dust and cigarette smoke. Yuri sat behind an old beat-up desk, watching him in silence. Ivan leaned against a wall in the corner, an old, bald tire serving as his table for his drink.

Mika was clearly agitated and Yuri was content to let him vent. It always felt good to Yuri to come to this place, as this is where he'd started when he first arrived in the United States after fleeing Russia. The walls had pleasant memories of the chop shop operation he and Ivan had run in the 90s.

"I'm telling you, Uncle," Mika started, "those three people are major trouble. They need to be dealt with and dealt with firmly. That nosey Matt Whiteside and the other two are getting too close for comfort." He stopped and lit a cigarette. "Give me the order so I can take care of them."

Yuri held up his hand and Mika stopped. He poured half a glass of vodka into the tumbler he held and reached into the ice chest sitting on the desk. The ice plunked into his glass. He took a deep drink and set the glass on the table. He leaned forward on the desk and spoke. "Listen to me, nephew. I hear what you're saying, but the timing isn't right. I am close to getting the legal papers for the ranch in order to get the control I need. Be patient for two more weeks and then I will let you go to work. I want this Matt guy and his friends dealt with more than you."

Mika, still visibly irritated, said, "Uncle, with due respect, I will honor your wishes, but I think waiting is a mistake. They are getting into areas we don't want them to be."

"It's a mistake that needs to be made then," Yuri answered sternly. "Ivan, you have the documents my attorney prepared for me to sign to make everything legal, correct?"

Ivan reached down and patted the brown, weather-beaten

briefcase near his feet. "Everything is here. The affidavit, showing you as the surviving joint tenant, making you the owner of the ranch, is here. The executed death certificates and request for payment under the death clause from New Bedford Insurance Company are here. Finally, a notarized reconveyance form, showing the underlying loan as paid in full." He picked up his glass and saluted Yuri. "Once this is all recorded and you collect the insurance money, you will own the ranch free and clear of all debt. Well done, Yuri."

Yuri smiled and saluted back. "This is all good, but we're not quite finished. Ivan, I haven't gotten the notification for approval of the extra water allocation yet. My attorney says we are still a couple of weeks away from that. Once we have the allocation, we will have the power we've been seeking." He looked at everyone around the room with a stern eye. "Until then, we still have work to do. Let's keep a low profile." He looked at Mika. "Don't anybody do anything stupid."

Two cyclists whizzed by along the American River bike trail, about thirty feet from the wooden picnic table where Yuri sat. Twenty yards behind him, the American River lazily flowed westward toward the confluence with the Sacramento River and then on toward the Delta. The bike trail was a popular spot for runners, bike riders, and nature lovers, with its scenic and close access to the river. Numerous magpies, their black and blue plumage shining from the afternoon sun, pranced noisily back and forth across the trail, flying out of harm's way at the last minute as a bike rider rounded a blind corner.

A bucket of fried chicken sat on the table, next to Yuri, along with some coleslaw, which his grandchildren, Nickolas and Annicia, were busy devouring. Their hair was wet from their swim in the river and each had a beach towel draped over their shoulders as they ate.

Yuri pulled two peppermint sticks out of his pocket and set them on the table. "See what Papa brought you for desert?" he asked, smiling broadly. "Once you finish your lunch, you can have the candy."

The two children paused for a second, eyeing the candy, then vigorously dove back to the chicken pieces they were working on. Nickolas cocked his head. "Thank you, Papa. Can we go to the toy store on our way home today? We've been very good."

Annicia chimed in. "Yes, Papa, we've been angels."

Yuri leaned back and gave them a concerned look. "You know, we didn't get to the toy store last week, did we?" He looked sternly from child to child, and then he broke into laughter. "Of course we can go to the toy store. As soon as you two finish, we'll head over there."

Nickolas and Annica jumped up and hugged Yuri, wrapping their small arms around his large waist. In each of their hands, they held a chicken drumstick, staining his pressed slacks with chicken grease. "Thank you, Papa, thank you!" they squealed in unison. He put his arms around them and hugged them.

Yuri felt his cell phone vibrate in his pocket and he pulled it out. He didn't recognize the number but answered it anyway. "Hello, Yuri here."

A female voice spoke from the other end. "Yes, Yuri, Caroline Bennett here. I don't think we've had the pleasure of meeting, but I understand you are now the new owner of the Johnson ranch thanks to the untimely and unfortunate demise of the Johnsons. I'm your neighbor."

Yuri stiffened as he listened.

She continued as if speaking to a petulant child. "I don't know how you pulled this little caper off, nor do I care, but I want you to know you're not getting any extra allocation of water that you have applied for and have been banking on."

"What do you mean?" Yuri asked, his voice rising in anger.

"Don't play dumb, Yuri," she answered. "When I heard you

saved the Johnsons from foreclosure by lending them money, I knew I smelled a rat. Let me tell you what will happen next at the Johnson ranch: nothing. I know many people at the California Water Resources Board, and your little application for more water will go nowhere."

Yuri listened in silence as Caroline droned on about herself and her plans. The more she talked, the angrier he got.

He finally cut her off, "I wouldn't be so sure of yourself." He flipped the phone down on the table next to the bucket of chicken. "Come on, kids, let's gather our things. Papa has to go back to work. We'll have to change our plans for the toy store, but I'll take you there tomorrow, I promise."

They both moaned in disappointment but did as they were told. Yuri stepped away from them as they were gathering their stuff together. He reflected on the conversation a moment, and then dialed his phone. "Ivan, get ahold of Mika and Marc. Tell them to meet at my office in an hour. Things have changed. I'm moving up our timetable."

TWENTY

Caroline sat behind her desk in a white sleeveless blouse and a pair of dark slacks, a white pearl necklace gracing her neck. She set her phone back in its cradle and clapped her hands with joy. Mellissa, sitting across from her in the office at the ranch, smiled a wicked smile, as if they had both just pulled off some schoolgirl prank.

The afternoon sun shone brightly through the picture window behind her, making the office unusually bright. A vase of freshly cut white roses stood at the end of her desk, and everything on it was neatly stacked. An ornate, gold-framed photograph of her father taken when he was in his mid-fifties hung on the wall behind her. She could almost feel him looking over her shoulder. Unconsciously she tugged at the necklace.

"Oh, Mellissa," Caroline raved. "I wish I could have been a fly on the wall when I told him what I was up to. He didn't say much, but I could tell he was seething."

A grandfather clock clicked and started to slowly chime the hour. After the third and final chime, it stopped, the sound reverberating through the office. Caroline leaned back into the thick leather chair and smiled. "I never get tired of hearing that clock, as it reminds me so much of Dad. It brings back fond memories of me playing in this office while he worked when I was a young girl. I wonder what he would think of what I've done with his ranch."

"Oh, I'm sure he would be so proud of you, Caroline," Mellissa gushed. "He might not be so happy with your politics, but everything else would be good." She slapped her hands on her thighs and pleaded, "Please, Caroline, tell me your plans. I've wracked my brains trying to figure out New London, but I can't figure it out. I can't stand it anymore."

Caroline leaned forward in her chair, focusing on her friend. I'm so glad I didn't agree to meet at Del Paso Country Club like Mellissa suggested, she thought to herself. She is such a dear to me, but I can't seem to get through to her about her hygiene or her choice of clothing. And those cats; oh my god, those nasty cats! They rule her life! It's been years since I was in her house, and it was in bad shape *then*. I can only imagine the condition it's in now. Oh well, she is who she is and I love her. I couldn't get half the things I want to accomplish without her help. No matter what the obstacles are, she soldiers on. She is a true friend.

"Hold on, Mellissa. Before I tell you everything, it's time to celebrate." She reached for a small silver bell sitting to her left and gave it a firm ring. A minute later, a tall, good-looking young man with moussed brown hair with blonde tips, appeared at the door. Caroline admired how his well-built, ripped chest filled out his pale blue polo shirt. "Monte," she asked. "Would you open a bottle of Cristal and bring us two glasses? I want to propose a toast."

He bowed and left the office.

Mellissa put the back of her fist to her mouth as she watched him leave. Without taking her eyes off him, she asked, "Caroline, where do you find these guys? He's so gorgeous." She turned back and put her hand on the desk. "If I was of a different sexual persuasion," she said, as if it were understood, she wasn't, "I'd definitely enjoy a romp with that."

Caroline smiled and thought, I don't think so, old friend. I don't think young Monte is your type. And you definitely aren't his. "Well, fortunately for me, you don't prefer men," she said playfully, "so I get him all to myself." They both laughed.

Monte came back with the champagne, setting a glass in front of Caroline and then pushing a glass across the desk to Mellissa. He poured Caroline's slowly but couldn't get Mellissa's into her glass fast enough, giving her a wide berth before leaving.

"Well, Mellissa," Caroline spoke as she lifted her glass, "here's to the first phase of our plan. So far, so good." They clinked glasses and sipped the champagne. Caroline closed her eyes and savored the bubbly drink. Setting her glass down, she leaned forward on the desk. "Okay, are you ready for this?"

Mellissa nodded excitedly. Caroline opened the middle drawer of the desk and handed Mellissa a five-page document. "Go ahead and read this. I think you'll get an idea what I have in mind for the Johnson ranch. Take your time, it's somewhat complicated."

Pulling the papers to her lap, Mellissa reached into her handbag by her feet and put on a pair of granny glasses. Caroline watched her pour eagerly over the documents, running her finger across each sentence in an effort to read each and every word. After ten minutes of silence, she stopped, took off her glasses, and stared at Caroline. "I can't believe it! This is genius. Caroline, this is pure genius. I would have never figured this out, but this it is so perfect. Where do we start this process? What is our next move?"

"The next Board of Supervisors meeting is in two weeks. Mellissa, you are to be the point person and be in charge," Caroline said. "You are going to shine, and you'd better plan on being in the media a lot in the next month or two. They will be all over you." Caroline let the information soak in, then added, almost as an afterthought, "We may need to upgrade your wardrobe a bit though."

"Oh, Caroline, this is so exciting. I just can't wait. I'll dress however you want me to. You know I love it when you help me with my wardrobe for these occasions."

Caroline pulled out a pen that was sitting in a crystal holder and scratched some numbers on a pad. She thumbed through her iPad and jotted down a few more. She leaned over the desk and handed the numbers to Mellissa. "You're to meet with these attorneys and these public relations people over the next week prior to the meeting. They will coach you on how to do your presentation. You're going to be great. I'll take you over to Nordstrom's next week and we can go on a shopping spree. It will be like old times."

Caroline set the pen back in its holder and folded her hands together. "There's something else. I want you to work for me full time after the next Board meeting, if that would be okay with you. I'll give you ten percent more a year than you're making at WMI."

Mellissa clasped her hands to her heart. "Oh, Caroline, I'd love to work with you. You're too kind to me." Mellissa handled the names and numbers as if they were precious heirlooms. She stood up and headed toward the door. "Thank you, Caroline, so much. I'm going to start right now and get ready. I want to make sure I do everything perfect. Oh, this will be so much fun, and I just can't wait to get started."

Caroline walked her out of the office and to the front door. She gave her a quick hug, holding her breath the whole time, and then watched her walk down the walkway to her car. Closing the door, she stood for a moment and contemplated her next move. Deciding everything could wait, she called out, "Monte, darling, come meet me in the bedroom!"

TWENTY-ONE

The speakers in the corners blared out the AC/DC song "You Shook Me All Night Long," as a heavyset woman in the center of the small dance floor, holding a microphone to her mouth, tried to follow and scream out the blue lyrics on the TV in front of her. She could have looked at any one of the five TVs that were situated throughout the bar showing the same lyrics, but she chose the big one ten feet in front of her. A couple of patrons sitting at the bar and close to the speakers put their hands over their ears to drown out the sound. The DJ at the far end of the dance floor was trying hard not to laugh, but was not doing a good job. In the small, dimly lit bar, the woman had the attention of all twelve of the people there. When she finished, the DJ tried to get the audience to clap, but he only got a half-hearted response.

Alan turned back to his beer sitting on the well-worn, wooden bar stool and commented to his companion occupying the bar stool to his left. "I've heard cats in distress that sounded better. Whoever told that woman she could sing should be locked into a room with her for three days with nothing but Neil Diamond karaoke songs."

His buddy laughed then tugged on his arm and pointed. "Oh no, look! She's putting in another song. I've got to tell the DJ that he needs to tell everyone his equipment is broken. I can't go through another song like that. I'd pay him twenty bucks not to play her a song."

Alan turned to look. "You've got to love Club 45, Brian. There's never a dull moment here, especially karaoke night." He signaled for the bartender. "It's time for another shot, birthday boy." Alan slapped him on the back. "You don't turn forty every day!"

Brian groaned. "You'll kill me with that stuff. I'll be speaking in tongues by the end of the night."

The door to the bar swung open and a tall, striking, redheaded woman in her early thirties stepped in. She was accompanied by two other female companions. She looked hot in formfitting jeans and a pink tube top. Her manicured red fingernails matched her lipstick and the pumps on her feet. Alan watched the women survey the bar for a second. Once their eyes grew accustomed to the light, they headed for a booth in the corner. Alan nudged Brian in the ribs and nodded in their direction. "Well, it looks like things are picking up in here tonight. I was beginning to lose faith in this place."

He gave them twenty minutes to order a drink and get acclimated before he sauntered over to their table. He stopped at their table and gave a slight bow. "Hello, ladies. How is everyone here tonight? My name is Alan, and I'm here to buy you a drink."

The women all looked at him, smiled excitedly and thanked him. The redhead stuck her hand out. "I'm Cheryl." She pointed at the other two. "This is Georgia and Patty."

"It's nice to meet all of you. Do you mind if I take a seat?" he asked.

Cheryl moved toward the middle of the booth, indicating he sit next to her. She batted her eyes seductively and cooed, "Have a seat, Alan. I'd like a martini."

He held up his hand. "Before I sit down, let me get you your drinks first. Georgia, Patty, what is your pleasure?" He took their order and came back with his hands full of cocktails. Once he settled in, Cheryl asked him, "What do you do for a living, Alan?" She fondled his green-striped tie. "You dress like an attorney."

Alan smiled as he sipped his rum and coke. "You're very perceptive. I am an attorney. I work for a firm that does land use law."

The redhead seemed impressed. She spent the next hour peppering him with questions. He pretended to be genuinely interested in her fingernail business, even complimenting her on the fabulous job she had done on her own nails. Every so often, Alan would order another round for the women and send Brian an additional shot of tequila at the bar. Eventually, he waved Brian over, and he settled in next to Georgia.

The five of them shot pool, listened to bad singing, and had a lot of laughs. The drinks came often and everyone seemed to be having a great time. At closing time, Alan whispered something to Cheryl and the two of them made their way out of the bar arm in arm and into the night.

The sound of Johnny Lee's "Looking for Love" blared from the speakers in each corner of the spacious bar. Numerous articles of clothing, everything from bras to T-shirts hung from the open rafters above the wooden dance floor. Hundreds of dirty autographed one-dollar bills were tacked to almost every inch of its paneled walls. A pair of cowboys danced a two-step gracefully across the dance floor while twenty other people performed a choreographed line dance in the middle of the floor. It was country night at Marco Polo's, a popular bar in Midtown, and the Thursday night crowd was getting a jump on the weekend.

Mellissa leaned across the walnut-stained bar and ordered a margarita. Next to her, a tall, slender woman probably in her mid-thirties leaned against her. Her short blonde hair, neatly groomed, was tucked into a dark cowboy hat. Her look contrasted with Mellissa's wrinkled muumuu, which hung about eight inches above her Birkenstocks sandals, and the rainbow headband she had over her unkempt locks. The tall woman was conversing with the two women standing next to her. Mellissa turned back from the bar with her drink and slid her free hand through the tall woman's front pocket. The woman smiled at her. Mellissa had to raise her voice to be heard over the music. "So, where was I, Bella? Where did I leave off?"

Bella squeezed Mellissa's hand affectionately. She leaned over and shouted into Mellissa's ear, "You were saying you were about to blow the lid off your boss's business. I think the last thing you said was you had a big file on everything that's transpired." The music stopped and the noise level dropped immediately, replaced by lively chatter, shuffling feet, and laughter. The other two women leaned in to hear the conversation. Bella continued, "You said you were ready to go to the media in the next thirty days with what you've learned about WMI? Aren't you worried your boss will fire you?"

Mellissa sipped her drink nervously. "Oh, I'm worried all right. But I'm worried he might do more than fire me, that creep. But he doesn't know that I've been compiling dirt on him, and by the time he finds out, I will be long gone."

"Do you have another position lined up?" Bella asked.

She nodded. "Caroline has asked me to come to work with her. I can't wait to drop the hammer on Yuri and get the heck out of that misery factory."

The lights from the bar flickered on and off. Mellissa glanced at her watch. "It's closing time already. Bottoms up, girls!" She tossed her drink down in one gulp and set her glass on the bar.

The women followed the crowd out the front door and stood at the corner under a streetlight outside the building, laughing and talking amongst the other patrons. Bella started across the street and called over her shoulder, "Come on, Mellissa. Let's get going."

Mellissa said a quick good bye to the others and stepped into the crosswalk. About halfway across the street, her sandal came off and she kneeled down to adjust it. A nearby car revved its engine and leaped out from the curb, its tires squealing and burning rubber. Mellissa looked up to see a pair of headlights bearing down on her at a high speed. Her eyes bulged out in fear, and her heart raced as she struggled to get up, instead stepping on her long dress causing her to stumble. The car barreled into her as she screamed in terror. The impact flung her up over the hood and smashed her face into the windshield as she flew over the car, landing with a thud in a crumpled heap in the middle of the well-lit street.

The car accelerated, turned left at the first street, and disappeared into the night. Bella shrieked and she ran over to Mellissa, furiously dialing her cell phone. She screamed into the phone, "Operator, operator, we need an ambulance at the corner of Twentieth and K Streets. My friend has been hit by a car. Hurry, please." She reached Mellissa's lifeless body and held her hand. She started sobbing as she gently caressed her. "Oh, Mellissa, please hang in there. I love you. Help will be here soon. Please don't leave me."

The sound seemed to be coming from somewhere to his left, a ringing noise that also had a musical quality about it. In the fog-like surroundings, he could hear the noise, but not see the source. He reached slowly outward and fumbled around with his left hand. The ringing grew louder, and the fuzziness of his mind began to clear. The room was pitch black, and his eyes adjusted to the tiny glow of light in front of him. He awoke on the third ring and stared blankly at the light, which glowed softly. The clock radio sitting on the night stand read 6:24. His cell phone rang for the fourth time, and Alan, seeing it light up, reached out and pulled it to his ear. "Hello," he answered, his voice gravelly and unsteady.

The familiar deep voice of his boss, John Parker, came through the phone. "Mellissa's dead."

Alan bolted upright, turned, and sat up on the edge of the bed, now fully awake. Holding the phone in his left hand, he turned on the lamp sitting next to the clock radio. The light blinded him temporarily and he had to shield his eyes.

"What did you say? Is that you, John? Mellissa? Are you kidding?" he croaked into the phone.

Alan felt something move behind him and he heard a soft female voice. "What's going on?" she asked.

He half turned and stared at the figure propped up on an elbow, squinting back at him. His mind raced as he tried to piece together the events that led to this stranger lying next to him in his bed. He thought, Oh damn, I'm remembering now. Last night, it was Brian's fortieth birthday party at Club 45. She was the redhead he'd met and shot pool with. How many shots of Jager did we do? Five, six? He reached up and massaged his forehead. What was her name? He held the phone to his chest, muffling it, and spoke to her softly. "Uh, it's nothing. Go back to sleep."

He heard John's muffled voice say, "Alan, I need you down at the office immediately. I've contacted Brian, Mark, and Stephanie. They will all be here in less than an hour. We need to huddle and figure out our next move."

"Jesus, John, how did this happen? We were just getting places with Mellissa."

"I'll explain it all when you get here. Hustle up." The line went silent.

Alan looked at the clock, which now read 6:26. Throwing the covers back, he stood up. "Damn it." He leaned over and gently rocked the woman by the shoulder. Oh boy, this isn't good, he thought. He looked over at the woman next to him and asked himself, What's her name? Cindy, Cathy? Then it hit him: Cheryl.

That's it, Cheryl.

He shook her shoulder softly. "Ah, missy, ah Cheryl, I need to get out of here, so you'll have to leave too. I'm sorry, but something important has come up."

The woman sat up, pulling the covers over her exposed breasts. Her hair was a tangled mess and she absently played with it. "What time is it? It seems awful early." Her expression changed from surprise to anger. "Hey, wait a minute. You promised we would go to breakfast at the Hilton and then go down to Old Town. What the heck is this, you throwing me out in the middle of the night?" She started to raise her voice. "I see how it is. Now that you've got what you wanted, you're kicking me out, right? That's garbage."

Alan grabbed the jeans that were at the foot of the bed and tossed them to her. He pulled his own off the chair sitting in front of the flat screen TV and started to dress himself.

"Look, I'm sorry, Cheryl, but this can't be helped. I've got a crisis to attend to and I can't leave you here. I'll make it up to you another time."

She flung the covers off her and stood up from the bed. The light fell across her naked body, exposing a tanned, slender, but shapely woman. Alan soaked in the sight for a minute before resuming dressing. Now I remember her, he thought. What a body. She turned and gave him a dirty look, and he noticed faded red lipstick smeared around her mouth.

She leaned down and snatched up her frilly pink thong, which was lying at the foot of the bed. "Make it up to me? You'll be lucky if I ever speak to you again. I can't believe I stayed here last night." She looked around the room as she wiggled into her jeans. Finding her strapless white bra and tube top in the corner by the night stand, she marched over and seized them. As she put them on, she stepped into her red pumps. She headed out of the bedroom through the family room, picking her purse up off the dark, marbled granite kitchen counter, and moved toward the front door. Alan followed her, noticing the half-full wine bottle on the counter with two empty glasses next to it. Looking at the label he thought, Oh no, I didn't open that Camus '03, did I? That was a 200-dollar bottle of wine. I must have gotten really drunk last night.

He walked to the front door and opened it. The woman glared at him for a second then breezed by him.

"Wait a second. How will I contact you? Can you leave me your number?" he asked.

The woman walked past him. She took her time as she stepped down the three steps from the entry to the sidewalk, holding the railing to keep herself steady. Her red curly hair bounced up and down with each step. She opened the driver's door to the white Camry sitting in the driveway, started the engine, and slowly backed out.

Alan watched her leave. He closed the front door and retreated back to the bedroom. His head was pounding as he looked around the room for his wallet. "Mellissa's dead. I don't believe this. After all this time and effort, after all the money we've spent, now this happens."

He spotted the wallet on the mantel above the fireplace. "I've got to hurry," he said to himself. As he walked back through the kitchen, he plucked his car keys off the holder that was hanging on the wall and exited the house into the garage. The shiny white Mercedes sat in the spotless garage. He hit the garage door opener and it sprang to life. "I guess it's time to get to work."

As he turned left onto 42nd Street, his street, he adjusted his mirror then accelerated. Alan reached for the rearview mirror to check out his face then returned his eyes to the road. The neighborhood was still asleep and the streets were empty.

He ran his hand through his hair and mumbled, "Poor Mellissa. She was our window to Caroline, our inside person. Yet she never knew it. This must have been an accident, right? But then who would want her dead?" Alan reached back into his memory to try to see if he could remember something that would have compromised Mellissa's position. He couldn't, but then his head hurt too much to think very hard.

He banged his fist on the steering wheel. "Man, I was with Mellissa last Tuesday. I had brought her along so well, and she was just beginning to feed us the info we were looking for. Now she's dead."

Alan pulled into the parking garage below a newer five-story building. As he pulled into the garage, he looked up to see one lighted window on the third floor. The rest of the building was dark. He waved his plastic card across the reader and waited for the gate to slowly open. He parked in a spot that read, Reserved Parker-Williams.

Alan pulled his briefcase from the back seat, slammed the door, and sprinted toward the elevator. Hitting the third-floor button, he waited nervously as the elevator sped to the requested destination. The door opened and he was through the glass office doors, with the painted gold lettering, Parker and Williams, before the elevator doors shut.

He glanced around the barely lit, empty foyer at two small couches off to the left and a coffee table heaped with copies of *The Sacramento Business Journal* and *Fortune Magazine*. The empty receptionist desk stood in front of him, and he walked past it to turn the corner where he could see the light coming from the conference room.

Stepping inside, he saw three faces lift up from a stack of documents and look at him.

Alan looked first at John Parker who was wearing a rumpled white shirt with baggy grey slacks and had a pair of eyeglasses perched on the tip of his nose. "You made it. That was fast," John said. He turned and pointed to the corner of the conference room where a coffee machine sat with five empty cups and some bottled water. "If you want some coffee, it should be done soon. I just started it."

Alan threw his coat over a chair and moved toward the counter. "Thanks, John." As he poured some of the steaming brew into a cup, Brian moved over to join him. Alan moved to his left to let him get in. He couldn't help but notice, even at this early hour, Brian was immaculately dressed in a blue polo shirt and dark dress slacks. Even his black hair was moussed perfectly. As he poured some cream into his cup, Alan nodded to him. "How'd you get so dolled up, Brian?" he whispered. "Last I saw you, you were knee deep in a Jagermeister and couldn't put a sentence together."

Brian just shrugged and moved to the conference table.

Stephanie sat quietly across from John Parker, in a pair of jeans, green blouse, and white flats. Even though she must have hurried to get to this meeting, she still looked as if she had just stepped out of beauty parlor. He mused.

"It sounds like we've got a mess here, Brian," Alan said.

"Uh, I think that might be an understatement," he answered.

Mark, the third man in the room, spoke to the two of them. "Come on over here and let's get going. Time is not on our side."

Alan took a sip of the coffee and moved toward where the others were standing. "What do we know, John? How did this happen?"

"We're still trying to determine that," John answered. "Here's what I do know. I received a call about an hour ago from Fred Douglas, Sheriff Cranston's assistant. Ever since you filled me in on this whole Johnson Ranch fiasco, I thought it prudent that Fred be in the loop of what we're up to in case things got out of hand. He's always been helpful to me, especially since I sponsor his bosses' golf tournament every year, so he's happy to help out in any activity that might involve us."

He shuffled some papers around in front of him. "It seems our girl Mellissa was out on the town last night, with a couple of her friends, and one of the places they stopped at was Marco Polo."

Alan set his cup on the table. "You mean the gay bar?"

"Yes." John answered. "Marco Polo is a popular place and has a wide clientele of all kinds of people: gay, straight, bisexuals, you name it. It was no secret Mellissa was a lesbian. She told everyone. Anyway, she and her friends were there until closing time and spilled out of the bar about 1:45. Mellissa started to cross the street when a dark European sedan, not sure of the make or model, came ripping up 20th Street and knocked her out of her sandals. She was thrown over the top of the car and was probably dead before she landed on the street. The car never slowed down and hasn't been seen since. The witnesses' descriptions of the car are all over the place, but no one saw the driver, as the windows were tinted. "

John pulled a handkerchief from his pocket and nervously wiped his forehead. "Is it possible this was just an accident? I mean, hit and runs aren't that uncommon."

Brian looked at him, raising his left eyebrow. "Come on, John. This was no accident. Mellissa was targeted. The real question is who knew about her and how much do they know?"

John sat down and leaned back in his chair. "That's the million-dollar question right now. Alan has spent months grooming Mellissa, and she gave us some useful info that we can start to use. This situation is taking our investigation into a different arena. We initially thought it would uncover some deep financial shenanigans on Caroline's part, but now it looks like it could be murder. It raises the stakes, don't you think?" He glanced around the room.

Alan shifted his weight. "When I met with Mellissa, she promised me she was preparing to drop a bombshell at the next Board of Supervisors meeting. She had filed all the papers and was set to present them to the county next week for a formal application."

"Did she tell you what it was she was filing?" Brian asked.

Alan shook his head. "No, only that it would be huge." He looked at Stephanie. "Mellissa kept referencing something called New London. Stephanie and I have discussed this and nothing comes to mind. Does anyone here have any idea what she might have been referring to? I've got to believe this filing has something to do with that."

John leaned back in his chair and stared at the ceiling. "New London, New London, why does that name seem familiar?" The room was silent for a second, and then John snapped his fingers and slammed his hands on the table. "Wait a minute. There was a Supreme Court ruling regarding the town of New London in 2005. The case was Kelo v. New London. The court ruled that the public use of the takings clause of the Fifth Amendment permitted the use of eminent domain for economic development purposes that provide for public benefit. That might be what they are talking about here. Eminent domain."

Alan stared at him blankly. "Could you put that in nonlegal form so the rest of us might understand?"

John laughed but grew serious. "The Supreme Court ruling gave public entities, like cities and counties, the legal authority to take land or land entitlements from a private owner and give it to another person or entity, as long as the use of that land or land entitlement could be proven to be for the public's benefit."

Stephanie had been taking notes on a yellow legal pad. "So how does eminent domain fit into this situation? What would the Board of Supervisors in Yolo County be taking from someone? What would it have to do with Mellissa?"

John stroked his chin. "The Board of Supervisors can't bring an action like eminent domain themselves. They need a citizen, or someone who is not employed by the county, to file the papers for an action by the board. Maybe Mellissa was to be the person to file the action. But what would she be trying to get the county to take over by this action? If this is what got Mellissa killed, it must have been something big."

Alan turned to Stephanie and asked, "Didn't Caroline say she wanted to grow more rice but didn't have the water allocation? I know Mellissa mentioned she had spent a lot of time at the Water Resources Board doing research."

"She did say that." Stephanie nodded in agreement. "Does eminent domain cover water rights, John?"

He nodded. "Water rights would fall under that clause. If the county could prove the taking of water rights from a property would be for the public's benefit, they could use this provision to do that."

"Then maybe this was Caroline's plan," Alan stated. "The Johnson Ranch to the south of her ranch only uses half the allocation of water they are allowed. If Caroline could get Yolo County to take that water allocation, she could apply for that water and use it at her ranch, as she could claim the water usage would be used for public benefit: more local farming."

Stephanie tapped her pencil nervously on the pad. "Two things come to mind. The Johnsons died two weeks ago, as did their lawyer a few days later. All of these deaths have been labeled suspicious. Because of the way title had been changed, the new owner of the Johnson Ranch is a man named Yuri Kletcko. The Johnsons' ranch was supposed to be donated to UC Davis as stipulated in the Johnsons' will, but that document has yet to surface. Kletcko had the Johnson's apply for a larger allocation of water from the Water Resources Board for their ranch a few months ago. Is it possible he got wind of the Mellissa's filing and decided to do something about her? If that's the case, was he also behind the Johnsons' deaths, and their attorney? Who will be next? Caroline?"

Alan cocked his head. "So Yuri Kletcko was Mellissa's boss at WMI. She told me she was about to expose his mortgage operation to the media. She was keeping a file on them because she thought they were doing things illegally. Maybe he found out about her plans and decided to squash them."

He pointed his pencil at Brian. "I want you to get involved in the investigation of Mellissa's death. Get with the sheriff and see how close to the bottom of this you can get. Whatever you do, don't attract attention."

John stood up and shuffled the papers in front of him, stacking them neatly. He looked intently at Stephanie. "I need you to follow up with Caroline. I want to know how she handles this situation or what her next move is. If the eminent domain theory is correct, then she will need someone new to make the filing. Maybe you could volunteer to do that for her, but be careful. If all these things are connected, you will hear from Yuri or one of his goons soon. Do you know if Mellissa had any friends or coworkers we could talk to who might give us some info we don't have?"

Alan flipped through his notepad a second. "She mentioned a woman named Amber Behrendt. She worked with Mellissa at WMI. I can try to get in touch with her."

John crossed his arms. "All right, get in touch with her and report what you find out as soon as possible." He looked around the room. "We all need to keep our antennas up. We may be dealing with a dangerous situation."

TWENTY-TWO

Yuri stared down from the window of the seventeenth floor of the Wells Fargo Building in downtown Sacramento at a yacht as it sailed lazily up the Sacramento River. A streaming cup of coffee was in the chubby fingers of his left hand, and in his right, he held a glazed donut. The glaze was still sticking to his prickly moustache from a previous bite. *It's only Tuesday at 9:00 a.m. I wonder where those lucky bastards are heading. I hope they get stuck on a sand bar in the middle of nowhere.*

This was the main office of WMI and he only made it here once a month unless it was necessary for him to step in and take control of things. He preferred to work out of his small office in Fair Oaks with Ivan and his close inner circle. Today it was necessary for him to step in.

"Excuse me, Mr. Kletcko, were you saying something to me?"

Yuri spun from the window to see Jennifer, his administrative assistant, standing at the doorway to his office. Her black skirt hugged her slender frame, and the white coifed blouse allowed her ample breasts to peek out, not enough to appear sexy, but more than a business environment would dictate. With her brown hair in a bun and her glasses, she could pass as a school teacher, albeit a rather slinky one.

"Oh, no, Jennifer, I was just talking to myself." He subconsciously rubbed his mouth with the back of his hand, almost getting the glaze from the donut off his face. His eyes took a walk across her body, starting at her neck and ending at her ankles. He didn't care that his gaze was obvious or what she thought about it. Well, that is one good reason to come down to this office, he thought.

He smiled a tight smile and put his coffee down on the massive dark walnut desk, trying not to spill any on the papers that were strewn across it. He walked behind the desk, pulled out the black leather chair, and sat down. He folded his hands across his big belly and leaned back. Although he wore a white custom shirt and a red Ralph Lauren tie, he didn't seem to fit well into his clothes. Most of his employees made fun of the way he dressed behind his back. One of their favorite nicknames was Mr. Magoo.

"What have you got for me today, Jennifer?" he asked. "Did we record the State Bank loans this morning? I spoke to Warren before I got to the office and he assured me it would go down."

Jennifer walked forward, her arms full of files, and gently set them on his desk. If there was any awkwardness felt by his lecherous stare, she didn't let on.

"First Republic Title called a few minutes ago to confirm the recording," she said without emotion. "Congratulations, you now own $65 million in mortgage loans that are in default and are all part of a security that no one knows which part is which. Uh," she paused for a second, pulling on a small silver necklace, "are you attending Mellissa's funeral?"

Yuri looked up from a set of documents he had been reading. "Nope, I don't have time. If I went to every personal event for my employees, I'd never get anything done." He went back to his documents. "Send out an email to Rick and Darrell that I want to meet them in…" He glanced down at his Rolex. "At 10:30. I want to move fast on these deals. And bring me some more coffee, will you?" He held out his half-full cup.

Jennifer leaned over, taking the cup from his hand. "Of course, I'll handle it for you. Is there anything else?"

"That will do for now," he answered.

She turned and headed out of the office while Yuri ogled her fanny, licking his lips and rubbing his thighs. "One of these days," he muttered.

He cast his eyes around the room, eyeing the wall to his right that was covered with framed accolades of Wealth Management's exploits over the years. The wall to the left was floor-to-ceiling shelving with numerous pictures of Yuri and various celebrities. His favorite was the one with him and Mercedes James, the famous porn star who had made over 250 movies. She was barely clothed and was draped all over him. He loved reliving that day.

What a ride it's been, he thought. Who would have thought, four years ago, that I would be sitting here like this after the subprime mortgage fiasco? Now I'm making money hand over fist buying mortgages and foreclosing on a lot of poor saps. Whoever said money can't buy happiness probably doesn't have money. But I do, and it'll buy as much happiness as I can get my hands on.

Darrell Martin rapped softly on his door, and Yuri waved him in. Darrell was a soft-spoken accountant by trade but an invaluable executive to Yuri.

Darrell spoke, reading off a report. "Well, we've got the State Bank deal closed. I assume we're to follow the same pattern we did on the Oregon Mutual and California First mortgages, right?"

Yuri shifted some of the papers on the desk. "That's exactly right. I'm meeting with everyone in a few minutes to go over the game plan. I want to hit the ground running with these mortgages. The Oregon Mutual ones took longer than I wanted." He added, "That's what I wanted to talk to you about before we go crazy. The press has picked up on some of our foreclosure practices, and they are starting to give us a black eye. I don't know how they've found out this information, but they have."

Darrell took a sip of water and looked directly at Yuri. "Mellissa was in charge of making sure the correct signatures were being notarized and recorded properly," he said. "Her job was to get the documents ready for recording, even if the signatures weren't correct. Some of the people we foreclosed on were in the midst of loan modifications and were blindsided by our speed in taking their houses. As a result, they're not happy. Everything was going along smoothly until someone alerted the press. I think Mellissa's political activities were taking a front seat to her work, and I believe she might have been the one that leaked out the information."

Yuri picked at his fingernails, listening intently. "So what? All we're doing is just speeding up the process. In every case we've foreclosed, the borrowers were behind on their payments and loans were in default. That's how this game is played. You borrow money, and if you don't pay it back, bad things can happen. Not our problem." He looked up and smiled deviously. "Besides, I don't think she'll be leaking out anything anymore."

Darrell leaned forward, putting his files on Yuri's desk. "I understand the process." He waved his hand around the office. "We all understand the process. We all realize we are purchasing these faulty mortgages to make money and that it involves displacing a lot of people. I'm just saying we should be more careful how we do this, maybe make it look like we are trying to help people keep their homes, before we actually take them. Public relations can be a double-edged sword. The last thing we need is for some starry-eyed congressman to start making noise about reform and before long there will be a bill to curb our business."

Yuri leaned forward, picked up a pen, and waved it in front of Darrell. "Nobody from Congress is going to touch us. I own Steve Miner of the Senate Banking Committee. You keep kicking these deadbeats out of their houses and I'll take care of the politicians.

There's too much money to be made here and it's too easy. I want to make sure we make as much as we can before any competition gets wind of this business and starts horning in on our stuff. I need to make a few phone calls to pacify the press. I'll see you in the meeting."

Yuri turned his back to Darrell and snatched his cell phone sitting on the walnut credenza behind him. Darrell stood and backed out the door.

The conference room was spacious, with an oval, glass-topped table and fourteen leather-bound, high-backed chairs surrounding it. More framed pictures of Yuri and his wife, children and grandchildren hung on its walls. The room was surrounded by floor-to-ceiling glass walls, giving it a fish bowl affect to the balance of the office staff, all of whom could see what was going on, but could not hear anything.

Yuri sat at the head of the table. Darrell sat next to Greg Mattingly, the head of mortgages, and Amber Behrendt, his assistant, sat across from them.

Yuri looked at Greg. "Give me an update on Mellissa's accounts. What's going on with them?"

Greg cleared his throat and read from a sheet in front of him. He, like almost all the senior people at the mortgage division at WMI, was young, in his mid-thirties, a college graduate, attractive and athletic. Yuri preferred this type, especially the men, as they seemed to attract lots of women—lots of beautiful women.

"We took over the first 200 houses we foreclosed on in January of this year," Greg read off the sheet. "We're not sure, but 175 of those houses have questionable documents. Mellissa signed off on them." He looked up from his documents and addressed Yuri. "You authorized her to go forward with the action and she did. This will be a problem if any more information leaks out."

Yuri nodded approvingly but raised his voice. "It's too late. The press has already started sniffing around. This could cost us a fortune if we get caught. How do we distance ourselves from Mellissa? How do we shift the blame to her as if she was a rogue employee?" He pointed his pen at him. "What's our game plan?"

Greg straightened his necktie and took a sip of the bottled water sitting in front of him. He glanced through the glass walls and could see the whole office; all forty-five employees were staring at the conference room. The sound of Yuri's voice was obviously carrying through the glass.

He spoke in a hurried tone. "The problem has always been getting all the documents for the foreclosure in order so it can be presented to the court for filing. We've had to hire two extra people to go through and verify that the homeowners were served the notices of default correctly, that their signatures are verified, everything to put the files in a complete state to present to the court."

Yuri was getting irritated. "This is worthless legal garbage and it takes too much time. Here's what you're to do, Greg. Now that we don't have our departed sister Mellissa to do our dirty work, I want you to hire someone who's a notary public, anyone who's a notary public, and we're going to stick them into that third office by the kitchen." The whole room turned to follow where he was pointing. "And all that person will do for eight hours a day, five days a week, is notarize your signature or Darrell's, stating that the information we put together is correct, the homeowners have been properly served, and we are entitled to take their homes for nonpayment. Mellissa did it, and we're going to keep doing it. If anyone asks, we'll just blame everything on Mellissa. She's won't care." He laughed out loud at his own joke. Everyone else in the room remained silent.

Amber kept writing on the empty notepad in front of her. She nodded her head to affirm she had heard what was being requested.

Yuri slowly surveyed the room. "Anybody got a problem with that?" his voice boomed. "We are sitting on a mountain of money and I want this process expedited!"

The only movement in the room was Amber's pen squeaking as she scribbled notes as quickly as she could. Finally, she stopped and the room was silent again.

Darrell raised his hand and waited to be acknowledged. "Uh, Yuri, we are dealing with a lot of homes and a lot of dispossessed people. You know there'll be a backlash sooner or later. How are we going to handle it? Like I said in your office, this will be a PR nightmare. Are you sure you want to do this?"

"Look" His face was red, and sweat was coming down the side of his forehead. He had already loosened his tie and was looking more disheveled by the moment. "I told you nobody can touch us. Quit making excuses and do what you're paid to do. Clean up Mellissa's messes with as little fanfare as possible, and let's keep doing what we were doing before she died, except do it more carefully this time."

Yuri pushed his chair out and exited the conference room. All the employees outside the conference room leapt to attention, and they started making themselves look busy. Yuri stopped for a second, glared at them, then walked across the main office floor and headed out of the office. His cell phone rang before he hit the front door, and without stopping, he pulled it out of his front pocket, glanced at the number on the screen, and put it to his ear. "Carlos Diego, good to hear from you. I'm glad you returned my call."

TWENTY-THREE

A mber knelt in the fifteenth pew of St. Mary's Church, along with approximately fifteen other employees. Her dark hair was pulled back in a ponytail, and she wore a dark blue skirt with a light colored blouse. No matter how she tried, she couldn't hide the fact she was an attractive young woman. As she absently thumbed through a hymn book that looked like it had seen better times, she took in the sight of the church. The brown casket, draped with dozens of red roses, stood in front of the white marble and gold adorned altar. Three large floral wreaths stood out among a sea of flowers. Five candelabras with white beeswax candles flickered silently above the altar. A thick prayer book with the gold-leafed pages opened to a passage that was to be read during the ceremony sat in the center of the altar. On the walls perpendicular to the altar was a series of stained glass windows, which let soft, filtered light into the church and upon all who were in it. At each window was a carved scene of a particular station of the cross, where Jesus Christ carried a heavy cross through the streets of Jerusalem, up to Mount Calvary, to be put to death by crucifixion.

Amber noticed an older couple in the front row of the church, both in black, and assumed they were Mellissa's parents.

She turned and sat down on the bench of the pew. Ahead of her sat a well-dressed woman in her early forties, accompanied by a much younger handsome man. The woman looked familiar to Amber. As she looked closer, she recognized Caroline Bennett, Mellissa's close friend. Caroline's eyes were red and she dabbed a handkerchief around the corners. They had never met, but Mellissa spoke so much about her, she felt she knew Caroline.

The church, although three quarters full, was quiet except for a few muffled voices. As she waited for the service to start, her mind drifted.

It seemed like yesterday Mellissa met me for drinks at the Rio Café in Old Town. I don't remember ever hearing Mellissa complain about a bad day, just a bad boss. She was always so cheery, so happy-go-lucky, a wonderful friend. I wonder what will become of her cats. Oh, those cats. Mellissa treated them as if they were her children. She sighed.

Her thoughts were interrupted by the sound of people standing, and she watched a priest come through a side screen door and stop behind the altar. He raised his hands and looked skyward. Amber could hear more than a few muffled sniffles and found herself tearing up. Out of the corner of her eye she could see Caroline softly crying.

The priest started, "Dearly beloved…"

After the service, Amber rode with coworkers, Mary Prentiss and Jennifer, in Jennifer's silver Honda Accord to the house of Mellissa's parents for the reception. Looking out the back window at the neatly mowed lawns of the house they drove by, Amber noted how much they resembled her own parents' home in another part of town.

"That was a nice ceremony, wasn't it?" Jennifer spoke to no one in particular as she followed a string of cars, driving down the residential street in a procession. "I hate funerals, but as they go, this was kind of nice. The priest said some nice things about Mellissa. You got the impression he knew her personally."

Amber turned to look at Jennifer. "I don't know. I never knew Mellissa to step into a church the whole time I've known her. It wasn't that she didn't like them or talked bad about them, just that she never went."

Mary turned in her seat and threw an arm over the back rest. "Maybe she knew him from his younger days. Hey, Jennifer, why didn't Yuri, show up? I mean Mellissa only worked for him for three years. Doesn't that count for something?"

Jennifer turned and noticed cars were parking up ahead at a two-story, brick home. "I think we're here," she said. "I don't know why Yuri didn't show up, and I really don't care. He made some lame excuse about being too busy. I don't think Yuri has a compassionate bone in his body. All he thinks about is money and chasing women."

Amber crinkled up her nose. "Ooh, how disgusting. The thought of that fat, curly-haired perp putting a hand on me makes me sick. How do you think his wife puts up with him? I mean, he is so obvious."

"I don't think divorce is part of their culture," Jennifer answered. "I don't think she has a choice to leave him. I get the impression there's not much intimacy in that relationship."

Amber looked down at the card she was holding. It had a picture of Mellissa and the dates of her birth and death. "Jen, do you ever notice how Yuri looks at you? He's undressing you with his eyes whenever he sees you. Sometimes I just want to slap that pig."

Jennifer stopped the car and put it in park. She shifted the mirror to adjust her makeup. "Of course he's a pig. And of course I know what he's doing in his mind. But he pays well and I need the money, so I play along. But make no mistake. If he ever tried to touch me with those fat, dirty fingers of his, I'd bite one off and spit it at him.

Then I'd rear back and kick him right in the balls. That would wake him up!"

Amber and Mary started laughing. "I'd pay to see you do that, Jen. Please, god, put me in the room when that happens." Amber took a deep breath and opened the car door. "Seriously, I wouldn't want to be in a room alone with him. He scares me. I think he has a dark side." She sighed and clapped her hands. "Well, I guess we should go in and mingle with the family. We can't stay too long, remember. Yuri only gave us two hours off." She glanced down at her watch. "We only have about fifty minutes left."

Mary threw a small purse over her shoulder and headed down the sidewalk towards the home, not waiting for the others. "Don't worry. I only want to get something to eat and a glass of water and I'll be ready to go. I hope they have some good food."

Amber picked at the few items on her plate as she stood by the entrance to the kitchen. The house wasn't large, and with mourners moving between the kitchen and dining room where food sat on the table, space was tight. She had studied the family pictures hanging on the walls of the hallway that led to the bedrooms in the comfortable home. Seeing pictures of Melissa as she grew up, brought emotions flooding back again. Amber held back her tears, but not without a great effort. She waited patiently for Mellissa's mom to finish talking to the priest who had performed the service.

She finally saw her chance and walked up to the woman. The woman's silver hair was done in a bob, her dress was a fashionable black, but her eyes were red, obviously from crying. She held a white handkerchief firmly in her left hand.

Amber stepped forward and extended her hand. "Mrs. Burns, I'm Amber Behrendt, a friend of Mellissa's. We worked together at WMI. I'm so sorry for your loss. Mellissa was such a wonderful person."

"Amber." She grabbed her hand with both hands. "Please, call me Joan. It's a pleasure to finally meet you. Mellissa spoke of you often. What a beautiful woman you are. You look like Scarlet O'Hara's sister."

"Thank you, Joan. Mellissa and I got to be close friends, and we did a lot of things together. I really miss her. You really raised a wonderful daughter. You should be very proud of her. She has done a lot of good things in her life."

Joan patted Amber's hand softly. "We are proud, dear, we are." Another woman came up wanting to speak to Joan. The mother let go of Amber's hand and said, "Excuse me for a minute. I'd like to talk in private with you sometime. Please keep in touch, Amber."

"I promise I will," Amber answered.

Someone tapped her on her shoulder and she spun around to see a tall good-looking man standing before her.

"You're Amber, right?" He held out her hand to shake. "I'm Alan Hubbard, a colleague of Mellissa's. She mentioned you a few times, and when I saw you standing here, from her description, I knew you had to be Amber."

Amber thought for second. This has to be the guy doing the documentary. Mellissa gushed about him and I can see why. "Oh, nice to meet you, Alan. It's too bad we have to meet under such circumstances. Mellissa told me about you."

"Yeah, I've met with Mellissa many times, and she was such a sweet person. She was a big help to me." Alan looked down at the floor. "What a waste she had to die like this."

"It sure is," Amber said. "She was excited about the project you are working on. I saw her at the office almost every day, but I hadn't talked to her at length for about a week before she died."

"Did she ever confide in you about her misgivings at WMI?" Alan asked.

She glanced around the room nervously. "I'm not comfortable talking here. Could we talk sometime later? I've got some things of Mellissa's and I need some help getting them to the right hands."

Alan leaned in and whispered in her ear, pressing a business card in her hand. "Absolutely. You can call me, and I'll help you out." He leaned back and shook her hand. "Hopefully we'll meet under better circumstances."

"I hope so too, Alan."

Amber watched him as he slowly made his way through the crowd and disappeared.

Jennifer came up and put her hand on Amber's shoulder. "You okay?"

"I'm fine, thanks. I was just feeling melancholy." She threw her purse over her shoulder. "I guess we should head back to the office before we get into trouble."

Jennifer nodded toward Alan, who was exiting through the front door. "Who was that? I don't think I've seen him before. What a hunk."

Amber was still looking in the direction Alan disappeared. "Uh, that was Alan Hubbard. I guess he was doing a documentary on a friend of Mellissa's." She glanced down at her watch. "We better move."

"Yeah, I think it's that time. I'll go find Mary." She took a last sip of her wine and set the glass on the dining room table. "Meet me out front in five minutes."

"Okay, I'll be there." Amber walked over to the hall and took a final look at the photographs on the wall. Feeling a wave of sadness, she sighed deeply, then headed for the front door.

TWENTY-FOUR

The Bellagio Hotel in downtown Las Vegas was a landmark on the strip. It rose in a semicircle around a massive lake that was home to the legendary Las Vegas Show of Water, which entertained visitors strolling down the sidewalk in front of the hotel every thirty minutes. The dancing fountains shot jets of water high up in the air against the background of the Las Vegas's skyline, with a choreographed performance timed to twenty-nine different musical arrangements.

Towards the top of the hotel sat the Chairman's Suite, a 4,000-square-foot suite of pure luxury. Yuri, a cell phone to his ear, stood in the living room next to a window overlooking the fountains as they went through one of their routines. Behind him was an indoor garden, complete with a fountain, quietly pumping a burst of water over boulders that ran down a small river bed into a Koi pond filled with colorful gold and white fish.

An L-shaped bar with a granite counter top was to his left. Two bottles of half-filled Opus 1 were sitting on the bar next to a couple of wine glasses, one of which was lying on its side, its contents spilled onto the bar. An open bottle of Crown Royal Blue sat next to the wine.

From where he stood, Yuri could see into the master suite, where clothes and an empty whiskey bottle had been strewn about. A slender young man lay on his back on the bed, motionless. He was wearing only a G-string and had a belt wrapped tightly around his neck. His lips were blue, and his purple tongue lay outside his gaping mouth. His eyes bulged from their sockets, staring lifelessly at the ceiling.

Morton Bain, in white briefs, a dirty wifebeater shirt and brown cowboy boots, lay on the floor curled in a fetal position across from the bed. He was weeping uncontrollably and mumbling incoherently, clutching a half-full glass of whiskey.

Mika sat on an oversized sofa across from Yuri, smoking a cigarette and staring alternately at the doorway to the master suite and Yuri. Yuri spoke firmly into the phone. "Greg, I need you to move that block of foreclosed homes quickly. I agree with Darrell, we should be cautious when we go forward with these foreclosures. Mellissa has brought the spotlight on us, which we don't need right now. Get those houses moved this week and then let's meet to figure our game plan going forward."

He shut the phone off and walked into the bedroom, stopping at the entry. Mellissa had a big mouth, he thought, and it caught up to her. He strode up to Morton and kicked the bottle out of his hand, sending it flying onto the marble floor of the bathroom, shattering into a thousand pieces. "Quit whimpering, you gutless wimp." He spat at Morton. "Pull yourself together."

Morton crawled over to Yuri and clutched his trouser leg. "I swear I don't know what happened, Yuri. We were playing a little rough, but I never meant to hurt Miguel. I loved him; I wouldn't ever harm him." He sobbed and wiped his nose on the fabric of his pant leg. "I don't remember anything, Yuri, I don't remember."

Yuri shook him off his leg. "Let go of me!" he snarled. "Get up and get yourself cleaned up. Take a shower, get dressed, and catch a flight back to the Bay Area. I'll meet with you next week. I'll handle this mess you've made here, but you'll owe me." He kicked Morton in the side, which made him wince as he scurried away from Yuri. "I told you I wanted you to get that snoop Matt off my ass, and now I want you to make it happen. He's been getting too close to my operation. All I need is a few more months and we can all relax."

Morton looked up at him with bloodshot eyes. "I'll make sure he doesn't bother you, Yuri. I'll fix it first thing Monday morning." He reached out toward the body on the bed. "I can't believe what I've done to Miguel, I loved him so." He started sobbing, burying his head in his hands.

With his foot, Yuri pushed a suitcase standing at the edge of the bed toward Morton. "There's three hundred thousand in cash in this suitcase. Take it down to the cashier's cage and pay off your marker. This hasn't been a good weekend for you."

Morton nodded meekly and crawled off toward the shower.

Yuri yelled at him. "Sober up, damn it. Don't drink another thing until you're at home in California." As soon as he rounded the corner and was in the bathroom, Yuri snapped his fingers at Mika. "After he's cleaned up and I get him out of here, you've got work to do. Are your boys capable enough to handle this job?"

Mika crushed out his cigarette and stood. "They're here at the hotel and are ready to go, Yuri. They're cooling their heels down by the laundry area, waiting for me to give them the signal to come up."

Yuri picked up a TV remote and switched on a Fox News show. He sat down on a puffy leather chair and pushed it into a reclining position. "You'll need to do this the same as you did for the Wilson job. After I get Morton out of here, take his boyfriend to the bathtub and quarter him up. He's got to fit onto that laundry cart." He pulled a thick cigar out of his breast pocket, bit off the end, and lit it with a gas lighter. He waved the cigar in a circular manner. "Do you understand?"

Mika smiled. "I got it. When I'm done with the body, they'll rush the cart up here, pick it up, and take it back down to a van that's waiting by the docking area behind the kitchen. It shouldn't take more than fifty minutes from start to finish."

Yuri nodded satisfactorily. "Don't forget to clean this room thoroughly. I don't want any type of forensic evidence left behind. Then take him to the spot past that old gas station thirty minutes outside of town. Make sure you bury him at least a half mile from the main road and at least five feet deep. I don't want any rodents or coyotes finding your handiwork." He pointed at the half empty bottle of Crown Royal Blue sitting on the bar. "Is that the one you put the drugs in, Mika?"

Mika nodded, smirking. "Yes."

"Good job, but make sure you dispose of it. If anyone found that bottle, it would be tough to explain away."

"I'll make sure it's gone, Yuri, and I promise you no one will find him," Mika said, smiling as if he were waiting to open a birthday present. "We dug the hole last night and it's off the beaten path."

"Use lots of bleach in the tub," Yuri commanded. "Come back here tomorrow early before room service gets here. Fill that tub up twice more and let it drain out. This place needs to be spotless."

Mika leaned in to look inside the bedroom. "When did you get here?"

Yuri flipped to another channel. "Morton called me this morning, babbling the same way he's been doing since you got here. He was so out of it when I showed up, he didn't notice I would have had to already be in town to get here so fast. He thought I was in Sacramento and flew here to help him."

"So Morton doesn't suspect anything?" Mika asked. "They were both passed out when I got here last night. It was almost too easy."

"He never saw you. When he woke up and found Miguel, his first call was to me. He thinks he accidentally killed Miguel." Yuri looked up at Mika. "But the good news is, after we clean up this mess, we own Mr. Morton Bain completely. We'll be doing a lot more business with General Technologies, whether Matt Whiteside likes it or not."

Yuri smiled a thin smile. "Mika, everybody has a weakness. You just need to find out what it is and exploit it." His phone rang and Yuri answered. "Hello?"

"It's Ivan. I filed the documents and sent the death certificates to the Great Northern Life Insurance Company in regard to the policies for the Johnsons. I followed up with the company to see if they received them and they confirmed they had indeed received the forms and all is in order."

"That's all good, but when can we expect the money?" Yuri asked. "I got a call from Artie Tennelli, Carlos Diego's lap dog, inquiring about repayment of the loan on the ranch from the insurance proceeds. Carlos doesn't like to wait for his money."

Ivan took a deep breath on the other line. "Uh, normally it takes some time. The insurance company does its due diligence, and once they're satisfied that the deaths were caused by a car accident, a check can be issued in two or three weeks." There was a moment of silence. "There's been a new development in the case. The movie director who was meeting with Caroline has made some inquiries with the Yolo County Sheriff's Department about the car crash and whether it was an accident or not. She also told them about the Johnsons' will. Now people are looking for a will that designates the ranch be donated to UC Davis."

Yuri tossed his cigar on the table in disgust. "They won't find that will, because we had it and it's been destroyed. Who is this woman who's making all these inquiries?"

"Her name is Stephanie Bernard," Ivan answered. "I don't know anything else about her."

"How long will that wild goose chase go on?" Yuri asked.

Ivan answered, "I don't have that answer either, but that's not all. Someone has filed the papers to start an eminent domain process on the Johnson Ranch with Yolo County. The county's going after all the excess water rights for the ranch."

Yuri shot out of his chair. "I knew that's what Caroline would try to do," he yelled into the phone. "She'll try to steal my water through the county! Let me tell you something, Ivan. She's just started a fight she won't win. I'll take care of Caroline Bennett! I'm on my way out of here in a couple of hours. Meet me in my office first thing tomorrow morning."

He kicked the coffee table in disgust. "Stephanie and Caroline, you don't know who you're dealing with!" He stared at the table for a second. He slowly looked up, his eyes squinting. "And Amber. She's got to be in all this up to her eyeballs."

"Is it bad news, Uncle?" Mika asked.

"It's nothing I can't handle," he answered. "How long do you think it will take you to clean up everything here and be back in Sacramento?"

Mika shrugged his shoulders and looked around the room. "Today's Wednesday; I can be back there by Friday afternoon."

The sound of the shower from the other room could be heard and steam started to slowly creep out from the bathroom. Yuri nodded in the direction of the shower. "I'll make sure he leaves here cleaned up and dressed." He leaned over and picked up the briefcase that was lying on the bar. "Let me know immediately if you run into any problems. Take your time and don't leave anything."

Mika nodded. "Don't worry, Uncle. I'll handle everything as you've asked."

Yuri's Fair Oaks office was quiet, except for the muffled sound of the landscapers mowing the lawn outside the window. Down the walkway, a man with a leaf blower for a backpack worked the nozzle back and forth across the walkways. Ivan stood next to the window watching, his hands behind his back.

Yuri sat at his desk, reviewing some documents. Ivan spoke to him without looking. "Is everything going well in Vegas?"

Yuri signed a document and flipped over to a new page. The landscapers had finished and had moved to another part of the office complex, leaving the two of them in quiet. "I spoke to Mika an hour ago," Yuri answered. "Everything went according to the plans, and he is sticking around to make sure the suite is spotless before he leaves."

"How did you drug Bain?" Ivan asked.

"That was easy. He'd been losing money all weekend at the craps tables, so Mika had one of his guys dressed as room service go up to the suite with a complimentary bottle of Crown Royal Blue." Yuri looked up from his papers. "It's expensive stuff. Morton knows the casino considers him a 'whale,' one of the big time gamblers that every casino covets, and just figured they were trying to keep him happy. Morton loves that stuff; it's like crack to him. We put the drugs in the Crown bottle."

Ivan turned away from the window. "That's pretty simple, but obviously effective. Now, what are your plans with Caroline?"

Yuri sipped some steaming coffee from a Starbucks cup. He leaned back in his chair, put his hands behind his head, and answered, "I would have thought Mellissa's demise would have given Caroline some pause. Apparently I was wrong. Maybe she hasn't connected the dots yet. What are your thoughts, Ivan?"

Ivan turned and walked toward Yuri's desk. "Well, we could fight her in court, which could take years to sort out, would be expensive, and you might lose. Or we could get the county to see the errors of their ways and withdraw the application. That would be harder than fighting them in court."

"What would cause the county to change their minds?" Yuri asked as he tossed a pen on top of a stack of papers. "They've already decided it's a good idea to take my water rights and have started the process. The only thing I can think of is Caroline needs to be convinced she can't win. Or she needs to be convinced it is not in her best interest to pursue this filing with the county."

Ivan held up his hand. "Hold on, Yuri, let's not get ahead of ourselves. I think it would be smart to start with legal action and try to fight the filing. It would look fishy if all of a sudden Caroline or one of her clones pulled the filing abruptly without ever getting a hearing or without some kind of negotiated consideration." He paced in front of Yuri, his hands behind his back. "I know someone will leak out that they yanked the filing because they were under duress and the spotlight would be turned on us, which is the last thing we need."

Yuri stared at him a second, soaking in what his friend was telling him. "You're right, Ivan. It would look too obvious if the county dropped this action all of a sudden at Caroline's request. Let's follow the legal route for the time being. It will buy us some time, which we need badly."

TWENTY-FIVE

The conference room at General Technologies was simple and high tech. The rich mahogany conference table was surrounded by ten chairs of simple aluminum frames, with compact, cushioned seats and back rests. Eight tiny low-wattage LED lights hung from a suspended frame above the table. Framed pictures of various projects hung from the off-white walls, along with a cabinet full of awards for individual achievements of employees. Matt sat at the middle of the table, a pile of files stacked in front of him. Diane Amory sat on his left. He handed her a file and waited silently while she thumbed through it, then handed her another as she set the first one down.

Matt pointed to the middle of a report she was studying. "That is an income and expense statement from a project not managed by WMI. Those numbers are in line with the numbers that were shown to the investment committee prior to the approval to purchase."

Diane set the file down and studied the next one. "How many projects are WMI managing for us currently, Matt?"

Matt counted the list of projects on a notepad. "They manage thirty-five at this point. But we are scheduled to close on fifteen more projects next month and I've been told WMI is scheduled to take them over." He leaned away from her, chewing on the end of his pen. "Who brings these projects to the investment committee, and who pitches them? Is it the same person every time?"

She set the file down. "The deals come from a variety of real estate brokers. They are pitched to our asset managers, who vet them out and then send them to the committee. I don't think there is any one broker who dominates the winning projects."

"Do we know if WMI has acted as a real estate broker on any of these deals and has been paid a commission upon closing the deals?" Matt asked.

Diane's eyes widened. "I don't know, Matt, I had never thought about that. Can you look into it and see what you can find? That might shed some light on these deals. You know, I've been getting more pressure from Morton Bain to have you leave these projects alone. He's even made threats about your and my employment here. But the more you keep digging up, the more I want you to continue." She leaned back in her chair, tapping her nails on its armrests. "I still don't understand why he is trying to get involved in these apartment complexes. He's got to have a tie to all this."

A young woman tapped at the glass door and Diane motioned her in. "Excuse me, Mrs. Amory, your 2:00 appointment is here."

Diane held up her hand. "Okay, Betsy, tell him I'll be with him in a minute."

Matt waited for Betsy to close the door. "There's one other thing I want to show you, Diane, and it's strange one. A year ago we bought this little water company called Goshen Water for 450,000 dollars. It's located in a small town just above Bakersfield." He flipped over a page in his notebook. "It services about 500 clients and seems an odd asset for us to own. We sold it a month ago for 140,000 dollars to a company called Terra Investments."

He paused to let her absorb the numbers. "Terra Investments, WMI, and Centennial, Inc. all have the same physical address. Morton Bain was the person who signed off to approve the purchase of the water company for us and also on its sale. I'm wondering a couple of things. Yuri Kletcko owns WMI and Centennial, Inc. Does he also own Terra Investments? Is there a connection between Mr. Kletcko and Morton Bain, and if there is, what is the nature of it?"

Diane started gathering her things and stood to leave. She had a worried look on her face. "That's a good question, Matt, and I don't have the answer. I think you'll have to find out what is going on here. But please remember we are talking about a sitting member of the Board of Directors of this company, and a powerful member at that. We had better be absolutely positive with rock solid backup information before we go around accusing Mr. Bain of any wrongdoing. He's not a person we want to anger. He wields a lot of influence in our industry. He could easily blackball us if we're wrong, but keep digging."

She patted him on the back as she left the office. Matt sat there by himself, thinking, Yuri is involved in a lot of things. I wonder what Stephanie has found out about him. Thinking of Stephanie gave him pause. He hadn't spoken to her for a few days and was trying to figure out a reason to dial her up. It's time to talk about Yuri and that would be a good excuse to call her. There're too many things swirling around with Yuri's name on it to make them all a coincidence.

The afternoon traffic going over the Bay Bridge East towards Sacramento was slowly making its way across the water. The cloudless sky made those pushing through the stop-and-go traffic wish they were somewhere else. Matt steered his shiny BMW into the second lane from the left as it made its way past Treasure Island and onto the last leg of the trip across the San Francisco Bay. He checked out his window every couple of miles to see the fleet of ships moored at the Port of Oakland, one of the busiest on the west coast. By the time he reached the town of Berkeley, the traffic was moving at a normal clip. His phone rang, and he threw on his Bluetooth headphone. "Hello?"

"Hi, Matt," Kathy Ann cooed into the phone. "Where are you?"

Matt adjusted himself in his seat. "I'm just outside of Berkeley. I was in San Francisco earlier."

"Why don't you stop by on your way home? I've got a six pack in the refrigerator with your name on it. I haven't seen you for a while."

Matt didn't answer for a second. What the heck, I can swing by for a minute or two. I've got nothing else to do. "Okay, I'll come by there in a couple of hours."

"Great, I'll be waiting for you," she replied, almost whispering the words.

Matt hung up and stared down the freeway. Kathy Ann is like a bad penny, he thought, she never goes away. She was the thing he wanted when he couldn't have it. Now that he could have it, he wasn't sure if he wanted it. I can't help feel that this woman will cause more problems than she'll solve. Well, Matt, you've asked for it now. What are you going to do?

He made the drive in less than two hours and pulled into Kathy Ann's apartment parking lot. As he walked up the stairs to her unit, she opened the door wearing a yellow mini skirt and loose-fitting blouse and holding a Coors Light in her hand. Her face and hair were perfectly done and she smiled sweetly.

He paused, a step from the top. "Hi there," he said, his eyes following her long legs to the bottom of her skirt that barely concealed her. "You look really nice." He said it in a way to not seem too complimentary, feeling the need to choose his words carefully.

A little girl's head poked around the corner, her eyes wide as she looked at Matt.

"Hi, Brittany, how are you?"

She smiled shyly and spoke in a soft voice. "Hi."

Kathy Ann turned. "Brittany, I told you to stay in your room. Get back there before I paddle you."

The girl looked up at her mother with fearful eyes and scampered away.

Kathy Ann turned back to Matt, smiling. "If I could only get my looser ex to come take her once in a while, it would be nice. I'm stuck with her twenty-four seven." She reached out and grabbed his hand, pulling him inside her apartment. "Come on in. Here, take your beer."

Matt took the beer from her hand apprehensively and followed her into the apartment. Her reaction to the child caught him off guard, and he felt uncomfortable. As he looked around, he noticed a couple of children's books on the couch along with a pair of dolls in frilly dresses. A laundry basket full of unwashed clothes poked out from behind a lazy-boy chair. He could see the kitchen from where he stood, and its counter had dishes scattered about. Well, he thought, she's not a great housekeeper or a patient mother; so much for that fantasy.

Kathy Ann saw his glance and kicked the laundry basket farther behind the chair. "Here, have a seat and make yourself comfortable." She surveyed the room and commented, "I need to tidy this place up, but Brittany keeps making messes faster than I can clean them up. I wish she would be neater."

Matt looked around the room and thought, I don't think Brittany did this all by herself.

Kathy Ann put her hands over Matt's. "You look good, Matt. I'm glad you came by, and I miss seeing you." She poured herself a tall glass of white wine and looked into his eyes. "I've been thinking. You're still living with your parents and your grandmother in Rio Linda. I know that can't be a great situation for you. Why don't you move in with me and Brittany?" She reached down and rubbed his thigh, smiling and batting her eyes. "It would be like old times." She paused and whispered, "And I know you liked the old times, didn't you Matt?" She smiled, seductively running her tongue across her lips.

Matt nervously took a sip of his beer before answering, "Uh, I don't think that would be such a great idea, Kathy Ann. Living with my folks isn't the best, but it works for me."

Kathy Ann let go of his hand and gave him a disappointed look. She got up and opened a drawer in the kitchen. She pulled a cigarette from a pack and put it to her lips.

"What are you doing?" Matt asked, an astonished look on his face. "Since when did you start to smoke?"

She lit the cigarette and inhaled deeply. "Oh, Matt, come on. I used to sneak smokes when we were dating. You just never caught me. When I married Keith, he used to smoke dope all the time, along with cigarettes. When he got to try out for the NFL, he flunked a drug test prior to his rookie season. That's why he was cut."

"And I always thought it was because he had lousy hands," Matt mumbled.

Kathy Ann continued to puff away, filling the apartment with smoke. "Well, there was that, too, which didn't help his cause. But I just began to smoke a little more when I was with him, and now I smoke probably less than a pack a day. I can quit anytime."

Matt looked surprised. "I can't believe that, Kathy Ann. You used to be so health conscious." He looked in the direction of her bedroom, where Brittany was playing. "What about your daughter? What about this secondhand smoke you're creating and she's breathing? Don't you worry about that at all?"

Kathy Ann waved her hand dismissively. "Nobody's ever proved that type of smoke is harmful. Besides, I won't smoke forever. I'll probably quit soon."

Matt waved his hands in an attempt to dissipate the smoke. "Please, let me open a window, I can't stand the smell." He stood up and lifted open the kitchen window, allowing a breeze to come in. He turned to her. "Listen, Kathy Ann, thanks for the beer, but I need to get going. I've been out of town for a few days and I've got some work I need to finish at home." Matt knew that was not completely true. He was caught up with work, but he wanted to get out of her place. "It was nice seeing you again."

Kathy Ann crushed out her cigarette and came up to Matt, hugging him tightly. "Oh, Matt," she whispered, "can't you stay for a while? I can put Brittany down and we can play. I've been thinking about your body for days." She put her hands on his butt and pulled him tightly against her. "I really want you, Matt. Come live with me," she whispered in his ear. "You won't regret it, I promise."

Matt reached around and pulled her hands off his body. He stepped back and moved toward the door. "Look, Kathy Ann, I enjoyed seeing you and all, but things have changed; we've changed. I'm in love with someone else, and trying to recreate something we had long ago is not going to work." He opened the door and stood at the entry looking at her. "I need to get home. I wish you and Brittany well. Good bye."

By the time he had reached his car, he wanted to kick himself. What was I thinking? I put a relationship with the most beautiful, caring woman in the world in jeopardy for something that was just an illusion in my head, somebody I had created but didn't exist. "Matt," he spoke out loud, "you'd better hope it's not too late to salvage this relationship with Stephanie. You've got some major work to do to win her back, and I wouldn't blame her if she told you to jump in a lake."

TWENTY-SIX

Yolo County's Sheriff's Department was located on a quiet street in downtown Woodland, a three-minute walk from the old courthouse. A single-story brick building with a charcoal, composition shingle roof, it sat back off the street. A slew of white patrol cars with yellow and green letters were parked on the right side of the building, each with the seal of Yolo County on the front door along with their motto, "Service without Limitation." Inside the building and past the reception area, was a large open room with forty individual office cubicles portioned out. The walls sectioning off each cubicle were only about four feet in height and allowed a standing person to see across the room. Detective and sheriff personnel busily manned phones and computers in an effort to keep more than 200,000 Yolo County residents safe. At the center of the room sat the main conference room, surrounded by frosted glass windows on all sides.

Stephanie sat at a worn conference table next to Alan. Across from them sat John Cranston, the Yolo County Sheriff. Both he and his assistant, Detective Fred Douglas, wore an olive green uniform with a sidearm strapped to their side. Fred had just finished reading the field report of the Johnsons' auto accident out loud. He looked up from the report and addressed Stephanie and Alan. "Do you have any questions? I'll answer them if I can."

Alan spoke first. "I've read the 911 transcript, and the Johnsons were obviously being traumatized by someone in a black sedan with a gun. Your report mentions that the Johnson vehicle had some damage on the driver's side of the car, indicating it might have been sideswiped prior to the impact with the oak tree." He scanned some notes from his notepad. "Have there been any new leads regarding the black sedan?"

Fred replied, "There was a witness who saw the car chasing the Johnsons. He could only describe it as either a dark Mercedes, or a BMW. He wasn't able get a license number on the dark, dimly lit country road. Our officer, who was attempting to respond to the 911 operator, couldn't find the Johnsons location initially. He arrived about three minutes after the witness showed up at the scene."

He pulled out a series of eight-by-eleven photographs from a manila envelope and handed them to Alan. "You can see the damage done to the driver's side of the Johnson car. We've put an alert out to all body shops around the Greater Sacramento Area to see if any of them have seen a black sedan with passenger side damage. So far, we've had no response."

Stephanie looked over Alan's shoulder at the photo. She looked at John Cranston. "Have you looked into the business connection between the Johnsons and Yuri Kletcko?"

"Until you called me with the information, we did not know Yuri Kletcko existed. But now that you've brought it to my attention, we are looking at him as a suspect, as we would at any person who stands to gain monetarily from an untimely death. You mentioned a life insurance policy. Do you have additional information on that policy?"

Stephanie shook her head. "No I haven't, but I did call the company's headquarters in Omaha, Nebraska and alert them that this might not be just an accident. They wouldn't give me much information, as they're not authorized to give that out to just anybody." She paused to take a breath. "They didn't say as such, but I got the impression from the person I talked to that a claim had already been made for the money on the policy."

The room was quiet except for the humming of the overhead lights in the ceiling. "Stephanie, you mentioned something about the ranch being donated to UC Davis. Has anyone seen a will from the Johnsons?" Fred asked.

Alan answered. "Nothing has surfaced yet. After we're done here, we have an appointment with John Roth's administrative assistant, Bonnie Jacobs, to see what kind of light she might be able to shed on that issue." He slid the photographs back into the folder and handed them back to Fred. "Have your people found out anything further about the cause of Mr. Roth's death?"

"Other than it is suspicious, no," answered John. "We should have the results of the autopsy in a week or so. We also haven't tracked down the client who was with Mr. Roth when he died. These are all rather strange circumstances."

Alan flipped over a sheet on his pad and continued writing notes. "Have you talked to the Sacramento City Police Department regarding the Mellissa Burns hit and run death that happened a few weeks ago? I sent over the information I had gleaned from *The Sacramento Bee*." He turned and nodded in Stephanie's direction. "We're both convinced these three incidents are related."

John leaned back and put his hands behind his head. "We don't have very much evidence to go on right now, but what I've seen and heard from you two makes me think you might be onto something." He turned to Fred. "When is Mr. Kletcko supposed to come in for an interview?"

Fred scanned his notes. "He comes in the day after tomorrow at 10:30 a.m. Bruce Adams and I are scheduled to meet with him, and you're welcome to join us if you wish. It should be an interesting interview." He flipped his notepad over to the front page and set it on the table. He looked across the table at Alan. "It would be really helpful if you could get us a copy of the Johnsons' will."

Alan watched Stephanie as she spoke to both detectives. "We know there was an original in Mr. Roth's office, but there's got to be another copy floating around. We're hoping Bonnie Jacobs might know about the second copy and where to find it."

John put his hands on the table and pushed himself up. "You both have been extremely helpful, and we appreciate your efforts. Be wary of Yuri. If these events are related, he could be dangerous. Fred and I will continue to work on these cases, and we will let you know if anything comes up. If you two discover something you think is relevant, let us know immediately."

Stephanie raised her hand as if she were back in school. "Sheriff, before you go, there is one other thing. The Johnsons' neighbor, and now Yuri's neighbor, is Caroline Bennett."

"The chairwoman of the Yolo Board of Supervisors? I've known Caroline for many years." he said.

"Yes, she is pursuing having the county take some of the Johnson Ranch water rights by eminent domain. It's a long legal process, but if Yuri retains ownership of that ranch, the action will not sit well with him, and he will not allow that to happen without a fight. Those water rights are worth a lot of money. We're worried about Ms. Bennett's safety. If Yuri is as ruthless as he appears, she would be the most logical person in his crosshairs."

John gripped the back of his chair. "Fred, what do you suggest? This is getting more complicated by the minute. I know all about the action the Board is trying to take. Should we suggest they wait on the eminent domain action until we get a better handle on all these events?"

Fred tossed his pen down on his pad. He shook his head, smiling. "Come on, John. Caroline has never been a fan of cops or of our department. She and her crew on the Board are always trying to cut our budgets every year. I doubt she would listen to anything we suggest." He looked over to Stephanie. "Besides, I think it's too late. The Board already has acted on the filing of eminent domain, right, Stephanie?"

"That's correct," she answered. "At their last hearing, some resident of Yolo County made the filing for the eminent domain action, and it was passed by the Board five to four. If Mellissa were killed to stop that action, which seems a stretch, it didn't work. Alan and I will speak with Caroline and let her know what we know. Maybe she will take this threat seriously and recommend they pull the eminent domain action."

John turned and reached for the conference room door. "I think that's a good idea, Stephanie. All right, we'll talk again soon."

Stephanie looked at the downtown area of Woodland through the open window on the passenger side as Alan drove his white Mercedes 300 down Main Street toward the southbound exit of I-5. She loved the idyllic nature of the town, almost untouched by time. Her mind started to wander, and she noticed a men's store as they drove. Something about the mannequin in the front window reminded her of Matt. Was it the blue polo shirt or the youthful look on its face? She wasn't sure, but she began to wonder what Matt was doing at that very moment. Did he think of her as much as she thought of him, or was he back with his old girlfriend? The thought of him with someone else is tearing me apart, she thought. I would like to see him again, but can I trust him? If the relationship is over, I should forget him and move on with my life. Why can't I do that?

As he hit the accelerator, Alan remarked, "If someone told me all these events in this story and then said it's all related to one person, I would say to them it's not believable. How could Yuri stay under the radar so well? If we hadn't been investigating Caroline for the board's performance regarding development projects, this would have slipped through the cracks."

Stephanie snapped back to the present. "Speaking of the other matter, will Mr. Parker allow you to continue this investigation now that's it's changed from its original mission?" asked Stephanie. "I mean, it's not totally unrelated, but it has changed from investigating Caroline's reasons for being antidevelopment."

Alan steered the car into the carpool lane. "Mr. Parker definitely wants me to continue on, and he wants to become more involved. He feels we are on to something, and one way or the other we will be able understand Caroline's agenda. He might even lend his legal services to the board for the eminent domain action if Caroline's willing to compromise on future development projects he might bring before her board." He leaned into her playfully. "For a fee of course."

Stephanie pushed his shoulder playfully and laughed. "You attorneys kill me. If you can't beat them, then go work for the side that pays you best."

Alan gave her a wink. "Everyone knows we're a bunch of whores, so why does it surprise people when we act like them? We just don't go around advertising the fact."

"You don't have to advertise," Stephanie said. "Certain things don't have to be explained."

Alan pulled into Old Town Sacramento and found a parking spot in front of John Roth's office. Alan stepped into the bright sunlight, his Ray Ban sunglass fending off the glare. He stood on the wooden sidewalk and waited for Stephanie to join him before opening the office door for her and following her in. Bonnie was sitting at the front desk, boxes surrounding her as she gingerly packed items for moving. She smiled at them halfheartedly. "Good morning, I'm Bonnie. You must be Stephanie and Alan." She extended her hand. "I apologize in advance for my demeanor, but I'm still in shock from everything."

Stephanie answered, "We completely understand, Bonnie.

Thank you for seeing us on such short notice. We promise not to keep you long." A lone ceiling fan spun lazily, while Rush Limbaugh's voice could be heard ranting about something on a radio in John's office.

"I'm glad to meet with you. Can I get either of you a cup of coffee or a water?" she asked.

They both declined. She waved them into John's office. "Come on in here. I'm sure John wouldn't have minded." She went around the desk and sat down slowly in John's old seat. She indicated to the seats in front of the desk for them to sit. She made a big sigh. "Well, what can I help you with?"

Alan and Stephanie took their seats and each pulled out a notebook and pen. "We're sorry about Mr. Roth, Bonnie," Stephanie said softly. "It's such a tragedy." She surveyed the office, noticing all the photographs of politicians and family lining the walls. What a nice office, so quaint and proper, she thought. I'll bet Mr. Roth met a lot of interesting people in his lifetime. Volumes of law books, all leather bound with gold leaf lettering, filled the shelves on one wall.

Stephanie took a deep breath. "The reason we're here, Bonnie, is because of the Johnsons, one of your boss's clients. I had interviewed the Johnsons a few days before their death, and they told me about their arrangement with Yuri Kletcko and their loan with him on the ranch."

Bonnie made some idle scribbles on a pad as she listened. Stephanie continued.

"They indicated to me they wanted to donate their ranch to UC Davis upon their deaths and that this was stated in their will. So far, as far as we can find out, nobody at UC Davis has heard anything about this arrangement, and we don't know if their will was ever produced."

Bonnie clasped her hands together in an exasperated manner. "I've torn this place apart for those files. The very first thing John told me to get him that Monday after the Johnsons' accident was all their files. I had set them on his desk just before his first appointment. He then collapsed, and in all the excitement and confusion, I forgot about them until you called. I've looked everywhere around here and I can't find them." She threw her hands in the air. "Those files have disappeared, and I'm sure their will was in them."

Alan crossed his legs and spoke. "Have you contacted the client John met with the morning he died? Maybe he saw something."

She shook her head frowning. "No, it was strange. This was a first-time client. He paid me five hundred dollars in cash for the consultation, which was odd. When he came out of John's office, asking me to call 911, I vaguely remember him having what looked like files under his arm. I didn't remember seeing then when he went into the meeting with John. He disappeared right after I called 911, and I haven't been able to track him down. The phone number he gave me when he made the appointment has been disconnected."

"Could it be possible that he took the Johnsons' files?" Alan asked.

Bonnie shrugged her shoulders. "I don't know. But they were there before he showed up and were gone afterwards, so I'm guessing he took them."

"What did the man look like? Had you ever seen him before?" Stephanie asked.

"No, I'd never seen him before that morning. He was a young man, stocky, with a bald head. He had dark eyes, and he seemed nervous while he was waiting. He wore dark slacks and a dark shirt, which I thought was odd for a warm summer day. He also had a mole on the left side of his face. "

Stephanie turned to look out the window of the office to see a horse pulling a frilly carriage filled with tourists as they soaked up the sights of Old Town. A man in buck skinned clothes with a dirty cowboy hat sat half sideways in the front seat of the carriage as he steered the horse pulling the carriage and filled in his passengers with historical facts.

She turned back to Bonnie. "Do you know if there is another copy of the Johnsons' will somewhere, Bonnie?"

"Yes, there was an extra one," she said. "Mr. Kletcko wanted it to be a confidential document, with the only original document to be left with John. He was a bossy individual, that Kletcko, and not very friendly. I had a bad feeling about him." She leaned forward, as if letting them in on a big secret. "I gave the Johnsons a copy anyway."

Alan perked up at this information, putting his notepad down on his lap. "Do you have any idea where that copy might be found?" He looked at Stephanie and raised his eyebrows. "This is big."

Bonnie looked at both of them, surprised. "I would imagine it is probably somewhere in their ranch house. A long time ago, Betty Lou told me she had a special place for all important documents, in a fireproof box. Unless somebody found it, it's probably still there."

Alan abruptly stood up, trying to act nonchalant. "Thank you for your help, Bonnie." He handed her a business card. "If you think of anything else, give me a call."

Stephanie hurried behind him as they left the office. He paused before opening the car door and leaned on the roof, looking back at John Roth's office. Noticing what an attractive man he was, Stephanie wondered what he was really like away from work.

She was startled when he said to her, "What are you staring at? Do I have something on my face?"

She blushed and gave him a big smile. "Oh, I'm sorry, I was just thinking." She turned more serious. "Let's hustle over to the ranch house and see what's going on there. I hope that Yuri hasn't tried to go through it and remove all their belongings. He does own it now."

"Yeah, I was thinking the same thing." He ducked his head into the driver's side and slammed the door. As he turned on the ignition, he asked her, "What happens if he's already there? What do we do next?"

Stephanie shrugged. "I don't know. We probably should let someone in law enforcement know we are there in case we run into trouble, don't you think?"

Alan nodded. "Yeah, that's a good thought. I'll alert the sheriff, just to be safe."

❖

Thirty minutes later, they were sitting in the car on Road 26A, looking down the long gravel driveway to the Johnsons' ranch house. They could see two vehicles in the circular driveway of the house: one a truck of some sort and the other a blue Audi. Three men wandered in and out of the house, carrying boxes.

Stephanie sighed. "I think we might be too late. It looks like they're already going through the place."

"It appears they are," Alan said as he watched the activity through the windshield. "Do you think they're looking for the will?" he asked. Before she could answer, he answered himself. "I doubt it. I bet they are only looking for any valuables. As far as Yuri knows, he's got the only copy. There still might be time to find it."

Stephanie thought back to the time when she drove Matt to break into Taylor Whitney's home in Granite Bay to look for computer files regarding a loan scam they had been hired to check out. Matt found the files, but they found themselves in a wild adventure that neither of them had bargained for. I wonder if we should try that tack again, she thought. I might as well ask.

"Do you think we should break in at night and try to find the will?" she asked.

He turned to her with a surprised look. "What, break into a house? Are you serious?"

She kept looking down the street. "I am absolutely serious. How else will we get in?" She turned and stared at him coldly. "The only way we're going to find that will is if we go look for it, and Yuri won't be giving us the keys to the house so we can search it." She gave him a smug look. "I know just who to bring in for this task: Matt. We should do it soon, like, tonight if possible. We can't afford to wait."

Alan turned on the ignition and turned the car around. "I hope you know what you're getting us into. I'm not convinced this is such a good idea."

"I do," Stephanie said. She pointed out the car window to the south. "Let's drive over to Caroline Bennett's house in Davis. I told her we might be dropping by. I think she needs to be made aware of what's going on around her, and be prepared."

Alan gripped the wheel and steered toward I-5 south. "Okay, we'll be there in few minutes. I just hope Caroline takes us seriously."

Fifteen minutes later, Alan and Stephanie were sitting at a patio table next to Caroline's shimmering pool surrounded by colorful apricot daylily and blue agapanthus blooms. Five towering palm trees stood watch over the pool, their brownish grey pods hanging down, forming grass skirts around the upper trunk. The yard overlooked the fifteenth green at the El Macero Golf Course, and a foursome of golfers drove by in dark green golf carts.

Caroline lay on her stomach on a lounge chair in a turquoise bikini, the back undone, while a young man rubbed suntan lotion on her back. He was tanned and buffed, and wore teal Billabong swim trunks with a wide white stripe on each side. A half full Mai Tai rested on a small table nearby.

Stephanie watched the man as he worked the lotion into Caroline's back. He looked less than enthusiastic as he moved his hands back and forth, rubbing the lotion into her skin. She sure likes them young, Stephanie thought. She glanced at Alan, who looked back and shrugged his shoulders at her.

Stephanie cleared her throat and spoke. "Caroline, we've heard about the eminent domain case the board is pursuing for the water at the Johnsons' ranch."

Caroline turned her head to the other side to face Stephanie. "Ah yes, isn't that just great. I just wish Mellissa were here to see this; she would be so thrilled." She paused for a second and sighed. "God, I miss her so much." She adjusted her Gucci sunglasses and continued. "The county ordered the appraisal of the value of the water rights two days ago. It won't be long before there will be a dollar amount to wave in front of Mr. Kletcko's greedy face."

Stephanie looked down at her lap. "That was tragic what happened to Mellissa, Caroline. But that's one of the reasons we're here. We're not convinced it was an accident, neither was the Johnsons' death nor their attorney's. If they are connected, your new neighbor, Mr. Kletcko, could be involved, and if he is, he's a dangerous man and you could be next. We don't know anything for sure, but we think you could be in serious trouble."

Caroline lifted herself up on her elbow and grabbed her drink, not caring she was topless. "I'm aware of all that has gone on with the Johnsons and their attorney, and I also don't think Mellissa's death was accidental. But what do you think that greedy Russian is going to do to me? Murder me?" She tossed her head back and laughed. "I don't think so. He would be crazy to try something that stupid. He has to know there are a lot of eyes looking into all these events, and if something were to happen to me, he'd be the first person the authorities would track down. No, he'll watch while Yolo County takes his water rights and puts it up for the public's benefit. And since I have great standing with the Water Resources Board and would use any additional water allocated for raising crops for food, I'll get that water. He'll get compensated, but I'll get the water." She lifted her drink as if in a salute.

Alan tried to keep his eyes above her neck, but couldn't. "Caroline, please think about this. Do you think a man like Yuri Kletcko will allow you to take his water without a fight? He knows you're behind this, and he will do whatever it takes to stop you. He obviously has designs on that water, and it's more than just for raising crops. He'll go sell it on the open market."

Caroline pointed her finger at Alan. "That's exactly right, and that's why I'll get the water. This is why the eminent domain is the proper way to deal with this issue. The best use of the water is right here in Yolo County, not somewhere else down the Delta." She wrinkled her nose. "Or even worse, to those fools in Southern California. My board has authorized the county to go get that water and keep it under our government oversight. That will ensure the water stays here in Yolo County, where it belongs." She took another swig of her drink. "I might be the one who started this boulder moving, but now that it's in motion, it's bigger than me."

She sat up and crossed her legs on the lounge. She handed her glass to the young man and said dismissively, "Here, Monte, go make me another one." She turned to Alan and Stephanie. "Are you sure you won't have one with me?" She smiled sweetly. "Monte makes them yummy."

"No thanks, Caroline. We've still got work to do today," Stephanie answered. "Here's the problem. You are the most visible target in this action by the county. Mr. Kletcko didn't fall into owning that ranch by accident. He had a plan, and so far everything has gone according to that plan up until the eminent domain action. Now things have changed. Be aware of that and be careful."

She waved her hands at them as if scolding them. "You two are such dears worrying about me, but I'll be fine. I was raised on a ranch and am very comfortable around guns, and I have plenty of them within reach. I'm not some dainty damsel who can't take care of herself. I've dealt with bigger brutes than Mr. Kletcko and have held my own. My only regret is those damned hillbillies, the Johnsons, didn't hang around long enough to see Yolo County take their water rights. I would have loved to see the expression on their faces when they found out I was behind it all." She clapped her hands and threw her head back laughing.

234

Stephanie stood up and dusted off her slacks. "Well, please be careful Caroline. If you need our help, let us know."

Caroline gave a faint wave as Monte handed her the Mai Tai. "Don't worry about me, you two. If it makes you feel better, I promise to be vigilant and on the lookout for anything out of the ordinary. Keep your eyes on the newspapers. All sorts of things will be going on in Yolo County."

TWENTY-SEVEN

Yuri paced back and forth behind the desk, his hands behind his back. Ivan sat across the desk in a chair, waiting for him to say something. A copy of the morning newspaper sat on the desk, opened to the headlines of an article stating, "Local Firms Foreclosing Illegally." The lengthy article explained how firms specializing in foreclosure property were taking homes illegally from desperate homeowners. Wealth Management, Inc. was mentioned in the second paragraph. Yuri stopped and pointed angrily at the paper. "I can't believe they print this rubbish! This is still a capitalistic country. I have the right to do business. If I buy a block of loans at a discount, it should be my business what I do with them. If people don't pay their mortgages, I have a right to foreclose!"

Ivan put his hands up. "Calm down, Yuri, of course you have the right to do business how you like. These reporters are just on a fishing expedition. It'll all blow over."

Yuri continued his pacing. "I hope you're right, but I'm not so sure. I thought we took care of the person who was leaking information to the press and this stuff would stop. What happened?"

Ivan sighed. "I don't know, Yuri. I thought we'd shut down that leak also, but maybe we were wrong. This is not an easy operation to keep quiet."

Yuri continued to pace. "If the press figures out how WMI works, it will be a problem." Dark sweat stains appeared on the armpits of his light blue Hawaiian shirt, and beads appeared on his forehead. "The press is really going to howl. I got a call from Artie Tennelli this morning, and he told me Carlos Diego is watching the situation closely. Carlos thinks it's time to get out while we're ahead." Yuri stopped and slapped his fist on the desk. "I don't want to get out just as we are just about to hit it big. Unfortunately, since Carlos and his cartel lent me the money to get these ventures started, whatever he says goes. Remember the golden rule: He who has the gold rules!"

He went over to the bar in the corner and poured himself a glass of Vodka. "Artie said Carlos wants to know where the insurance check from the Johnsons is."

Ivan winced. "Did you tell him we've hit a snag?"

"Not yet," he answered. "Carlos doesn't like to hear that sort of news, nor does he take it well. I've stalled him off."

The office door opened and Mika came in. He was out of breath and his red silk shirt was soaked from sweat. "I'm sorry, Yuri, but I had to get over here quickly. The movie directors who are doing the documentary on Caroline Bennett were parked outside the Johnsons ranch this morning. They sat there for forty-five minutes watching us." He wiped his forehead with his sleeve. "I don't know if they saw anything. It's a distance from the road to the house. I knew you would want to know."

Yuri came over and patted him on the back. "Thanks, Mika, you did the right thing." He motioned to Ivan with his open hand. "These directors are getting too close for comfort. I wonder what they're interested in. Ivan, do you think there might be another copy of the will around?"

Ivan shrugged. "I hadn't thought about that. Did you find anything of value there?" he asked Mika.

Mika nodded. "There is some turquoise jewelry that looks valuable, and I think a lot of the furniture pieces are antiques."

"Did you find a safe?" Ivan asked.

"No, Ivan," he answered, "but we weren't looking for a safe. It's a big house and things have been stored there for years. I don't think I've ever seen so much stuff."

The room was silent as Yuri walked back behind his desk. "Start looking for a safe or a file cabinet, Mika. They probably keep their personal records somewhere on that ranch. What about security at night? Is the house well locked up?"

"No," Mika replied. "The Johnsons didn't lock anything, and there's no alarm. I've scheduled an alarm company to go out in a couple days to alarm the place. Until that happens, I've stationed Andre near the entry to keep guard. He's to call me if there's anything suspicious going on."

"Good," Yuri replied. His cell phone rang and he answered it. "Hello?"

"Yuri, it's Morton Bain. Something has come up."

Yuri plopped down in his chair, putting a finger to his lips to notify those in the room to stay quiet. "Go ahead, I'm listening."

Morton cleared his throat nervously. "I got a call from William Thompson, the Chairman of the Board of General Technologies, this morning. He wants me to be in San Francisco in their office a week from Wednesday to meet with him and the rest of the Board, along with Matt Whiteside and Diane Amory. They want to discuss my relationship with you and WMI." The pitch in his voice rose and started to quiver. "I'm really worried, Yuri. What shall I tell them?"

Yuri paused to think. *That jerk Whiteside raises his head again. I thought he had been called off a month ago. I need to buy some time.* "Relax, Morton, nothing will happen with your board. You'll explain to them that our relationship is an old one and we've done numerous deals in the past, all of them successful." He quickly changed the subject. "How will this meeting with your board affect

238

our contract on the new projects General Technologies just purchased?"

"Nothing has changed yet," Morton replied. "But I feel they may pull those from you. Things are getting hot around here for me, Yuri."

Yuri slammed his drink on the desk, spilling vodka on the newspaper article. Damn that nosey Whiteside! I was counting on that money. I can't let Morton go in front of that board; they will press him, and he will fold like a lawn chair, spilling everything. He's been a mess since the Las Vegas incident, and putting him under a spotlight like that will cause him to crack for certain. He's become a liability.

"Morton, listen to me. I'm going to send my plane for you tomorrow morning, and we'll fly to Vegas together. We can prepare for this meeting with your board there and figure out what you're to say to them. Be at McClellan Air Force Base here in Sacramento at the general aviation terminal tomorrow at 8:30 in the morning, and I'll pick you up. I'll get you a room at the Hyatt for the night."

Morton replied excitedly, "Oh, that's a good idea, Yuri. I knew you'd figure out the best way to approach this. I'll be there tomorrow bright and early."

Yuri hung up and looked at Mika. "Pick up Marc and meet me at McClellan Air Force Base tomorrow at 7:30. Bring the things we discussed yesterday."

TWENTY-EIGHT

The yellow cab pulled into an enormous metal hangar and parked under the wing of a sleek twin engine Aero Commander 690B. The bright sun shone down on the fuselage, which was artic white and had a blue ribbon running from the tail to the front of the plane. The wings sat on the top part of the plane, leaving its belly about two feet off the ground. Its three-bladed props shined like a newly polished fine silver set. Yuri had let Morton use the plane numerous times before, and he was always in awe of its power and beauty. With two Honeywell TPE331 turboprop engines, it easily cruised at 270 knots, fast enough to get to Vegas in an hour and a half. With a range of just under 1200 nautical miles, it could fly to a variety of destinations Morton liked to frequent. Morton was an avid skydiver and loved jumping out of planes, but he wasn't crazy about flying without a parachute on his back. Still he liked the convenience of a big, fast plane, so he subdued his fears with alcohol.

A uniformed captain was slowly walking around the plane, getting it ready for flight. Morton leaned across the front seat and handed the cabbie two twenty-dollar bills. The cabbie reached for his wallet when Morton patted him on the shoulder. "Don't worry about it. Keep the change."

He slid out the door and stood at the base of the three steps that led to the plane. He looked up into the cloudless day, shielding his eyes from the sun. Yuri was standing in the doorway above him smiling. "I hope you had a good night here in Sacramento," he said.

Morton looked up at him. I wonder if I should tell him I got drunk at Marco Polo last night and woke up with a strange man in my bed. No, he thought, that would be a bad idea in the best of times. Yuri has a strange look about him this morning, Morton thought. He looks in too good a mood given all that's swirling around him. Things don't feel right. "I had a great night thank you." He smiled. "The suite you set me up in at the Hyatt was awesome, thank you."

"I'm glad you liked it." Yuri stood to one side of the doorway to the plane. He waved his arm in a grandiose gesture toward the inside of the plane. "Shall we get rolling?"

Morton nodded and climbed up the stairs. He paused at the top to catch his breath. He looked in and saw Mika and Marc sitting facing him in captain's chairs, their backs to the front of the plane. He nodded to them. Why did Yuri bring these two thugs?

Marc got up and hopped into the copilot's chair, putting a pair of headphones over his ears and fastening his seatbelt. He began conversing with the pilot, and together they reviewed a map that was spread out between them.

Morton watched all this and stood frozen at the entrance for fifteen seconds, not sure if he should step all the way into the airplane or bolt back down the stairs.

Mika smiled and held up a glass with a full drink. "Hey, Morton, join me for a Crown and Coke. There's nothing like a little eye opener in the morning."

Morton licked his dry lips. His hangover pounded his temples and he knew a little whiskey might be just what he needed to calm his nerves. He nodded at Mika. What am I worried about? He thought. Yuri needs me. He moved slowly into the plane. With shaking hands, he reached out to Mika and took the glass. He lifted it to his lips and with eyes closed took a big gulp. He wiped his mouth with the back of his right hand. Smiling, he took a seat across from Mika.

He started to take another swig and stopped, sniffing the drink. He looked at Mika with a quizzical face. "It smells funny."

Mika sniffed his and then took a drink. "It's probably the off brand of Coke we got back there. Some of that stuff has been around for months."

Morton nodded. That makes sense, he thought. He finished off the drink and held it out for another. Mika reached down below his seat for the bottle and poured him another. Morton could feel the warmth of the alcohol going through his body, and he started to relax. He watched out the window of the plane as it rolled down the runway, picking up speed and slowly rising into the air. As they left the residential areas of North Highlands and flew over the northern part of Sacramento, he looked down upon a sea of green that stretched all along the horizon. Rice fields, he thought, the crop of money.

The plane banked to the left and headed west, then south. He looked down and recognized the causeway, dissected by I-80 and I-5 farther south. It was flooded with water, and thousands of waterfowl were flying around it.

The causeway got farther and farther away as the plane climbed. To the east, he could see the Sacramento River snaking around towards downtown, where it would meet up with the American River.

Numbness slowly came over his body and he slumped against the window. He could think clearly, but he had little feeling in his limbs. He tried to lift his arm, but it didn't respond. Fear gripped him. They drugged me, he thought. "Yuri, what did you give me?" he slurred drunkenly. He tried to turn his body, but couldn't.

He heard Yuri's voice from the seat across from him. "It's

nothing to be alarmed about, Morton. I only gave you a muscle relaxer. A little GHB, as it's known on the street. You probably know it as the date rape drug. I know how you don't like to fly, and I just wanted to make you comfortable."

Yuri put his hands on Morton's chair and stood over him. "I'm really disappointed that you didn't follow my orders and get Matt Whiteside off my ass. Now he's stuck his nose in places that are disrupting my business."

Sweat beaded up on Morton's forehead and he started whimpering. "Yuri, I tried my best. He was given orders, in no uncertain terms, to quit. He must have acted on his own. My next move will be to have him fired." He started to crave another drink and thought about asking for one. His heart was pounding in his chest.

"You should have done that a couple of months ago," Yuri said, almost spitting. "That would have saved us all a lot of problems. Now we must go in a different direction."

Morton looked down at the farmland below through the window and noticed they weren't flying very high.

His hands shook uncontrollably, and he asked in a frightened voice, "What direction are we going in, Yuri? I don't remember flying this way to Vegas. We should be farther east." He pleaded with Yuri. "Tell me what you want me to say to the board and I'll say it. I won't tell them anything about our arrangement, I swear."

He felt someone pulling on his arms and strapping what felt like a large backpack to his torso. Someone reached around his waist and pulled the strap tightly, cinching the device to him. He tried to envision what it was on his back but drew a blank. He saw Mika out of the corner of his eye, adjusting something behind him. "What is that, Mika, a bomb? Are you trying to blow me up?"

Mika burst out laughing. "Come on, Morton, why would we strap a bomb onto you while in an airplane? We'd all get killed." He slapped Morton on the back. "No, you're in for a fun surprise."

The steady humming of the twin engines was the only other sound in the plane. Morton recognized the landmarks below them as they flew over: Elk Grove, Galt, and then Lodi. He noticed they had been following Highway 99 south, and he immediately recognized the Lodi Airport, which sat at the north end of the town by the many times he'd skydived from the place. As he stared out the window, he could see an older twin engine plane lifting off from the end of the runway, full of parachutists. It flew to the west, climbing for altitude.

Morton felt the plane banking to the west as it started to circle above the airport. Suddenly, he felt a rushing wind blowing over him, and he realized someone had opened the plane's door. He felt panic and he struggled to move. As the plane circled, he could see the other older plane a few hundred feet under them, and one after another, the parachutists jumped out, free falling down to earth for a few seconds before pulling their rip chords and releasing their colorful parachutes.

Morton felt a pair of hands roughly lift him up by the straps of the backpack, and a different set of hands lifted his feet. He was held parallel to the floor and rotated 180 degrees until he was facing the open door, the wind blowing in his face so hard he had to squint. His heart was racing, as he desperately tried to move his uncooperative limbs. His mouth twitched and he felt wetness between his legs as his bladder gave out.

Mika leaned into his ear and yelled, "Don't worry, Morton, you're in good hands. We bought you this brand new Icarus Safire parachute. As a skydiver you know, it's one of the best available, with a nine cell elliptical canopy, and it's in your favorite color, blue. We used your American Express card to buy it and at twenty-two hundred bucks, and it's the best parachute money can buy. Now here's the really good news: If it doesn't work, we'll get you your money back." He heard Mika and then Yuri laugh heartily as he felt himself being thrown from the plane. The onrushing burst of wind smashed into his body, causing him to tumble head over heels, catching a glimpse of the plane every second or so as he fell away from it. He managed to right himself so that he was facing the ground, which, through the slits of his eyes, he could see was racing up to him.

Out of the corner of his right eye, he caught sight of the bright parachutes floating below him. In two seconds he screamed past them as the startled parachutists stared down at him in disbelief. He struggled to breathe, his heart palpitating in his chest. He kept attempting to control his arms, which were being whipped back and forth across his body like a child's ragdoll. After what felt like an eternity, he began to gain some feeling in his right arm, and he fumbled with the backpack in an attempt to find the rip cord. The ground was coming at him at an alarming rate, the buildings and ground growing larger by the second. Suddenly, his fingers reached the cord and he started to pull. His eyes bulging, his heart racing, his jaw clenched, he screamed out, "Pull! Pull!" With every ounce of energy left in his body, he strained to yank the cord. With one final effort, he felt the rip cord disengaged and he felt the parachute start to fall out of the backpack. He closed his eyes and shrieked, "I got it! I'm saved!" One second later, the final thing he heard was honking horns and screeching tires as he splattered across the southbound lane of Highway 99.

TWENTY-NINE

The night was still, and a brilliant moon sat up high in the star filled sky. The muted light from the harvest moon gave the area an eerie glow. A few crickets were rubbing their legs and creating their own kind of racket. The deep croaking sound of some bullfrogs could be heard in a nearby pond, their voices carrying in the crisp fall night. Matt sat in his car and stared through a pair of binoculars at the ranch house across the field. He'd worn dark Levis, a black shirt, and a dark sweatshirt to be sure he would not be seen. Stephanie, sitting next to him, and Alan, in the back seat, also wore dark clothes. They all stared in the same direction, trying to detect any type of movement. He handed the binoculars to Alan. "I don't see anyone. See what you think."

Alan scoured the area around the house. After a few seconds, he pulled the binoculars down. "You're right. I don't see anything either. There's no car in the driveway." He handed the glasses back to Matt. "What are you thinking of doing?"

"Stephanie and I will go into the house in about thirty minutes and see if we can find that will," Matt replied. "Bonnie told you guys that the Johnsons put important papers in a fireproof box somewhere. I think we'll start in the master bedroom. Let's be thorough." He turned around, facing the back seat. "After we leave for the house, take the car and hide it behind that stack of hay bales over there." He pointed in the direction behind the back of the car. "I want you to watch down this road. If you see anyone coming down it, call us so we can get out."

He tapped Stephanie lightly on her thigh. "Are you ready?"

Her eyes showed fear, but she nodded bravely. "I'm ready."

"All right, Alan, we'll see you in a little while. Be alert."

Matt bent over and steadily walked across the recently harvested alfalfa field, his feet crunching the frosty ground as they headed toward the house. Stephanie kept pace a few feet behind him. Every hundred yards, he would stop and kneel on one knee to survey the area. He turned to Stephanie and asked, "Are you okay?"

"I'm good, Matt," she answered, breathing heavily.

He looked at the silhouette of her beautiful face lit by the soft moonlight. I wish I had a camera for this moment, he thought.

She had moved up beside him and knelt. A few cows could be heard mooing in the distance and the smell of freshly cut alfalfa hung in the air.

Stephanie whispered to him, "How far do we still have to go?"

Matt looked toward the silhouette of the house in the distance. "It's still about a quarter a mile away. Let's keep going." He reached out to take her hand. She smiled at him as he led her towards the house. After fifteen minutes of steady walking, they reached the corner of the garage.

They followed the garage and ended up by the back door. The bottom half of the door was wood paneled while the top half was made up of six glass panels. Matt shined the light into the house. Seeing nothing, he handed the light to Stephanie. He put on a pair of leather gloves, pulled a sheet rock knife from his coat, and started to cut the small frame holding the glass panel just above the door handle. He followed the outline of the panel with the knife all around the window. After working the knife around the window numerous times, the frame came off along with the glass window panel. Matt stuck his hand through the opening, turned the handle, and opened the door. He turned to Stephanie and made a sweeping motion with his arm. "After you."

Walking softly, they slowly made their way to the master bedroom. Matt flashed the light across the room. After a twenty minute search yielded nothing, Matt got up and sat on the bed. "What do you think, Stephanie? We've looked at all the logical places. We've looked in the dressers, the drawers, under the bed, in the closet."

She sat next to him and surveyed the room. "We must be overlooking something. If you had a ranch in the middle of nowhere and wanted to keep something safe, where would you put it? You certainly would not put it in a drawer or a closet. You wouldn't put it under the mattress or in the bathroom." She looked down at the floor were a throw rug covered an area about three feet around and under the bed. She got on her knees and pulled the rug back, shining the light from the flashlight across it. "Nothing here."

Suddenly they heard a car coming up the driveway, fast. Matt felt the phone in his pocket vibrating. He didn't need to answer it to know what it was ringing for. He quickly turned off the flashlight and looked around the room. "Quickly, Stephanie, we have to find a place to hide here. We don't have time to get outside." He grabbed her hand and headed to the closet. He found a section where a group of long dresses were hanging, and he pulled them back. He and Stephanie slid in and pulled the dresses back to conceal themselves, bending down to hide their faces.

He whispered to her, "This isn't very good, but we don't have many choices. Let's hope whoever's here doesn't need anything back here." She leaned in closer to him and squeezed his hand tightly.

They heard the car stop at the front of the house and the occupant get out. The front door opened and a light was turned on.

The person walked from the family room into the kitchen, and they could hear them switch on a light. Matt held his breath. I hope they don't see that the window is gone. He tried to remember if he left the window pane inside or outside the house. I think it was outside, but I'm not positive. We'll find out soon enough if I left it inside the door.

They heard the person walk down the hallway toward the master bedroom, then stop midway. Matt could feel Stephanie's pulse racing in her hand. His own breathing was quickening and he worried if his heart was pounding loud enough for the person to hear it.

A man's voice started talking, which startled Matt and made Stephanie gasp. She immediately put her hand to her mouth. The man spoke loudly into a cell phone. "Mika, I'm at the ranch house." There was a pause, and then he continued. "No, I haven't found anyone in the house, but I have a feeling someone's been here."

Matt could barely make out Stephanie's face, but he could see from the look in her eyes she was terrified. He felt the hair on the back of his neck rising, and his hands felt sweaty. He tried to think of what he might use as a weapon if the person were to continue farther down the hall. He strained his eyes to see if there might be any object heavy enough to use as a club. With his right hand, he slowly felt outward. He felt the tip of an umbrella and gripped it firmly.

The hall light was turned on, and it filtered into the bedroom. Footsteps started down the wooden floor of the hall towards them. A man appeared at the doorway to the bedroom and stopped, casting a long shadow across the room that ended at the entry to the closet. He continued speaking into his phone. "I was here an hour ago, Mika, when you called and asked me to pick up your girlfriend at the airport. Everything was quiet before I left. I don't know why it feels different, but it does." There was some muffled speaking from the other end of the phone. "Okay, Mika, I'll take another look around here and call you if I see anything."

A car horn started blaring from down the road. The man had taken a step into the bedroom and stopped upon hearing the noise. He reversed himself, walking back down the hall, flipping the lights off as he went and opening the front door. Good job, Alan, Matt thought.

"What's that?" Stephanie whispered.

"It's Alan. He's trying to get the guy's attention. Get ready to move."

They both heard the man walk out the front door and down the walkway, his boots grinding on the concrete. The horn stopped then started up again. The car in the front of the house started its engine. Matt grabbed Stephanie's hand. "Let's go."

As Matt stepped out of the closet, the floor beneath his foot moved and he stumbled forward, bumping his head on the wall. He yelled out. "Ouch!" then froze.

Stephanie turned to him and whispered, "Are you okay? What happened?"

Matt put his finger to his lip and listened. He waited a few seconds, hearing nothing. "I hit my head. I'm fine, let's keep moving."

They inched down the hallway with their backs against the wall. When Matt reached the kitchen, he stopped. He listened carefully but heard nothing but chirping crickets. The horn kept blaring in the distance. Finally it stopped and there was complete silence. Matt opened the door and they both slipped out. Matt reached down and put the pane of glass back in its spot on the door, carefully securing it with its trim. Walking quietly, they rounded the house the same way they came in. As they came around the garage, they saw a car heading toward them. Matt and Stephanie pressed themselves against the garage as headlights swept by, and they watched as the car sped down the driveway, its red tail lights glowing in the dust.

Matt bent over to slow down his breathing, his breath

vaporizing in the frosty air. Stephanie clung to his arm tightly.

"I don't think we should we go back inside, Matt. I don't think I've ever been this scared in my life."

Matted patted her hand. "I agree. It wouldn't be a good idea tonight. We can come back another night. Let's get across this field and find Alan."

❖

The next morning, Matt sat studying some charts on his computer. He rubbed his eyes, yawned, and sipped on a cup of Starbuck's coffee. His phone rang and he answered. "Hello?"

A woman's voice came on the phone. "Matt, it's Diane. I don't know if you heard, but Morton Bain was killed over the weekend in a skydiving accident near Lodi."

Matt sat up in his chair. "Really, Morton Bain? I didn't know he did daredevil activities. He always seemed kind of wimpy to me."

"I had heard he skydived," Diane said. "There are some irregularities about the accident that the authorities are looking into. His parachute was brand new, but it was barely open. He wasn't on the flight manifest that morning. Even though some of the other parachutists on the flight knew him, none of them saw him on the plane."

Matt wrote some notes on a notepad. "Do they think it's foul play?"

"The authorities aren't saying much right now," she said, "but they're investigating. Apparently, that particular skydiving company has had some problems before and has been fined in the past, so it could be legitimate. I guess we'll have to wait and see."

"What do we do about WMI?" he asked. "Our presentation in front of the Board was to have Morton explain his relationship with them and to shed light on what services they are providing. By the way, did you read that article I sent you from *The Sacramento Bee*

251

regarding WMI?"

"I did," Diane answered. "They're putting a lot of homeowners out of their homes, and it doesn't sound like they're doing it legally. That doesn't look good, and I'm sure the Board will want to distance General Technologies from that activity. They don't like bad publicity."

Matt took a sip of his coffee. "So I assume we are still on the calendar to make the presentation to the Board next week?"

"Yes, it's still on. I can tell you they will want to terminate WMI's contracts immediately."

Matt thought about that for a second. That will not go over well with Yuri Kletcko, and that's not going to be a pleasant phone call. "Who will be telling WMI that they are fired?" Matt asked.

Diane laughed. "Why, you of course, Matt. You're the one who discovered the issues with them, so you should be the one that breaks the news."

"Thanks, Diane," he said glumly. "I'm looking forward to that."

"It's my pleasure. Well, I'll let you know if I hear anything further about Morton's death. In the meantime, send me the draft copy of the report you're presenting, and we can discuss it later in the week."

Matt hung up the phone and set it on his desk. He folded his hands together and rested his chin on them. There have been so many unexplained deaths around here lately. If Yuri's behind them, does that mean I'm on his list? His felt a shiver go down his spine.

The Olive Garden in Citrus Heights, a suburb of Sacramento, was bustling for a Tuesday evening. Servers bounded around the restaurant, taking orders and delivering dishes. The smell of fresh bread and garlic permeated the air. Matt and Stephanie sat at a table with a lone red carnation rising from a white vase sitting in the middle of the table. He sipped a beer and studied the menu in front of him. He looked up. "What do you feel like tonight, Steph?"

"I think I'll go with the soup and salad. I'm not that hungry." She set her menu down. "When do you think we should go back to the Johnsons', Matt? I'm almost over being scared out of my wits." She halfheartedly smiled at him.

Matt stared at her for a second. "Tomorrow night might be a good night. I wanted to let a few days go by before we went back, so they'll relax their defenses." He leaned forward and raised his eyebrows at her. "Tell me again how you talked me into this adventure."

She grinned and took a sip of her wine, locking her eyes with his. "I brought you in because you're a pro. You've done this before, remember."

Matt made a grimacing face. "I remember, but I also remember Mr. Whitney ended up dead. I would prefer not to meet the same fate. So what was it you were going to tell me tonight about the Johnsons' case?"

Stephanie leaned in and spoke softly. "Alan spoke to the Sheriff of Yolo County today." She paused. "He thinks they've found the car that sideswiped the Johnsons' at a body shop in Rancho Cordova."

A server came up and put a basket of bread at their table. She waited until he left. "The sheriff got a tip Monday and they picked up the car yesterday. The forensics team is going over it as we speak."

Matt raised his eyebrows in surprise. "How long will it take them to figure out if it's the right car?"

She cast a quick glance over her shoulder and continued. "Alan thinks they are pretty confident it's the right car, but there's something else. The front end and bumper had a big dent in it, as if it had run into a large animal."

"Guess who the car is registered to?"

"Was it Mika Menski?" asked Matt.

"No, not to him, but close. It was registered to the WMI Corporation. It's a black Mercedes, the same type as the one Mika drives."

"What else did Alan say?"

Stephanie tapped her fingernails on the table nervously. "He thinks if the sheriff's department finds anything significant, they will convene a grand jury and get an indictment. But it could take a few weeks to do that. Here's what I'm worried about. If Yuri gets ahold of the will before we do, he will keep that land for himself. With the land go the water rights. Caroline is positive she can get those rights through Yolo County's pending action, but Yuri won't let that happen, either by legal or other means." She paused, looking at him intently. "We both have seen his other means."

Their food arrived and they slowly picked at their food. Matt spoke between bites. "Here's another interesting thing I found. Yuri bought a small water company just north of Bakersfield from General Technologies. One of our directors was in cahoots with him, and that director just turned up dead in a suspicious skydiving accident."

Stephanie's eyes grew wide. "Another person connected to Yuri turns up dead? You're kidding?"

Matt shrugged and continued eating. "No, but it's starting to come to me why Yuri wanted that water company. He'll take the water allocation he gets for the Johnson ranch and sell it to a company called Southern Cal Water through his water company. Southern Cal Water will probably pay double what any local entity or Northern California company would pay, because they need the water badly."

"Can he sell water to Southern Cal Water?" Stephanie asked.

Matt nodded. "I'm not sure, but if I was a betting man, I'd say yes. Why else would Yuri want a Podunk water company in the middle of nowhere? Selling the water down south won't be a popular move around here. If news about it ever got out, it would give

Caroline some populist backing in her quest to get that water through eminent domain."

A young couple sat at the table across from them, and their small child started screaming. Both Stephanie and Matt winced at the ear piercing screams. The father picked up the child, chiding her calmly, and headed out of the restaurant.

Matt looked at Stephanie with raised eyebrows. "Did you mention to me once that you wanted kids?"

She threw her head back and laughed. "I did, but I only want angels, not brats."

He smiled at her. "I'm sure that's what every prospective parent wishes for." He pointed at the door where the child and her father went out. "But many end up with that instead."

"Maybe," she said. "But mine will be different, you'll see. So what do we do about Caroline? I don't think she realizes how ruthless Yuri can be. I think she believes, since he will get compensation from the county for his water, all will be good. I'm sure Yuri doesn't feel the same way."

Matt held his hands apart. "You're right, Stephanie. We're talking millions of dollars annually. If Yuri sells the ranch with the increased water rights, he would stand to make a huge profit. He won't settle for the chump change the county wants to give him."

Matt reached over the table and placed his hand over Stephanie's. She looked up at him, surprised. "I'm sorry how things have turned out, but I want to make it up to you. I want to see you more, to be with you more. I love you, Stephanie, and I don't want to be without you."

Stephanie pulled her hand back and set it on her lap. Her eyes welled up with tears. "Do you realize what you've put me through, Matt? These past few months have been hell. I've been sleepwalking through the days. Now all of a sudden you want to forget everything and pretend nothing has happened? What about your old girlfriend? What happened to her?

Matt ran his hands through his hair. "I know I've acted like an ass, and I'm sorry. I never meant to hurt you, Stephanie, I swear. Kathy Ann was a figment of my imagination, and she will never interfere in our lives again. I don't expect you to forgive me right away, but I want to earn back your trust and your love. Can you at least allow me to do that?"

Stephanie shifted in her seat and dabbed her eyes with her napkin. She looked Matt in the eye. "We can move slowly in that direction, Matt. I'm not diving back into this relationship only to find out you changed your mind again. Yes, you can earn my trust, but it won't happen overnight. I need time to see if you are sincere."

Matt leaned back in his chair and smiled. "That's fair enough. I'm only asking you to give me another chance, but I promise you this won't happen again. I've learned my lesson."

"We'll see, Mr. Whiteside." She checked her watch. "We should go. I told Alan I'd meet him at 7:30 tomorrow morning at the Hyatt to compare notes and see what our next step is." She stifled a yawn with the back of her hand. "I'm really tired. It's been a long week."

Matt felt a twinge of jealousy at the mention of Alan. Knock it off, he thought to himself, you're the reason we're not together. It's not her fault other men desire her.

He looked around for the waiter to bring him the check. "I'm with you. We've still got a long week ahead. I'll pay the bill and we can get out of here."

THIRTY

The traffic on J Street was steady at the noon hour. It was a beautiful sunny day. The trees in the park were turning yellow, orange, and bright red as they clung to the last days of their life cycle. The farmer's market was in full swing in Caesar Chavez Park, just down from the State Capitol. Local farmers were selling their fresh tomatoes, celery, onions, garlic, and other produce from booths covered by white canopies. Office workers on their lunch hour browsed from booth to booth, picking over the fresh produce. A few yards north of the produce section, a group of food vendors served up everything from sushi to tacos. Although the park was bustling with people, the steady traffic surrounding it was the sound heard above everything else.

Alan sat on a bench just past the food vendors, finishing up a homemade tamale, trying not to spill anything on his light green Bill Bass shirt. Several pigeons strutted around him, hoping for a piece of tamale. They were joined by two more of their feathered brethren, all prancing in circles around Alan's feet. A couple yards away, a homeless man slept soundly under a fir tree, his worldly possessions stuffed into a rusty shopping cart parked by his head.

Alan wiped his hands on a napkin and tossed it into a paper bag.

He took a swig of bottled water and surveyed the park. He thought he spotted Amber making her way through the market towards him, a couple of files under her arm. At a distance, her tiny figure made her look like a small child. Wearing a brown business suit with a white ruffled blouse and a frizzy blonde wig, she moved briskly through the crowd, pausing every twenty steps to look over her shoulder. Large, dark sunglasses hid her eyes as she surveyed the park.

I wonder how she became friends with Mellissa, Alan wondered. I know they worked together, but they seem so different. He waved at her and she acknowledged him, walking with the same steady gait. Alan stood when she reached him and stuck his hand out for her to shake. "Thanks for meeting me, Amber. I appreciate your time. Nice outfit, I might say. I barely recognized you."

Amber set the files next to Alan and sat down. "That was the idea, Alan."

"Did you get a chance to eat?" he asked "I can get you something here if you're hungry."

She shook her head, looking around the food court. "No thanks. I don't have a lot of time, so let me show you what I've got." She glanced around the park nervously then sat down on the bench. She lifted up the first file and handed it to Alan. It was at least an inch thick. "That one is the file Mellissa kept on WMI's activity. She was very thorough. In it she has written names, dates, events, banks, and who was doing what."

Alan thumbed through the file slowly. Without looking up, he asked, "Can you give me a summation of what she was trying to prove in these files?"

Amber sighed. "This is why the mortgage division of WMI is in existence, to make money off the backs of distressed homeowners. They are buying bundled mortgages from numerous banks at ten cents on the dollar. The banks want these mortgages off their books because if they don't sell them, the Federal Deposit Insurance

Corporation could render the banks insolvent, and the banks could be liquidated. At the same time, the banks don't want to be foreclosing on every loan they have, because it's giving them a public relations black eye. So they sell a large portion to investors like WMI."

Alan kept reading the contents of the files.

"So how does WMI profit from these loans, you might ask? If banks foreclose on these loans, they're stuck with a huge amount of undervalued houses and no market to sell them. They lose a lot of money and look like bullies in the court of public opinion in the process." Amber looked around the park again before continuing. "However, if the banks sell these loans at a discount to WMI, the banks can claim they don't own the loans and that they're only servicing them. That allows WMI to foreclose on the homes, turn around and sell them, and put in a claim to the TARP program of the Federal Government for the difference between the selling price and the full amount of the loan. The TARP fund pays WMI back, and WMI pockets the difference. Quite a deal, I might say."

Alan did some calculations in his head. I'd say it's a good deal, he thought.

Two teenagers swept by on skateboards, dodging in and out of the people wandering on the sidewalk that lead to the center of the park. There were a couple of near collisions and some choice words thrown in their direction. Alan paused for a second, watching the chaos.

"So far it doesn't sound like anything illegal is being done. If anything, it sounds like a smart business strategy."

"It would be, except the banks are stringing the homeowners along," Amber said as she checked out her nails. "They supposedly are trying to help modify these people's loans so they can stay in their houses, but WMI is pushing the foreclosures through the back door, and getting the courts to drop the gavel on the foreclosure action. The next thing the homeowner knows is the sheriff's department is at their door forcing them to evacuate their homes. It's heart wrenching to watch these people lose everything."

"That's interesting," Alan said. These guys are slaying it, he thought. They have a guaranteed profit from the Feds and could care less about the homeowners. No wonder the people who've lost their homes are up in arms. I'd be angry too if it happened to me. He set all the files in his briefcase. "And everything is here in these files, all the illegal activity?" he asked.

"I don't know about everything, but it looks like she has covered a lot, and she outlines pretty well what the program is at WMI. I'm just happy to get them out of my possession. I keep thinking one of Yuri's henchmen is going to show up at my doorstep any day and demand I give them up." Amber slapped her hands on her lap. "I guess that does it for me. You know everything I know."

"So do you think Yuri knows you have these files or knows that Mellissa confided in you?" Alan asked.

She nodded. "I'm sure Yuri knows that Mellissa and I were good friends. I'm sure he would assume the worst, so I'm not waiting to find out what he is planning to do to me."

"Do you think these files had anything to do with Mellissa's death?"

Amber shook her head. "I don't know, Alan. Mellissa didn't hide the fact that she was not happy with what she was being forced to do for her job. She hinted to anyone who would listen, that she would blow the whistle someday. But would that cause someone to want her dead? I could see her getting fired, but not killed. You tell me."

Alan nodded. "Yeah, that is a radical way to shut someone up. The old fashioned way would be to fire them. I'll pass these on to District Attorney Jan Wilson to see where she wants to take it." He picked up the last file. "So tell me about this file, the one that is named 'New London.'"

Amber shifted her weight nervously. "New London is an eminent domain case that went to the United States Supreme Court.

Caroline Bennett, Mellissa's best friend, was to use that action to get Yolo County to take the water rights for a neighboring ranch. Mellissa was the person who was to bring the action to the board. She thought the idea was brilliant and had done a ton of research on the case. After she was killed, Caroline got someone else to bring the action to the board."

"Did she think Caroline can pull off this action?" Alan asked. "If you ask most people, it would seem like using the county to take water rights from one person and giving it to another is paramount to stealing. That doesn't seem right."

Amber rubbed her hands together nervously. "The way Mellissa explained it to me, it was all legal and for the public good." She tapped the file with her index finger. "She explains it all in the file."

A fire engine, its siren blazing, came roaring up J Street heading away from downtown. Both Alan and Amber turned to watch it go by.

Alan looked at her. "I understand the thought process of utilizing the water rights, but I'm still stuck on how the county will be able to convince a judge that it is in the best interests of the public to take one person's rights and transfer it to another."

"Well, the county will compensate the ranch owner for the rights," Amber said. "The value is determined by an independent appraiser, so it's not like they steal them."

"I'm sure an appraisal will be done, but it will be low and in the favor of the county. That is where the court battle will be."

Amber stood up and extended her hand. "That's all above my pay scale, Alan. I'm leaving town. The tension at WMI is high, and Yuri is sure I'm the one who's leaking things to the press."

Alan looked up. "Really?"

"Yes, really. Thank you for taking these files off my hands. I didn't know who to give them to and I'm glad to get rid of them."

"Where are you going?" he asked

"I'm sorry, Alan, but I'm not telling anyone. You've got my

private email, so if you need to get ahold of me, contact me through that."

"Thank you for your help, Amber. Take care of yourself. There is a lot of money at stake, and the people Caroline is messing with aren't nice. If anything strange happens, call me immediately."

Amber sighed deeply. "I'm really scared, Alan, but I will call you if anything comes up."

He stood and watched her walk back across the park and disappear around the corner of a building. He sat back on the bench and opened up his briefcase. *How is Caroline going to pull this off?* he thought. *She knows there will be an enormous court fight, and it could take years to sort out. Is she trying to bluff her neighbors into selling their rights?*

His phone rang and he picked it up. "Hello?"

"Alan, it's John Cranston. I wanted to let you know the car we impounded from that body shop is the same car that ran into the Johnsons' car."

"It is?" Alan said.

"We also found some clothing fibers that match the clothes Mellissa Burns was wearing the night she died. They were found on the driver's side headlight, which is consistent with the eyewitness's account of where she was struck."

Alan raised his eyebrows. "Any idea who was driving the car?"

"There was only one set of fingerprints in the car: Mika Menski. I've issued a warrant for his arrest."

Alan started walking rapidly toward his office, knowing he needed to tell Stephanie about this. "This Menski guy is loose cannon. Do you have any idea where he might be holed up?"

"We think he's over at his cousin's place in Rancho Cordova. I've got an APB on him right now." He paused for a second. "The autopsy came back for John Roth, the Johnsons' attorney. He had large amounts of the anthracylines, daunorubicin, and doxorubicin in his system. Those drugs are used to treat cancer but can induce a heart attack. It looks like he might have been murdered."

Alan started running toward his office, his phone held tightly to his ear. "Thanks for the info, John. Please let me know the minute you catch Mika. I've got to go." As he ran, he thought, This is starting to become clearer. I need to get the information Amber gave me on WMI to the district attorney. Yuri and his band of merry miscreants will be trapped in a corner soon, and I don't think they will roll over without a fight.

He rushed into his office and handed the files to the receptionist. "Make a copy of these and get them over to District Attorney Jan Wilson's office immediately," he shouted to her as he ran by. "Give the original to John Parker and have him send a copy to Dave Flour at *The Sacramento Bee*. I know John's in court, but have him call me when he gets out. Have Jan call me as soon as she reads the file." He bolted into his office and dialed his phone. It rang five times, and then he heard Stephanie's voice come on as it went to voicemail. "Stephanie, it's Alan," he spoke, trying to catch his breath. "Call me immediately when you get this message. It's urgent."

He hung up and plopped down in his chair. Where would she be? he thought. I know she and Matt had talked about going back to the Johnsons' ranch tonight, but they need to wait until Mika is in custody. He's out of their league, and they don't need to cross paths with him right now.

Alan opened his desk drawer and found Matt's business card. He dialed his number only to get his voicemail. He cracked the knuckles of his hands and nervously tapped the desk top. "I can't stand sitting around waiting," he mumbled. "I need to do something." He pulled his Glock out of its holster and checked its clip. It was full with fifteen ten-millimeter bullets. Satisfied, he slid it back in the holster and headed out the door.

THIRTY-ONE

Yuri held his cell phone to his ear as he paced back and forth behind his desk. Ivan sat across from him stiffly, trying to catch any of the conversation coming through the phone. Even though he was five feet away from Yuri, he could hear an agitated voice. When Yuri finally spoke into the phone, his voice was shaky. "Look, Artie, I'm doing everything I can. I've called the insurance company twice a day. Everything was on schedule and they were going to cut a check last week. At the last minute they were tipped off that there might be an investigation into the accident, and they've used that as an excuse to stall us."

"You've told me all that before, Yuri, and I've passed that information on," Artie replied. "You don't understand Carlos Diego. He doesn't care about your problems. You got him to invest in the Johnson ranch with the guarantee he would be repaid immediately after the Johnsons were taken care of. It's been over a week since they died, and he's not happy."

Yuri glanced over at Ivan with a nervous look. He wiped his forehead with a handkerchief. "I'm not happy either, Artie, but I can't fly to Omaha and cut the check myself. Tell Carlos to give me some time and I'll get it handled."

"I'll ask him, Yuri, but I don't make any promises. Carlos also wants you to buy him out of WMI. The press is bad and the heat is getting too intense. He and the Cartel don't want to get dragged into an investigation of the company. He'll take twenty million for his share, which he feels is a bargain for you."

Yuri continued wiping his forehead. His upper lip trembled and he started to stammer. "Twenty million, Artie? That may be a good deal, but it's money I don't have this minute. I need some time. In two months, I'll be receiving a big check for water rights on the ranch after I get the new allocation."

The phone was silent for a minute. Yuri could hear paper rustling on the other end. He strained to hear. "Uh, from what I'm reading here in *The Sacramento Bee*, that may be a problem for you." He paused as the paper rustled some more on the other end of the line. Artie continued. "There is some noise about a will that leaves the Johnson ranch to UC Davis. Then there is the issue of Yolo County going after your water rights through eminent domain. That doesn't sound to me like you'll be getting any big checks soon. What is your plan B?"

Yuri put his hand over the mouthpiece and whispered to Ivan. "Get ahold of Mika. Tell him to be ready; I'm going to need him tonight." He lifted his hand and spoke into the phone. "There are a couple of people here that are standing in my way, I'll admit, but I'm preparing to deal with them. Ask Carlos to give me two more months and I'll be able to pay him back."

"I will relay your message, Yuri, but I'll give you some unsolicited advice," he said sternly, as if talking to a child. "If Carlos gives you the time and you don't come through with the money, you might want to think about moving away; far away. Carlos will send someone to find you."

"Thanks, Artie, I'll keep that advice in mind." He hung up and flipped the phone on the desk in disgust.

"I assume Carlos Diego is not happy with the current state of events," Ivan stated, nervously wringing his hands. "What are you planning to do, Yuri?"

Yuri wandered over to the window and stared at storm clouds gathering in the distance. A pair of businessmen in suits and ties holding briefcases walked in front of his window on their way to the parking lot. They were in deep conversation and never noticed him looking at them. "It's time to make some moves. Tell Mika and Marc to meet us at The Firehouse restaurant in Old Town at eight o'clock. We'll make our move tonight."

The bar in The Firehouse Restaurant was quiet. Historic photos of Sacramento's early days hung on the walnut-stained, paneled walls. A piano sat silently in the corner, covered with a black leather tarp. The bar was dimly lit, with wall sconces giving off a yellow light, and the low-wattage under-cabinet lighting above the stepped liquor cabinet was the only other light. At the center of each of the fifteen small circular tables, a lone battery-operated candle in a cranberry-colored bowl flickered silently. Yuri, Ivan, Marc, and Mika huddled around one of the tables in the far corner of the room. An older man in a Hawaiian shirt and shorts and a youthful-looking woman sat at the bar conversing with the twenty-something bartender.

Yuri swirled ice around in his drink. In a low voice, Ivan spoke in Marc's ear as he listened stone-faced. Yuri finally spoke discreetly. "I've tried to avoid carrying out what I'm about to do tonight, but I'm out of options. Let me lay out the plan for all of you."

He pulled out a small notepad and wrote as he spoke. He first addressed Marc, giving him written instructions. He then went over the plans with Mika, underlining a few points for emphasis. Finally, he gave Ivan his instructions. "All right, you all know what's at stake," Yuri said. "Mika, you and Marc go first. After you finish, all of you will meet me on the tarmac at McClellan Air Force Base, where my plane will be waiting. I will leave the vehicle gate open for you. We will be wheels up within minutes after your arrival."

Mika asked, "Excuse me, Uncle. Are you sure they're going to be there? How long should we wait if they aren't there?"

"They'll be there, Mika, I promise you," he answered. "They will also have the document we've been searching for. Whatever you do, get that document and head to the airport. Call me when you're en route."

He looked from face to face. "Okay, go out and do your job and I'll see you in a few hours."

Mika and Marc got up and left the room.

Yuri turned to Ivan. "You and I have a few minutes to kill. How about another round, old friend?"

Ivan smiled. "That sounds good. I'll buy." He got up and moved toward the bar. Yuri folded his hands together and pressed them against his temples knowing he had one shot to salvage the operation.

THIRTY-TWO

Classical music played from the Bose stereo system sitting on the ornate table in Caroline's formal living room. A stained glass Tiffany lamp with dangling crystal stalactites threw a soft light around the room. A large oil painting of a fox hunt, complete with hounds and formally dressed hunters on horseback in their red coats, white pants, and black knee-high boots, hung above the colorful couch. Caroline sat sipping her champagne, as she listened to Stephanie explain the recent events of the past few weeks. Matt sat in a chair next to her, his hands folded, listening intently. Both wore dark coats that had small water beads on them from the light rain that was falling outside.

Caroline subtly looked Matt up and down, admiring his good looks and wishing this were a private meeting. She turned her attention back to Stephanie and listened to her explain about Yuri, the Johnsons, Mellissa, and John Roth. She stifled a yawn. Mr. Kletcko is bad news alright, but I don't think he's stupid enough to rough up a sitting board supervisor, and certainly not stupid enough to touch me.

Stephanie stopped talking and looked at Matt. "Did I miss anything, Matt?" Before he could answer, she spoke to Caroline.

"We think you should stay away from your ranch for a few days, to be on the safe side."

Matt jumped in. "Stephanie's right, Miss Bennett."

Caroline held up her hand. "Please call me Caroline, Matt. Miss is just so formal."

Matt nodded. "Okay, Caroline. Until the authorities have Yuri Kletcko in custody, you should stay away from here. There are too many things that have his fingerprints on them. If Yuri is what we think, violence is in his DNA."

Caroline clasped her hands together. "I understand what you are telling me, and I appreciate your concern for me. And here I thought all you were doing was a documentary about me, Stephanie." She smiled.

Matt slowly looked at Stephanie, and she cleared her throat before she spoke. "That was what we were doing initially, Caroline, but things have changed, and we couldn't let what we found out not be told to you."

Taking a sip of her champagne, she studied Stephanie. Something tells me you're not telling me everything, sweetie, she thought. But that's all right. This isn't my first rodeo, and I'm not afraid of some two-bit developer, wanna-be gangster. I can handle myself, thank you.

Caroline set her glass on the table. "Don't get me wrong. I'm grateful for you telling me all this, and I take what you're telling me seriously. But I'm not ready to jump to the conclusion that somehow my life is in imminent danger. I'll be careful, but more than likely I'm going to stay put. I'll see if Monte can stay the night with me, and I'll try to get my ranch foreman to stay over in the ranch office. Unfortunately, I've got a lot of things going on around here that need my attention, and I can't just disappear for a few days."

Stephanie stood up and picked up her purse, which was sitting by her feet. "It's getting late." Matt followed her lead. "Thank you for hearing us out. Matt and I both hope we're wrong, but we want you to stay safe. Please call if you need us."

Caroline walked them to the front door. "I will surely do that. Keep in touch if anything new transpires." Caroline stood by her front door and watched them walk away through the shadows of the trees. After they drove off, she shut the door and refilled her glass.

What if they're right? she thought. What if Yuri is crazy enough to try to harm me? She wandered into the office and pulled open the second drawer from the top. Picking up the Kimber 1911 pistol with its Lasergrip, she checked the Bullet Bore clip to see that it was full. Holding it to the light and moving it around in her hands, she turned the gun toward the Tiffany lamp in the living room. She aimed the barrel at it and made an imaginary bang while lifting the gun back as if it had recoiled.

Checking to see if a bullet was chambered and seeing that it was, she walked to her bedroom and stuck the gun under her pillow. Nothing like a bit of insurance, she thought. If anybody tries to visit me, they'll be in for a surprise.

Yawning, she headed to her closet. I'm tired. Tomorrow is a big day with the appraisal of the water rights being available to the public for the first time. It's sure to be a riotous meeting, and I'm going to need some sleep. It's going to be a long day.

She heard her own voice telling Monte to turn the light off and to get into bed. He wouldn't pay attention, so she yelled at him, "Monte, turn off that damn light!" Her voice awoke her and she looked groggily up to see the lamp by her bed on and the silhouette of a man standing next to her nightstand. She froze in terror. She looked at the other side of her bed and saw no one was there. Her mind raced in different directions, and then she remembered the gun, grab the gun. She reached under her pillow and fumbled around. Feeling nothing, she ripped the pillow back and stared at the empty space. Her heart was racing as she started to panic. Where did it go?

The man dangled the Kimber handgun in front of her face. "You lookin' for this?"

Instinctively, she lunged and tried to grab the gun from him, but he pulled it back and slapped her across the face with it. Stunned, she tasted the blood that trickled from her mouth and felt the right side of her face swelling. "Who are you, what do you want?" she shrieked. "Get out of my bedroom before I call the police."

"Shut up, Caroline, and do as you're told if you don't want to get hurt." The man spoke gruffly as he stuffed the Kimber into his waistband. "Get your ass out of bed."

"How do you know my name? What do you want?" Her breathing was labored as she tried to calm herself. Her eyes grew wide as she tried to focus on the man in the dim light, but she didn't recognize him. She scanned the room, looking for something to defend herself with, hoping against hope that she might have left something useful around.

"Hurry up," the man barked at her as he waved the gun in front of her. "I don't have all day."

Caroline did as she was told, throwing the covers off and exposing her long tanned legs. Her Victoria's Secret baby doll pajamas barely covered her. She stood before him shivering, and wrapped her arms around her waist.

"Turn around and put your hands behind your back," he snarled.

Turning, she felt the intruder yank her hands together. He slid a plastic zip tie over her wrists and tightened it. "You're hurting me," she cried out.

He roughly loosened the cuffs a little, and then he yanked her forward, causing her to stumble. "Come on, we're going for a ride," he grunted.

"Where are you taking me?" she pleaded. "Can I get a coat please?"

The intruder shoved her forward. "Just shut up." He pushed her toward the door, and as she walked he ogled her fanny. "Anyway, I like the way you're dressed. He thrust out his hand and groped her. "You know, for an old broad, you have a nice ass."

Caroline turned as she shuffled forward, giving him a nasty look but still shaking with fear. "Who are you and what are you planning to do with me?" she asked again, this time with more angst.

"I'm Mika, but it's not important who I am. You're what's important. I told you we were going for a ride and that's all you have to know." He directed her out the front door to a waiting black Crown Victoria limousine. Another man sat in the driver's seat with the ignition running. He nodded at Mika as he led Caroline into the car. She slid over and Mika joined her in the back seat. He pulled a cloth from his pocket and tied it around her mouth.

"Okay Marc, we're all secure back here. Let's advance to stage two." He slapped Caroline on the thigh. "This will be fun."

Caroline recoiled. She stared at Mika then at Marc. Mika leered at her lustily. Oh my god, she thought, what are they going to do to me?

THIRTY-THREE

The haystack stood about twenty feet tall and ran almost thirty feet in length. The moon peeked through the clouds with just enough light to cast a shadow across the field and light up the silhouette of the house in the distance. Matt rested on his haunches, his back against the haystack and looked through the binoculars. He put them down and turned to Stephanie, who was kneeling by his side. A soft rain fell upon them, creating small drips off the bills of the baseball caps they both wore. "Everything looks quiet. Let's go see if we can find that will."

Bent over and trying to keep a low profile, they started across the alfalfa field. Every so often, they would slip on the wet ground. "This feels like déjà vu, except for the rain," he said as they crept forward. "The only thing missing is Alan, waiting at the end of the street."

"Do you think the will is still there, Matt?" Stephanie asked. "I wonder if they are still looking for it."

Matt turned to her and answered softly, "I know they are looking for it, if they haven't already found it. If the ranch were to be donated to UC Davis, it would make Kletcko a very unhappy man."

They made their way slowly across the field until they reached the front corner of the garage. Like the time they had been there before, there was no activity around the house and it was completely dark. The rain had stopped and they shook themselves like dogs to get the water off. Matt moved around to the back door with Stephanie on his hip. He looked down at the door then back at Stephanie. "It looks the same as we left it the other day. Let's go in."

He pried the trim away from the window pane, pulled the pane off, and reached in to open the door. They wiped their feet furiously on a well-worn mat at the base of the door and went in. He turned on his flashlight briefly to get his bearings and then headed to the master bedroom. He turned the flashlight on the floor to the doorway. They spent the next hour going over every inch of the room but came up empty.

Matt sat down on the edge of the bed, looking dejected. "I don't know where else to look. Maybe we should go to the living room."

Stephanie came over and sat next to him. "That sounds as good a place to look as any."

As Matt stood, he stared into the closet. He moved to where they had hidden from the stranger the last time they were there. "Wait a second, Stephanie." He held the light and pulled back the string of long dresses hanging on the pole. He stepped to the back of the closet and pushed down hard with his foot on the floor. He continued probing the floor with his foot until he hit a spot that gave in. "Stephanie, come here," he whispered with some urgency. "Hold my light."

Stephanie shined the light on the floor as Matt felt around the area with his hand. He stopped, rubbed the floor, and then pulled the pocket knife out of his coat. He pried at a seam between boards with the knife and slowly lifted open a small door. He reached down, finding a false floor, and pulled a metal box from inside it. Stephanie could see him smiling in the light. "Well looky here. This is what I tripped on the other night. We'd have never found it if I hadn't stood right on this spot and made the floor cave in."

He moved out of the closet and set the box on the floor in the middle of the room.

Stephanie kept the light on the box and looked at him. She smiled a big smile and said, "Let me open it. Let's see what we got."

Matt took the light and watched while she slowly opened it. She pulled out a dozen stock certificates, two life insurance policies, and a folded document. She carefully unfolded it and read the top: Final Will and Testament of Betty Lou and Kenneth Johnson. It was signed by both Johnsons and witnessed by John Roth. Stephanie scanned the document, flipping to the second page. She stopped reading and brought the document closer to her face. Smiling, she looked up at Matt. "There it is, right there on page two. They left the ranch and everything on it to UC Davis. This will confirm it."

Matt reached out. "Let me look at it." She handed it to him and watched as he studied it. "That's it alright. Okay, let's get out of here."

He had just put the lid down on the box when the silence was shattered by a loud explosion from a gunshot coming from the bedroom doorway. Stephanie screamed and Matt jumped about two feet. Smoke and cordite filled the room, making it difficult to see. Matt could barely make out the figures of two men standing in the doorway, one with a smoking gun in his left hand. One of the men moved over to a lamp standing by a chair and turned on the light. The room lit up. The man spoke in a taunting voice. "I want to thank you for finding the copy of the will for us. We've been looking all over for it."

I know that voice, Matt thought. "Well, Mika, we finally meet," Matt said matter-of-factly. Stephanie stared at Matt with a terrified look, then back at Mika. Matt continued. "I'm glad we helped you find the will, but we have to get it to the proper authorities. They've been looking for it too. I'm sure you understand." He started to get up. "Now, if you don't mind, we'll be on our way."

Mika laughed and pushed Matt back to the floor with his foot.

"Oh, I understand." His voice turned serious. "Unfortunately, the proper authorities, as you say, will never see that document." He leaned over and snatched the will from Matt's hands. He opened it, looked at it quickly, and then stuffed it into his jacket. He pointed the gun at Stephanie. "I didn't know you kept such nice-looking company." He bent down and pulled her head up by her chin, studying her face. "I can see this is shaping up to be an enjoyable night." Matt tried to come at him, but Mika whacked him in the head with the solid steel butt of his gun, a Ruger SP .357 magnum revolver, knocking Matt on his back. He pulled himself up on his hands, shaking his head to clear it.

Stephanie cried out, "Matt!" She crawled over to him and cradled his head. He was bleeding from a cut above his eye. He shook his head again and focused his eyes. "I'm okay, Steph." He looked up at Mika. "Okay, what now? You got your document, now let us go. You don't need us anymore."

"Oh you are so wrong, my friend. We are far from done with you. Didn't you know that snitches get stitches?" Mika turned to the second man and snapped, "Tie him up, Marc, and take him to the car." Mika turned back to Stephanie. He reached for his belt and loosened it. "I've got some business to discuss with the young lady here."

Marc stepped forward and grabbed his hand. "Don't be stupid, Mika. We're on a tight schedule. Wait until we're in the air."

Mika gave him an ugly stare, but he re-buckled his belt. Marc kicked Matt in the back and pushed him to his stomach. He roughly clasped Matt's hands behind his back, binding them with a plastic zip tie. He grabbed Matt by the arm and pulled him up. "Get up and let's get moving. Hurry up, Mika. Get her tied up and let's go."

Matt's head throbbed from the drubbing he took from Mika's gun. He tried to think of what they might have in store for them. We have nothing of any value. They can't possibly want to rob us. What did he mean by wait until we're in the air? As Matt was pushed through the front door, he saw a black limousine parked in the driveway. It looked like there was another person inside the limo, but because of the limited light, he couldn't make out who it was.

Mika opened the door and roughly threw Stephanie in first. Matt heard her cry out, "Caroline! Are you okay?" The answer was garbled. Matt was thrown in next. When his eyes adjusted, he saw Caroline, still in her pajamas, huddled in the corner of the limo, a gag across her mouth. Her eyes were as wide as saucers, and when she tried to speak, it only came out as a muffled sound.

Stephanie slid over to her, speaking excitedly. "How did you end up here? Did they get you at your home?" Caroline nodded yes, excitedly.

Mika stuck his head in the door, waving the Ruger revolver menacingly in front of the three of them. "Welcome to WMI limo service. Our drive to the airport will be about forty minutes. Sit back and enjoy the ride." He leaned in and breathed on Stephanie's neck. "I've got a special evening planned for you, gorgeous." He tried to lick her ear, but she pulled away. He snarled at her. "That's okay, pretty lady, go ahead and play hard to get. I like feisty women."

Matt kicked at him. "Why don't you lick me? It's easy to be a bully when you've got a gun."

Mika spit at him. "Shut up, Matt. You're lucky my uncle wants you alive because it would give me great pleasure to blow your head off." The door slammed, and the tinted window separating the driver and the passengers rolled up, leaving Matt, Stephanie, and Caroline in silence. Matt felt the limo jerk forward and then accelerate. Mika said we were heading toward the airport, he thought. What airport and where are they taking us from there? He tried to reach into his back pocket to retrieve his cell phone, but it was gone. In the confusion, Mika must have taken it. "Stephanie, did they get your phone?" he asked.

She felt around her jeans and shook her head. "Yes, it's gone." She got up on her knees and felt with her hands for the gag on

Caroline's mouth. She found it and, after a few moments of tugging and pulling, got it loosened. Caroline shook her head back and forth and finally got it off her mouth.

She looked at Matt and then Stephanie with an exasperated face. "I'm so sorry I didn't listen to you and now look at the mess I've gotten you into."

Matt shook his head. "You didn't cause this; we brought it on ourselves. They were looking for the Johnsons' will and we found it first. Now the question is, what are they planning for us?"

He looked out the window as the traffic raced by. He could tell they were on I-5 headed south. Sacramento International Airport was only fifteen minutes away, so they weren't going there. He looked up at the ceiling of the limo and noticed a sun roof. He got on his knees and tried to open the plastic shield with his head. It slowly slid back, revealing a darkened glass window.

The window behind the driver started to come down. Matt jumped back into his seat. Mika stuck his head into the back, checking things out. Seeing nothing going on, he backed out and rolled the window back up. Matt got back on his knees and looked for the switch to open the sun roof. He spotted it but stopped to figure out what was his next move.

Okay, I get the window open, and then what? He thought. I can't jump out onto the freeway from a speeding car. Is there anything around that I can use as a signal?

"What are you looking for, Matt? You're not thinking of going out the sun roof, are you?" Stephanie asked anxiously.

"No," he answered, "I'm trying to find something to use to draw attention to ourselves."

Stephanie suddenly sat up straight. "Matt, wait a minute. I've got that GPS tracker with me in my jeans. Help me get it out and we could alert Alan." She turned around in her seat. "See if you can get it out. It's in the back pocket on my left side."

Matt maneuvered over to her and felt around her backside. The zip tie was tight and he could only move his fingers back and forth. He found the pocket and managed to get his middle finger and index finger into the pocket. "Steph, can you turn yourself a little to the right? I feel the tip of it, but I can't grab it."

Stephanie adjusted herself and waited. "You're almost there, Matt."

Matt strained and finally touched the device. With two fingers, he clamped down as hard as he could. Slowly, he started to raise his hand out of the pocket. Matt clamped his fingers hard but could feel his grip was tenuous. Just as he got the device out of the pocket, his fingers slipped and the device fell, bouncing off the seat and onto the floor. The tinted window to the front seat started to lower. Matt and Stephanie quickly hopped back into a sitting position, recovering just as the window was fully opened.

Mika stuck his head through the window and looked around. He smiled an evil smile and asked, "Hey, have any of you ever skydived?" Nobody responded; they just stared at him dumbfounded. He threw his head back and let out a guttural laugh. "Well tonight might be your lucky night!" He pulled back to the front seat and raised the tinted window back up.

Caroline looked at Matt and asked in a high-pitched voice, "What did he mean by skydiving?"

Matt leaped off the seat and was looking around the floor of the dark limo. I don't have an answer, Caroline," he answered. "The guy is a sicko. I wouldn't take what he says seriously." He didn't want to say what he thought.

Matt fumbled around the limo's floor until he found the device and picked it up in his hands. He pulled himself up to the seat and turned his back to Stephanie. "Can you see the button to activate it, Steph? I can't feel it."

Stephanie leaned in closer to look. "Move your finger a quarter inch to the left." She guided him as he maneuvered his fingers. "That's it, a little more, a little more. There, that's it. Push in with your thumb."

Matt did as she instructed and waited a second. Nothing happened. He pushed again and waited.

"You did it, Matt," Stephanie cried. "The red light is on. Now we have to hope Alan has his phone nearby him."

Matt let go of the device and it fell to the floor, the red light blinking. He tried pushing it under their seat, out of sight, with his feet. "Did Alan tell you how this thing works?" he asked.

"He just said it will beep at his phone and he can find our position and know where we are located," she answered. "I don't know how much farther we're going, but I hope he can get to us fast."

Matt glanced outside the window to get some bearings on where they were. "We just passed Sac International, so we aren't going there. I would guess they would take us to the next closest airport, which is McClellan Air Force Base. That's about twenty minutes away. I hope Alan has enough time to get to us. It would be impossible for anyone to help us if they get us into the air."

Thirty-Four

A lan stood anxiously on the porch at Stephanie's house. He rang her doorbell and nobody answered, so he dialed her cell again. It went to voicemail, so he tried Matt's phone again. He didn't pick up either. They'd said they were going to go to the Johnsons' either tonight or tomorrow. "I better head out to the Johnson ranch and see if I can catch them there before Yuri does."

He hopped into his Mercedes and headed for I-80 west toward Woodland. He pushed the 248-horse-powered engine hard as he dialed Sheriff Cranston's number on his cell phone. "John, it's Alan. Have your guys picked up Yuri yet?"

The voice came through his Bluetooth headset. "No, not yet. He wasn't at home in El Dorado Hills. My officers are heading to his office as we speak, but I doubt he would be there this late in the evening."

"Where are you, John? I think I could use some backup. I'm headed to the Johnsons' to see if I can find Matt and Stephanie. Neither of them has returned my calls for a couple of hours and I'm worried about them. They could be in big trouble."

"I'm at home. It's right on your way," John answered.

"You got it. I'll be there in five minutes. You might want to bring some heat. I'm not sure what we're going to find."

"I understand. I'll be at the curb waiting for you."

Suddenly Alan's cell phone started beeping. He checked it and saw the GPS had been activated. Alan hit the accelerator and watched as the speedometer hit ninety-five. He stayed in the fast lane until the turnoff to Sheriff Cranston's house. He came up to the driveway and slowed long enough for John to jump into the car, toting a shotgun and a portable red light. In less than a minute, he was back on the freeway speeding north. Alan handed his cell phone to John. "That's Stephanie's GPS, John. I told her to activate it if she ever got into trouble. Check it out and direct me to her."

John studied the phone for a few seconds. "They're coming down I-5 and are just north of I-80. We're about eight miles apart. Keep driving this direction; if they stay on I-5, we'll catch them in about seven minutes."

Alan's hands were sweaty on the steering wheel as he gripped it tightly. His windshield wipers held a steady rhythm as they went back and forth, wiping the windshield clean of the rain, which had started coming down harder. "That part is good, the part about catching up to them. The next question is bad: What do we do when we do catch up to them?"

THIRTY-FIVE

The Aero Commander 690 sat at the end of the runway, its low profile fuselage hugging the runway as its turboprop engines whirled away into the rainy night. The blue lights that outlined the runway, combined with soft-white lights spread out along the field next to the runway, shed a soft, diffused light on the plane's silhouette. Yuri stood on the ground next to the steps to the plane, a cell phone at his ear. He looked up at Ivan standing at the plane's doorway, his arms folded and a concerned look on his face. The plane rocked slightly from the power of the spinning propellers. Yuri shouted into the phone sternly, trying to be heard over the noise of the engines. "How far away are you? We're behind schedule."

Mika's voice came over the phone and Yuri strained to hear him. "We're about six minutes away, Yuri. We just got off I-5 heading east on I-80 and are about four miles from the Watt Avenue exit. Which runway are you located at?"

Yuri looked at the sign twenty yards from where he stood, squinting to read it in the low light. "Runway 16," he yelled into the phone. "It's at the south end of the airport. You can't miss us. It's the only plane around with its engines running." He glanced around the airport nervously. He reached into his coat pocket and subconsciously fingered the Springfield 45 pistol there. "Did you have any problems?"

Mika laughed. "No, not at all. Everything went the way you said it would. None of them saw it coming."

"That's good," he shouted. "Tell Marc to leave the limo after you get here. We won't need it anymore after tonight. Be ready to hustle. I don't want to hang around here any longer than necessary." He hung up and climbed the stairs into the plane.

"I can't believe this, Ivan," he said exasperatedly. "Everything was going perfectly. Why wouldn't Carlos give me more time? I was about to make him millions."

Ivan threw his hands up. "I don't know how he thinks, Yuri, but the real problem has been those people meddling in your affairs. If they'd have minded their own business, you wouldn't be dodging an arrest warrant. When the cops found Mika's car, I knew there would be issues."

Yuri pounded his fist. "I know that. I told Mika to take that thing to Gustoff's, but he had to give it to his chop shop buddy, Bennie, because he's so particular about it."

I need to think about what I'm to do with Mika, Yuri thought. He's become a pain in the ass. If he would have done what I instructed, I wouldn't be in this dilemma. WMI, the ranch, the insurance money are all in jeopardy because of his foolishness. When I get back, I'm going to deal with him.

"Ivan, I need a drink. Pour me a vodka, would you?" He looked over to the tower across the airport. He felt like someone was staring at him. Come on, Mika, he thought. Hurry up. Ivan handed him a glass and he eagerly drank it up. It calmed him somewhat, but he was still anxious. He spotted a pair of headlights near the tower, heading in their direction. That's not the entrance Mika would be coming in, he thought. That has to be the airport authorities. We need to get moving soon. Come on, Mika, hurry up!

Mika hung up the phone and nervously fingered his Ruger revolver. "Is everything alright?" Marc asked apprehensively.

"Yeah," he answered. "Yuri is antsy to get out of here." He pointed out the windshield. "That's the street we turn onto, Peace Keeper Drive. I think I'll check on our passengers to make sure they're nice and comfortable."

He pressed a button and lowered the window. He got on his knees and stuck his head and upper torso through the window. Matt, Caroline, and Stephanie were in the same positions as when he'd last checked on them. He waved his gun around the limo and asked sarcastically, "Is everybody enjoying the trip?" He turned to go back to the front seat when something caught his eye. He tilted his head and saw a tiny red light blinking under the seat. He glared at Matt and pointed the Ruger in his face. "What the hell is that? Get that thing and give it to me, now!"

Matt didn't move. "Why don't you get it yourself?"

Mika's face turned red and his eyes grew wide. He reached over and grabbed Stephanie by the neck, pulling her against him. He reached down and yanked her blouse, ripping it open, and grabbed her left breast with his free hand. "How about you do what I say and I don't kill your girlfriend," he snarled.

Before he finished the sentence, Matt sprung forward and smashed his forehead into Mika's face, breaking his nose and spraying blood everywhere. Mika's head flew violently back, hitting the back of the window frame, and he crumpled back into the front seat. Blinded by blood and full of rage, he aimed the gun into the window opening and fired wildly into the back seat area, causing ear-numbing explosions and filling the air with smoke and gunpowder. His face was pounding as he screamed, "I'm going to smoke you, fool. I don't care what Yuri wants, you're a dead man." Screams of pain and fear came from the back seat as Mika started to dive back. Marc grabbed his arm and yanked him hard toward the front.

"We've got problems, Mika," he said looking into his side mirror. "We've got a cop tailing us."

Mika turned around in his seat and looked out his side mirror. He saw a white car with a flashing red light on its dashboard. "Turn left at this street and hit the gas," he yelled at Marc. "The plane is just down the road." He rolled down his window, leaned halfway out of the car, and shot three times at the car behind them. It swerved to the left to avoid the shots then corrected itself. Mika tumbled back to look out the front window of the limousine. In the distance he could see the plane sitting on the runway, both engines running. "There they are," he yelled, pointing towards the plane with his gun. "There's the gate to the right. Keep up the pace. I'll take care of this guy driving behind us."

Alan pushed the accelerator as hard as he could as John clung to the dashboard for balance. He pulled the Mercedes right up behind the limousine. "Are you going to hang back and see where they lead us to?" John asked.

"No, they're headed toward that plane up ahead and we've got to stop them," Alan answered. John watched as the front window on the passenger side rolled down. He saw Mika lean out of the window and take aim at the Mercedes. The rain got in his eyes and he tried to wipe them with his sleeve. "Swerve left, Alan, he's got a gun!"

Alan swerved just as three shots exploded past the window. "Can you take a crack at him, John?" he screamed. "I can pull around him!"

"No, Alan, you need to take the shot," John yelled back. "He's on your side. Take my shotgun and I'll hold the wheel. Wait until he sticks his head out again and then speed up to him."

John handed the shotgun to Alan, and he put it between his knees with his left hand on the stock. Alan rolled his window down and rested the barrel on the opening. "Okay, John, let me know when to hit it."

John watched through the windshield intensely. He saw Mika lean out again, blocking the rain with his forearm. "Get ready, Alan," John yelled. Mika took two more shots, one hitting the windshield a few inches above John's head, splattering glass around his face. "Okay, Alan," he screamed. "Gun it."

Alan hit the accelerator, sliding the shotgun through the window. The cars came up to each other five feet apart. Mika leaned out again, his body bouncing back and forth from the moving limo and trying to steady the gun in his outstretched arm. Just as Mika squeezed off a shot, Alan hit the brakes, causing Mika to miss. John steered the car toward the limo, and Alan pointed the shotgun at Mika, firing at almost point blank. Mika's face exploded backward in a burst of flesh, bones, and blood. His head snapped back and bounced off the top of the car door, and then he fell forward, his body balanced precariously, half in and half out of the open window. Blood flowed down the car door, mixing with the rain water and painting the door a streaking crimson red.

Alan looked up and saw the airplane on the runway thirty yards up the road. He reloaded the shotgun and fired at the right front tire of the limousine, blowing it out and causing the limo to swerve to the left then correcting itself to the right. The limo slowed and suddenly came to a stop.

Alan had stopped his car too when he saw Marc jump out and start running for the plane. John hopped out of the car, clamped two hands around his gun, and steadied it on the roof. He yelled as loud as he could. "Stop! It's the police!"

Marc, still running, turned and fired a shot at Alan's car. It hit the windshield between John and Alan, spaying exploding glass all over the front seats. Marc turned again, and John squeezed off two shots. One hit Marc in the chest and the other hit his shoulder. They watched him take two steps forward and collapse. He started crawling on his belly toward the plane, his left arm extending out for help. Gravel and dirt from the prop wash spayed into his face and eyes as he cried out, trying to be heard above the roar of the engines.

Alan dusted off glass from the windshield. John revved the engine. "Hang on, John. We need to stop that plane." Alan hit the gas again and got to within twenty-five yards of the plane before it started rolling down the runway. He watched Yuri pull up the stairs just as Marc had reached them and closed the plane's door, leaving Marc bleeding profusely on the tarmac. The plane started picking up speed as it moved down the runway, with Alan and John closing in from behind. Alan got to within five yards of the plane before it started pulling away and lifted off. Alan slowed the car down, watching the craft fly off, and then he turned the car around.

"Let's check out the limo," he said to John.

They parked about four feet away from the limo, and he and John cautiously approached it. Mika, obviously dead, still hung out the passenger window. Alan opened the passenger door and stuck his head inside. He pointed his Glock around until he recognized everyone in the limo was friendly. A look of relief came across Matt and Stephanie's faces as they recognized him. "Is everyone okay?" Alan asked anxiously as he holstered his gun.

"Oh, thank god it's you, Alan," Stephanie sighed as she slumped back in her seat.

"You are a sight for sore eyes, Alan," Matt said, smiling. The gash on his forehead was still oozing blood, and it drizzled down his face. "We need an ambulance though. When Mika fired the gun, we all hit the floor, but Caroline took a shot in the shoulder. She's lost a lot of blood."

"I'm on it, Matt." He pulled out of the limo and yelled to John, "Call an ambulance. We've got a gunshot victim." Alan ran back to his car and pulled a towel out of his gym bag in the back seat. He leaned into the limo and pressed the towel against Caroline's shoulder. "Hold this tight, Caroline." He replaced her hand where his was. "You're going to be okay; help is on the way." He patted her thigh tenderly then backed out of the limo. Matt crawled awkwardly out of the limo with Stephanie following behind him, their hands still bound by the zip ties.

He turned and tried to hold his hands so Alan could see them. "Do you have a knife or something?"

Alan retrieved a knife from his car and cut the ties loose. "Do you know where they were going to take you, Matt?"

"I don't know, Alan, but I don't think they wanted to keep us alive for long. I knew we were in for a bad flight."

Matt went over and gave Stephanie a hug and kissed her forehead. "You've got to quit getting me involved in your schemes. It's bad for my health."

Stephanie smiled back and gave him a squeeze. "Come on, Matt. You like the excitement, admit it."

He pulled back and laughed. "I don't like it that much." He let go of Stephanie and walked over to Mika. He nudged him and, getting no response, gently reached into his breast pocket and lifted out the Johnsons' will. He handed it to Stephanie. "We don't want to forget this." He turned to Alan and asked, "What will happen to Yuri? Will the authorities be able to catch him?"

"I'm sure they'll track him down. John called in the plane's ID to the FAA. He's got to land somewhere, and someone will be waiting to take him into custody. I wouldn't feel safe with that guy running around free."

Matt nodded in agreement. "No, neither would I."

THIRTY-SIX

Colorful leaves from the trees that lined the streets in midtown Sacramento were falling in record numbers with the end of the fall season, and the first hint of winter temperatures was in the air. UC Davis Medical Center was located just off a residential district, and visitors often used the streets of the older but well-manicured neighborhood to park their cars before entering the red-bricked building. Nurses and orderlies in light blue uniforms scurried about the busy corridors, checking charts and patients with equal regularity. Matt found himself sitting in a leather-bound chair in a comfortable suite on the top floor of the hospital, reserved for well-to-do supporters and other dignitaries. Stephanie sat next to him in a similar leather-bound chair as they watched Caroline. With her left shoulder bandaged and her left arm in a sling, she finished her lunch of soup and Jell-O. Her hospital bed was tilted and she was supported upright by many pillows.

Caroline pushed the tray that was holding her food to the side and smiled. "Eating this stuff for almost a week is an extreme way to lose weight, don't you think? I'll be able to eat real food again when they release me in the next day or two. I can't wait to get my hands on a nice fat chicken breast."

Stephanie laughed. "Come on, you were in great shape before. This will just make you look that much better."

"Yeah," Matt added. "You are looking great considering all the blood you lost. Do you feel as well as you look?"

Caroline reached behind her and adjusted one of her pillows. "Yes, I feel a lot better. My shoulder still hurts from the wound, but every day I seem to gain a little more strength. These nurses work me to death in therapy. They're tough, I tell you. I'll be glad to get out of here though. As much as I appreciate the attention the doctors and nurses give me, I hate hospitals. I want to get home."

"Well, that will be soon," Stephanie said. "Did you hear that UC Davis is going to be your new neighbor?" Caroline looked surprised. "They formally petitioned the probate court to take possession of the Johnson ranch," she continued. "I don't think you will have the same problems with them as your previous neighbors."

Caroline put her hand to her shoulder. "God, I hope not. Getting shot is no fun, let me tell you."

Matt leaned on the back of his chair. "I don't want to press into your business, Caroline, but now that you're dealing with the University, maybe you could strike a deal with them to purchase the water you're looking for. It would be much less costly than having the county grab it through the eminent domain process."

Caroline's face turned into a look of disappointment. "But think of all the recognition Yolo County would get if they were successful. New London was a huge case, and it put that city on the map. I think those water rights would greatly help the citizens of Yolo County, and I've always been told there's no such thing as bad publicity."

"Maybe," Matt answered, "but at what cost? It will take a fortune to fight the University because it's no longer a secret how much those rights are worth, and they won't just roll over. There is also no guarantee that a court will look at this action the same as the New London case. California courts are way different than Connecticut's. New London went all the way to the Supreme Court, and it took years to do so. There might be a better way is all I'm saying."

Stephanie stood up and gave Caroline's hand a squeeze. "You've got plenty of time to figure things like that out. Right now all you should concentrate on is getting better." She picked up her purse that was hanging on the chair. "Matt, shall we leave the patient so she can get some rest?"

Matt bowed to her and gently patted the bed. "I think you are right. It's time for her to get back to healing."

Caroline held up her hand. "Before you go, do you know if there is anything new on Yuri? Did they find him yet?"

Matt looked at Stephanie, then back at Caroline. "No, I talked to Alan yesterday and there is nothing new there. He thinks Yuri's fled the country, but no one knows for sure. There are a lot of people looking for him though, including his wife. It appears he left her high and dry, and she's not too pleased about that. She's been more than helpful to the authorities in regards to his business dealings."

Caroline nodded her head. "I would feel a lot better if I knew he were in jail. All right, I should probably rest up. I'll talk to you two later."

Matt held Stephanie's hand as they left the hospital. He scanned the older homes that sat way back off 42nd Street and pointed to one as they passed. "I love the architecture of these homes down here. They sit in front of these mature trees and they have so much brick. There is something very charming about this neighborhood."

Stephanie looked at the home he was staring at. It's a great area. I would love to live here."

Matt put his arm around her waist and hugged her. "Maybe that dream will come true someday. You never know."

She looked into his eyes and smiled. "This is true, you can never tell."

When they reached Matt's car, he glanced at his watch. "It's almost 11:45; do you have time for some lunch? Why don't we go get something at De Beers Irish Pub, by your office?"

"That works for me as long as you're buying."

Matt held her door and smiled. "Of course I'm buying."

❖

Their waiter had picked up their lunch plates and dropped off a dessert menu, which they both glanced at briefly and then closed. Matt sat silently and studied Stephanie's face. He squirmed in his chair and reached across the table to touch her hands. "Umm, Stephanie, can I ask you something?"

She held his gaze and raised her eyebrows. "Sure."

He spoke softly. "I've always loved you, and you have never left my thoughts. I felt overwhelmed by all the events involved in a wedding, and I truly made a mistake." He swallowed hard before continuing. "Will you forgive me for being a moron and marry me? We haven't lost that much time. If you'll allow me, I'll take care of all the venues and vendors to get us back on track. We could have a June wedding."

Stephanie didn't flinch and remained silent for a few seconds. Finally she spoke, her eyes locked into his. "I never stopped loving you, Matt. When we put the wedding on hold, I had hoped you would clear your head and we could be together. Yes, I'll marry you. I've always felt we should be together." She smiled mischievously. "You're going to be a busy man if you're going to put all the pieces of this wedding together. You better pay this bill and get after it."

Matt stood up and leaned down, kissing her hard on the lips. "You're right, I'd better get going. I'll see you after work. I love you, Stephanie! You can get back to your office on your own, right?"

"I think so, seeing as it's right on the corner." She put her hand up flat and blew him a kiss. "I love you Matt."

THIRTY-SEVEN

C aroline sat at her desk signing a stack of checks that were sitting in front of her. Elliot Spencer, her ranch manager, dressed in his usual dark slacks and white shirt, stood quietly behind one of the chairs in front of her desk. He waited patiently while she silently did her work. Without looking up, she asked, "Tell me again what you are requesting?"

He took a deep breath and spoke. "When we spoke a few months ago, you gave me the go ahead to plant the ten thousand acres of rice even though we didn't have the water or the workers to handle it. I tried to procure the seed to do that, but it came late and we weren't able to get the majority of the crop in the ground."

He paused. "It was a good thing because the housing facilities here are not in a condition to handle the additional workers." He cleared his throat and continued. "I understand you will have more water this spring and therefore we can be fully prepared to plant more rice. I need to fix up the housing, Caroline. The workers deserve to live in sanitary conditions." He pleaded to her. "It's only fair."

She set down her pen and leaned back in her chair. "How much money do you need and how long will it take?"

He stepped around the chair. "If you give me 150,000 dollars, I swear I will be able to house more than enough workers to handle the extra rice crop. I can get it done by April at the latest."

Caroline let out a big sigh. "Okay, Elliot, you win. Get the housing fixed." Then she pointed her finger at him and said to him sternly, "But you better deliver a bumper rice crop for me."

He reached out and shook her hand enthusiastically. "You can count on me. I'll make sure we knock it out of the park."

She nodded and returned to her checks, indicating to him with a dismissive wave of her hand she was done with him. After Elliot left the room, Caroline looked up and called out, "Alan, are you ready?"

Alan stepped into the room. She bit on her pen as she eyed him standing in the door way. This man knows how to dress, she thought as she checked out his Armani slacks, white polo shirt, and red-and-black-striped tie.

"Are you ready for me, Caroline?" he asked.

If you only knew, she thought smiling to herself. "Sure, take a seat." She indicated he sit in the chair across the desk. "What can I do for you?"

"Well, first off, I'm glad to see you've healed up so well. That was quite an ordeal you went through."

She smiled. "Thank you, and thank you for coming to our rescue. I might not be here without your heroics. And thanks for visiting me in the hospital. That was nice of you."

Alan shifted in his seat, trying to change the subject. "It was no problem, I was glad to help." He cleared his throat. "The reason I'm here, Caroline, is John Parker wants to lend his services to you and the Yolo County Board of Supervisors in their quest for the water at the Johnson Ranch." He paused for a second. "I know you're aware of Mr. Parker's firm and how he is one of the eminent land use attorneys in the state. He could be very useful to your cause."

I'll bet Mr. Parker thinks he could be useful, she thought. Especially when there are millions of dollars in attorney's fees involved. She smiled to herself. How quickly he changes sides, but obviously he doesn't know I've cut a deal with UC Davis to buy their water once they receive title to the ranch and that Yolo County will be dropping the eminent domain action when the Board meets in three weeks. He probably doesn't know I've been nominated for the vacancy on the Water Resources Board either. I think I'll keep Mr. Parker in the dark for now.

Caroline shuffled some papers on her desk. "Of course I'm aware of Mr. Parker's reputation. Everybody around here knows about it. Even though we've held adversarial positions in the past, I've always respected him." She smiled sweetly at Alan. "I'm sure I could use his services, provided you are the person I'm working with." She winked at him.

Alan was caught off guard. He nervously adjusted his tie. "Uh, I'm sure Mr. Parker would have no problem keeping me on your account, if that is your wish."

Caroline uncrossed her legs slowly under the desk. Oh yes, that is my wish, she thought. At least that is part of my wish. There will be more to come. As she stood up, she watched Alan eyeing her in the tight black leather mini skirt she wore, with the white sleeveless blouse and black pumps. This outfit never fails me, she thought. Keeping her eyes locked on Alan's, she strutted over, exaggerating her swinging hips, and picked up a crystal liquor decanter sitting on the mini bar. "Well, now that that's settled, how about a celebratory drink?" She lifted the glass to her eye level, looked over the glass at Alan, and poured a drink.

Alan, catching her drift, stood up and smiled. He held up a matching crystal glass and saluted. "Absolutely, let's celebrate! Here's to a fun and profitable relationship."

THIRTY-EIGHT

Rows and rows of neatly pruned grapevines, as far as the eye could see, stretched across the rolling landscape. An asphalt driveway wound up and over a hill past a large pond where a flock of ducks, green headed mallards and colorful teal cavorted in the muddy water while a pair of snow white herons majestically patrolled the shore. When Matt had visited the newly constructed winery three months before, he was enchanted with how the low-slung wood buildings with corrugated metal roofs blended seamlessly with the surrounding scenery. Supporting out buildings, all in the same architectural style, containing the barrel room, wine press, and bottling facility, sat empty and quiet. The winery was located just outside the town of Sutter Creek in Amador County, an area just east of Sacramento. Matt and Stephanie loved this up-and-coming wine region, and the Helwig Winery was steadily making a name for itself in the industry.

It was late in the afternoon on this particular Saturday in June. The temperature was in the high eighties, but a soft breeze drifted up from the Delta, making the evening very pleasant. Down below the winery, at the base of an amphitheater, groups of people stood in front of neatly spaced rows of chairs with white covers hanging over them. They watched the young couple in the white gazebo, as they stood against a backdrop of a cloudless sky. It was a beautiful scene of grass-covered rolling hills, and a brilliant sunset of orange and red. Ten or twelve swallows with purple backs and rust-colored breasts darted back and forth from the main building to the water feature behind the gazebo, loading up their bills with mud to perfect their nests.

Matt stood military-straight in his charcoal grey Anthony Franco tuxedo, complete with white shirt, black bowtie, and shiny black Bostonian shoes. A single white rose boutonniere with light purple breath of heather was pinned on his chest. His hair was neatly trimmed and moussed, as if he had just came out of an Abercrombie and Finch photo shoot. Next to him stood Drew, his best man, in a similar tuxedo, and the two of them made a striking picture of youth and good looks. Their smiles and the ease at which they carried themselves made the setting that much grander.

Father Michael, a white-haired Catholic priest who had baptized Stephanie and her brother, stood between them reading the wedding vows they had both chosen. Matt had watched Stephanie walk up the aisle on the arm of her brother, John, with unbridled love and could only think of how proud her father would have been if he were still alive. He felt he was the luckiest man alive and vowed to do everything in his power to be a loving husband.

Matt's father, mother, grandmother, and younger sister sat in the front row, each dressed in outfits of pastel colors and each looking happy. His mother would periodically dab a white handkerchief to her eyes as she watched her only son take his new bride.

Matt held Stephanie's hand as she stood facing him. Her white silk Oscar de la Renta strapless wedding gown hugged her curves and flowed around her long legs. A white ruffled veil with a long train followed behind her. Underneath the lace veil, her face radiated joy as she stared into Matt's eyes. Behind Stephanie stood Mary Wilson, a tall pretty woman in her late twenties, her roommate from college. She held Stephanie's bouquet of white Sahara roses with Casablanca lilies and adjusted her train so she wouldn't trip as she maneuvered around the gazebo.

He heard the priest say to him, "Matt, do you take Stephanie to be your wife, to love and to cherish, in sickness and in health, until death do you part?"

Matt answered in a resounding voice that echoed across the crowd. "I do!"

Father Michael turned to Stephanie. "Stephanie, do you take Matt to be your husband, to love and to cherish, in sickness and in health, until death do you part?"

Stephanie paused, took a deep breath, and whispered, "I do."

They exchanged rings, which the priest blessed. He then announced to them, "I now pronounce you man and wife." He turned to Matt and said, "You may kiss the bride."

Matt lifted up the lace veil and gently placed it over Stephanie's head. He pulled her close and kissed her on the lips. He slid his arm around her waist and kissed her forcefully enough to bend her backward as he held her waist. With his free hand he waved to the crowd, which responded excitedly with applause. He let her back up, and she, smiling to the crowd, adjusted her veil. They turned and faced the audience, and Father Michael announced, "I now proudly introduce to you for the first time, Mr. and Mrs. Matt Whiteside." The crowd stood up and erupted in applause again, and they proceeded to exit joyously between the rows of chairs as an organist played the Wedding March.

The wedding party returned to the gazebo for pictures while the guests walked back up to the winery to the open-air patio where the reception was to take place. Waiters in white jackets, white shirts, and black bow ties meandered through the crowd with trays of champagne and plates of miso-seared pineapple and truffled quail eggs benedict with fennel hollandaise.

Matt and Stephanie struck different poses and, after about

twenty minutes and a hundred photos, made it back to the reception. The first people to greet them were Matt's parents, Barbara and Stan. Barbara kissed her daughter-in-law on the cheek and held her hand. "You look so pretty, Stephanie. We can't be happier to have you in our family."

Stan came up and gave her a kiss on the cheek. "You do look beautiful today. Congratulations."

Stephanie blushed but smiled broadly. "You both have been so kind to me. I can't thank you enough."

They stood in the receiving line for a half an hour before retiring to the head table. Circular, white linen-covered tables spread out across the concrete floor. Large floral arrangements of yellow roses, daffodils, and ranunculus sat in crystal vases on each table. A full Vera Wang place setting, set off by a silver charger sat in front of each seat. Crystal glasses for water and wine added sparkle to each setting. In the other corner of the room, a disk jockey played soft music as people mingled around the room. The sound of clinking glasses and laughter floated in the air.

An ice sculpture of a Chinese dragon was placed next to the head table with ten different types of sushi. Matt tried to squeeze in bites of prime rib and mashed potatoes, while Stephanie worked in a bite or two of Caesar salad and rosemary chicken before they were interrupted by well-intentioned guests.

At the end of dinner, Drew stood up to offer a toast. Matt cringed as he worried about what his good friend might tell. To his relief, Drew went easy on him and didn't offer anything salacious. He asked the guests to rise. Raising his champagne glass, Drew said to them, "I want to wish both of you, Matt and Stephanie, a long and happy married life. You are two of the most wonderful people I know. We all wish you a great future together."

When John, Stephanie's brother, got up and gave a moving speech about their life growing up and how much he and Stephanie both missed their father, Matt had a lump in his throat. I can't imagine what my life would have been like without my father, he thought. He's been such a rock for me and has been so helpful to me over the years.

The disc jockey announced that he was about to play a song for the bride and groom's first dance. Matt grabbed Stephanie's hand and led her to the dance floor as the Beatles' John Lennon sweetly sang the words to "In My Life." Matt held Stephanie tightly as they swayed slowly across the dance floor to the beat of the music. Their eyes locked together. "What are you thinking, Mrs. Whiteside? Can you believe we are finally married?"

Stephanie buried her head into his shoulder. "Oh Matt, I couldn't be happier. I love you so much. I can't get used to being called Mrs. Whiteside yet." She pulled her head back and kissed him on the lips. "But I know I can get used to it quickly."

Matt whispered, "You look so beautiful today. I couldn't be a happier man." The song ended and another one started. The bridal party joined them on the dance floor, and before long Drew came waltzing by with Mary Wilson in his arms. He was talking to her, and she was laughing as they moved gracefully together. As they glided by, Drew gave Matt and Stephanie a knowing look.

Matt watched him disappear into the crowd. He shook his head and laughed. "Good old Drew. He knows how to show a woman a good time."

Stephanie looked over at them and smiled. "I wouldn't worry about Mary. She can handle herself very well. Besides, they make a cute couple. I hope Drew gets to know her."

"You know Drew. He usually doesn't keep women around for too long. But maybe he'll surprise me."

They made it back to their table when Caroline came up with Alan in tow. "What a wonderful party you've thrown. I'm a pro at these things, and you guys put me to shame."

Matt smiled at her. "Thank you, Caroline. I'm glad you guys made it."

"Are you kidding?" Alan said. "We wouldn't have missed it. Hey, I forgot to ask you in all the confusion last week, but Mr. Parker has another case he wants to hire you for when you get back from your honeymoon. Do you want to hear about it?"

Stephanie looked at Matt and they both said in unison, "Wait 'til we get back!"

They all laughed together. Alan looked at Matt. "Do you mind if I have a dance with the bride, sir?"

Matt extended his hand toward Stephanie. "I'm sure she would love it. Be my guest."

Alan half bowed and stuck his arm out. Stephanie slipped her arm through his and they headed for the dance floor.

"I guess congratulations are in order, Caroline," Matt said. "When do you get sworn onto the Water Resources Board?"

Caroline sat in Stephanie's seat. She pumped her fist, a broad smile on her face. "A week from next Tuesday I'm officially a Board member. I'm so excited I can't see straight. I resigned from Yolo County's Board of Supervisors last week, so Alan's boss doesn't have to worry about me turning down any more of his client's projects." She looked over at Alan on the dance floor. "Now I just need to figure out how I can use his services."

"Mr. Parker's, or Alan's services?" Matt asked.

She turned and laughed. "Both!"

"Has Alan heard anything further about Yuri?" Matt asked. He took a sip of a beer.

Caroline spun slowly around and faced him. "There has been nothing new. It's like he disappeared into thin air. They never tracked his plane to any airport in the U.S. He hasn't returned home, and his family is just as perplexed as anyone." She looked back at Alan and Stephanie, then back. "I understand the family is struggling, as he didn't leave them access to any money or assets. A real class act."

"Do the authorities think he's still in the country?" he asked.

She shrugged. "I don't know, Matt. Nobody's said anything. But Alan told me there are some interesting characters besides the police looking for him. Yuri better hope the police find him first."

THIRTY-NINE

The thick adobe walls had cracks running from the floor to the ceiling. The light-brown colors barely hid the dust that had accumulated in the undulations of the uneven texture. Where the plaster had broken away in large chunks, the thick brick walls that lay under the plaster showed through. A single light, with a circular aluminum shade, hung twelve inches down from the seven-foot ceiling, casting light three quarters up the wall with the balance of the wall in a shadow. A single dusty, four-paned window centered on the wall let in a small amount of sunlight from the outside into the room.

The man sat silently on a rectangular steel table, which was covered by a single sheet of white butcher paper. He lifted his right hand to his cheek, softly touching the plaster bandages that covered his face. He resisted the urge to scratch his face, even though it screamed for attention. Across from the table sat a brown steel chair full of dings and dents, as if it had been used as a prop in a staged wrestling match.

The door burst open. A short man with black hair, brown eyes, and an olive complexion came right up to the table and shook the sitting man's hand.

"Buenos dias," he said cheerily. His long white coat lay open and he carried a chart under his arm. Without waiting for a reply, he examined the man's face without speaking, stopping ever so often to softly poke a spot here and there. Finally he stood back and spoke. "Well, today is the day. You have been through a rough time. Are you ready to get the bandages off?"

The man sitting on the table nodded silently, blinking carefully through the open slits left for his eyes.

The man in the coat set the chart on the table and continued studying the man's face. "Good. Everything has been taken care of. Your friend outside has paid everything in full, and after these bandages are off, you will be free to go." He pulled a pair of tape-cutting scissors out of his pocket and held them in front of his patient's eyes. "I will go slow and take my time, so relax."

The man on the table felt the scissors at the back of his neck move slowly up the side of his head. He felt the pressure being relieved on his face as the plaster bandages fell away. He sat still for an hour as the scissors went back and forth around his head and face.

Finally, the man in the white coat pulled the last piece of bandage off. He stepped back, admiring his work. He turned his head at an angle and circled the man on the table. When he came back to his original position, he clapped his hands together and smiled. "Ah, I've created another masterpiece!"

He handed the man a mirror and watched intently as he slowly examined his face. The man held the mirror and carefully touched his face, softly rubbing the stubble of his beard. "Well, amigo, this is the last time I'll see you. I've given your friend everything you need to take care of your wounds. He's got all your medicine, and if you follow my instructions for the next six weeks, you'll be good as new. Follow me, and I'll escort you out."

They exited the room through a dark corridor to a reception area where a third man was sitting sifting through some old magazines. He looked up, staring at the patient for a moment, and did a double take. He smiled widely.

The man in the white coat motioned with his arm towards the door. "You may take your friend with you now, and I wish you luck. Do as I instructed you to help this man, but don't try to contact me." With that, the man in the coat turned, went back through the swinging door, and disappeared.

The man's friend, still holding the magazine, watched the door swing back and forth. He turned and spoke. "Well, old friend, shall we get you home? I can't believe it's you. As a matter of fact, if I hadn't seen this with my own eyes, I wouldn't believe it was you."

The patient reached to his face and rubbed it softly. A smile slowly came across his face. "What do you think? Do you think anyone will recognize this face?"

The friend shook his head, smiling. "Not in a million years, my friend, not in a million years. Your own mother," he made a solemn sign of the cross, "may she rest in peace, wouldn't recognize you.

They stepped out through the dirty entry door onto a dusty street. The building where they had just exited from had no sign hanging from it, no type of identification of any kind. Across the street, a heavyset Mexican woman with lots of makeup on her face spotted them and called over to them in Spanish. "Come over, amigos," she said. "Come buy me a drink. Let's have some fun tonight."

A mangy dog lying next to her lifted its head, not sure whether to bark or get excited. It reached with its hind paw to behind its ear and began to scratch itself furiously. It then turned and bit itself numerous times on its haunches before it got up, stretched, and slowly started to cross the street.

The two men ignored the woman and walked to an old sedan parked twenty yards down the street.

"*Dos hotos*," she yelled at them, and then she spat on the ground.

The friend opened the passenger door and held it. He pointed to the gold Rolex the patient was wearing. "You might want to put that away."

The patient looked down and nodded approvingly as he unclasped the watch and slid it into his front pocket. He paused and rubbed his face gingerly as he looked up and down the street. He spoke out loud. "Everybody has a weakness. I just need to find it and exploit it." He nodded to his friend. "I've got some scores to settle. Let's get started."

He ducked into the car and his friend gently closed the door. The friend ran around to the driver's side and hopped in. They drove off slowly down the dirt street, a small cloud of dust trailing the car, followed by the mangy dog, who kept pace at a comfortable trot.

Club Pheasant's Chicken a la Cacciatore
Courtesy of The Palamidessi Family

3 lbs. chicken (one whole), cut into pieces
1/2 tsp. salt
1/4 tsp. pepper
3/4 cup flour
olive oil
1 medium onion, peeled and diced
4 cloves garlic, peeled and minced
1 Tbsp. fresh rosemary, chopped
1 lb. whole button mushrooms
2 bell peppers, seeded and chopped
3 Tbsp. chopped parsley
1/2 cup sherry wine
1 (14.5 oz.) can crushed tomatoes
7 oz. can tomato sauce
1 cup chicken broth

Salt and pepper chicken pieces: roll in flour, and shake off excess.

In a large skillet, heat oil and cook chicken on all sides, until well browned. Remove chicken from pan and set aside. Add more oil to skillet (if needed), and add onions, garlic, rosemary, mushrooms, diced pepper, and parsley. Cook 5-8 minutes.

Add wine to skillet and cook for 5 minutes, scraping bottom of pan: add tomatoes, tomato sauce and chicken broth. Cook 5-8 minutes. To the skillet, add browned chicken pieces and cook for about 30 minutes.

Pismo's Coastal Grill
Swordfish Steaks on the Backyard BBQ
Courtesy of Dave Fansler

This is one of the easiest and tastiest fish dishes you can do yourself on your backyard grill. Cooked this way, you would think the swordfish is a New York Steak. Even novice seafood eaters love this method.

Four 1" thick or thicker swordfish steaks
Marinade:
one cube salted butter
4 Tbsp. dry white wine
2 Tbsp. fresh squeezed lemon juice
2 garlic cloves pressed
1/2 tsp. white pepper
2 Tbsp. chopped fresh parsley

Slowly melt butter and then add wine and lemon juice next. Then add garlic and parsley. Cook on medium low heat until thoroughly melted for at least 2 minutes for the flavors to combine. Pour into a ceramic dish and let cool on kitchen counter.

Submerge swordfish steaks into marinade so they are almost covered for 3 minutes...then turn for another 3 minutes.

Make sure barbeque grill is freshly oiled...take swordfish out of marinade and discard.

Grill swordfish for a few minutes until it's well marked, then turn over to finish until firm to the touch...do not overcook!

Yianni's Bar and Grill
Steamed Mussels in White Wine Sauce
Courtesy of Nic Pantis

2 cups dry white wine
1/2 cup minced shallots
6 medium garlic cloves
1/2 tsp. chopped fresh ginger
2 tsp. fresh lemon juice
1 bay leaf
5 lbs. mussels, scrubbed and debearded
1/2 stick salted butter
2 Tbs. chopped fresh parsley leaves
2 Tbs. chopped fresh basil leaves

Put the wine, garlic, shallots, and bay leaf into a large pot and simmer for about 4 minutes. Increase the heat and add mussels. Cover and cook, stirring every few minutes, until the mussels open (should take about 6-10 minutes).

Remove the mussels and set in a large serving dish. Throw out any mussels that didn't open. Add the butter into the broth, swirling it around to make an emulsified sauce. Add the lemon juice, parsley, basil and ginger, and let simmer for 4 minutes. Pour the broth over the mussels and serve immediately with warm garlic bread.

Cream of Mushroom with Leek Soup
Created by Owen Sullivan

12 oz. Monterey or Button mushrooms, chopped (about 4 cups)
½ cup yellow onions, chopped
One leek, white part only, chopped
2 cloves garlic, minced
2 Tbsp. salted butter
1 Tbsp. flour
½ tsp. salt
¼ tsp. pepper
2 cups chicken broth
1 ½ cup half-and-half
1 Tbsp. dry sherry

Melt the butter in a deep saucepan and add leeks, onion, mushrooms and garlic. On medium heat, cook about 3 minutes or until the onion is translucent and mushrooms are soft. Add flour, stirring quickly to blend, then add salt and pepper.

When flour is absorbed, add chicken broth and half-and-half, stirring constantly until it thickens and starts to bubble.

Turn down heat to simmer for 6-7 minutes. Pour in sherry and mix thoroughly. Garnish with the leek strips if desired. Serve immediately.

Owen Sullivan brought you

the struggle for water

in Liquid Gold.

Now delve into a cesspool

of deceit, as those who prey

on the most vulnerable

among us, make a killing

in his latest novel...

Deed of Trust.

AVAILABLE SPRING 2014

OWEN SULLIVAN

Have you read the award-winning novel
· *The House's Money?*

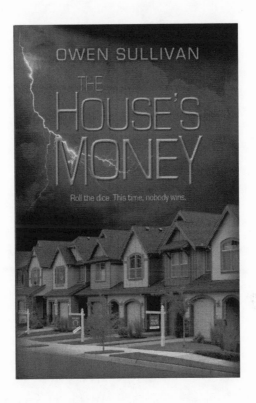

The House's Money, explores the world of high finance and
mortgage-backed securities, a world of greed, power and status.
To learn more about this five time award-winning novel, visit:
www.TheHousesMoney.com

With a degree from USC's School of Business in Real Estate Finance and Marketing, Owen Sullivan has attacked almost every corner of the real estate industry for over 35 years. From one tip of California to the other, he served as Senior VP for one of the largest builders in the country. In 1987, he ventured off to start his own company, developing and selling in excess of $300 million in real estate ventures.

Owen is an avid football fan and spends his free time playing guitar, entertaining friends and cooking. He lives in Orangevale, California, with his wife, Genevieve, and their dog, Joey.

To learn more about Owen, read his blog, or to find more recipes like the ones included in this book, visit: TheHousesMoney.com

Made in the USA
San Bernardino, CA
21 August 2013